UNLOCKING FREEDOM'S DOOR

A Novel

K. P. FOX

Flat Pond
Publishing

Unlocking Freedom's Door

Copyright © 2016 by K. P. Fox

Published in the United States of America
by Flat Pond Publishing

Cover design concept by Andrew Newman Design
Cover and Interior production by BookWise Design

Hardcover ISBN: 978-0-9979179-0-1
Paperback ISBN: 978-0-9979179-1-8
eBook ISBN: 978-0-9979179-2-5
Library of Congress Control Number: 2016952748

www.unlockingfreedomsdoor.com
www.flatpondpublishing.com

Massachusetts

*This book is dedicated to
Karen, Megan, Ryan and Lisa for their support,
encouragement, and patience,*

*To my mother and father for instilling in me sensitivity,
compassion and tolerance,*

and

*To all the teachers
who open doors for so many!*

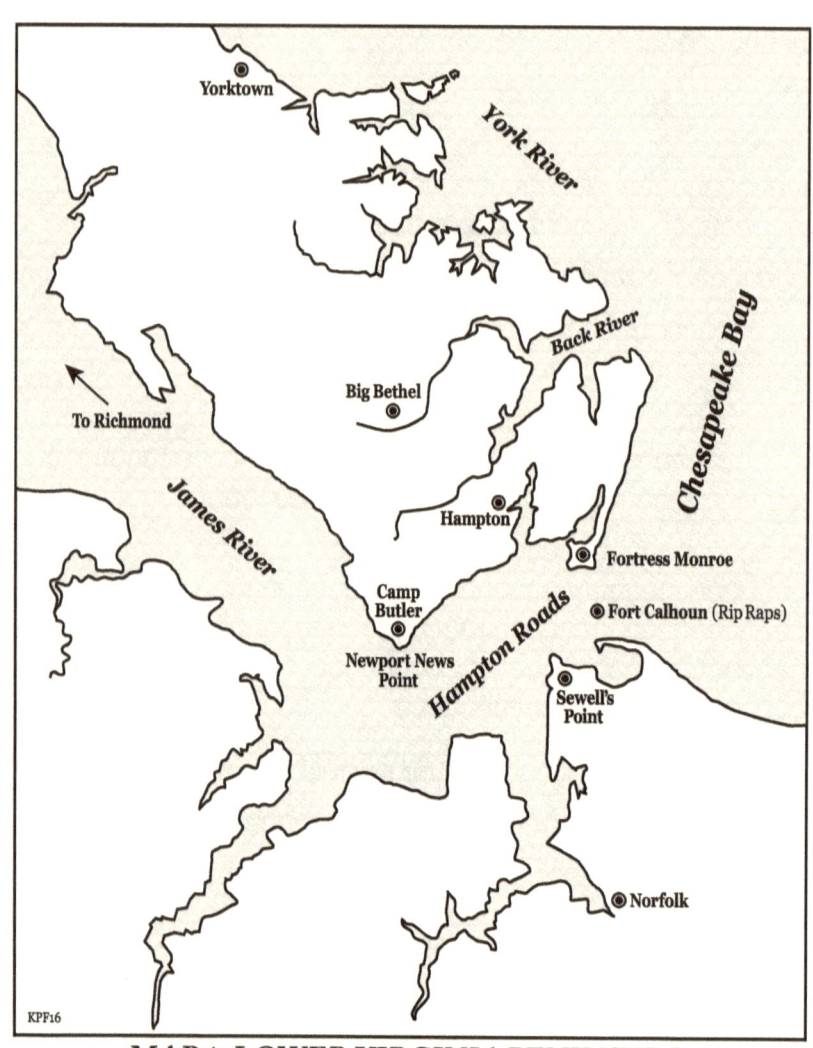

MAP 1: LOWER VIRGINIA PENINSULA

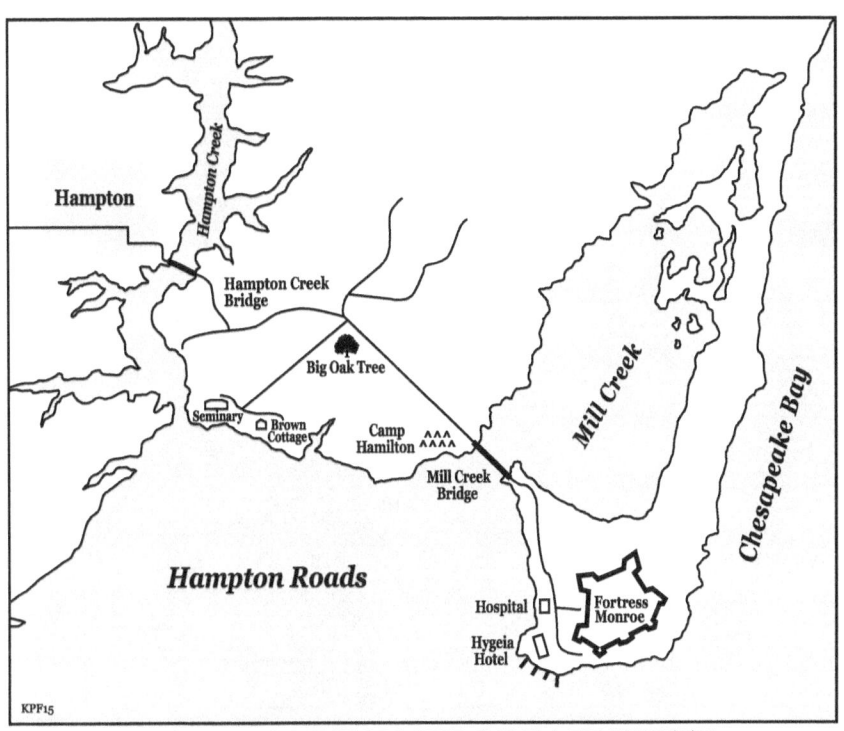

Hampton Creek

Hampton

Hampton Creek
Bridge

Big Oak Tree

Seminary

Brown
Cottage

Camp
Hamilton

Mill Creek
Bridge

Mill Creek

Chesapeake Bay

Hampton Roads

Hospital

Fortress
Monroe

Hygeia
Hotel

KPF15

MAP 2: HAMPTON, VIRGINIA VICINITY

*"Education is the key
to unlock the golden door of freedom."*

GEORGE WASHINGTON CARVER

PROLOGUE

Christmas Day, 1861—

I hate closed doors.

They always stop you from going where you need to go.

THE ROUGH WOOD OF MAMA'S DOOR SCRATCHES my ear. Dr. Browne's in there. Again! He comes by almost every day now. He and Mama tell me she's getting better, but I don't believe them. I can see it in their eyes. Mama had that same look when she told me Grandpa John would be fine. But he died.

Yesterday, I saw Papa. He was leaning against a tree crying. He thought no one was watching him. I don't ever remember seeing him cry before. He's such a big, strong man. I wanted to go over and hug him, but I think he wanted to be alone. Most days I get sad. Sometimes I get angry.

I want to go into my mama's room, but it's always dark in there and smells like the seaweed that washes up on the shore.

When I press my ear up against the door, I can hear them talking.

"Mary, I'm concerned about your weight loss. You need to eat something if you want to regain your strength. Your students are eager for you to return to the classroom. And I know it's important to you as well."

"I'm not hungry, Doctor. But I can't wait to get back to my classroom. Other than Daisy and Thomas, my students mean everything to me. I'm feeling a little better. I should get ready for the Christmas Festival. Daisy has a solo performance. I'm so excited."

Mama has another coughing fit. The floor in this old house is squeaky so I need to be still. I hate this house. It's dusty and cold, and everything creaks and groans. Sometimes critters come down the chimney. Papa and I chase them around the house and try to shoo them out. Papa says they lived here before us so they still think it's theirs. I guess they have as much right to be here as us. We used to have a really nice house. But that was before the great fire. We lost everything—our home, our furniture, and most of our clothes. I get sad just thinking about that day.

Worst of all, I lost my bird book. It used to belong to my mama when she was a little girl. I loved to read about all the different birds and try to find them when I was outside.

Birds are kind of like people. They come in all sorts of colors, sizes, and shapes.

Birds are lucky though. They don't have doors. They're free to go wherever they want. They only have to decide where to land.

"Mary, I'm sorry. You need to stay in bed and rest. Hopefully you'll regain your strength and be back teaching your students soon." Sometimes I feel like kicking Dr. Browne right in the shin.

I open the door just a crack. Mama's holding a needle and thread and is busy taking in her dress. Since she's been losing weight, all her clothes are too big now. She leans on her elbows and tries to sit up. "But, Doctor, I must attend the festival. It'll break Daisy's heart if I'm not there. It'll break my heart too."

Oh, darn floor. I hold my breath.

"Daisy, is that you?" my mama says.

I have no choice. I open the door wide enough to poke my head through. The room is so dark it feels almost like nighttime, but it's still the afternoon. I want to pinch my nose closed with my fingers but I don't. It might make Mama sad.

"Hi, Mama. How're you feeling today?" I can tell she's been crying. Her eyes are all red and puffy. Mama used to be so pretty. Now her body is small and shrunken in the bed. It almost looks like nobody's in there except her head on the pillow. She reminds me of an owl with her big eyes and tiny face.

Mama always used to fix her hair so nice. Now it's always matted down and stuck to her head like it's glued. Some days her hair pokes up in the air like a belted kingfisher.

"Come over here and see me, baby. You look just like an angel in that pretty white dress." I walk over to her bed. She puts her sewing down on the blanket with her skinny arms. Her hands are like bony bird claws. "Let me retie your hair ribbon. It's coming undone."

"How come you're not getting ready, Mama?" I heard what Dr. Browne told her, but I don't care. He's always telling her what to do. He's not the boss of her. I know my mama wants to come and see me sing.

"Oh, baby, I'm feeling a little bit better, but the kind doctor wants me to stay in bed and rest." She holds my hands and looks at me through her shiny brown eyes. "So I won't be able to go to the festival. I'm so sorry."

"But, Mama, you promised you'd come. This is a special party." I stamp my foot on the floor so hard the bottles on the table clatter. I look at the doctor and give him my mean look. He turns away and looks out the window. I want to go over and sock him in the belly.

"I know, Daisy. Please don't be upset. I'm disappointed too. But Papa will be there to see you." I can feel my lower lip quivering. My mama's eyes are getting watery. "Perhaps you can come here after the festival and sing your solo for me," my mama says.

"It won't be the same as you being there."

This isn't just any year of the festival, and Mama and I both know it. This is the first time us colored children get to sing in front of everyone. Before only the white children got to sing at the festival.

Dr. Browne starts fussing with all the little medicine bottles. I know he wants me to leave. He cares a lot for my mama and is always looking after her. Even though I get mad at him sometimes, I know he means well. "Daisy, I think you should go now and let your mama finish her meal and get some rest. Besides you need to get ready for your big performance tonight."

I stare at Dr. Browne and point my finger at him. "I'll go. But I'm coming here after the festival to sing for my mama." I put my hands on my hips to let him know I'm serious. I give him my mean look again. He turns away shaking his head. I can see he's grinning though.

"I can't wait, baby." My mama smiles at me, but it's not a happy smile. It's a scared smile.

As I walk out of my mama's room, she starts another coughing fit. I look back and see Dr. Browne wiping something dark and red from my mama's mouth onto a white cloth. He puts a hand on her shoulder. My mama starts to cry.

I close the door and look through the keyhole.

"Doctor, do you think I'm getting worse?"

"It's hard to say, Mary, but let's be positive and hope for the best. Try to eat. Perhaps after a good night's rest you'll feel a little stronger."

I open the door just a crack. Dr. Browne walks over to the basin near the window. He washes his hands while looking outside. "Just look at that spectacular sunset. I'm not sure I've ever seen a sky so beautiful."

My mama turns her head and looks out the window. The cottage is near the shore of Hampton Roads. Some days you can hear the waves crashing against the rocks. The big boats look like toys bobbing up and down in the water. Their white sails are pink against the red sky. "Oh, Doctor, I know it's supposed to be beautiful, but it only reminds me of blood and this awful war. I hope it ends soon."

"We all believed it would've ended by now, Mary. Hopefully it will soon. Let's not worry about that now though. Get some rest, and I'll finish tidying up the room. Maybe you'll feel well enough tomorrow to visit with your students."

"Oh, that would make me so happy, Doctor."

I close the door quietly.

Mama loves to teach. She says a person with no learning is like a closed door. They have nowhere to go. She says it's her calling to open the door for all the children of Hampton.

And when General Butler arrived at Fortress Monroe and Mama heard what he did, she said he was the key to unlocking freedom's door.

Several months earlier—

M ARY TURNED UP A TREE-SHADED LANE clutching Daisy firmly by the hand. The satchel slung over her shoulder, containing books and a blanket, swung back and forth with each stride. Daisy's small legs struggled to keep up with her mother's brisk pace. "Slow down, Mama. You're hurting my arm."

Quaint wooden homes and shops—white, gray, and red—lined the cobblestone road. In a few weeks, flower boxes would be overflowing with brilliant colored blossoms and lush foliage. Mary treasured their morning walks through the tranquil streets of Hampton. But her town was changing. Mary couldn't see it, but she could certainly feel it. People were on edge. Many were suspicious. It had been five days since the Union surrendered at Fort Sumter. Only a day ago, on April

17, the Virginia General Assembly voted to secede from the United States, joining seven other Southern states.

Mary was too anxious to notice her daughter's pleas. She was certain two men had been following them since they left home that morning. White slave patrols roamed the town enforcing laws that forbade the teaching of all black people. Even children. She suspected the two men tailing her were seeking some type of incriminating evidence. Mary knew she risked severe punishment or even imprisonment for educating the deprived children of Hampton. She considered tossing the books into the bushes as they walked but felt confident she and Daisy could elude the two men.

Turning the next corner, Mary glanced over her shoulder and yanked on Daisy's hand. They quickly darted up a small dirt path. Mary whispered, "I'm sorry, Daisy. I didn't mean to pull on your arm so hard. We need to hide here for a few minutes, baby."

Mary felt Daisy grab her forearm. "Why do we have to hide, Mama? Why are you whispering? You're scaring me."

"I'll explain later, Daisy. Just do what I say and follow me." She guided Daisy behind some thick bushes where they both squatted down. Until now Mary hadn't realized how fast they had been walking. With each breath, she tried to control her heart pounding against her insides. Drops of perspiration trickled down her forehead, the sides of her face, and the back of her neck. Even on this cool April day, she could feel her dress sticking to her back.

Mary put her finger to her lips as the footsteps of the two men grew louder and then stopped. She was certain they stood only a stone's throw away where the dirt path turned up from the road. One man called out, "I think they turned up this way. They can't be far. I don't want to lose that stinking bitch again. Go check down the street. I'll look up here."

She heard the fading footsteps of one man. Mary couldn't hear the other man but suspected he was slinking up the dirt path. Mary looked down into Daisy's widening eyes and, again, put her finger to her lips. She could feel Daisy trembling. Mary put her arm around her daughter, stroked her hair, and kissed the top of her head. The sweet lemon scent of Daisy's hair, usually providing comfort and solace to Mary, only heightened her concern for her daughter's safety.

Mary craned her head to look down the path. She heard Daisy whimper and turned back. Daisy had one hand over her mouth and was pointing to Mary's arm with the other. Mary looked down. She could feel her wrist rubbing up against something soft and sticky. It was an elaborate spider's web spanning several small branches. A massive brown spider with a bristly body had crept onto Mary's dress and was making its way up her arm. She was about to brush off the spider when she heard rustling in the nearby bushes. The man was just a few feet away. Mary froze. She stared into Daisy's eyes, tears pooling in the corners.

Mary looked back at the spider. It inched up her arm. She watched the eerie movements of its eight legs, working in unison to navigate the folds in her sleeve. Her legs began to cramp from squatting. Perspiration from her forehead trickled down her nose. A drop lingered at the tip, urging a sneeze. Mary did all she could to fight the impulses of her body. Nerve endings screamed. Mary willed herself to stay still. *I must protect Daisy.*

Mary blew on the tip of her nose. The drop of perspiration flew into the air. Mary felt some relief. This gave her an idea. She turned her head and blew on the spider, hoping to encourage it to retreat. Instead it raised its front legs in defiance. Mary could see its beady eyes and tiny fangs moving in a pinching motion. She mustered all her strength to resist jumping up and screaming. She could feel Daisy's tears dripping onto her hand.

The man reached into the bush narrowly missing Mary's head. She was almost resigned to being caught. Mary now wished she had thrown the lesson books into the bushes, eliminating any evidence.

Mary could feel something tickling her neck. The spider continued creeping towards her ear. Goosebumps rippled across her shoulder and down her back. Her body shuddered. Her legs throbbed. She could hear and feel blood pulsing in her ears. She couldn't fight it anymore. She had to jump up.

A man's voice called in the distance. "Grover, I looked all the way to the end of the damn street. There's no sign of that bitch. They're long gone. Let's go. We'll try again tomorrow morning."

The man withdrew his hairy arm from the bushes. Mary closed her eyes and said a silent prayer. Footsteps shuffled away.

Unable to wait any longer, she swiped the side of her neck, sending the spider reeling into a nearby tree trunk. Mary's legs shot out into a seated position to relieve the cramps. With a soft moan, she messaged the backs of her thighs and calves. She grabbed the edge of her dress and scrubbed her face, neck, and hands. Her body convulsed.

Slowly Mary regained control. She looked over at Daisy, who was staring at the spider's web and seemed to be in shock. They remained hidden for a few more minutes. Mary leaned her head and kissed Daisy on the cheek. Daisy was as rigid as a statue. In a gentle whisper, Mary said, "Daisy, it's okay, baby. They're gone. We're going to be fine."

She put her hand on Daisy's shoulder. "You stay here. I'm going to check to make sure it's safe to leave." Daisy looked into her mother's eyes and grabbed her arm. "It's okay, baby. I'll be right back," Mary said. She carefully removed Daisy's clutching hands.

Mary maneuvered out from behind the bushes and walked down the dirt path. She peered out into the main street, looking both ways. The two men had just disappeared around the corner at the end of the block. Mary came back to retrieve Daisy, who looked from her mother's face to the spider's web. She held out her hand and guided Daisy onto the dirt path. Daisy wrapped her arms around Mary's legs. Mary leaned over and caressed her back.

With some coaxing by Mary, they inched their way down to the corner. Mary scanned both directions one more time. With a softer grip on Daisy's hand, they headed in the opposite direction of the two men. Mary chose side streets and narrow paths, even though it would make the journey longer. When they had to go on a major street, Mary made sure they walked on the shaded side hidden in the shadows.

Gathering two more children along the way, Mary and Daisy approached a large white home in an exclusive neighborhood of Hampton. It was owned by Confederate Colonel Charles K. Mallory, head of the 115th Virginia Militia, and they proceeded to the rear of the impressive property where the slaves resided.

Mary passed the rundown shanties and could see dirt floors through the open doors. Rotting wooden walls, in desperate need of paint, held up sagging roofs. She thought that the structures were barely suitable for farm animals, never mind humans. Waiting in the shadows were two men, Frank Baker and James Townsend, each with their two children. They looked around suspiciously as Mary approached.

Mary greeted them. "Good morning, Frank. Good morning, James."

The two men responded in unison. "Morning, Miss Peake."

James leaned over with his hands on his knees and a broad smile. "Good morning, Miss Daisy."

Daisy attempted a smile, wrapped her arms around Mary's leg and buried her face in her mother's dress.

Mary placed a hand on Daisy's back. She looked at the four children and said, "Are you ready for your lessons today?"

They looked at their teacher and nodded.

Mary, still shaken by the earlier encounter, turned to James. "Has anyone been asking where the children have been going during the day?"

"The Master's wife asked one day last week. I told her they were running an errand." James shrugged his muscular shoulders. "She seemed okay with that. There are plenty of folks here to do the work, so them being gone hasn't been a problem—especially the younger children. Besides there's a lot less work to do these days." James frowned. "You look upset, Miss Peake. Are you and Miss Daisy okay?"

"We're fine, James. Thanks for asking though." She looked down at her daughter. "We just had a close call with a slave patrol." Mary attempted a faint smile.

"Miss Peake, we all appreciate what you've been doing to educate our children. But we sure don't want you to get in trouble or get punished," James said.

"James, there's no need to worry. We'll just have to be more careful." Mary put her arm around his son, James Jr., one of her favorite students. The tall twelve-year-old flashed a toothy smile at her. Due to his age and size, he was often required to work on the farm and could only attend Mary's classes once or twice a week.

While the group stood in the shadows, a young slave in his early twenties wandered over. Under his breath, James whispered, "Oh, damn!"

"Miss Peake, this is Shepard Mallory. He's new here," James said.

While bearing the same surname as their owner, Colonel Mallory, there was no known blood relationship between the white Confederate officer and the slave. But Shepard arrived a few weeks ago, at a time when declining chores required fewer slaves, not more. His features were small and refined. His skin was a lighter brown than the other slaves. James suspected there was more to Shepard's relationship with their owner.

Mary watched the young slave's head swivel from the two large men to the group of seven children. His gaze rested on Mary's face. "What're you all doing here? You all look as guilty as a naked man suffering with quickstep in a cotton field. Why're you all talking in these shadows?"

James liked the young slave but wasn't sure if he could trust him. Frank, more gullible and most likely concerned that Shepard would eventually discover the truth, said, "Shepard, Miss Peake is teaching our children reading and writing. You got to promise to never tell anyone. We could all get in bad trouble—especially Miss Peake here."

"Reading and writing?" Shepard looked at each man and then to Mary. "Did your brains turn to cow chips? Slaves aren't supposed to be learning that stuff. You all are playing with fire. Besides I'm not the one going to get in trouble. I've got nothing to do with this crazy plan."

"Shepard, shush up. Just promise you won't tell anyone," James said, putting his hand on the young slave's shoulder and squeezing.

Knocking his arm away, Shepard said, "I won't tell anyone. Don't be worrying. I don't want anything to do with this." Shepard looked at Mary. "But Miss Peake, you can get twenty lashes for what you're doing. Or worse. You can get locked up in jail for a long time."

"It's okay, Shepard. I'll be fine. Besides it's only a few children."

"Yeah, well a spark can turn into a fire mighty quick. You all better be careful." Shepard shook his head.

"Shepard, it's important our children are prepared for a day when they might be free. They'll need to be able to support themselves and contribute to society." Mary squinted, watching for Shepard's reaction. "A person without an education is like a closed door. I'm trying to open that door for the children of Hampton."

"If you're not careful, the only closed door you're going to see is from the inside of a jail cell." Shepard frowned as he crossed his arms. "Besides I wouldn't be holding my breath for us all to be free."

"Miss Peake, Shep's right. You need to be careful." James swatted at a fly buzzing around his head. "And starting next week, you'll need to see our missuses when you pick up our children for lessons." Mary frowned as the big man spoke. "Our master, the Colonel, is sending us to Sewell's Point starting Monday. It's across Hampton Roads on the south shore. What with the war breaking out and fewer crops being planted, there's not much heavy work on the plantation anymore. The master can make good money lending us to the Confederate troops. They're going to put us to work building a fort against the Union."

Mary placed a hand to her mouth. "Oh, I'm so sorry. How long will you be gone?" She reached out and touched James's arm. Towering over most men, his broad shoulders and intimidating appearance masked his gentle, kind spirit. With a thick forehead, high cheekbones, and broad nose, James was ruggedly handsome. Mary cherished her friendship with the sensitive, compassionate man. Despite his lack of a formal education, she knew James possessed raw intelligence and endless potential.

James looked at his two children. "They're telling us it could be a few months." Mary watched James Jr. kick up some dirt.

"That's terrible." Mary looked from James to Frank. "I'll certainly pray for your safe and quick return back to Hampton and your families."

"What about me?" Shepard stared at Mary. "I'll be going too. Are you going to pray for me?"

"Of course, Shepard." Mary smiled at the young man. "I'll pray for all of you."

After exchanging goodbyes and well wishes, Mary rounded up the children and set out across town. They carefully navigated the back roads of Hampton, avoiding any busy streets. She was concerned that with a larger group of children in tow it would be more difficult to evade the slave patrols. The playful shoving by the boys did little to keep the group inconspicuous. Mary had to corral the children several times along the way to discipline them.

Arriving at the outskirts of the scenic town, Mary led the group over the Hampton Creek Bridge. This was the most vulnerable part of the trip. Mary knew the group was exposed as they crossed the wide waterway without the protection of trees or shade. James Jr. and Frank Baker's son pretended to throw the smaller children in the water. One of the boys pulled on Daisy's pigtail, and she shrieked. Mary turned and said, "Children, it's important that you behave and walk quickly and quietly until we get to the tree." Her warm smile but stern eyes produced instant compliance.

Reaching the other side of the bridge, the group stayed along the edge of the main road. Several minutes later, they turned down a grass path. The excitement grew as they came upon a small field dominated by a huge oak tree. The children ran over to their outdoor classroom and began chasing each other around the massive trunk.

Mary cherished this location. She discovered it several years earlier while hiking through the fields. The large tree, with its extensive limbs, was a sign of strength and comfort. It also gave her hope in a way Mary couldn't explain. Daisy loved the tree, too, because it housed so many species and families of birds.

Lobes of the brilliant green oak leaves unfurled in the warm sunshine. Catkins drifted to the ground like snowfall. While Mary spread a large fluffy blanket on the damp ground, the children tried to catch the yellow, wormlike flowers.

The children settled on the big blanket, forming a semicircle around their teacher. Daisy always sat to Mary's left. Mary turned and smiled at her daughter, who eagerly knelt with her hands on her knees. The other children always tussled to sit to Mary's right. This day James Jr. was the quickest to occupy the coveted position.

Classes usually started with a song to calm the children down and help them focus. With an age span of almost ten years, planning lessons for the diverse group was sometimes challenging. Ironically, the younger children, who were able to attend classes almost daily, were more advanced. The older children often had to work on the farms and attended Mary's classes less frequently. At only five years old, Daisy was the star pupil, having benefited from Mary's constant attention.

Mary slipped a lesson book out from the satchel. Turning to her right, she smiled and handed it to James Jr. Her gaze swept across the other students. "Sarah finished Chapter Three yesterday. So this morning, James is going to read Chapter Four to us."

Some of the younger children groaned. They knew the next thirty minutes would be slow and painful as James Jr. struggled to sound out almost every word. Mary said, "Now, children, James doesn't get to join us very often. It's important that each of you has an opportunity to practice reading. You're going to have to be patient. Remember we all had difficulty learning to read." She turned to James Jr. and smiled. "I'm sure before long James will be reading fluently. Now, why don't we get started?"

James Jr. frowned at his younger sister, Millie, who still had her hands over her ears. He looked down at the page and placed his long finger under the first word. "T-t-h-h-e-e the f-f-farm ani-ani-ani-." There was an explosion of laughter, interrupting James Jr. in midsentence. The children pointed at James Jr. as they rolled around on the blanket.

"Children, that will be enough," Mary demanded. "I won't tolerate anyone making fun of James or any other child as they learn to read." Mary turned to Daisy with a stern look. "And Daisy. You should know better too."

"But, Mama." Daisy pointed to James Jr. with one hand and covered her mouth with the other hand. Two long catkins, twisted together, had floated down and landed on James Jr.'s head. The greenish-yellow clusters fluttered in the breeze like fuzzy, rabid caterpillars.

"Oh, for heaven's sake," Mary said. She reached over and plucked the catkins out of James Jr.'s hair. Mary turned to Daisy and threw them onto her daughter's head. Laughter erupted again.

Back at the Mallory farm, James, Frank, and Shepard were preparing to travel across Hampton Roads to Sewell's Point. They hoped they would be back with their families before the start of summer.

GENERAL BENJAMIN FRANKLIN BUTLER WAS NOT invited to sit down. He stood at attention with his arms by his sides. He balled his hands into tight fists. His jaw was clenched. General Winfield Scott, head of the U.S. Department of the Army in Washington and Butler's commanding officer, sat behind his desk with his hands folded across his ample waistline. The aging officer, at seventy-four, was clearly enjoying dressing down the younger Butler.

Butler shifted his weight from one foot to the other while the old man ranted. Although forty-two years old, Butler felt like a child back at Exeter Academy being scolded by his head schoolmaster. And he resented it. After all, he was a highly successful lawyer from Lowell, Massachusetts, where he practiced, as well as in Boston. Butler felt deep pride in his role as originator of the Massachusetts Brigade. He had even secured a bank loan to fund their provisions and travel. Governor Andrew had rewarded his efforts by appointing him in command of the newly formed brigade.

Only three days earlier, on May 13, Butler had entered Baltimore with two Union regiments. Acting on orders from General Scott's office to capture military stores in the hands of Rebel forces, he occupied the city without incident. Two days later, he was awoken by an aide. An important dispatch had arrived from General Scott.

Still in his nightclothes, Butler sat up in bed and reached for his reading glasses on the side table. He was certain Scott had sent a congratulatory letter on his first military encounter—and a successful one to boot. His short stubby fingers tried to neatly unfasten the flap of the envelope. After several failed attempts, he grabbed the envelope with one hand and ripped off the edge with the other. He removed the letter so quickly it partially tore. His hands were shaking. Butler unfolded the letter and read the first few lines.

"Your hazardous occupation of Baltimore was made without my knowledge and, of course, without my approbation. It is a godsend that it is without conflict of arms."

Butler put the letter down. "How can this be?" he mumbled to himself.

Leaning forward and pounding his fist on the desk, Scott proceeded to chastise Butler. "You had no authority or business entering Baltimore. You took a great risk upon your troops and the Union. And you thwarted my intention of taking Baltimore. How can you ever be entrusted with anything in the army again? You didn't even give me the courtesy of a reply to my message."

Butler watched Scott's sagging jowls quiver as he opened and closed his mouth. Spittle clung to his lips as he spoke, spraying onto the cluttered desk. Butler looked around the office littered with dusty relics from prior wars. The room even smelled tired and old. While Butler's anger brewed, sadness also crept in. He looked down at the old man whose eyelids sagged so heavily Butler could barely see his dull, gray eyes. Butler wondered if Scott was just a future, washed-up version of himself.

For the first time, Butler questioned his desire to follow in the military footsteps of his ancestors. His patience was worn thin. Under the circumstances, perhaps it would be best to leave the army and return to Massachusetts and his law practice. Butler advanced two steps, pulled Scott's letter out of his pocket, and threw it onto his desk. He leaned over and placed his hands on the edge of Scott's desk. "I didn't answer your communication as you didn't know what you were talking about. You say my movement was a hazardous one. I fully disagree. There was not the slightest hazard, and I knew it. I had sent a scouting party to determine what was going on in Baltimore."

Having tried many cases in Boston, Butler felt he himself was now on trial and needed to present a strong defensive argument. "You told me it wasn't necessary you should know beforehand what my Department of Annapolis did, and I was acting within the full limits of my department. I had orders from you to get the arms, which had been sent from Rebel Virginia to the Rebels in Baltimore. How did you think I would get them unless I went where the guns were? Your order itself told me the specific location in Baltimore where I would find these munitions. I agree that I didn't report to you in a timely manner, but I hadn't a moment to spare. I retired after almost two days' sleeplessness to get a little rest and was awoken to receive your insulting dispatch."

Butler could see the old man's jaws quiver and his bushy white eyebrows flutter in agitation. He thought about the countless times he had met with Scott and how frustrating many of those interactions had been. He continued. "What was the use of my reporting to you, anyway? I'd been before you several times in the past, and, as in the past, I doubt whether you'd keep awake long enough to listen to me."

Butler spun on his heels and, without saluting, marched out of Scott's office. Feeling light-headed, he leaned against a corridor wall. Officers walked by and nodded or saluted, depending upon their relative rank. Butler returned the greetings and pretended nothing was wrong.

Back at his hotel room, Butler thought after such an auspicious start, how could his military career unravel so abruptly? And disastrously? He threw his clothes and personal effects into his travel trunk.

Later that day, Butler arrived at his temporary quarters in Annapolis. He opened the door and was greeted by his wife, Sarah. "Benjamin, what a surprise! I wasn't expecting you until tomorrow." Sarah looked at her husband's bloodshot eyes. "What's wrong, Benjamin? Are the children well?"

Butler walked over and embraced his wife. "The children are fine, Sarah. I just had one of the worst days of my life"

"Oh, Benjamin. What happened?" Sarah said.

"Yesterday, I received a scathing message from General Scott regarding my occupation of Baltimore. I went to see him this morning in Washington. The interaction was quite heated, and I'm afraid I have no choice now but to leave the army." Butler squeezed Sarah's shoulders and buried his face in her neck.

"Benjamin, I don't understand. Everyone is talking about how successful you and your troops were. They're saying you were able to prevent a rebellion by those loyal to the Confederates. And without bloodshed. Why would General Scott be upset?" Sarah hugged her husband. Butler, again, felt like the ten-year-old child, this time being consoled by his mother. He felt a tear trickle off the tip of his nose and watched it disappear into his wife's thick hair.

Butler stepped back, cleared his throat, and wiped his eyes with his hands. Pacing the floor, he tried to explain. "Well, with Washington at risk of attack from the Rebels, Scott wanted to make an overwhelming show of force by marching several thousand Union troops into Baltimore himself. Several thousand! Can you imagine? It was a ridiculous plan." He swung his arm through the air as he spoke. "There wasn't even any opposition there. I suppose my actions deprived the old General one last display of his rank and power." Butler dropped his arms and shook his head. "Needless to say, the old man was livid. And I, also, was angry in return. The exchange was quite passionate."

"But I don't understand, Benjamin. Why do you have to leave the military?"

"That's not all of it, I'm afraid." Butler walked over and sat down in an armchair. He leaned over with his head in his hands, massaging the back of his neck. "Scott's relieved me of my command as a result of my actions in Baltimore. He's reassigning me to Fortress Monroe." Butler looked up at his wife.

Sarah walked over and sat in the chair next to her husband. She gripped the wooden arms. "Fortress Monroe? Isn't that in Virginia? Why, that's in the middle of Confederate territory." Sarah placed a hand over her mouth in disbelief.

"It's about eighty miles from Richmond and, yes, the surrounding area is occupied by Confederate forces. I'm sure I'm being punished and banished to some irrelevant island." He waved his hand in the air and looked at Sarah with a forced smile. "But it doesn't matter. I've decided to leave the military and return to my practice."

"Benjamin, you know I would pack right now and leave first thing in the morning for home. Besides you haven't seen our children in over a month now. I'm sure you miss them. And I know they would love to have their father back home." Sarah looked into her husband's eyes. One of his eyes drooped inward. Growing up, children made fun of him for being cross-eyed. Sarah found that to be one of his many peculiar but charming features. "But are you sure this is what you want?"

"Sarah, I don't know what I want anymore. All I know is my legacy to follow in the footsteps of my ancestors is finished. My grandfather fought in the Revolutionary War, and my father fought in the War of 1812. I lasted for all of what—four days?" Butler stood up, walked over to the window, and looked out onto Chesapeake Bay.

"It seems so unfair, Benjamin. Isn't there anyone you trust in Washington that you can talk with?"

"Trust? Ha! Sarah, I'm a Democrat. The administration is Republican. I'm not sure I can trust anyone there."

The conversation was interrupted by a knock at the front door. Sarah walked over and opened it. Butler's military secretary, Richard Fay, stepped in. "Mrs. Butler, I have a dispatch for the General. I think it's important. It's from Washington, ma'am. Secretary Cameron."

Butler stepped into the foyer. "Good day, Richard. What would the Secretary of War want with me?"

Fay handed the document to Butler. "This just arrived, sir."

"Thank you, Richard." Butler nodded. "Oh, Mrs. Butler and I may be returning to Massachusetts tomorrow. We should know later this evening."

"Of course, General. I'll wait to hear from you. Sir. Ma'am." He nodded and left.

Sarah followed her husband back into the sitting room. Butler opened the envelope. He took his reading glasses from his pocket. Butler read the letter and looked up at Sarah with a frown.

"Well, what does it say, Benjamin?"

Butler shook his head. "Now I'm totally confused. It says 'You are hereby informed that the President of United States has appointed you Major General.' It's a promotion, Sarah."

"Benjamin, I'm so proud of you. This is wonderful."

"Or is it irrelevant?" Butler threw the paper into the air. It fluttered to the floor.

Sarah walked over and picked it up. She read the dispatch and looked down at her husband. "Benjamin, I think you should write to Secretary Cameron. Explain to him what's happened. Perhaps you should go back into Washington to meet with him. You could even request a meeting with President Lincoln. I'm sure between the two of them, you could get to the bottom of this. How can you be relieved of your command and then get promoted? All in the span of a few days! It makes no sense, Benjamin." She walked over to Butler and held his face in her hands. "Write to Secretary Cameron tonight, dear. You can leave for Washington in the morning. I'll go pack your bag."

Butler placed his hands on top of his wife's hands. "I thought you wanted me to leave the military and go home. It sounds to me like you're trying to make a case for me to stay."

"Benjamin, there's nothing I want more than to go home. Believe me. But I know you. I fear you won't truly be happy unless you take this new commission at Fortress Monroe. At least write the letter and go to Washington. You may get to the bottom of what's going on, Benjamin. Or you may not. Besides what harm can it do?"

After dinner that evening, Butler sat down to write to Secretary Cameron. As he thought about phrasing the letter, all the emotions of the day resurfaced. Even though his new commission sounded impressive—Major General of Fortress Monroe and the Departments of Virginia and North Carolina—Butler was convinced he was being punished.

Butler wrote, "What does this mean? Is this a censure of my action? If my services are no longer desired by the Department, I am quite content to be relieved of command, but I will not be disgraced. To be relieved of command of a department and sent to a remote fort, without a word of comment, is something unusual at least. Am I so poor a soldier as not to understand it otherwise than in light of a reproof? At least, I desire a personal interview with you and the President before I accept further service."

On the morning of May 18, Butler entered the office of Simon Cameron, Lincoln's Secretary of War. Although the nature of business in the room was to either defend against acts of violence or to initiate them, the decor was surprisingly warm and comfortable. Aside from the large desk and American flag, it could have been a sitting room in one of the many beautiful homes around the District. After greeting the Secretary, Butler took a seat directly across from Cameron and got right to the point.

"Secretary, my dispatch to you summarized my dreadful meeting with General Scott." Butler sighed. "If my services are no longer needed, I intend to report home to be with my family."

Butler watched Cameron shuffle papers on his desk. "General, I kindly beg that you not leave the services of your country." Cameron looked up. "You'll only regret this. You've come into the service as a leading Democrat. Others who are prominent Democrats have followed your example. If you leave, your action may make the war a Republican, partisan one. Besides you are being put in command of one of the most important departments of the United States, including Fortress Monroe and the Department of Virginia and North Carolina. Why would you assume your services are no longer needed?"

Butler described the emotional meeting he had had with Scott. Cameron covered his mouth with a hand and suppressed a smile. "General, surely being young, you are capable of forgiving the outbursts of temper of a disappointed old man. Confidentially, General Scott will not long remain in command of the army due to his infirmities."

"Secretary, all this sounds well and good. But it doesn't change the facts. Fortress Monroe is isolated, far from any real action. And surrounded by Confederate territory." Butler stood up with his arms crossed. Thick veins stuck out of the side of his neck. "I feel I'm being punished. I won't be humiliated or insulted."

"General, I understand your frustration. Your dispatch to me was quite clear on this. I contacted the President and he is eager to meet with you. Let me assure you, this is not a trivial assignment. I suspect the President will make this clear." Cameron stood and extended his hand.

Later that day, Butler called on President Lincoln. "Mr. President, thank you for taking the time to see me regarding this unfortunate situation. As you know, I am being relieved of my command of the Department of Annapolis and am being reassigned to Fortress Monroe and the Department of Virginia and North Carolina. I believe this is in retribution for my actions in the taking of Baltimore, which was necessary and well within the limits of my department."

Standing together, President Lincoln was a good foot taller than the diminutive officer. Lincoln smiled, sat on the edge of his desk, and folded his arms. He rubbed his bearded chin. "Certainly, General, this administration has done everything to remove any thought of reproach upon you; and I wish very much that you would accept the commission. Why, I'm surprised you believe your new assignment to be so trivial. You will find great historical significance in Fortress Monroe and will soon understand its strategic importance. It's the only Union fort in the south not to fall into Confederate hands."

Lincoln paced the floor as he continued. "The fort is ideally located on Hampton Roads. To the west is the James River. It's the only sea passage to the major Confederate cities of Norfolk and Richmond." He stopped directly in front of the General. Butler looked up into the President's deep-set eyes and detected a sly smile forming. "General, whoever controls Hampton Roads commands all sea traffic inland to major population areas of the Confederate territories." Lincoln placed his hand on Butler's shoulder. "And Fortress Monroe is perfectly located to restrict all water passage in and out of the James River."

Butler considered Lincoln's persuasive comments. He also recalled the discussion he and his wife had had a few days earlier. Sarah was usually reluctant to give advice about military matters and Butler's career. But when she did, it was on the mark. "Well, Mr. President, I did consult with the mother of my children regarding this difficult decision. She will support whatever I decide but believes I would be most unhappy and discontented if I don't take this new commission."

"Certainly you couldn't have done a better thing than consult with your wife who will also bear the burden of your new commission," the President said. "Her advice is sound and similar to my own beliefs in this matter, General."

Butler looked out the window of Lincoln's office at the unfinished Washington Monument in the distance. He turned to the President. "Then I will accept the commission with many thanks to you for your personal kindness and patience. But there is one thing I must say to you,

as we don't know each other well." Butler took a deep breath and let it
out slowly. "As a Democrat, I opposed your election and did all I could
for your opponent. But I shall loyally support your administration as
long as I hold your commission. If I find any act that I cannot support,
I shall bring the commission back at once and return it to you."

"That is frank and fair." Lincoln smiled and stood up, once again
towering over Union officer. "But I want to add one thing. When you
see me doing anything that, for the good of the country ought not to
be done, come and tell me so, and then perhaps you won't have any
reason to resign your commission."

"I will certainly do so if the need arises, Mr. President, and do
thank you for your kind words of support." Butler shook hands with
President Lincoln and returned to his hotel room.

The steamboat cruised down the Potomac River and entered
Chesapeake Bay. The crisp morning air greeted the lingering fog,
hugging the distant shoreline. A shroud of marbled gray and white
clouds threatened the spring day, but the waters were unusually calm.
Well out of range of Confederate guns, the large ship made good
progress as it passed the York River to the west on its way around the
Virginia Peninsula.

Only four days after meeting with President Lincoln, General
Butler stood on the main deck. His wispy hair fluttered in the sea
breeze. His hands rested on the starboard railing. Butler closed his
eyes, took a deep breath of the fragrant Virginia air, and tried to relax.
Looking at the large pine and cedar trees dotting the distant landscape, he was reminded of his home and the New England coastline.

It had been only five weeks since leaving Boston, but it seemed
much longer. So much had happened in that short time. He missed his

children and still questioned whether he should have left the army and returned home. But he knew it was too late to change his mind. Sarah remained in Annapolis to supervise the packing of their personal possessions. She would join Butler at Fortress Monroe in a few days.

The sound of seagulls broke Butler's trance. He had been replaying the events of the past few days over and over again in his mind. Thinking of his encounter with General Scott, his hands were gripping the railing so tightly his knuckles were white. Butler flexed his hands, trying to return circulation to his fingers. Even his jaw muscles were sore from being clenched.

He contemplated what awaited him as the steamboat continued south around the Virginia Peninsula. After his discussion with the President, Butler was intrigued to learn about the historical significance of Fortress Monroe. Through careful research and conversations with others knowledgeable of the area, Butler learned that Fortress Monroe was on a large spit of land at the tip of the Virginia Peninsula. He had metaphorically joked that he was being banished to some remote island. Near the town of Hampton, the fort was surrounded by a large expanse of water called Hampton Roads, at the southern end of Chesapeake Bay. He snickered to himself as he thought, *I guess I am being sent to a remote island.*

He considered the briefing he had received in Washington, carefully avoiding puddles of sea spray as he walked the deck. The current fort was the most recent of several built on this location since the early 1600s. Earlier versions succumbed to the forces of nature or were burned down. After the British Fleet sailed into Hampton Roads during the War of 1812, sacked Hampton, and formed a blockade of the waterway, Congress realized the need to fortify the location and to protect the region and Chesapeake Bay. The construction of a masonry fortification was approved, with work commencing in 1819. Named after President Monroe, the fort was essentially completed in 1834.

A weakness of Fortress Monroe was that it couldn't command the two-mile wide channel leading into Hampton Roads. To remedy this, another stronghold, Fort Calhoun, was constructed on an artificial island of stone in the middle of Hampton Roads, about a mile from Fortress Monroe.

Butler was also aware that the Confederates were building a fortification on the south bank of Hampton Roads at Sewell's Point. Despite the great guns of Fortress Monroe, the Union could not fire across this long distance. The strategic importance of Union-controlled Fort Calhoun to fully command sea traffic in the area was evident.

Stretching his neck from side to side, Butler shook off the stiffness of the voyage. The dread of his new assignment had gradually been replaced by anticipation. He was looking forward to getting started in his new post.

Butler spotted the top of a lighthouse. As the steamboat reduced speed, Fortress Monroe slowly came into view. Although he had heard about the enormity of the Union fortification, the massive granite walls and turf-covered ramparts were truly stunning. Butler knew that Fortress Monroe, jutting out into Hampton Roads, was surrounded by Confederate forces on the mainland. Consequently, Union forces could only access the fort by sea. Due to its location and the Union's control of the surrounding waterways, however, they could resupply the fort at will.

Union naval vessels were moored in the waters leading into the James River further west. Several structures bordered the waterfront, wedged between the Hampton Roads and Fortress Monroe. Butler could see the hospital and a sprawling, elegant hotel—incongruous against the hard, cold, stonewalls of the Union stronghold.

As the steamboat pulled up alongside the wharf, he was pleased to recognize three men awaiting his arrival. Captain Peter Haggerty, a military officer under his command in the successful occupation of Baltimore, waved. Major Richard Fay, his military secretary, stood with his arms crossed. Edward Pierce, a close acquaintance from Boston and a private in Company L of the Massachusetts Regiment, saluted. The three men would be part of his new staff at Fortress Monroe.

General Butler disembarked and the four men exchanged warm greetings. Making their way onto the waterfront, Butler was welcomed with a military salute. "General, we've arranged an escort for you to your quarters," Fay said. "I'm sure after your travels, you must be in need of some rest."

"To the contrary, Major Fay. The sea was quite calm, and we made steady progress. It'd do me good to walk and stretch my legs."

The four men headed towards a bridge that crossed a large waterway. Butler stopped midway and looked down over the side.

"General, we're crossing a moat that's about eight feet deep and a hundred feet wide here. It's controlled by a gate system fed by water from Mill Creek on the north side." Fay pointed to his left. "This is the largest moat-encircled masonry fortification in the United States."

Butler was impressed with the exterior layout. He knew that the government had made a substantial investment constructing the fortification, which covered sixty-three acres. "It certainly is a scenic location, with the open sea and attractive buildings surrounding the fort," he said.

Fay smiled. "Despite its luxurious setting, General, let me assure you this fort is designed for only one purpose. As you can see, the fort has an unusual shape. There are seven walled fronts with a bastion at each intersection. The design provides the capability to protect the fort from any angle using direct, flank, and crossfire."

Butler looked up at the high granite walls as they approached the entrance. "I notice the walls are quite thick," Butler said.

Fay stopped and put his hand on the hard stone. "Yes, sir. They're thirty-five feet high and ten feet thick at the base. The walls we're passing through surround the entire fort. The total circumference is over a mile long. Can you imagine?"

After passing through the gate, Butler could see the huge expanse within the protection of the massive granite walls. Butler found the setting quite pleasing, noting the broad, partially shaded walks and numerous oak and flowering trees planted throughout. The dogwoods were in full bloom. To his right, he spotted an attractive chapel. It reminded Butler more of a peaceful New England village than a military fortress.

As they walked, Butler could see houses of various styles and sizes dotting the landscape. They were surrounded by beautiful, flowering gardens. Many were covered with mature vines. Large shade trees sheltered the porches. Butler looked up at the granite walls. The serene residential setting made an unsettling contrast to the grave purpose of the fort.

They passed by a street with white houses set close together and alike in appearance. The orderly homes were uniformly spaced and set back from the road, as if at attention and awaiting inspection. Butler stopped in front of one. "Are these the officers' quarters, Major?"

"Yes, General. Some of the officers also occupy quarters in the casements built into the walls under the ramparts. We can inspect them on the north side of the fort if you wish," Fay said.

Butler noticed that, until reaching the north end of the fort, the ramps and ramparts were in good condition. Fay continued. "The fort is designed for 412 guns with a water battery containing forty guns to concentrate fire on vessels before they enter the channel." Butler pointed to the north-facing wall. "Major, I'm noticing the guns only face the sea. I don't see any armaments for inland protection."

"You're correct, General. The fort was established to protect the waterways. It was never conceived the fort would be assaulted from the land-facing side to the north. At least until now, that is." Fay grimaced.

Butler wiped the sweat off his upper lip. "My initial determination is this fort doesn't meet wartime standards, Major. Particularly under the unfortunate circumstances our country currently faces. Have sandbags placed on the walls facing land to cover the magazines. If the Confederates ever fired upon us, the magazines would be without protection."

Fay led the group into one of the officer's quarters built into the rear wall. Butler wandered over to an embrasure penetrating through the exterior wall. Intended primarily for firing guns through the slanted exterior opening at enemy forces, the guns were currently withdrawn. This allowed the gentle breezes to flow into the otherwise stuffy room.

It took a few minutes for the men's eyes to adjust to the darkness. Butler peered out the opening into the moat that surrounded the north side of the fort facing the town of Hampton beyond. He noticed that the wide, deep moat seen on the south, sea-facing side of the fort was much narrower and quite shallow on this north side. The moat walls were eight feet high and designed to hold six feet of water. Yet there were barely one to two feet of water in this area.

Butler could see a considerable population of oysters in the moat. He recalled hearing that this area of Virginia was known for its delicious seafood. As he examined the moat, he turned to Fay. "Major, I notice the moat in this area is quite shallow. It's not clear that it would be very effective if we were attacked from this side."

While awaiting a response, Butler heard the sharp sound of something hitting a rock. He immediately hugged the wall. Butler's initial reaction was that Rebel forces might be firing on the fort from the mainland. He suspected the sound might be from Rebel fire ricocheting off the large granite walls.

Butler carefully looked out the opening again and saw an empty oyster shell sailing through the air. It struck a pile of shucked oysters in the shallow moat. Growing up near the New England coast, Butler knew that gulls picked up clams and oysters, flew high into the air, and dropped them onto rocks. After striking the hard surface, the shells would break open revealing a tender meal.

Another shell flew by the window. Based on the horizontal trajectory of the shell, he concluded it couldn't be the result of a bird. He estimated the shell came from the left, possibly from an adjacent room. Butler turned to Fay. "Major, I would like to inspect the quarters just to the west."

"Yes, sir." They exited the room back into the bright sunshine. Butler shielded his eyes. They walked a short distance and entered the adjacent officer's quarters. Squinting into the darkness, Butler could make out the silhouettes of two men sitting on stools near the embrasure, huddled over what looked like a large bucket.

Butler watched one of the men reach into the bucket, remove an object, and insert a knife in a prying motion. He brought the object to his mouth, slurped the contents, tossed the empty shell out the window and let out a deafening belch. The sound echoed throughout the stone structure. The two men roared with laughter.

"Ahem," Major Fay cleared his throat.

Startled, the two men turned and immediately came to attention.

"Gentlemen, is this your idea of defending the fort against Rebel forces—pelting them with oyster shells?" Butler said, looking from one man to the other.

"No, sir. We've been on duty all night and are on our respite. We find the oysters more tasty and satisfying than the fort's rations, sir," one of the men said.

Butler turned to Major Fay. "Major, open the gates and restore the moat to its required depth. Also, insure that our soldiers are adequately fed so they no longer have to scavenge the moat for food."

"Yes, sir."

As the men followed Butler out of the room, Fay looked over his shoulder and gave the two soldiers a stern look

Back outside in the bright sunlight, Butler shielded his eyes and looked down the street. He pointed to a large wooden structure. "Major, I'd like to visit the stables and inspect the horses."

Fay looked at Butler then down at the ground. He kicked up a small cloud of dirt. "General, while the fort has excellent stable facilities, there are only a few horses there."

"Are they being exercised or on an excursion into the Virginia countryside, Major? If so, we can come back at a later time."

"Well, not exactly, sir."

"I'm sorry, Major. I don't follow. What're you trying to tell me?"

"Well, General, the fort only has a few horses presently."

Butler was stunned. "How can that be, Major! We've over 4,000 soldiers and anticipate doubling our size shortly. Clearly the stables should be teaming with cavalry horses."

"General, it appears requests have been made but the requisitions have gone unfulfilled."

"Major, this is unacceptable," Butler said, glaring at the empty building. He turned to his aides. "Let's make this an urgent item to address at our staff meeting in the morning. If you could show me to my quarters now, I'd like to unpack and take a rest."

DAISY WAS LYING ON HER STOMACH ON THE floor. Her feet swung back and forth as she turned the pages of a bird-watching book. "Oh, look, Mama. This is one of my favorites." She held up the book to show her mother. "It's a cardinal. They like to eat berries and seeds and all types of bugs. That's so disgusting. It's such a pretty color though. I love red. I think it's my favorite."

"It is a pretty bird, Daisy. That's the male, right?" Mary looked at her daughter and smiled. She was so proud of Daisy, who had started to read when she was only three. Now, at five, she could almost read fluently.

"Yeah, I guess so." Daisy put the book back down on the floor. "The male attacks other birds to protect its nest." She turned back to her mother. "How come all the boy birds have the best colors? Girl birds are always an ugly brown or gray color." Daisy flipped the page. She rolled onto her side with her head in her hand. The pointer finger of her other hand moved across the page as she read.

"That's how God made them, baby. I think you're pretty, and you're a girl." Mary carefully pinned a dress pattern to some fabric.

"Yeah. But even I'm brown." Daisy flipped the page. "Do you know what bird you are, Mama?" Daisy softly giggled as she pointed at her mother.

"What bird I am? You think I'm a bird?" Mary looked up from the dress she was making for Daisy.

"No." Daisy put her hand over her mouth to conceal her gaping smile. "I always pick birds for people I know."

Mary eyed her suspiciously. "Okay. So what bird am I?"

"You're a mockingbird," Daisy said, giggling. Her two front teeth were just filling in after a painful month of being teased by her friends.

Mary put the light blue material on her lap and placed her hands on her hips, pretending to be shocked. "A mockingbird! Why am I a mockingbird?"

"Because they sing the best. They go on fence posts or on top of houses and sing to everyone. Just like you. And you sing better than anyone I know."

Mary couldn't deny that she loved to sing—at home, at church, and in the garden. Or sometimes just walking down the street. "Well, thank you, baby. That's a very good reason. But mockingbirds don't have pretty colors like the cardinal." Mary's lower lip drooped.

"How do you know? I didn't show you the picture." Daisy quickly covered the page with her hands.

"You forget. That book used to be mine. I spent lots of time looking at the pictures and reading all about birds when I was your age. It was my favorite book." Mary picked up her shears and starting cutting along a pattern through the fabric.

"Was it your favorite because you like birds?" Daisy turned on her side to face her mother.

"Yes. And because my father gave it to me when I was a small girl. He brought it from his home in England." Mary looked out the front window and was momentarily startled. She thought she saw a shadow pass by.

A loud knock on the front door interrupted their conversation. Mary leaned forward in her chair and pointed. "Baby, can you get that? I don't want to lose my place here."

Daisy jumped up and ran to the door.

Mary heard her daughter call out, "Mama, it's Mr. Dennis."

Dennis was one of the slaves up at the Boyd plantation.

"Come in, Dennis. I'm in the sitting room. Please show him in, Daisy."

Dennis followed Daisy into the cozy, well-lit room. Mary placed the fabric on her lap. "Hi, Dennis. I hope everything's all right with the Boyds."

"Mrs. Boyd sent me here to fetch you, ma'am. She says it's an emergency." Mary watched Dennis look around the room.

"Oh, dear! I hope there's nothing wrong with her."

"Ma'am, she said to tell you to bring your sewing kit." Dennis arched his eyebrows and shrugged his shoulders.

"My sewing kit? Now?" Mary put the fabric and shears on the side table and stood.

"She said right away, ma'am." Dennis looked uncomfortable.

Daisy went over to her mother and put her arms around Mary's waist. "Mama, you said you would read the bird book with me when you finished."

Mary rubbed Daisy's back. "I'll be real quick, baby. We can spend as long as you want reading when I get back." Mary looked at Dennis. "Please tell Mrs. Boyd I'll be along shortly. I need to bring Daisy to our neighbor's first." Mary took Daisy by the hand.

Dennis nodded, took another quick glance around the room, and walked out.

"Daisy, bring your book. You can read it until I get back."

Through the window, Daisy watched Dennis climb into a carriage and drive away. She turned back to her mother. "Why does Mrs. Boyd always have to ruin our day? I hate that woman."

"Daisy, you shouldn't use that word. Mrs. Boyd may not always be pleasant, but that's no reason to dislike her."

"But Mama, I don't like the way she treats you. And Mr. Boyd is a really scary man," Daisy said.

Mary stared out the window. She crossed her arms and watched the carriage disappear around the corner. Swirls of dust blew across the road. Mary knew Daisy was right, particularly about Mr. Boyd. She had managed to evade the slave patrols for over a month since her close encounter. She suspected Mr. Boyd was somehow connected with the incident. Visiting the Boyd home was always draining, even though it meant more business and much-needed income. The Boyds always made Mary feel inferior. She placed a hand to her mouth and turned away from the window.

Weston Boyd paced the floors of one of the largest mansions in Hampton. "Melinda, how can you wait until we're just about to leave to get dressed? You know how important this event is. Where's that stupid woman anyway?" He took a sip of vintage Château Latour Bordeaux from his lead crystal glass and set it down on the table.

Melinda Boyd walked across the sitting room and spun in front of a large mirror. "Weston, this dress must've shrunk. I wore it only a few weeks ago, and it fit just fine." She strained to fully inhale. "I can't imagine what happened."

Weston Boyd struck a match and lit the expensive European cigarette hanging from his lips. His inventory was slowly dwindling. Soon he would have to smoke American cigarettes. After a deep inhale, he tilted his head back and blew gray smoke high into the air. He examined the tight dress. "Don't you have anything else you can wear? And why do you use that damn Negro woman anyway?"

"It's simple, Weston. She jumps when I tell her to, and she's cheap. Even you can understand that. Besides she does good work. And she's a mulatto not a Negro. Not that that makes any difference, of course." She put her nose in the air, turned sideways, and admired her full figure in the mirror.

Weston sat down on his gold embroidered settee. He placed his arm along the back and looked around the magnificent sitting room. Weston felt immense pride in the wealth he had inherited. He relished his role as a leading citizen of the town. "Well, I don't trust her. We know she's been teaching some of those damn slave children. We just haven't caught her yet. But I have some men following her around. We'll get her eventually. And when we do, we'll give her something she'll never forget."

"Weston, don't hurt her. At least wait until my dresses are all altered." Melinda Boyd was aware most of her wardrobe no longer fit. With the Union blockade, European cigarettes and other fine goods were in short supply. There was a shortage of elegant American and European fabric, and Melinda's dresses would be difficult to replace.

Weston looked at a portrait of his deceased grandfather, a successful plantation owner who had amassed great wealth. "Who does she think she is? Just because she's a free woman, it doesn't mean she can violate the laws of Virginia. She may be half-white, but she's still half-Negro too. And that makes her a dirty Negro."

Melinda unbuttoned the midsection of her blue satin dress and took a deep breath. As she exhaled, flab bulged through the opening like bread dough. "I heard a new Union General arrived at Fortress Monroe today. And more and more men from the North keep coming."

Weston extinguished his cigarette in a marble ashtray and stood up. He started pacing again. For the first time in his life, he felt threatened. Weston had heard about the Union forces arriving almost daily. As of the third week in May, local folks estimated there were 4,000 armed men at the massive Union fort. Weston stopped and pointed a finger at his wife. "If those Yankee bastards think they can change our way of life, they have another thing coming. The institution of slavery is critical to the South. Why, those stupid Negros wouldn't know what to do with freedom even if they had it. It won't happen anyway because we'll crush those Yankee scum."

Dennis lingered by the door to the sitting room until Weston noticed him. "What is it, Dennis?" he growled.

"Mr. Boyd, sir, Mrs. Peake is here. Should I show her in?"

"Of course not. I don't want that woman in this room. Bring her into the kitchen. And Melinda, take that damn dress off so it can be fixed and we can leave."

Melinda turned her nose in the air and walked out of the sitting room. "I have to leave it on so Mary can see where it needs alterations."

Mary stood outside the side entrance to the mansion—the servants' door. She always felt conflicted when she went to the Boyds' home and to the homes of her other white customers. As a free woman of mixed race, she felt entitled to enter through the front door. She made that mistake once with Mr. Boyd. When he opened the door and saw her standing there, he slammed the door shut in her face. Afterward Melinda Boyd instructed Mary to always use the servant's entrance.

Dennis escorted Mary into the house. Walking by the massive foyer, she always had the same thought. With its large staircase spiraling to the upper floors, several people could walk arm-in-arm up the stairs and still not touch the banisters. The extreme lavishness was as impressive as it was repulsive.

On this visit, Mary caught a glimpse of the sitting room through a large arched doorway. She couldn't ever remember seeing anything so exquisite, not even when she lived in Alexandria as a child. Being a seamstress, she appreciated the magnificent fabrics that bordered the tall windows and the richly colored upholstery on the furniture. She was proud of her own home, but the comparison to the drab browns and grays of her furnishings was startling.

Mary's eyes followed the staircase up to the second and third floors. She was certain her entire home would easily fit in just the foyer. She wondered how some families could have so much while others struggled to feed and clothe themselves. And some of those fortunate families, with so much, seemed to always want more.

The thought of Daisy's earlier comments made her smile. Female birds may have brown and gray feathers, but they are also humble and demure. The colorful feathers of the male birds just reflected their flashy and aggressive behavior. Mary was fine with her browns and grays.

Melinda Boyd burst through the kitchen door. "Mary, what took you so long? We've been waiting and waiting. I need this dress altered immediately. Now hurry and take your measurements so I can get out of this thing."

"I'm sorry, Mrs. Boyd. I came over as soon as I could. Let me see." Mary did a quick walk around Mrs. Boyd. She knew she had let this dress out within the last month. She couldn't believe it was already bursting at the seams. The Bishop sleeves, which were supposed to be gathered at the shoulders, widening at the elbow and narrowing at the wrist, were snug the entire length. "Mrs. Boyd, I'm not sure there's enough material left to let out. I can try moving the buttons, but I'm not sure that will suffice."

"Wait 'til I get a hold of Rebecca. She must've shrunk the dress when she cleaned it," Mrs. Boyd said.

Mary recalled letting this dress out at least three times in the past several months. Even from a few feet away, Mary doubted the dress had been washed recently, if ever. After Melinda Boyd disrobed and handed the dress over, Mary adjusted the buttons and seams as best she could. Upon finishing, Dennis escorted Mary to the servants' door. Weston Boyd intercepted them. "Leave, Dennis. I want a word with her."

"Yes, sir." Dennis left the room with a concerned glance over his shoulder.

Mr. Boyd set down his wine goblet and crossed in front of Mary. His face was full of grim fury. "You must think you're something special. We know what you've been doing. And we're going to catch you. When we do, you'll get a beating like you can't imagine. I'll ruin you and your family. When I'm through with you, you'll be begging the slaves for food and shelter."

"Mr. Boyd, I'm not sure what you're referring to." Mary could see the rage in his eyes. As frightened as she was, she didn't want to look away and appear guilty.

"You know damn well what I'm referring to. You're teaching those damn Negro children to read." Weston placed his hands on his hips.

"Mr. Boyd, all we do is go on nature walks and sing songs." Mary's back was pressed against the doorjamb. Her heart was pounding like a freight train.

He pointed his finger inches from her face. "That's a bunch of damn hogwash and you know it." Veins bulged in his forehead. His eyes were bloodshot. His sour breath sickened Mary.

"I'm sorry, Mr. Boyd. I don't know what you're talking about. Good day, sir." Mary slid past Weston and stepped outside. She hurried around the side of the house and down the long stone path bordered by perfectly manicured hedges. She dared not look back.

Blossoming dogwood trees graced the front lawn. She was relieved to smell their sweet scent after being in the warm, stuffy kitchen. Reaching the road, she turned back to the enormous brick house with its white columns framing a massive porch and supporting a second floor balcony. The beauty of the home and surrounding landscaping was breathtaking, despite the people who occupied it. Rundown slave shanties leaned precariously in the back of the home. The contrast was always startling to Mary.

Weston Boyd, with folded arms, stood in the doorway of his mansion. Mary could see him talking to two men. She wasn't certain, but they looked like the same men who had followed her and Daisy a month earlier. Weston Boyd pointed in her direction. The two men turned. Meeting their eyes, Mary lowered her head and hurried up the tree-lined road. The sight of the two men and Weston Boyd's threats played over and over again in her head. Her throat was tight and her head throbbed as she held back tears.

The further she walked, the more determined she became. After several blocks, the brisk exercise and bright sunlight seemed to have a calming effect on Mary. Despite her encounter with Weston Boyd, seeing her home in the distance, she couldn't help smiling. Mary always looked forward to the comfort of being at home with Daisy and her husband, Thomas.

Mary thought about her earlier conversation with Daisy and her clever daughter's penchant for comparing people to birds. She grinned. *Weston Boyd is a vulture—he feasts on the weak and needy. Melinda Boyd is a peahen—strutting around in her fancy feathers, with her big bosom thrust out, and screeching constantly.*

JAMES TOWNSEND YAWNED AND STRETCHED his arms high into the air. A sharp spasm shot through his back. He doubled over, supporting the weight of his body with both hands on his thighs. Every muscle in his body was on fire. His hands throbbed. James winced as he examined his fingers. Half the nails had been torn off from hard labor. Even the thick callouses that took years to develop and once protected his hands had deserted him. In their places were large patches of open, raw flesh.

He noticed a flap of skin just under his left thumb. Wanting to prevent it from catching on a shovel handle, he carefully tore it off. James immediately regretted the decision as he created another gaping, bloody gash. He'd wrapped strips from an old flour sack around his shoes to protect the sides of his feet that protruded through large splits near the soles.

It had been well over a month since he'd told Mary that Frank, Shepard, and he were headed to Sewell's Point. James still remembered her reaction and hoped she was keeping her promise to pray for the three men. He certainly prayed for her well-being as she evaded slave patrols to teach his children and the other slave children of Hampton.

James couldn't recall the last time he had had a good night's rest. His days under the hot sun were long and exhausting. His nights were spent sleeping on a dirty old blanket on the ground. He knew living conditions in the shanty behind the Mallory estate had been far from ideal, but compared to living like field oxen, it almost seemed like paradise.

The three men were part of a slave brigade, constructing a Confederate fortification on the opposite shore of Hampton Roads, about three miles southwest of Fortress Monroe. Although much of James's body ached, his heart hurt worse. He hadn't seen his wife and children since leaving Hampton.

Frank Baker hobbled over. "Morning, James." He inspected his hands, which were in the same horrible condition as his friends. He let out a low groan as he flexed his fingers open and closed.

"Hey, Frank. How you feeling today?"

"Pretty much hurting everywhere. I'm not sure what hurts more— my back, my hands, or my feet. How about you?" Frank said as he stretched.

"Yeah. It sure wasn't easy on the Mallory farm, but compared to this, it was almost bearable." James put his hand on his friend's shoulder.

Colonel Mallory was less severe with his slaves than most area farms. He permitted his slaves to work at their own pace and without supervision, provided all work was performed satisfactorily. He also let his slaves move freely around Hampton when their work was completed. They were allowed to marry and have children, although the families had no legal standing.

A change from growing tobacco to cultivating grains and vegetables, along with the escalating conflict on the peninsula, left Mallory with excess slaves. Colonel Mallory told James, Frank, and Shepard that the construction of the Confederate fortification on Sewell's Point and the critical need for hard labor there presented him an opportunity to loan the three slaves to the Confederacy and generate much-needed income. He further explained that they were selected because they were strong, healthy, and attracted a premium rate.

James, in his midthirties, and Frank, six years older, were devastated at the thought of being away from their wives and children, but they had no choice. If they resisted their master's demands, they risked being sold off and separated from their families forever.

Shepard, only twenty and not married, was relatively new to the Mallory farm. Shepard never talked about his background, but it was obvious to the other two men that he didn't trust anyone. Not even them. They had seen the deep scars on his back one day and suspected that whatever happened to him probably contributed to the young slave's guarded behavior.

While Frank and James stood talking, Shepard came hobbling over. His breath ran ragged just from the short walk. "No way I'm going to be able to work today."

James grimaced at the young slave. "Shepard, are you crazy? We're all hurting. They aren't going to let you rest while we all work ourselves to the bone."

"Yeah. But I'm really hurt. My back's broken." Shepard stooped with is hands on his knees.

"Shep, your back isn't broken, you fool." James looked around to see if they were being watched. "You're going to get yourself whipped silly if you pretend being hurt."

Frank looked at Shepard and back to his friend. "James, it's too late. This boy's already silly." The two men laughed so hard they had to clutch their backs in pain.

"Well, I'm sick of this. I can't do this much longer. I want to go back to the farm." Shepard looked across Hampton Roads at the town of Hampton in the distance.

"Listen, Shep," James said. "This dang wall's almost finished. Maybe it'll be done in a few days or a week at the most. After that, we're sure to go back to the Mallory farm. Just keep your head down and do what you're told."

They shuffled over to retrieve their tools and start another long day reinforcing the breastworks. Rags wrapped their hands to protect the open wounds. A Confederate officer strutted over with his arms crossed in front of his chest. "We're making good progress, and we're almost done. I figure we'll be finished in a day or two," he said. "We've got maybe another fifty feet of digging to do. The harder you work, the quicker you finish. So get your carcasses out there and stop your whining."

The three slaves gave each other a furtive glance. "Thank the Lord," James muttered. He could only think of seeing his wife and children and enjoying a home-cooked meal. He couldn't wait. Yet, after what he and his two friends had been through the past month, he knew they could manage a few more days. After all, James thought, what choice did they have?

James thrust the shovel into the hard earth and threw a heap of soil over his left shoulder. The sun's rays beat down on the slaves. Perspiration drenched their shirts, and they longed for water to quench an agonizing thirst. With the anticipation of being home before the end of May, though, they labored on with renewed vigor.

The distant sound of cannon fire echoed over Hampton Roads. James looked up and spotted a trail of smoke coming from a ship a half-mile offshore. A loud explosion sent dirt, rocks, and splinters of wood high into the air, raining down onto the three slaves and others close by. James saw Frank dive into the trench they had been digging and cover his head with his hands for protection. Shepard stood up to peer out into the waterway. James grabbed his arm and yanked him into the trench just seconds before another explosion, only ten feet away, buried the three men in debris. Despite ringing in his ears, James could hear the muffled commotion among the Confederates as they barked out orders and readied their guns.

"Just stay down until the shelling stops! We don't need to get killed just when we're about to get out of this hellhole," James yelled with his arm over Shepard's back, pressing the young man against the ground.

A Confederate soldier spied the three slaves hunkering down in the trench. He ran over and kicked James in the side. "Get the hell out of there and start repairing the damaged breastworks!"

James looked up in disbelief as projectiles from Union gunboats whizzed over their heads. The three men remained motionless. "I said get up. You either move now, or I'll shoot you where you lie. This hole will be your grave," the soldier said. James shot a glance to Frank and nodded. He tapped Shepard on the shoulder. They crawled out of the trench and scurried behind the breastworks, joining other men rebuilding the fortification.

The two sides continued exchanging fire until darkness arrived. During the night, the Confederates worked frantically to make rapid progress on the breastworks. Frank, James, and Shepard worked all night until daybreak. They hadn't slept for twenty-four hours straight. After a two-hour break, they were back working at the breastworks.

That afternoon, the two sides resumed the bombardment. This time the Confederates were ready and were much more accurate firing their guns. Incurring a few cavernous holes in its hull, the Union ship limped back to the safety of its port.

"Dang, that was close," James said. He, Frank, and Shepard were coated in dirt and sweat but, fortunately, uninjured.

"I can't wait for the next few days to be over so we can get out of here," Shepard said. "I'm so tired, I might just sleep until then."

"Well, I suspect all this commotion just added at least three to four more days to our work here. Those explosions destroyed a big part of the breastworks we've been working on this week." James pointed to several gaping holes in the earthen wall.

The three men picked up their dusty blankets and spread them out on a level patch of dirt. Despite the hard ground, they were soon fast asleep.

DELIGHTFUL AROMAS OF BAKING BISCUITS AND smoldering oak wood permeated the kitchen. Daisy was covered in flour. White powder coated the table and the floor where she stood. "My, my! You look just like a ghost," Mary exclaimed, shaking her hands in the air. "W-w-w-o-o-o-o," she howled. Daisy doubled over in laughter.

Rivers of happy tears flowed down Daisy's face, washing away flour that stuck to her skin. "Now you look like a white tiger with brown stripes," Mary said. Another round of laughter filled the kitchen.

Daisy ran up to her room to look in the mirror. Mary could hear the tapping of Daisy's feet as she ascended the wooden stairs. "Hey you, get back here. We're not done. There are a lot more biscuits to bake today." Mary smiled as she carefully arranged the tray in the wood-burning, cast-iron stove.

She cherished her stove and used it often. Thomas had come home with it a year earlier. The owner of a large mansion in Hampton had renovated his kitchen, and Thomas had bartered with the man, exchanging his labor for the stove. Mary placed both hands to her mouth to hide the broad grin, as she recalled the day Thomas had surprised her.

Daisy walked into the kitchen with a freshly cleaned face. "That looks better," Mary said. "Let's mix some more dough. We need to make two more batches of honey biscuits. And let's try to keep the flour in the bowl this time." Mary walked over and kissed her daughter on the top of her head, lingering as she inhaled the lemon scent of Daisy's hair. Mixed with the aroma of fresh biscuits, Mary thought the two made a pleasant combination.

"Mama, why do we need so many biscuits?" Daisy cracked eggs into a bowl and watched a piece of shell fall in. "Whoops." She covered her mouth with her hand. Daisy grabbed a spoon, scooped the shell, and mixed the eggs with the other ingredients. A puff of flour leapt out of the bowl and landed on her nose.

"The Daughters of Zion are providing each family with biscuits and jam later today. Our job is to make the biscuits. We need to be there by three," Mary said. "Oh, Daisy." She walked over with a cloth and wiped flour off her daughter's tiny nose, softly squeezing it as she finished. Moving to the oven, Mary opened the door a crack and checked so make sure the biscuits were rising and not burning.

In addition to teaching, Mary's other main passion was the Daughters of Zion. She had heard about the organization and set about originating a chapter of the benevolent society in Hampton several years earlier. Its primary mission was to serve the poor, the sick, and the needy. When Mary wasn't teaching, she could often be found at a small chapel used as a meeting place for the Daughters. They formally met every Monday evening but informally got together at various times during the week.

Mary and Daisy each cradled a large basket covered with a red cloth. Mary was setting a brisk pace on the way to the chapel off Court Street. Daisy fell several paces behind, busy watching several goldfinches splashing in a nearby puddle. "Mama, my arms are killing me. I think they're gonna fall off."

Mary stopped and turned to her daughter. "Daisy, please don't say *gonna*. And your arms aren't *going to* fall off. We only have one more block to go. You can do it. You're a strong girl." She noticed bugs buzzing around Daisy's basket. "Make sure you keep the cloth over the biscuits. We don't want any flies feasting on them."

The chapel was humming with activity. Tables were set along two walls below large tapered windows. Used clothes, organized by gender, size, and garment type were neatly stacked on one table. Another table was lined with clear, glass jars, filled with three different types of jam—raspberry, strawberry, and blueberry. Mary and Daisy walked over to the jam table. Mary set her basket down. "Baby, you can put your basket right here." Mary pointed to a corner of the table. Daisy set the heavy basket down. She rubbed her forearm where the handle had made a deep imprint.

James Townsend's wife, Hannah, was busy organizing the used clothes. Spotting her friends, Hannah walked over to greet them. "Good afternoon, Mary. Daisy, those biscuits smell heavenly. Did you help your mama bake them?" Hannah put her hand on Daisy's shoulder. Daisy flashed her teeth and nodded her head up and down.

"Have you heard any word from James?" Mary bit her lower lip.

"Oh, Mary. I'm so worried. I haven't heard anything since they left in mid-April. It's been over a month now. I don't sleep at night, and the children seem so sad. I'm thankful that you keep them busy most days with their lessons." Hannah reached out for Mary's hand. "I try to stay busy to keep from fretting all day. There's word that Union boats fired on Sewell's Point yesterday. I haven't heard about any casualties. I pray James and the others are safe," Hannah said.

Mary put her arm around Hannah. "I'm sure they're fine. James and Frank are strong, smart men. They'll make sure they keep themselves and Shepard out of danger."

Hannah looked around the room and attempted a weak smile. "It's gonna be busy today," she said. "We have over thirty women coming." Someone called for Hannah from across the chapel room. "Oh, I should go see Charlotte. She may have heard something about Sewell's Point. Excuse me, Mary. I'll talk with you all later." She patted the top of Daisy's head and walked away.

"How come she gets to say *gonna* and I can't?" Daisy said with her hands on her hips.

"It's not correct grammar, Daisy," her mother said. "You know that. Now please help me unpack the biscuits." Daisy saw a friend and wandered away.

"Hey, where are you going?" Mary said.

"I'll be right back, Mama." Daisy skipped across the room.

Mary finished putting the biscuits on the table. Noticing a new pile of clothing that had just been dropped off, Mary walked over to help organize them.

A few minutes later, Daisy was back by her side. She pulled on her mother's arm. Mary looked down, "Oh, there you are. I was wondering where you went."

"Mama, what does 'uppity' mean?" Daisy said with furrowed brows.

"Uppity? Why, where did you ever hear that word?" Mary crossed her arms.

Daisy pointed across the room. "Those women over there. They said you were uppity because your skin was light and you think you're better than them."

Mary watched two dark-skinned women standing near the table, wrapping Mary's biscuits in a piece of white cloth. They placed several biscuits and a few jars of jam into soiled handbags. "Oh, Daisy. It's a complicated topic, baby. Of course, I don't think I'm better than anyone. We're all equal in the eyes of our Lord." She caressed the top of Daisy's head. "Some people have very difficult lives and, I'm afraid, say things that they think will make them feel better. We're very fortunate we have a nice home and enough food to eat. Some folks don't." Mary took Daisy's hand. "Now we need to get going to make supper for your papa. He'll be home soon."

They left the chapel room, hand in hand, each swinging an empty basket in their free hand.

Mary rarely gave much thought about her biracial heritage. She was always too busy. As an educated free woman, she felt comfortable in most settings and around most people. However, some white people, like Weston and Melissa Boyd, made it clear how they felt about her. Even with her lighter skin and delicate features, Mary knew they considered her beneath them. Whenever she left the Boyd home, feelings of melancholy and sometimes anger were only temporary. She knew the Boyds and others like them were just plain ignorant.

Even some dark-skinned women assumed Mary didn't understand their plights. Mary occasionally felt trapped between the two races, thinking she didn't really fit neatly into either. One thing was clear though. She deeply resented slavery and felt the laws were stacked against black people, whether free or not. She was convinced that, with an equal footing, they could thrive and contribute to society as effectively as anyone. These deep-rooted sentiments helped fuel her passion to teach the slave children of Hampton.

Later that evening, Mary sat in her chair, trying to sew by candlelight. Daisy was fast asleep after a busy day of school, baking, and then the Daughters' meeting at the chapel. Thomas watched Mary's eyes slowly narrow, squinting to see the needle and thread in the dull candlelight. Intermittently, Mary's eyes would close for several seconds and her head would slowly fall forward until she would awaken with a sudden shudder. A few times Mary even started to snore.

"Mary, why don't you just go to bed? You can barely keep your eyes open," Thomas said, hiding a grin behind his large hand.

She looked up at her husband and smiled. "Oh, I'm fine. Just tired from the long day, I guess. Daisy and I made several dozen biscuits this afternoon. There are happy families all over Hampton tonight who ate freshly baked biscuits, smothered in homemade jam." Mary pushed the needle through the material with one hand and pulled it out the other end with the other.

Through weary eyes, she looked at her husband, started to say something and then hesitated. "Thomas, do you think I'm uppity?" Mary pursed her lips.

"Mary, what are you talking about?" He sat forward. "You're the most generous, giving person I know. Why would you ever think you're uppity?"

Her eyes darted from the dress to Thomas's face and back. "Oh, I don't know." She shrugged her shoulders. "Just forget it." Mary looked up and made a crooked grin.

"I almost forgot to tell you," he said. "I was repairing a home in Fortress Monroe today and heard some of the soldiers talking. They said there's a new general at the fort. He's from Massachusetts. I think I saw him walking around." Thomas chuckled. "If it was him, he sure was short. And chubby. Not exactly what you'd imagine an important man with such a big job would look like, that's for sure."

Mary inched forward in her chair. "Thomas, did you hear anything about Union ships firing on Sewell's Point?"

"Come to think of it, I did hear these soldiers mention one of their ships was hit by Confederate fire and barely made it back to the wharf. I don't really know anything else. Why?" James said.

Mary put the material, needle and thread down in alarm. "Thomas, I told you. James, Frank, and the young slave Shepard were sent there in mid-April. It's going on five weeks now. I saw Hannah this afternoon. She's so worried about James. It's understandable. To go this long without even a word must be unbearable. I hope they're okay."

"Sorry, Mary. I forgot about that. It's been so long. Listen, I know James and Frank, and I'm sure they can take care of themselves. They'll be fine." Thomas leaned over and patted his wife's hand.

"That's what I told Hannah today. I sure hope we're right. And I hope this awful war doesn't escalate. Do you think the Confederates would ever attack Fortress Monroe?" Mary sat back in her chair.

"Well, if they tried, I can't imagine they would have a chance in Hades of succeeding. What with all the Union soldiers here and their large guns, the Rebels wouldn't stand a chance. I understand those guns in Fortress Monroe can reach all the way to Hampton. Can you imagine? That has to be over a mile away." Thomas shook his head in grateful disbelief.

"Well, I hope there are no confrontations near here," Mary added. "Actually, Thomas, I really don't want to see any fighting at all. I wish these men could find a more civil way to address their differences. We all want slavery to end, and my deepest hope is that these poor people can be free to live the lives they desire. But the thought of spilling blood—I just can't think about it." Mary picked up her sewing and looked out the window into the darkness.

Thomas paused a moment and licked his lips. "I know, Mary. But some things are worth fighting for. And this is one of them." He stood up and extended his hand. "What do you say we go to bed now before you poke yourself in the eye with that needle?"

Thomas chuckled as he helped Mary up from the chair.

BUTLER AWOKE EARLY, STIFF FROM HIS VOYAGE the day before. Despite a restless night, he was excited to confront the challenges of his new command. He closed the door to his quarters. Standing on the porch, Butler gazed at the breathtaking expanse of the fort. The massive granite walls cast long shadows from the rising sun. The morning fog overhead was slowly burning off to reveal a deep blue sky. He set out for a walk around the interior perimeter of the fort—a daily ritual he would continue throughout his time there. Mentally rehashing a list of improvements underway at the fort, Butler was pleased that he was already making an impact.

He paused outside his office. Soldiers were marching in unison down the street. Men were atop the ramparts positioning the large guns. Butler realized that the advice he had received from the Secretary of War and President Lincoln was indeed sound. Fortress Monroe was most impressive. His ego was slowly being restored to be in command of such an extraordinary fortification, despite its geographic isolation.

He filled his lungs with air, thrust his shoulders back, and entered his office with a proud smile. The staff members waiting for him included Major Fay, Captain Haggerty, and Private Edward Pierce. As they all took seats around the table, Butler explained that he had three key objectives for his first meeting—review his orders from General Scott, understand the current and near-term troop levels of the fort, and address the shortage of horses.

"Gentlemen, my orders from General Scott are as follows. First, we're not to let the Rebel forces erect batteries to annoy Fortress Monroe. We already know that recently two of our ships fired upon Sewell's Point to destroy that fortification and its newly mounted guns. I understand that while the *Monticello* incurred extensive damage to its hull, it was able to lay waste to a large portion of the Confederates' breastworks being constructed there." Butler went on to list the remaining orders from General Scott, all designed to hinder and frustrate Rebel efforts in the area.

Butler stood up and walked over to the window. He opened it to let fresh spring air into the stuffy room. After returning to his seat, he held up a piece of paper. "I'm told a war garrison for Fortress Monroe is about 2,500 men. We'll soon have here, inside and outside the fort, nearly three times that many. Assuming 1,500 is an adequate garrison to resist any attack on the fort, at least for the next few months, we'll use the remainder of the forces for aggressive purposes. Our first engagement is to enter the Town of Hampton in order to disrupt the Virginia vote for secession taking place today."

Butler was anxious to test the resolve of the Rebels in Virginia. He knew the decision by the Virginia Convention delegates to secede from the Union was not an easy one, nor was it unanimous. After

Lincoln's election a year earlier on November 6, South Carolina was the first state to secede on December 20 that year. In their case, it was a unanimous 169 to zero vote by convention delegates to leave the Union over Lincoln's election and the restriction of slavery in new U.S. territories.

Six more Southern states followed over the next several weeks. South Carolina had opened the floodgates, and the young nation ruptured. Following the attack by Confederate forces on a small Union garrison at Fort Sumter, Lincoln declared a state of insurrection. The Confederates occupied the fort after the Union commander surrendered, leading Lincoln to call for 75,000 volunteers to quash the rebellion. The Northern states quickly answered the call. With their backs against the wall to take sides, Virginia delegates voted to secede from the Union on April 17. This was followed by an order from Lincoln to blockade all Southern ports.

Butler walked around the perimeter of the table with his arms crossed. "We know that the Virginia convention voted eighty-eight to fifty-five to secede from the Union. Only a few weeks earlier, a vote actually *rejected* secession." He paused to make the point. "The attack on Fort Sumter and the North's response was clearly the turning point in voter sentiment. The Virginia delegates voted to submit an Ordinance of Secession to the citizens for ratification or rejection. This vote is taking place today," he said, stabbing the table with his finger.

Butler continued, "I'm ordering the First Vermont Regiment, under the command of Colonel Phelps, to make a reconnaissance across Hampton Creek and into the village of Hampton. Phelps is one of the finest soldiers I've ever met. He's to enter Hampton with the intent to disrupt the secessionist vote and then return to the fort. Major Fay, relay these orders to the Colonel and have him ready his troops as soon as we finish here.

"Now let's move on to the current garrison population and expectations for additional forces." After a long discussion, the group agreed that additional land was needed to accommodate growing troop levels. Butler and members of his staff would meet in an hour to explore the countryside.

"My last topic is the issue of horses. What exactly is the current situation, Major?"

"General, we have seventeen horses, not all in the best of shape nor adequately trained."

"Major, in a few weeks we'll have almost 10,000 men in and around Fortress Monroe. How can we mount an effective campaign in the surrounding Confederate territories without horses?" Butler stood up and pressed his hands into the table. "Have a requisition for 300 cavalry horses prepared for my signature by this afternoon."

"Sir, there's an existing requisition for 120 horses that's been outstanding for three weeks," Fay said.

"Then we shall issue a second requisition for more horses, Major." Butler stared at his senior aide.

Colonel Phelps and his men assembled in Fortress Monroe to receive their orders. After mounting his horse, Phelps led his Vermont regiment through the main gate. The fort was connected to the mainland by a causeway about a half-mile long and then a wooden bridge some 300 feet in length crossing Mill Creek.

The causeway and bridge were property of the fort and therefore controlled by the Union. Beyond the bridge was Camp Hamilton and then a tract of land heavily wooded and scattered with farms. It was not unusual for Rebels to picket the mainland end of the wooden bridge. On this particular morning, this was not the case.

Phelps and his men proceeded up the dusty road heading into Hampton. He knew that the village of Hampton, with a population of about 1,500, was located about a mile northwest just over a second wooden bridge spanning Hampton Creek. The Union men were enjoying their first foray into the countryside. Until now they had been confined to the Fortress Monroe, Camp Hamilton, and the immediate vicinity.

As the Union men were approaching this second bridge, they could see smoke rising in the distance. Volunteers from the Virginia Militia had set fire to the wooden structure to frustrate the advance of the Union soldiers.

Phelps ordered, "Double quick, men. Disperse those men and extinguish the flames." The Vermonters were soon at the bridge scooping up water from Hampton Creek with their hats and dousing the burning timbers. Within minutes, the flames were out. However, the four Rebel agitators had escaped back across the bridge and into the village.

News of the advancing Union forces quickly spread throughout the town. White folks sympathetic to the South, particularly women, either hid inside their homes or fled into the countryside. The terrified slaves were mostly left to fend for themselves. In an attempt to maintain their loyalty, their masters had told them stories of captured slaves being tortured by the Northerners, sold and transported to Cuba, or even being eaten.

Most of the slaves hid where they could. A few, not believing the

Rebel lies, stood by the side of the road to witness the first Union incursion into Hampton. Mary Peake and her daughter, Daisy, were also with those waiting for a close-up view of the Vermonters. Mary's husband, Thomas, was at Fortress Monroe, building housing for the troops.

Mary and Daisy could hear a young boy nearby, pleading with his mother to hide. Mary looked to her right and recognized Frank Baker's wife and two children. Frank's son, a few years older than Daisy, was holding his mother's hand and trying to pull her away from the roadside and into the cover of nearby trees. Mary heard him say, "Please Mama, they're going to cook us and eat us. We need to go and hide now."

His sister's arms were wrapped tightly around their mother's leg. The poor woman seemed frozen in place. Mary wanted to go over to comfort them, but the Union forces were nearby and fast approaching.

Mary felt Daisy pulling on her arm. "Mama, are these men going to eat us?"

Mary laughed, "Of course not, baby. These men are going to save us." While she clearly didn't believe the lies told by the local white folks about the Northerners, she was going through a range of emotions herself. None of these emotions, however, was fear.

She felt defiance toward the slave owners and the Confederates trying to preserve their way of life and its dependence on slavery. She felt concern. Concern with how this escalating war would evolve and what the eventual outcome might be. But mostly she felt hope.

As Phelps and his men entered the center of the village, more slaves came out to the street to witness the encounter. Colonel Phelps rode over to an old man, slumped and leaning on a cane in front of a small masonry church. "Sir, can you please tell me where the voting is taking place today?"

"Yes, sir," the man looked up and pointed. "Further down this road you all can see a large white building. That'd be the courthouse. That's where the voting's taking place."

Phelps thanked the man and ordered his men to follow him down the road and to be on guard. As each row of Vermonters marched past Mary, Daisy, and the other bystanders, they removed their hats and gave a polite bow. Mary smiled and returned an acknowledging nod back to the soldiers.

The growing group of slaves by the roadside started shouting to the passing Vermonters: "Praise the Lord!" "Halleluiah!" "Bless you all!"

Phelps led his horse to the courthouse and dismounted. He entered through the front door with several of his heavily armed men. A short, burly man inside walked over to confront them. "What's the meaning of this? This is Virginia land and you have no business here, sir."

Phelps towered over the man. Although he could have easily overpowered him, Phelps showed the restraint of a seasoned soldier. "I have orders from General Butler, commander of Fortress Monroe, to close down these polls. Please disperse and leave the premises immediately."

The man looked around the courthouse at his fellow citizens. He turned back to Phelps. "By what right do you take this action, sir?"

The Colonel thrust his shoulders back and looked down his nose at the man. "My might is my right, sir. Now please vacate the premises. We don't want any violence but are well prepared to deal with any that might occur."

One of the town's men made a quick movement towards a back room. Two Union soldiers immediately drew their weapons and took aim. Realizing they were outnumbered and outgunned, the Hampton men grumbled as they filed out of the courthouse building. One man yelled over his shoulder as he left. "We'll see about this. This isn't over. You'll see."

Phelps and his men went outside, closed the front door, and watched the Southerners disperse down the side roads. He remounted his horse, instructing his men to again be on guard as he led them back down the main street of Hampton. By this time, the crowds had dissipated.

Butler, Fay, Haggerty, Pierce, and two guards mounted some of the few horses in the fort and proceeded down the causeway, across the wooden bridge spanning Mill Creek. Over the clopping of hooves against the boards, Fay briefed the General. "Sir, we established Camp Hamilton on the Segar Farm just up the road. It consists of tents and other temporary structures. The Second New York and First Vermont regiments are billeted there." Fay wiped his forehead and upper lip with a handkerchief. "While we can probably accommodate additional men there, much of the nine New York regiments arriving soon will require yet another encampment."

Sweat rolled down the sides of Butler's face. He unfastened the top two buttons on his jacket. His aides, anxious to get relief from the grueling sun, quickly followed suit.

Approaching Camp Hamilton and seeing its weak defenses, Butler frowned. "Is this Camp Hamilton safe from Rebel advances, Major?" he asked.

"Yes, General. There was little effort made to provide the camp with extensive fortifications as the guns from Fortress Monroe provide sufficient protection," Fay said, turning and pointing back in the direction of the large fort.

After a quick inspection of Camp Hamilton, the group proceeded north, further into the Virginia countryside. Butler swatted a swarm of mosquitoes circling his head. He slapped the side of his neck, leaving a streak of blood from the thirsty insect. "Damn these bugs!"

Butler stood in the saddle, giving his bottom some relief. It had been a while since he had ridden. His inner thighs were throbbing. His pants were drenched in sweat from the hot, sticky saddle. "General Scott indicated there might be a shaded pine forest north of here near the bay. Major, are you aware of this area?"

"No, sir." Fay unfastened a few additional buttons. "Actually, this is the first time any of us have been this far from the fort."

The group entered a partially shaded area. "Has there been any reaction by the Rebel forces to the buildup of Union men and supplies, Major?" Butler asked.

"General, we believe the Rebels are well aware of the men and provisions arriving daily." He turned to face Butler. "Without an effective navy, they aren't able to break our blockade of Hampton Roads." Fay replied, taking a swig from his canteen.

Sporadic trees grew denser. The group enjoyed the needed relief from the intense sun. They had arrived at the pine forest, almost two miles from Fortress Monroe. On a narrow strip of land next to the beach and between Miller's River and the sea, the area looked ideal. The group split up to investigate.

Pierce dismounted and stretched his legs. He led his horse near a swampy area along the edge of the tree line. One of his boots stuck in the deep mud. He bent over to dislodge it.

"My Lord!" Butler called out. His men quickly converged around their commander. "We're in the middle of a cemetery. Look here! Some of these graves are over half a century old. Why, they date back to the War of 1812."

Realizing the unsuitability of the location, they continued along the Back River. Butler informed the group. "Before leaving Washington, I studied some maps at the Congressional Library. There should be a high promontory at the junctions of the James River and Hampton

Roads. A map indicated a section of land jutting out into the bay and extending maybe four to five miles." He shifted his weight in the saddle.

The group followed the river, trying to stay in the shade of the trees. Approaching a clearing on a hill, Butler dismounted. His aides joined him.

Butler pointed. "Look there. That's the mouth of the James River in the distance. As you look to the west, you'll see a bluff stretching to a point. This is the junction of Hampton Roads with the James River—an area called Newport News. I estimate it's at least a half-day's ride. We won't have enough daylight to ride there so I propose we return to Fortress Monroe and set out promptly by sea."

They arrived back at Fortress Monroe in the early afternoon. Colonel Phelps met with the officers and briefed them on his successful mission into Hampton. What they didn't realize was that the white citizens of the village had slowly filtered back into the town from their homes or the surrounding woods. After gathering in the main street, they marched over to the courthouse, opened the front door and, in defiance, commenced with the polling. Outraged at the Union aggression, the citizens of Hampton overwhelmingly approved the Ordinance of Secession. The sentiment was similar in polls throughout Virginia. The only exception was in Western Virginia, where the population was more sympathetic to the Union.

After a hearty lunch, Butler, his staff, and twenty-five troops from Fortress Monroe headed down to the main wharf and boarded a steamship. Traveling west through Hampton Roads towards the mouth of the James River, Butler couldn't help but think of the irony associated with their current location.

Butler shook his head as he reflected. "Do you realize that the country is fighting a war over a dreaded practice whose origins may have begun in this exact location."

Haggerty leaned against the port railing. "How's that, sir?"

"I've been doing some reading. Somewhere near here, a Dutch ship arrived carrying Angolans captured from a Portuguese slave ship. I think it was around 1619 or thereabouts." Butler spat over the railing into the churning water. "It's believed to be the first introduction of slavery to the New World."

The group stood on the deck enjoying the smell of the sea air and the gentle breezes across Hampton Roads. The sound of a cannon, coming from the direction of Sewell's Point, jolted everyone. Captain Haggerty yelled, "Take cover!" Everyone scrambled to safety on the deck. Fortunately, the cannon shot from the Confederate battery fell short of the steamship. A large splash sent water high into the air.

Inside Sewell's Point, Frank, James, and Shepard were busy reinforcing the breastworks from the damage Union ships had exacted a few days earlier. The three slaves were in an optimistic mood knowing that their work there was almost finished, though the echoes of that cannon fire still kept them on edge. They labored harder than usual to ensure the timely completion of the fortification. The more quickly they returned to the Mallory farm and their families, the better. James stood up and leaned on his shovel. "Hey, Frank, what's the first thing you're going to do when we get back?"

Frank looked at his friend and gave him a mischievous smile. Just as he opened his mouth to respond, the light mood was shattered. The three slaves were only twenty feet from the deafening sound of one of the fortification's guns. Their first thought was that Union ships were back to shell the Confederate stronghold.

The men froze. James said, "Quiet. Listen for return fire. If you hear anything, head behind the breastworks lickety-split." They waited for a few minutes. Nothing. The three men didn't notice any usual commotion in the camp like they had encountered a few days earlier. James shrugged his shoulders and said, "They must be just testing the guns."

Back on the steamship, Butler was furious. He turned to Haggerty, "Are there any guns mounted on this vessel, Captain?"

"No, sir," Haggerty said. "We only have the small arms we carried with us."

"Then hand me my rifle. I'll show them not to be so damn reckless." Butler watched Haggerty run inside the cabin and return with his rifle. Butler placed the rifle on the port side railing, steadying his aim against the rocking motion of the waves. He held his breathe and gently squeezed the trigger in the direction of the Confederate fortification.

Shepard saw one of the Confederate soldiers pointing towards Hampton Roads. He wandered up and peaked over the revetment. Shepard scanned the wide expanse of the waterway and could see Fortress Monroe to the northeast and several boats. The sound of a rifle shot echoed in the distance. The bullet, from Butler's rifle, hit the wooden boards missing Shepard's head by inches, and splattering his face with splinters and dirt. Before he could react, James grabbed the back of his shirt and pulled him to the ground.

Frank hunched next to the two men. "Boy, are you daft! We got maybe a day or two until we're going home, and you're going to get yourself shot before we even leave. What's wrong with you, boy?"

Shepard's breath came in hard and fast. He wiped the dirt off his face and, trembling, felt around to see if there was any blood.

"You're fine, Shep. Now will you please just do what your told?" James pleaded, sitting against the earthen wall with adrenalin still pulsing through his body.

All eyes on the steamship watched for signs of additional canon fire. After they were certain they were out of range, Fay said, "We were lucky. Either that or their aim's bad."

Butler watched an osprey soaring high in the air. As it headed over the Confederate stronghold at Sewell's Point he thought, *If I could only see what you see.* Butler followed the large bird's flight, as it headed south and west over the Elizabeth River. He pointed and said, "Look, Norfolk is only seven miles up the river."

Haggerty turned to Butler, "General, it would be so simple to concentrate a Union fleet to attack the city."

Butler put his hand on his aid's shoulder and smiled. "Soon enough, Captain. Soon enough."

The steamship proceeded west toward Newport News Point, high on the bluffs. Spotting a small jetty, they carefully piloted the boat to avoid the shallow water. After disembarking, the men climbed the banks, swatting mosquitoes along the way. With faces drenched with perspiration and clothes stuck to their backs, they looked out over the sprawling view. They could see well north up the James River towards

Richmond, and across Hampton Roads to the Confederate southern shore.

Butler's expectations were more than realized. Across the way he saw a field of elm trees, perhaps greater than sixty acres. Between the trees and the bluffs was a large meadow of wheat, gently swaying from the soft sea breeze below. Butler saw that, from this vantage point, an armed fortification could command the James River north of their position. Satisfied with the results of their expedition, the group returned to the steamship and traveled a few miles further west towards Richmond, then turned around and proceeded back to Fortress Monroe.

"**D**AISY, ARE YOU READY? WE HAVE A BIG day ahead of us. Remember it's your turn to read today." Mary placed warm biscuits on Daisy's plate. She craned her head, listening for a response. Mary thought she had heard Daisy up early practicing her reading.

"I'm coming, Mama!" Daisy yelled down from her room.

"Are you reading your bird book again?" Mary smiled at her daughter's obsession with birds.

"Oh, darn." Upstairs, the girl closed the book and put it on the shelf. "I was reading about blue jays. I'll be right down, Mama." She slipped on her shoes and closed the door to her room.

Mary could hear her daughter running across the upstairs floor and down the stairs. Daisy skipped over to her mother and wrapped her arms around Mary's legs. "Mama, did you know blue jays sneak over to other birds nests and steal the babies? And then they eat them." Daisy pretended to bite Mary's leg. "They're mean."

Mary laughed and leaned over, kissing the top of her head. She was proud of her daughter. At only five, she displayed intelligence well beyond her years. "Hurry and eat your breakfast before your biscuits get cold. We have a busy day ahead of us," Mary said while placing two books and a blanket into her satchel.

A loud knock at the door startled her. She opened the door and was shocked to see Melinda Boyd standing there, perspiring and gasping for air.

Melinda Boyd had been on her way to an important women's breakfast. Her fancy carriage pulled up to an exclusive restaurant. She was a few minutes late to ensure everyone would witness her grand entrance. Dennis walked around to the side and helped her down the two steps to the ground. Mrs. Boyd began her grand, swaying entrance up the walk. She suddenly stopped and turned. Pointing to the slave and shaking her hand, she shouted, "Now be sure to pick me up in one hour. Exactly." Dennis nodded, returned to the carriage seat and pulled away, leaving a trail of swirling dust.

Strolling up the stone paved sidewalk, Mrs. Boyd spotted a small coin in the dirt. As she bent over to retrieve it, she heard a loud ripping sound. Mrs. Boyd looked around to see if anyone heard the telltale sound. Straining to put her chubby hand behind her lower back, she felt a wide tear extending several inches below her waistline. She tried to push her protruding undergarments back through the opening.

Realizing she was already running late and only a few blocks from Mary's home, she made a quick detour. Unfortunately, Dennis had already left with the carriage. She didn't like walking through the poorer area of Hampton but had little choice.

With a hand awkwardly behind her back, Mrs. Boyd pushed her way past Mary and Daisy, and stepped into the house. Mary slipped the satchel strap off her shoulder and set it on the floor. She grabbed Daisy's hand. Mary could feel Daisy tugging on her arm, trying to pull her out the front door. "One minute, Daisy." She looked at the woman. "Mrs. Boyd, what a surprise. Is everything all right?"

Mrs. Boyd looked down her nose at Mary's daughter, clinging to her mother's arm. "Of course everything's not all right." She looked back to Mary. "Why else would I ever come here?" Glancing around the room with disdain, she continued, "You need to mend my dress, Mary. I'm in a hurry, so I need it done right now." She pointed a finger at the floor and stomped her foot.

"Oh, Mrs. Boyd." Mary smiled. "Daisy and I were about to—"

The woman immediately cut her off with a dismissive hand gesture. "If you want to keep my business, you'll do the work now and do it fast."

The buxom woman posed with her nose high in the air. Stepping around Mrs. Boyd to examine the tear, Mary discreetly shook her head at the woman's imperious expression. She put a hand over her mouth to cover the smile forming on her lips. Mary thought Mrs. Boyd's rear end pushed against the fabric like a wild, caged animal trying to escape bondage. She found the woman's behavior intolerable, but unfortunately, she needed her business.

Daisy pulled on her mother's arm. "Mama, we need to go. We're gonna be late."

"I need to fix Mrs. Boyd's dress first, baby. And please don't say *gonna*." Mary patted her head and left to retrieve her sewing kit.

Mrs. Boyd glanced around the tiny sitting room with its tattered furniture and dull upholstery. Daisy was standing by the door with her arms crossed, staring back at Mrs. Boyd through a wrinkled brow. When Mrs. Boyd turned away, Daisy stuck her tongue out. Daisy spotted the long tear in the dress and let out a giggle before covering her mouth with her hand.

An hour later, Mary clutched Daisy's hand as they hurried down a hedge-lined side street. She noticed gray clouds forming on the horizon and hoped she would finish her lessons before the weather deteriorated.

Following her usual circuitous route, Mary stopped at several slave shanties scattered throughout the town to pick up children. With her young students in tow, she entered the bridge crossing Hampton Creek. Her thoughts wandered to the unexpected events that morning—the surprise visit by Mrs. Boyd and then the Union troops entering Hampton. Both had made her late. She smiled as she recalled how the soldiers had greeted her and Daisy as they marched down Court Street.

A gust of wind blew one of the boys' hats over the railing and into the churning waters of Hampton Creek. Mary heard the children's shrieks and turned to watch the current swiftly carry the hat away. "Oh, Tommy. I'm so sorry. I think your hat is gone. Children, hold onto your hats. And be careful of this railing. We don't want to get any splinters."

Daisy pointed to the opposite shoreline. "Look, Mama. An osprey. They're mean. Just like blue jays. They eat fish." The large white bird, with its distinctive black mask, flapped its wings, hovering high above the water. Then, with talons extended, it plunged feet-first into the water. In an instant, the bird exploded into the air carrying its prey. "Look! It caught a big fish."

The children jumped up and down on the bridge and shook their fists. "Drop it." "Get free, fish." "Fight back."

With talons deeply embedded in its victim's flesh, the large bird pumped its wings vigorously. The head of the captured fish faced forward, observing the panoramic views below. Mary shuddered as she wondered if the fish knew its fate. The osprey glided higher into the sky. Soaring past a grove of tall cedar trees, it headed south towards Hampton Roads.

An even larger bird, watching the deadly encounter, swooped out of a cedar tree and gave chase. "Mama, look. An eagle. It's chasing the osprey. Get him, eagle." The children cheered the eagle on, not realizing the fate of the fish was sealed either way.

Reaching the eastern shore of the bridge, a chilly wind off the Chesapeake Bay kicked up blinding swirls of dirt. Mary paused briefly to cover her eyes. She turned to survey the bridge and water's edge, and steered the children onto a nearly concealed grass pathway. The children sprinted into the open field and chased each other around the big oak tree. Distracted by the late start to her day, Mary hadn't noticed two men hiding in tall reeds just south of the bridge.

The children finished singing. Mary reached into her satchel and pulled out her lesson books. She turned to her left and handed a book to Daisy with a wink. "For the past week we've been reviewing our vowel and consonant sounds. This week we'll start working on our grammar. Soon we'll all be ready to start reading. Isn't that exciting?" She looked from child to child, as they all smiled and clapped in anticipation. "And today, it's Daisy's turn to read to the group." Mary turned back to her daughter but noticed she was distracted by something to Mary's far right. She followed Daisy's gaze and saw two men, with grizzled beards and wearing filthy, torn clothes, lumbering towards them. She could see their rotting teeth through gaping smiles.

Mary's surprise turned to panic when she realized they were the two men who stood outside the Boyd home only a few days earlier. They were also the same men who had pursued Mary and Daisy in mid-April. Mary pushed Daisy to her feet, "Run into the woods, Daisy. Run, children!" The children jumped up and ran screaming past the large oak tree and into the trees beyond.

Mary stood to confront the men. One grabbed her roughly by the shoulders. She desperately tried to pull away from the man's pungent smell of stale beer and tobacco. "Let me go! I wasn't doing anything wrong."

"You're teaching those Negro children, bitch. We saw you. We've been watching you for weeks and finally caught you. Maybe we should whip your hide right here."

"Leave me alone." Mary tried to push the man away.

The other man chuckled through a mostly toothless grin. "Let's do it, Grover."

Grover pulled Mary's body close to his and ran his filthy hands slowly down her waist, to her hips and then firmly cupped her buttocks and pulled her into him. Mary recoiled in disgust as the man moaned. His mouth touched her left ear. "Well, you're right pretty for a dirty Negro."

Mary's body tensed as the man's tongue slithered down her neck to her shoulder. She turned away and prayed, looking up at the big tree limbs that normally brought her strength and comfort. He reached up with his right hand and slid the dress off her left shoulder. With another moan, his tongue followed the contour of her chest, towards her left breast. Mary turned and slapped the man.

"Don't you hit me, bitch." Grover struck Mary across the face with his hand, knocking her to the ground.

Wilbur leaned over Mary and ripped the dress from her back,

revealing smooth, light brown skin. "Maybe we should have some fun first, Grover."

Mary bit the man's arm. Wilbur pulled it away and kicked Mary in the side. "Whip her, Grover!"

Grover pulled out a whip and raised his arm high into the air. Mary curled into a ball, protecting her face and bracing for the sting of rawhide. She could only think of Daisy and hoped she would remain hidden. Mary saw the whip coil back. With eyes squeezed shut and teeth clenched, she anticipated the tearing of her flesh.

She heard a large groan.

A few seconds passed.

Mary peered out from under her arm. She could see the man's feet dangling in the air. She looked up. A large man was clasping Grover's throat. Grover's feet flailed, attempting to touch the ground. Gasping for air and turning blue, Grover spat into his captor's eyes. The man head-butted Grover and threw him to the ground. Mary slowly sat up and looked around. At least twenty armed Union soldiers surrounded her assailants.

Wiping the spit off his face with his sleeve, the man walked over to Mary. He extended a massive hand. "I'm Colonel Phelps of the Vermont volunteers. Are you hurt, ma'am?"

Grateful for the help but embarrassed, Mary pulled her dress up around her neck with one hand. She tried to close the back of the dress with her other hand. Colonel Phelps helped her stand. "No, thank you, Colonel. I think I'm all right." Mary had some difficulty keeping her balance. She was in shock and still dizzy from the blow to her face. "Thank God you arrived when you did. How did you know we were here? This field is well hidden from the road."

Colonel Phelps cocked his head towards her assailants. "We were returning from Hampton and spotted these two near the bridge. They and a few others tried to burn the bridge earlier this morning to stop us from entering Hampton. We tracked them here and heard children screaming and running through the wooded area near the road."

Clutching her dress against her body, Mary attempted a weak smile. "My name's Mary. Mary Peake. I believe I saw you this morning, Colonel. You and your men were very kind to my daughter Daisy and me as you paraded into Hampton."

Phelps nodded and turned to the two men. "You two tried to burn the bridge this morning."

"What's it to you?" Grover said while he rubbed his forehead with one hand and messaged his throat with the other.

Phelps turned to Mary. "These men won't be bothering you anymore, Mrs. Peake."

Grover struggled against his restraints. "We're gonna get you and hurt you bad, bitch. And you, Yankee, we're gonna make you all suffer. You'll see!"

"I'd be impressed if you accomplished all that from a jail cell in Fortress Monroe," Phelps smirked. He ordered his men to take the two away. He turned to Mary. "Do you and the children need an escort back to town, Mrs. Peake?"

"No, thank you, Colonel. We should be safe now thanks to you and your men." Daisy came running over and wrapped her arms around her mother's legs. Mary reached down with one hand and embraced her daughter. "Colonel, this is Daisy, my daughter."

Phelps squatted down to her level. "It's nice to meet you, Miss Daisy. I remember seeing you when we marched into town this morning. You and your mother are very brave." He patted her on the head and stood up.

"We'll take these men away. It's unlikely you'll ever see them again." He paused and looked at several other children slowly entering the clearing. "Well, I need to get back to the fort. Are you sure you'll be okay? I can have some of my men accompany you back to town."

"Thank you, Colonel, but no, really, that won't be necessary."

"Very well. I hope we meet again, Mrs. Peake. Good day." He smiled down at Daisy. "And good day to you, Miss Daisy." Phelps turned and followed his men to the road.

Mary gathered up the children, many still crying. She regained her composure as she tried to console them. Mary dreaded telling her husband that evening but knew she had to be honest with him. She pinned the back of her dress to hold it together until she could mend it later.

Daisy pulled on her mother's arm. Mary leaned over and kissed her daughter's cheek. Daisy cupped her hands around her mother's ear. "Mama, that Colonel is an eagle."

Thomas was late arriving from Fortress Monroe. He quickly washed up, sat at the table, and filled his plate. "We've been working hard building more living quarters for all the troops. There must be hundreds of them arriving each day it seems." He looked over at Mary and Daisy. Their plates were still empty, and their heads were both bowed. "The two of you are awfully quiet. What's going on?"

Mary looked up, meeting Thomas's eyes. "Oh, Thomas. I…I was assaulted today."

Thomas jumped up and squatted down next to his wife. Mary had been careful to hide the left side of her face when Thomas walked into the kitchen. He looked at the red imprint of a big hand. "What happened? Who did this? Are you all right?" He held her hands in his.

"We're fine. Fortunately, some Union soldiers were in the area and rescued us."

"Us? Who else was there, Mary?" Thomas looked over at Daisy and back to Mary. "Mary, was Daisy with you?"

"Yes," Mary said with a soft voice.

Her lower lip began to tremble. Thomas stood over Mary and put his arms around his wife. "You're home now and safe."

Between sobs, Mary described the horrible event.

Later that evening, Thomas sat next to Mary on their bed. "Listen, I know how important your teaching is to you, but it's becoming too dangerous. This isn't the first time you've been followed. You've had other close calls. Next time, God knows what might happen to you or Daisy."

"Thomas, I should've been more careful. I was late and in a hurry. I was distracted. It won't happen again. Besides the soldiers took those awful men away to be locked up," she said. Mary put her arms around her husband. "Please don't make me stop teaching."

"Mary, there are more slave patrols all over the town, and they're growing by the day." Thomas took one of her small, soft hands in his massive, calloused ones. "If these two men knew about you, chances are others do as well. You said Mr. Boyd threatened you. He won't give up on this. He's rich and powerful. Please just stop the lessons. At least for a few days."

"I'm not afraid of the consequences, Thomas." Mary stood up and pulled down the sheet and climbed into bed.

"You should be, Mary. Twenty lashes is a brutal punishment. And you could be imprisoned for God knows how long. Or worse. Besides this involves Daisy as well. It's not just about you." Thomas gritted his teeth. Mary could tell she was trying her husband's patience.

"I can leave Daisy with Hannah Townsend while I give my lessons during the day. Later in the afternoons and evenings, I can teach Daisy at home." She turned on her side.

"Mary, don't you understand? My handyman business is mostly for white folks. And so is your seamstress business. If you get caught and are punished, these folks will stop hiring us. Mr. Boyd will see to it. You told me he threatened that the other day. We could lose everything."

Thomas eased onto the bed next to her. His voice softened. "I know how passionate you are about teaching these children. And I admire you for that, I truly do. But you have to look at the risks, not just to you and Daisy, but to the other children too." He shifted closer to where Mary was lying. His fists were clenched. "I'm not going to forbid you from teaching, Mary, but I'm asking you please lie low for a few days. Think of some other way, a safer way, you can do this."

Mary turned to Thomas and hit her pillow with her hand. "Thomas, it'll break my heart to stop teaching them." She put her head down onto the pillow and stared out the window into the darkness. In the top corner a spider was busy outside, encasing a struggling moth in its web. Mary shuddered and turned away. "It's been a long day, Thomas, and I'm tired. Can we please wait until morning to talk about this?"

Thomas placed his hand on Mary's shoulder and kissed her softly. "Sure. I only thank God that you're both all right."

THUNDERHEADS HOVERED OVER CHESAPEAKE Bay on the distant horizon. Frank, James, and Shepard shuffled back to the clearing that had been their home for over a month. They finished what they hoped was their last day of hard labor at Sewell's Point. The damage to the breastworks from the Union bombardment was finally repaired.

The three men were busy digesting another dry and tasteless meal of hardtack. They were so filled with the anticipation of going home that they didn't even complain about their painful backs or their mutilated hands and feet.

The mixed news of the day trickled through the slave brigade at Sewell's Point. The ability of the slave population to communicate quickly and over relatively long distances was uncanny. Unsure how the Yankees would treat them, the anxious bystanders were relieved at the polite and friendly greeting by the Vermont Regiment as they marched into Hampton. News of the cheering crowd lightened spirits throughout the area. They hoped this was a positive sign of things to come.

On a more troubling note, though, the results of the secession vote were now well known by everyone on the peninsula: Virginia had officially voted to join the Confederacy. Rebel soldiers at Sewell's Point were busy celebrating their independence from the Union, as well as the near completion of the fort.

James looked at his two friends. "I'm not sure whether to feel good or to be scared. I'm looking forward to going home, but this vote is sure to cause more trouble." He sat down, examining his cracked and bloody hands while shaking his head.

Shepard pointed in the direction of several Rebel soldiers. "I don't give a rat's ass about no fool's vote. I just want to get away from these goobers and back to the farm in one piece."

The three men stopped talking when they spotted their Confederate supervisor walking toward them. Eager to hear instructions regarding when and how they would be transported back to Hampton, the three slaves stood up and gave the Confederate soldier their full attention.

"You boys all did a fine job on these here earthworks." The three slaves exchanged big grins. "Given that this war is expected to grow now that Virginia is officially part of the Confederacy, we have to be prepared for a bigger confrontation with these stinking Yankees. We've talked with Colonel Mallory. He's agreed to let us keep you to work on fortifications in the South. In the morning, you all'll be leaving for North Carolina, so get a good night's sleep." The soldier turned to walk away.

James reached out and grabbed his arm. "You can't do that. We're supposed to be going back home to our families."

The man swung his arm, releasing James's hold. "Boy, I don't give a damn about your families. You'll do whatever we tell you," the soldier said, pointing his finger into James's chest.

The Confederate soldier was a large man, but James was imposing and towered over him. James pushed the man's arm away from his body.

Frank intervened, trying to deescalate the confrontation. He pushed James away with one hand and held up the other hand to the soldier. "We don't want any trouble."

The soldier rested his hand on his holstered pistol. "You're worth more to me alive than dead, boy. But that won't stop me from putting a bullet through your forehead. You lay your hands on me again, and that'll be the last thing you do. Now you'll do what we say, you worthless piece of garbage. You all are going south, and when we're done, maybe we'll send you home. Or at least what's left of you." He laughed mercilessly.

The soldier turned to James and spat into his face. Frank grabbed his friend's shoulders. James's nostrils flared, and his body tensed. Frank did all he could to restrain him. The soldier smiled. "Yeah, go ahead. You just try it. I'll shoot you where you stand and throw your ugly carcass into Hampton Roads for the crabs to feast on."

The soldier turned and walked away. The three men looked at each other in disbelief. With tears in his eyes, Frank looked at James. "They're gonna work us 'til we're dead. For sure, we'll never see our families again if we go south."

James wiped the spit from his face onto his sleeve. "I'm not doing this any longer, Frank. I'm plum worn out. And it's only a matter of time before I take a swing at one of them. No way I'm staying away from my family any longer. No way! I'll be leaving as soon as it's dark."

Frank swiveled his head around to make sure they couldn't be heard. "James, what in blazes are you talking about? How're you gonna get out of this place? There're guards everywhere. Besides we can't swim back to Hampton. And we're surrounded by Confederate territory."

Shepard was listening to the exchange. "If we escape and get caught, we'll be whipped 'til we're dead."

Frank looked at Shepard and back to James. "And they can go after our families in Hampton. Our families could pay the price if we escape, James."

"Don't you want to see your family again?" James said. "What's wrong with you? You said the truth yourself, Frank. They're gonna work us 'til we're dead. You all can stand here jawing, but I'm leaving. Now!" With that, James glanced around and started moving towards the shadows of the trees.

Frank and Shepard jogged to catch up with him. "Where would you go even if you got out of here?" Frank said.

"See that over there?" James pointed. The two slaves followed his finger.

"What're you pointing at, James?" Frank asked. "I only see water." Frank and Shepard looked out over the expanse of Hampton Roads. The sunset, reflected in the breaking waves, looked like red-hot flames crashing onto the shore.

"No, over there. On the other side of Hampton Roads," James said.

"That big fort?" Frank grabbed James's arm. "Are you crazy?"

"I'm not crazy, Frank. I'm going straight to that fort over there." He stabbed the air at the immense Union fort, three miles away, on the other side of the choppy water. "Fortress Monroe! You heard how the Yankee soldiers treated the colored folk in Hampton today. They treated them with respect, Frank. If we can get there, I just know we'd be safe."

"James, you're daft." Frank looked around. He could hear the laughing and yelling from the partying Rebels nearby. "Even if we make it to the fort, they can't keep us. They got to return us back to here. It's the law! Any slave that's ever escaped to the Yankee side has always been returned, James. Besides how do you know the big bugs running the fort will treat us like the Yankees marching into Hampton? And how're we gonna get across that water? Walk?" Frank shook his head. "We sure ain't Jesus."

Shepard, unusually quiet and intently listening to the conversation, said, "Why're we going there? I hear the Yankees treat colored folks worse. They send them to Cuba. I hear they even make them pull carts like oxen."

"Don't you get it? We got no choice," James said emphatically. "These greybacks are busy celebrating their independence. They're getting all liquored up. They won't notice we're leaving 'til we're long gone. I know a path that leads to the water's edge. I've seen some small boats there."

"How do you know this, James?" Frank stared at his friend in disbelief.

"You think I've been busy building this dang place? I've been busy looking for a way to escape while we're breaking our backs. I snuck down to the water yesterday."

In the darkening skies, the three men crept through thick reeds down a path that led to the water's edge. Two small skiffs had been dragged well onto the beach to avoid floating away at high tide. Inside each was a set of oars. James said, "These boats are kind of small, but we're better off just taking only one. The three of us should fit."

Frank looked at the boat and scanned the vast waterway. "James, these boats are probably fine near the coast, but I don't think they're made for the open sea. You think they can make it to the other side of Hampton Roads? Those waves look awfully big out there."

"What if the boat tips over? I can't swim," Shepard said. "I'm thinking you're the one that's all liquored up, James."

"None of us can swim, Shep," James said. There was grim determination in his voice. "But we're going anyway."

Shepard looked into the shifting waves and back to the two men. "I don't know. I'm as nervous as a cow with a bucktooth calf." He could hear the partying getting louder behind them. Without warning, celebratory shots rocketed into the air. Shepard eyes were wide with alarm. "Okay, let's do it."

The three dragged one of the skiffs to the water's edge and got ready to push off. James said, "Wait!" He ran up the rocky beach to the other skiff and took out the oars. He was about to throw them into the deep reeds when he heard footsteps coming down the path. He tried to get Frank's attention, but he and Shepard were too far away and busy talking near the water's edge. James squatted behind a patch of sea grass.

A Confederate soldier, obviously intoxicated, staggered over to a tree and started relieving himself. James watched the man closely, hoping they would go undiscovered. It seemed like an eternity, but the man finally finished his business and fumbled with the opening in his pants. James let out a quiet sigh as the man started to walk back up the path.

James prepared to toss the oars when suddenly, the man turned around. He squinted into the dusk sky in the direction of Frank and Shepard. Realizing there were two men there, the soldier yelled out, "Who's there?"

Frank and Shepard immediately froze. The soldier pulled out his handgun and walked towards the shoreline. James had no time to think. As the man passed within several feet of him, James swung the oars and struck the soldier in the back of the head with a sickening thud. It helped that the liquor dulled the man's reflexes. Blood splattered onto the oar from the deep gash. The soldier immediately dropped to the ground.

James quietly called to Frank, "Help me hide him." Frank hurried over.

After dragging the unconscious soldier and the oars to the other skiff into the deep reeds, James and Frank quickly ran back to the water's edge. James said, "Let's get out of here, quick! I hope no one heard that scuffle."

They pulled the boat into the water. Shepard climbed in. The hull immediately scraped bottom and wouldn't move. James pushed the young slave's shoulder. "Shep, you got to wait until the water's deep enough before you climb in. Now get your black ass out and wait 'til I tell you it's okay to get in."

Shepard looked into the dark water and reluctantly stepped out of the skiff. He kept looking around at the waves breaking at his feet.

Frank helped guide the boat into the deeper water. "What the hell are you afraid of, son? You look like you're stepping on hot coal or something. There's nothing in these waters that's gonna bother you. Now move it and fast."

Silently guiding the skiff offshore, the water was just above James's knees. "All right, now slowly climb in. Be careful not to tip it over."

With the two men in the skiff, James pushed it out further until the water was waist high. He leaned over the side and quietly rolled into the bottom. The boat rocked woozily from side to side. Shepard clutched the bow. "Damn, James! You almost knocked me into the water."

James was on his back lying on the bottom of the boat. "Shep, if you don't close your yap, I *will* knock you into the water."

James carefully sat up in the middle seat. He placed the oars in the rowlocks and started to pull. The boat made no progress. Waves crashed against the stern, splashing water onto Frank. The boat was slowly being pushed back to shore with each crashing wave.

"James, I think you need to sit the other way so you're facing me. I think that end needs to go first." Frank pointed to the bow where Shepard was seated.

James swung his legs around the other side of the seat facing the stern and Frank. He grabbed the oars and slowly turned the boat so the bow was facing out to sea. Awkwardly guiding the boat into the breaking waves, it was quite obvious James had never rowed a boat before. The pressure from the rough oars against his mangled hands made him wince with each tug. It took him a few minutes to coordinate the movement of the oars.

They moved slowly into Hampton Roads, farther from the noise of the carousing Rebels. For every few feet of progress, it seemed like the waves pushed the boat back to shore the same distance. About several boat-lengths from the shore, a high wave hit the bow of the boat, sending water over Shepard and the skiff high into the air. Shepard landed against James's back. As the skiff rocked from side to side, they were almost thrown into the water.

"James, what're you doing? You're gonna kill us," Shepard said. "There better not be snakes in this water," he added.

James pushed the young man forward toward the boat's bow and grabbed the oars. "Shut your face, Shep. I'm doing the best I can. You want to do this? Be my guest. You can take the dang oars. And if you don't keep your voice down, we're gonna have them big Rebel guns raining down on us."

They were finally nearing Fort Calhoun, the Union fortification in the middle of Hampton Roads. Voices could be heard coming from the fort. "We gotta be extra quiet. If we can hear their voices, they can hear ours," James said.

Frank looked at the island fort and pointed. "Why don't we just go there?"

James turned and looked over his shoulder. "They'll see us long before we can land this boat. They're armed to the teeth and will blast us out of the water. We need to get to the other side where we can land undetected. Then we'll decide how to approach Fortress Monroe. Besides we want to meet with the big boss. That's our best chance."

The three men rowed quietly towards Fortress Monroe. There were several schooners, tugs, and two steamships anchored in the waters. Lanterns were seen bobbing and swaying, so the men knew some of the boats must be occupied. They slowly navigated between the boats, paying close attention to any movement or noise.

After what seemed like an eternity of fitful and painful rowing, James stopped. They had a critical decision to make. Frank looked at James. "Should we row up to one of the wharfs serving the fort or should we land at the water's edge near the fort? The wharf would be closer and easier but leaves us exposed to gunfire if they think we're Rebel invaders."

James flexed his hands and said, "Landing on the coast will be safer and will let us investigate the area before revealing ourselves to Union soldiers."

He looked down at his numb hands and the sticky oars. Even in the dark he could make out the dark bloodstains on the oar handles. "We're gonna row over there." James pointed to the shoreline just west of the fort and several hundred yards away. "Quiet now. There could be guards stationed nearby." He guided the skiff around the west side of Fortress Monroe toward the shoreline beyond. They could hear faint music coming from the Hygeia Hotel adjacent to the large fort.

The skiff quietly approached the shoreline until the keel hit bottom. The three men slowly climbed out into the shallows and pulled the boat into nearby reeds. They waited a few minutes, squatting down until they could get their bearings and land legs. After the long ride through rough waters, the three men were feeling cramped and their stomachs were queasy. James's hands felt like they were on fire.

Frank pointed north. "If we go through the sea grass there, we can get to the bridge over Mill Creek. They usually have guards posted at the bridge. If we come from the landside, they're less likely to mistake us for Rebels. They have fires lit there, so they'll see we're colored folk."

James agreed. "Frank, you're right. That's the best way. Let's be really careful until we get to the lit part of the bridge."

They made their way through the tall grass about a hundred yards north of the bridge, and then doubled back down the main road leading to the Fortress Monroe.

Shepard grabbed James by the arm and pointed in the opposite direction. "Why don't we just go back to the Mallory farm? We can be there in no time."

James shook his head. *Would this boy never learn?* "Shep, there's nothing more I want than to see my family after being away all this time. But the town still has white folks and Rebels in it. We don't want to get caught and sent back to Sewell's Point after coming all this way. We need to go to the fort. It's our only chance at safety."

As they approached the bridge near Mill Creek, the Union guards spotted the three men. One of them called out, "Who goes there? Make yourself known or you'll be shot where you stand." The sound of a cocking pistol echoed in the night.

The three slaves stopped in their tracks. James said, "My name's James Townsend. This here's Frank Baker and Shepard Mallory. We're slaves from Colonel Mallory's farm."

"What's your business with Fortress Monroe? You should be back at your farm at this late hour not wandering around." The soldier waved his pistol.

"Sir, we came from the Confederate fort at Sewell's Point. We were forced to build the earthworks there. We escaped cause they were gonna send us south—away from our families in Hampton," James said.

"Why's that our concern?" Another Union soldier aimed his rifle at James.

James's heart was beating against the walls of his chest. "Sir, we only ask you let us talk to the commander of the fort. We can help him with what's going on at Sewell's Point," James said.

The Union soldier, seeing the potential of this information, lowered his weapon. After a moment, he said, "Wait here." Two other guards kept rifles pointed at the slaves, while the other walked across the bridge to the fort.

After consulting the officer on duty, the guard returned. The three slaves waited patiently. "You can stay until the morning, but I can't promise the General will see you. In fact, he's likely to send you back to Sewell's Point right quick."

"Sir, we would be much obliged to stay in the fort for the night," James said.

Two Union guards led the three slaves across the bridge, over the causeway, and through a gate into the expanse of Fortress Monroe. The three men were amazed at the size of the fort, even though it was difficult to see in the dark. They were led over to the stables where the stalls were mostly empty. "You can stay here for the night. Don't leave this building until someone comes to get you. There'll be a guard posted outside who will shoot you on the spot if you try to leave."

"Thank you, sir. We're much obliged," said James. Frank and Shepard nodded in agreement.

James waited until the two soldiers shut the stable door. He turned to Frank and Shepard, shrugged his shoulders and said, "Well, we're safe so far. Let's hope we can convince the boss man here that we know something useful to him."

The next morning, General Butler had just finished breakfast with Major Fay. They sat in his office and were comparing viewpoints about Colonel Phelps's excursion into Hampton and their own expedition to Newport News Point.

Butler felt good about the plot of land they had inspected high on the bluffs overlooking the James River. More troubling, however, was the vote by Virginia citizens to secede from the Union. He had hoped the disruption by his troops would have discouraged the voters. Unwittingly, it had only emboldened them.

Captain Haggerty knocked on the door and entered. "Excuse me, General. Three Negro slaves approached our picket at the Mill Creek Bridge late last night asking for sanctuary. They spent the night in the stables. Shall I have them returned to their owners?"

"Sanctuary?" Butler said. "Why would they want sanctuary here of all places?"

Haggerty entered the room and closed the door. "Evidently, they were in the service of the Confederates, who were using them to construct earthworks at Sewell's Point."

Butler tossed his napkin onto his plate. "That has to be a couple of miles across Hampton Roads. How on earth did they get here?"

Haggerty glanced uncomfortably at Fay before addressing Butler. "They said they found a small skiff on the beach and used it to cross."

Butler pushed his chair away from the table and stood up. "Well, they were certainly taking their chances! Based on my limited experience on the steamboat yesterday, those currents are quite rugged. I'd think it'd take a strong back to navigate those waters. How'd they escape?"

"While the Confederates were busy celebrating yesterday's vote and with nighttime setting in, they claim they were able to sneak off unnoticed," Haggerty said. "And, sir." Haggerty looked at his commander, biting his lower lip.

"What is it, Captain?"

"Sir, they've requested an audience with you." Haggerty scoffed.

Butler put his head down. He looked at the flowering tree outside his window. Butler watched the leaves flutter in the breeze.

"Shall I tell them no, sir?" Haggerty said, predicting his commander's reaction.

Butler stared out the window in deep thought. He turned back to Haggerty. "These men have taken extraordinary risks to come here. Not only did they escape the Confederates under grave consequences, they achieved an incredible feat crossing Hampton Roads. Least of all, they approached this fort in the dark, risking injury from hostile fire, or perhaps worse. I'd like to meet these three men before our staff meeting, Captain. I believe they've at least earned that much."

"Certainly, General." Haggerty hesitated for a minute.

"Is there anything else, Haggerty?

"Clearly, sir, we must return them to the Confederates or their owners."

Butler folded his arms thoughtfully. "As you well know, Captain, I was a lawyer before becoming a general. I'm well versed in the law and our obligations to the South. And, Captain, nothing is *clear* to me these days. Have them brought here in thirty minutes."

"Yes, sir." Haggerty paused for a moment, turned, and left Butler's office.

Fay quietly observed the exchange. "General, surely you're not considering giving these Negroes asylum."

"I'm not planning to do anything at this time, Major. At the very least, though, I'd like to understand what they might know about the Confederate fortification at Sewell's Point. As you recall, the Rebels now have functioning guns, clearly demonstrated by them firing upon our steamboat yesterday."

Despite the safety of Fortress Monroe, the three escaped slaves spent a restless night. They woke to the creaking sound of stable doors opening. Two Union soldiers entered. One said, "General Butler will see you shortly. In the meantime, you'll be fed breakfast." The three men weren't even sure how long it had been since they had eaten. James was particularly hungry after expending so much energy rowing across Hampton Roads. His stomach had growled throughout the night.

The Union soldier watched the three men scarf down their hardtack biscuits. "You should be prepared for the trip back to Sewell's Point after your meeting, so eat well."

Frank, James, and Shepard looked outside at the bleak, gray sky. They had been optimistic after successfully navigating Hampton

Roads and safely arriving at Fortress Monroe, but now, James thought, perhaps he had been unrealistic in his expectations. When the Union soldiers left, Shepard immediately turned on him. "I knew this was a bad idea! Now we're gonna get sent back to that damn Rebel camp and get our butts whipped."

"Hush up, Shep." James wasn't in the mood for Shepard's usual antics. He was having back spasms from hours of rowing the previous night. His body and hands were already a wreck from the hard labor at Sewell's Point, and the oars added and opened several new blisters. Despite the soldier's comments, James maintained a positive attitude. "We got this far, and we're gonna see the boss man. We need to stay cool."

"Well, I ain't happy about the smell of this place, but it sure beats the hard ground at Sewell's Point." Frank tilted his head back and threw straw into the air.

The three men sat on the ground, finishing the food provided by the soldiers. James looked at his two friends. "Let me do the talking when we get to this general. I got a plan."

"Oh, yeah?" Shepard said. "What's this big plan, James?"

"You just hush up, Shep. Don't you dare open your mouth when we're in there. And I'll let you know the damn plan when I'm finished thinking about it."

"You don't even have the plan figured out?" Shepard stood up, raised his arms, and spun around in exasperation. "Now I know we're in trouble!"

Frank looked up at the young slave. "Shep, you talk too much. We got this far. We're out of that Rebel camp, we crossed Hampton Roads, and we're in Fortress Monroe. I say we've done pretty good so far thanks to James. Now finish your food. We're not sure the next time we're gonna eat."

James stood up and grabbed Shepard's arm. "Shep, you got to promise you'll keep your mouth shut and your hands in your pockets."

Shepard looked down at the ground, pretending to be hurt by the harsh words. He looked up at James. "Yeah, well, there's no need for pockets on a dead man's coat."

The three men were escorted to the waiting area directly outside General Butler's office. As they stood looking around the room and each other, Captain Haggerty knocked and opened the door to inform Butler the three escaped slaves were present. The General, looking up at Haggerty, observed the slaves patiently standing behind him.

James looked over Haggerty's shoulder at the big boss sitting behind his desk. James was shocked by what he saw. He had anticipated that a Union general, and the head of such an impressive fort, would be tall, strong, and striking. What James saw was the opposite. Butler, for sure, was far from handsome. He had a large, balding head with drooping bags under his eyes and sagging jowls. Even sitting behind his desk, James could tell he was short in stature. James wondered if the general's feet even touched the floor. He was already feeling nervous about their prospects, and the sight of Butler didn't help. He braced himself for Shepard's reaction.

Shepard peeked around Haggerty and leaned over to James. "Now that's one ugly man. Why, he looks like the backside of a bull with them big hanging jowls! That man must have fallen out of an ugly tree when he was young and hit every branch on the way down." James didn't respond, but Shepard could see his eyes widen. Shepard quickly looked down at the floor.

The young slave turned to Frank and whispered, "That man's face is so ugly it could curdle cream."

Frank leaned into Shepard and muttered, "Shut your mouth or I'll flatten you like cow turd in a crowded pasture."

Butler stood. "Captain, show these men in."

The three slaves entered the office. Butler walked around to the front of the desk to greet them. "Good morning. I'm General Butler, Commander of Fortress Monroe and the Department of Virginia and North Carolina." James and Frank were almost a foot taller than Butler. Even Shepard, shorter than the other two slaves, could easily see over the head of the officer.

The three men nodded. James said, "Morning, sir. I'm James Townsend. This here is Frank Baker and Shepard Mallory."

Shepard noticed something strange about Butler's eyes; neither looked directly at him. Unnerved, Shepard shifted from side to side, trying to move his body into the line of sight of one of Butler's eyes. Seeing his movement, James discreetly reached a hand over and gripped the back of Shepard's arm. Shepard, startled, stopped moving but let out a small yelp.

Butler said, "Is everything all right, boy?"

"Yes, sir. I'm fine. Thank you, sir." Shepard looked down at the floor.

Butler walked back behind his desk and sat down. He waved a hand in the direction of his aides. "You met Captain Haggerty. This is Major Fay, one of my senior staff, and this is Private Pierce, a junior aide." The three slaves nodded their heads, acknowledging the men.

"I understand the three of you had quite a harrowing journey last night. I'm told that you escaped from the Confederate encampment at Sewell's Point and rowed a skiff clear across Hampton Roads in the middle of the night." Butler raised his eyebrows and waited to see who the spokesman would be.

"Yes, sir. That's what happened," James responded.

Butler was only looking at James now. "Why would you take such extreme risks? Not only are those waters dangerous, particularly at night, you could have been shot by the Rebels for escaping or possibly by my guards. And why do you think I won't return you to the Confederates, as I'm obligated to do?"

The serious look on the faces of the men before him reflected their deep and growing concerns. James said, "Sir, we were told that we were gonna be sent farther south to work on more Confederate forts. Most likely, we'll never see our families again. We had no choice but to escape."

"I see," Butler said. He placed his hands together. "How long have you been at Sewell's Point?"

"Sir," James said, "we've been there maybe five weeks." Frank and Shepard nodded their heads in agreement.

"And where were you before then?" Butler said.

"Sir, we belong to Colonel Mallory. We live on his farm in Hampton."

Butler knew of the man. "This would be Colonel Charles K. Mallory of the 115th Virginia Militia. Is that correct?"

"Yes, sir, I believe so," James said. "We've been working his farm for a long time. Work was slow, so he lent us to the Confederates to keep us busy and to make extra money."

"Interesting. So the Confederates are paying Colonel Mallory for your services?" Butler said, turning to his aides. He had heard that the Confederates were using slaves to compensate for the North's superior numbers.

"Yes, sir," James said. "There're lots of us slaves there."

"And you say they're going to send you to other fortifications to the south?" Butler was keenly interested in the Confederates' use of slaves to help their war effort.

"Yes, sir, to North Carolina," James said.

"You mentioned you have families. Are they on the Mallory farm in Hampton?"

"Yes, sir. I have a wife and two children. So does Frank here," James said.

"And you?" Butler looked at Shepard. James's body noticeably stiffened.

Shepard shifted his body from side to side to try to get into Butler's line of sight. James reached slowly steadying Shepard and gave him an extra squeeze to remind him to answer carefully. "I don't have a wife or children, sir."

Butler looked back at James. "Can you tell me what state the Confederate fortification is in currently?"

Shepard forgot James's instructions. Having just answered the Union officer's question, he was now eager to participate in the conversation. Shepard stood tall with his shoulders back. "It'd be Virginia, sir."

Butler let out a big laugh. "That's very funny." The other Union men joined in. James looked down at the floor, closed his eyes, and shook his head

Shepard wasn't sure why everyone was laughing.

"Son, I meant what condition is the fortification in? I'm pretty sure I know it's in the State of Virginia." Butler chuckled, shaking his head.

"Well, sir," James said, "there're two guns mounted and more in the works from the navy yard. Our part of the earthworks was completed so they're sending us on."

"Yes, we witnessed one of those guns yesterday," Butler said. The three slaves looked confused. "We were on a steamboat heading west towards the James River when one fired upon us. It fell well short of our boat, but it indicates a growing threat. I pulled out my rifle, steadied my aim, and gave my best return fire."

Shepard's eyes opened wide. He let out a gasp.

"Boy, is there something wrong?" Butler said.

Shepard stood still, unsure of what to say. James stepped in front of Shepard and said, "Sir, we were next to the gun when it fired. Dang near blew our eardrums out. And your return bullet, sir, well, it almost hit Shepard here."

Butler smiled deviously. "Well boy, what were you doing looking out over the battery? You could've taken a bullet to the head."

"That's what I said, sir!" James said, looking down at the young slave.

Butler continued his interrogation regarding the number of Confederate forces and any other information that might be helpful to the Union cause. Finally, Butler looked at James and said, "So, what am I to do with the three of you?"

"Sir, please don't send us back to the Rebels."

"Aren't you worried the Rebels will seek retribution against your families?" Butler said.

"Sir, we heard about the Yankees entering Hampton yesterday and how respectful they were to the colored folks there. We were hoping that somehow you all could protect us."

Butler looked over at Shepard, who was clearly distressed with the conversation. "Boy, is there something wrong with you?" Butler looked at James. "Is he a little barmy?"

James looked at Shepard and then back to Butler. "Sir, Shep is awfully nervous. We've been told all sorts of crazy, bad things that could happen if we come to this fort. Shep here kind of believes them."

"Like what?" Butler put a hand to his mouth, hiding his smile.

"Well, sir, we were told that Yankees would sell us to Cuba as slaves. Or that you'd make us pull carts like oxen." James shrugged his shoulders.

"Well, I never thought of that. I see no reason to send you to Cuba. And I'm not certain that this young man, Shepard, is strong enough to even pull a cart," Butler said with a sly smile, "So I see no cause for concern."

James and Frank chuckled at the comment. Shepard wasn't so pleased.

Butler turned to Haggerty. "Captain, show these men some suitable quarters and see that they're fed. I'll communicate with Washington on this matter and decide which course of action to take when I hear back."

Butler turned to the slaves. "We'll provide shelter and food until I get further direction. In return we could use your services. We're constructing a new bake house in the fort, and our mason is in need of assistance. Is this an acceptable arrangement?"

The slaves looked at each other and nodded. James said, "Yes, sir. Thank you, sir. We're happy to help. We're hard workers."

Butler sat down behind his desk. "Is there anything else I can do for you at this time?"

"No, sir. Thank you, sir," James said.

The three slaves turned to leave. Shepard stepped forward before James could restrain him. "I have a question."

"What's that?" Butler leaned back narrowing his eyes and crossed his arms.

"Well. We spent last night in the stables. How come there're no horses there?"

Butler grimaced at Fay and Haggerty. He turned back to the young slave. "Good day, Mr. Mallory."

Captain Haggerty opened the door and escorted the three men

outside Butler's office. James leaned over to Shepard. "You damn fool. You're gonna mess this up for us."

"I ain't done nothing wrong." Shepard turned away.

The two Union guards leaning against the wall quickly came to attention as their officer approached. "Take these men to the bake house and put them to work. See that they're fed at meal time and given suitable quarters," Haggerty said.

The two guards exchanged a confused look. "Sir, I don't understand. Don't we need to return them?" one of the guards said.

"You have your orders, private. Is something unclear?"

"No, sir." The one guard shrugged. He gently took James by the arm and guided him to the front door.

Haggerty returned to find Butler's office in the midst of a lively debate. Major Fay was standing near Butler's desk, one hand on his hip and the other vigorously gesturing. "Sir, this is a dangerous precedent! I've never heard of any Union fort keeping escaped slaves. Under every circumstance, the slaves were promptly returned to their owners."

Butler was standing by the window, looking at the nothing in particular but in deep thought. The skies were starting to clear, and the morning sunshine was now peeking through the clouds above the thick granite walls surrounding the fort. The stale room was heating up. Butler unlatched the window and opened it.

Butler could see soldiers exercising in the parade grounds in the distance. Fresh air, carrying the faint smell of nearby blossoming trees, started to fill the room. He walked back to his desk, leaned against it, and looked up at Fay. "Yes, Major, this may be true. But these three slaves were at Sewell's Point, effectively leased to the Confederacy. Technically, the Confederacy doesn't own them, so we're not obligated to return them there."

Fay looked at Captain Haggerty, hoping to enlist him in the effort to convince their commanding officer against this dangerous path. "That may be true," Fay said. "But Colonel Mallory does own them. We can at least return them to the Mallory farm."

Butler was inclined to stand and debate the Major eye-to-eye. But being several inches shorter than the Major, he decided to sit down behind his desk. "What will that accomplish?" he asked. "Mallory will just return them to the Confederacy to restore his revenue stream. And, I might add, the slaves will most likely be severely beaten or worse. You heard these men, Major. They have families." He waved his hand, continuing his thought. "Wives and children. If these men are sent south, they mostly likely will never see their families again. I think it's prudent on all fronts to keep them here until we get direction from Washington."

Fay took a seat in front of Butler's desk. "General, I'm as humane as you. I have a wife and children. I understand the dilemma of this situation and am repulsed by slavery as well. But this is no trivial issue," Fay said.

Butler retrieved a blank sheet of paper from his desk drawer. He uncovered his inkwell and picked up his pen. "Major, I do appreciate your passion. And I agree, it's not a trivial issue. I'll correspond with General Scott and others in Washington regarding an appropriate path." He looked up at the Major and set the pen down. "In the meantime, putting the slaves to work here helps us and prevents them from aiding the Confederates. Now give me an hour to construct my letter, and then we'll start our staff meeting. First on the agenda is the status of our horse requisition," Butler said as he winced.

GENERAL BUTLER STOOD WITH HIS HANDS IN HIS pockets. The sun was peeking over the horizon. His wispy hair blew in the gentle morning breeze as the steamship came to a standstill next to the main wharf. Several minutes later Sarah carefully negotiated the gangplank after traveling throughout the night. Butler smiled and walked towards her. He held out his arms, and they embraced. "I missed you so much," Sarah whispered into his ear.

"I missed you too. I know I only left Annapolis on Tuesday, but so much has happened. I can't wait to fill you in," Butler replied as they walked hand in hand to the carriage.

Soldiers loaded several crates. Sarah scanned the expansive horizon of Hampton Roads and Fortress Monroe. "Oh, Benjamin, this place is so beautiful."

Butler nodded. "Wait until you see what's behind those walls. You'll swear you're in a New England village." He helped his wife up the steps and into the seat.

Rolling along the waterfront and over the moat bridge, the carriage passed through the large arched opening. Sarah gasped in wonder. The sun's rays scaled the granite walls, lighting the tops of the oak trees. Spring flowers were in full bloom. The scent of fragrant blossoms filled the air. Her eyes darted across the landscape, as she squeezed Butler's hand.

They stopped in front of the last in the row of officers' homes, which was wrapped by a large porch. "Sarah, I must warn you, the house has potential, but it definitely needs a woman's touch," Butler said, helping his wife descend the steps.

Sarah smiled eagerly as they strode up the path to their new temporary home. Soldiers followed carrying their crates. "I'm sure it will be just fine, Benjamin."

By midmorning, the aroma of freshly brewed coffee filled the kitchen, and the couple sat across the table from each other. Butler poured his wife a second cup of coffee while he filled her in on the main happenings over the past two days. She was particularly interested in the plight of the three slaves. "Benjamin, what are you going to do?" She reached across the table and placed her hand on his.

Butler gulped the remains of his coffee. "I've written to General Scott for direction. In the meantime, we'll keep them busy working on the new bake house. Of course, we'll see that they have suitable quarters and are well fed." Butler stood up and put on his jacket. "I assume you received word that a gala is being planned to officially welcome us to Fortress Monroe? I tried to talk them out of it, but at least they agreed to not make it too extravagant."

Despite not sleeping much during the nighttime boat ride, Sarah was giddy with excitement. "Oh, yes. I was told before I left Annapolis yesterday. I understand a seamstress is coming by this morning to measure me for a new dress." She hugged her husband.

Butler left for his office in a cheerful mood. He was relieved Sarah was back by his side. He still longed to see his three children though. It had been over a month since he left Boston. He hoped they might be able to visit sometime during the summer. Butler did receive regular reports and knew they were safe and enjoying their stay with Sarah's sister.

His thoughts turned to the three escaped slaves from Sewell's Point seeking refuge. Butler was determined not to have the escaped slaves do any work that he wouldn't have his own troops perform. He thought that was only fair. Word from the Union soldiers overseeing the bake house construction indicated that the two older men, James and Frank, were hard workers. Although their hands were covered with open sores and blisters, they worked through the pain. The fort doctor did his best to bandage the wounds. Shepard, the smaller, younger one, however, was quite strong for his size but not particularly ambitious or trusting. Nonetheless, the bake house was progressing well.

Walking by the construction site, Butler nodded his head in the direction of the three slaves. James and Frank nodded back. Butler suspected the men were nervous about their future. He wasn't quite sure how things would transpire either. General Scott was unpredictable, and he and Butler hadn't parted on the best of terms. Butler could see Shepard eyeing him suspiciously until he disappeared around a corner. Butler shook his head and grunted at the young slave's brazenness.

After a causal stroll around the perimeter of the parade grounds, Butler entered his office. He cracked the window and immediately sat down to work. Butler reviewed plans for additional regiments from New York due to arrive soon. The need to secure the site at Newport News for a new encampment was becoming a pressing matter. Also, ever present on his mind, was the requisition for horses, without which he could not seriously pursue any offensive actions on the peninsula.

Major Fay knocked at his door and interrupted. "General, our guards at the north bridge have informed us that there is a Confederate officer bearing a flag of truce, requesting to meet with you."

Butler looked up. "Who is this person and what does he want?" He was not happy with the disturbance.

"Sir, he only informed our guards that he's a major and that his business is private between you and him. Should I send word that your schedule is too busy?"

"No, Major. I'm wondering if our expedition to Newport News a few days ago is the subject of the meeting. In any case, I don't want a Confederate officer in the fort where he can bear witness to the poor state of our defenses, particularly on the north wall. Tell this Confederate officer I'll meet with him in an hour at the north end of the Mill Creek Bridge," Butler said.

"Yes, General." Fay turned and exited through the door, closing it behind him.

Mary walked down the dirt road, past the field and large oak tree where she had been assaulted two days earlier. She shuddered as she thought about the horrific encounter. Approaching Camp Hamilton on her way to Fortress Monroe, she forced herself to think about more pleasant matters.

It was midmorning and the days were getting noticeably longer. Migrating birds had long returned to the Virginia Peninsula. The chirping sounds of new generations filled the trees with a soothing symphony. Parents were busy teaching their hatchlings how to fly, hunt, and survive. Mary sang as she approached Mill Creek Bridge.

Word of Mary's seamstress skills had reached the women in the Union fort. A hand-delivered dispatch requested her to meet with the fort commander's wife this morning. The note further explained that Mrs. Butler needed a new dress for an upcoming military gala and that some of the other officers' wives might desire her services as well.

Mary was excited with the potential new customer base but nervous to meet such important people. If the war continued or worsened, she thought, perhaps they would be a more reliable source of work than the Confederate-loyal women of Hampton. Thomas was certainly in high demand at Fortress Monroe helping the Union build and renovate housing for arriving troops. Mary beamed as she carried her bag filled with needles of various sizes, shears, a measuring tape, and multicolored spools of thread.

She stepped onto Mill Creek Bridge and stopped. The great expanse of the fortress walls rose into the sky in front of her. Thomas often talked about Fortress Monroe and the beehive of activity within. Mary was filled with anticipation. She had lived in Hampton for many years but had never set foot in or even near the great fortification.

Mary knew Thomas was delighted that she was keeping busy this day. After her assault, he had convinced Mary to take a break from teaching. It had been only a few days since the terrifying encounter, but she desperately missed her students. She wasn't sure when or under what circumstances she would be able to resume her clandestine classes.

After walking over the moat bridge, Mary arrived at the main entrance. She was impressed by the thick granite walls and thought about how much labor it must have taken to build the massive fort. Mary wondered whether slaves had been used in the process.

Entering the fort's interior, she had the same reaction as General Butler had days earlier. She had expected to see rows of large guns and mounds of cannonballs, clear signs of the growing conflict. Instead Mary thought she had stepped into a peaceful village filled with blossoming trees and beautiful spring flowers. The homes were well kept and looked so inviting. Seeing birds everywhere, digging for worms and scavenging twigs for new nests, Mary thought how excited Daisy would be if she were there.

She held up the dispatch to make sure she had followed the directions properly. Mary stood looking up at the attractive white house. *Are these Northern women going to treat me in the same demeaning way as the Boyds?* She looked around at the big granite wall surrounding the fort and noticed the large guns mounted on top, aiming out into Hampton Roads and Chesapeake Bay. Mary had the unsettling sensation of being trapped in a giant cage.

She took out her handkerchief and dabbed her forehead. Swallowing hard, Mary walked up the steps to the front porch. She raised her hand to knock but hesitated. *Maybe there's a side entrance, a servant's entrance, that I should be using instead*, she thought. She shook her head nervously and rapped on the wooden door with her knuckles.

Through the windowpane, Mary watched a pleasant-looking woman saunter to the door. Her dark hair was pulled up in a bun on the top of her head. The door swung open. "Good morning. May I help you?" the woman said.

Mary smiled politely. She looked down at the dispatch in her hand. Meeting the woman's steel-blue eyes, Mary felt her throat constrict. "I'm here to see Mrs. Butler. My name is Mary Peake. Is she at home?"

"Why, I'm Sarah Butler. It's so nice to meet you, Mrs. Peake. Please come in."

Mary stepped into the house. "Mrs. Butler, I was told you're interested in having a new dress made," Mary said. She looked around the large but rather plain room. A shabby sofa sat next to a damaged wooden table. Faded rugs covered worn wooden floors. Drab fabric framed dusty windows like old military uniforms. *Well, the Yankees certainly don't spend their money on extravagances of the home,* she thought. "What a beautiful home," Mary said aloud.

Sarah waved off the polite comment. "Oh, I just arrived this morning and haven't even unpacked our personal possessions yet. It's rather stark right now, I'm afraid. My husband arrived only three days ago, but I suspect he's spent most of his time at his office."

"How long will you be here?" Mary followed Sarah into the sitting room, enchanted by the woman's graceful, elegant strides. Her fair skin radiated beauty.

Sarah sat down and extended a hand. "Please sit down, Mrs. Peake. That's a difficult question to answer. I wish I knew." She flipped her hand, laughing. "I suppose we'll be here at least through the year but that depends on how this dreadful war progresses."

"Oh, it's so upsetting." Mary placed her hands together on her lap.

"Mrs. Peake, may I pour you a cup of tea? It was just brewed, and I was about to have some with sugar biscuits." Sarah poured Mary a cup of tea and handed it to her.

"Thank you. You're so kind." Mary took a sip. The warm fluid flowing down her throat to her stomach began to wash away the tension. She was surprised how attractive and young the woman appeared.

"Mrs. Peake, I hear you're quite talented. Where did you learn your seamstress skills?" Sarah took a bite of a biscuit.

"When I was young, I lived with my aunt in Alexandria to attend school. She was the one with the talent." Mary smiled and picked up a biscuit. "During the time I was there, I picked up whatever seamstress skills I could."

"Oh, how long where you there? Alexandria is such a wonderful place." Sarah dabbed her lips with a napkin.

"I attended school there for ten years until I was sixteen. When

Virginia annexed Alexandria, the laws forbade us from going to class."
Mary gently shrugged and looked down at her lap.

"What awful, oppressive laws! I sure hope the Union will soon
prevail in this conflict and find some way to put an end to slavery."
Sarah reached over and gently touched Mary's arm.

Mary looked up, not sure how to react. She was uncomfortable
with the conversation but relieved such an important woman shared
her perspective.

Sarah reached over to pour more tea into the cup while Mary
steadied it in her hands. "That reminds me. My husband told me
about the most amazing thing that happened right after he arrived
here. Three slaves escaped from a Confederate fort on the other side
of Hampton Roads. I think he said it was called Sewell's Point. Does
that sound right?"

Mary almost spilled her tea. She placed the saucer and cup on the
side table and leaned forward. "Yes, there is a Confederate fort there.
Did your husband say the names of the three men?"

"I'm sorry, Mrs. Peake. I don't believe he did." Sarah set the teapot
down. "Do you know someone there?"

"Yes. Three friends were sent there in mid-April. Their master
loaned them to the Confederates." Mary tried to hide her distress.
Tears filled the corners of her eyes.

Sarah reached over and held Mary's hands in hers. "There, there,
Mrs. Peake. I wish I knew their names. I'm sorry. The only other
thing I remember my husband saying is that he put them to work on
the new bake house."

Mary looked up. "You mean they're here? They weren't returned
to the Confederates?"

"That's what Benjamin said. He wrote to Washington for
instructions." Sarah patted Mary's hand and then stood up. "Well,

what do you say we get started? It's been a while since I had a dress made for me."

Mary rummaged through her bag for the measuring tape.

After almost an hour of processing paperwork, Butler exited his office and headed to the stables. He mounted his horse and, with Major Fay and Captain Haggerty accompanying him, proceeded toward the main gate of Fortress Monroe. As he passed by the bake house, James and Frank looked up to see the general and his two aides exiting the fort.

Word had quickly spread of the Confederate officer waiting outside for a meeting with Butler. James looked at Frank with slumped shoulders. He shook his head slowly. "Well, at least we tried, Frank. Looks like the Confederates have come for us. You know the Yankees have to give us back."

"Well, at least we had a few days away," Frank said. He picked up a stone and hurled it into a pile of sand.

Shepard was watching the two men. He put his shovel down and walked over, eyeing them suspiciously. "What's going on? I can see how you two are acting."

James looked at Frank and then to Shepard. "Nothing's wrong, Shep. Just keep working," James said.

"I know something's going on. I see how you're looking. You can't hide it from me."

"Shep, Just keep working. It'll be okay," James muttered. He put his large hand on the young slave's shoulder.

Butler and his two aides proceeded along the causeway leading to the wooden bridge. Crossing Mill Creek, Butler could see the Confederate officer mounted on an attractive, well-groomed horse at the far end. Union guards stood on alert near the man, clearly uneasy. As Butler approached, he thought the man looked familiar but couldn't place where they might have met.

The men dismounted, and Butler extended his hand. "Good day. I'm General Butler, Commander of Fortress Monroe and the Union Department of Virginia and North Carolina. I understand you wish to meet with me on some private matters."

The Confederate officer nodded his head. "Good day, General, I'm Major John Baytop Cary. Thank you for your time and willingness to speak with me."

Butler cocked his head and squinted. "Major, you look familiar. Is it possible we've met?"

"Yes, General. We met briefly at the Charleston Convention last year," Cary said. "Under more pleasant circumstances, however." The Confederate officer attempted a weak smile.

"Of course, Major." Butler recalled the pleasant nature of the formal Southern gentleman. "How may I be of service? What's the nature of these important matters?"

"General, would it be possible to talk in private while, perhaps, taking a gentle ride through the nearby countryside?" Cary asked. "Of course, your aides may join us to ensure your safety."

Butler agreed, and they mounted their horses. The two officers of opposing sides rode side by side with Major Fay and Captain Haggerty several horse lengths behind. Butler, short, dumpy, and slouched, presented a pretty sad figure on his horse. Major Cary, trim and fit, neatly dressed with an erect posture, looked like he was born on a horse. The two aides exchanged glances and smirked.

Cary looked to his left. "General Butler, I've been requested to meet with you for multiple reasons. The first, but not necessarily the most important, is to understand your intention to take possession of Virginia soil."

Butler was not surprised. He suspected the purpose of the meeting was related to the Union's incursion into the Virginia Peninsula. "Major, let me assure you, the Union has no intentions at this time to take possession of Virginia territory other than a limited area near Fortress Monroe to accommodate our growing needs. Furthermore, we have no plans for aggressive action—unless, of course, we are molested by Confederate troops."

Cary nodded. "On another matter, we have many families and citizens of Virginia who wish to go north to a place of safety. Would you permit passage through your blockading fleet?"

Butler was caught off-guard by the request. He pulled on the reins, bringing his horse to an abrupt halt. "Major, the presence of families of the belligerents is always the best hostage for their good behavior. One of the objects of the blockade is to prevent the admission of supplies and provisions into Virginia while she is hostile to the federal government. Reducing the number of consumers would defeat the purpose of the blockade. In addition," he waved his hand, "passing a vessel through the blockade would involve much trouble and delay. Why, each vessel would have to be examined to prevent fraud and abuse of privilege! I feel I must refuse your request."

Cary circled Butler slowly until the two horses and riders were face to face. "Will the passage of families desiring to go north be permitted?" The muscles in Cary's jaw tensed.

Butler shrugged his shoulders and shook his head "With the exception of interruption at Baltimore, which has now been disposed of, travel of peaceable citizens through to the North has not been hindered, and as to the internal passage through Virginia, your friends have, for the present, entire control of it. The authorities at Washington will settle that question, and I must leave it to be disposed of by them."

Butler could see the frown on Cary's face. "Your position is disappointing, General. But, I must say, not unexpected. Certainly you will agree with my last request."

Butler bristled. "That depends on your request, Colonel."

"General, I'm informed that three Negroes belonging to Colonel Mallory have escaped within your lines. I am Colonel Mallory's agent and have charge of his property. What do you mean to do with the Negroes?" Cary asked.

Butler knew he was legally obligated to return the slaves but felt compelled to do otherwise. Butler turned back to Fay and Haggerty, who were closely watching their commander and the Confederate officer, well outside of earshot. They nodded at Butler.

Butler had been emotionally wrestling over the fate of the three men. He continued to be astonished and impressed by their harrowing journey across Hampton Roads. Butler felt the safety of the three men should be a factor in his decision, but it shouldn't govern it. Having witnessed their contributions in advancing the construction of the bake house, he now realized how valuable the slave population must be in building Confederate fortifications. Butler looked at Cary. "Why, I intend to hold them."

Cary, reflexively, pulled on his reins. The horse's front hooves left the ground, almost rearing, and then obediently walked backward. Cary patted the horse's neck in an effort to comfort the large animal. "Do you mean, then, to set aside your constitutional obligation to return them?"

"I mean to take Virginia at her word, as declared in the Ordinance of Secession passed only recently. I am under no constitutional obligations to a foreign country, which Virginia now claims to be." Butler looked directly into the man's eyes.

"But you say we cannot secede," Cary replied in disbelief, "and so you cannot consistently detain the Negroes."

Cary, perhaps superior in appearance and skill as an equestrian, was disadvantaged to Butler's keen intellect. "But you say you have seceded, so you cannot consistently claim them. I shall hold these Negroes as contraband of war, since they are engaged in the construction of your battery and are claimed as your property. The question is simply whether they shall be used for or against the Government of the United States. Yet, though I greatly need the labor which has providentially come to my hands, if Colonel Mallory will come into the fort and take the oath of allegiance to the United States, he shall have his Negroes, and I will endeavor to hire them from him."

"Colonel Mallory is absent," Cary said. He stiffened on his saddle.

"Well, that is unfortunate then, Major. I believe I have clearly stated my position, and so it stands. If there's no further business you wish to discuss, then might I bid you good day?"

Cary clenched his jaw. "No, General, I have communicated the topics for which I have come. While your answers are certainly not to my liking, you have clearly and eloquently stated your position. I fear that this will ultimately be settled on the fields of Virginia. Good day, General."

The Confederate officer abruptly turned his horse towards Hampton and kicked its sides. The horse immediately went into a canter and, shortly after, broke into a full gallop, leaving a trail of swirling dust in its wake. Fay and Haggerty had their weapons drawn, having witnessed the testy exchange.

Butler watched the Confederate officer disappear around a bend.

"It was good to see you again, Major Cary," he snickered. Butler turned and rode back to where his aides were waiting.

"Sir, did you arrange a location to turn over the three slaves to their owner?" Fay said.

Butler looked at Fay quizzically. "Why would you think it necessary to give these men back to the Confederates? So that they may support the Confederate efforts against us? I plan to retain the three Negroes as contraband of war."

Fay and Haggerty were flabbergasted. "But sir," Captain Haggerty said, "on what basis can we claim to keep these escaped slaves as contraband?" Haggerty, while a young man, was a very good lawyer. "Do you know of any legal proposition or treatise that supports this position?"

Butler gently nudged his horse forward, not making eye contact with either man. "Not the precise proposition, but the principle is familiar law. Property of whatever nature, used, or capable of being used for warlike purposes may be captured and held either on sea or on shore as contraband of war. Whether there may be a property in human beings is a question some might doubt, but the Rebels cannot take the negative. At any rate, Haggerty, it's a good enough reason to stop the Rebels' mouths, especially as I should have held these Negroes anyway." Butler kicked the sides of his horse and broke into a canter. Hooves sprayed dirt and dust into the air, lengthening the distance between Butler and his aides.

The three men rode the rest of the way in silence, back across the wooden bridge and through the main entrance leading into Fortress Monroe. Approaching the bake house, Butler could see James and Frank intently watching him.

Butler rode over and dismounted. James wiped his hands on his pants. "General, we'll put our tools away and get ready to go." His voice was despondent.

Shepard looked from James to the General. "What're you talking about, James? We're not going anywhere. Right, General?"

Butler looked at the disheartened faces of James and Frank. Shepard, normally distrustful and pessimistic, radiated hope and optimism. "You're right, Mr. Mallory. I don't know why Mr. Townsend would want to leave. That is, unless he's unhappy here." Butler placed his hands on his hips.

James and Frank were dumbfounded. James nodded. "No, General. We're happy here. We don't want to leave. But I don't understand. I thought you were meeting with the Rebels to turn us over."

"Well, I did meet with them, Mr. Townsend. But I told them they couldn't have you back," Butler said, his smile showing his stained teeth below his mustache.

"Sir, we're happy about this, but I don't understand. Isn't it the law?" James asked.

"Well, there are many laws at play here, Mr. Townsend. All you need to know is that you'll stay here and help out where needed. In return, you'll be given quarters, meals, and be paid a fair wage. I hope this meets with your approval."

James and Frank nodded. Shepard said, "Of course it does. Right, James?"

James put his arm around the young slave. "It sure does, Shep. It sure does."

Time passed quickly as Mary noted the measurements needed to make the dress. She and Sarah discussed styles and fabrics. In the meantime, two officer's wives had arrived, who required only minor alterations to their dresses. The group finished a pleasant lunch and

Mary stood, anxious to leave. Sarah put her arm around Mary's waist and escorted her to the front door.

"Mrs. Butler, thank you so much for your hospitality. It was such a pleasure to meet you and the other women," Mary said as they walked.

They stopped at the door. "Mrs. Peake, I'm so happy to meet you. I hope we can become friends. And, please, call me Sarah."

Mary smiled. "I would like that, Sarah. Please call me Mary. We should be able to do an initial fitting in a week. Is that okay?"

"That should be fine, Mary. The gala's not for another three weeks." Sarah gave Mary a gentle hug. Mary's face flushed. She turned and walked across the porch. Her legs felt a little weak. She held the railing as she stepped down the stairs.

Sarah stood in the doorway. "Oh, Mary?" she called.

Mary stopped and turned.

Sarah pointed. "I believe the bake house is down that way. Go to the corner and turn right."

Mary looked down the street.

"And Mary, I do hope these three men are your friends."

"Thank you, Sarah." A warm glow engulfed Mary's body.

Mary hurried down the street. She turned the corner and saw a large group of men working on a stone building surrounded by scaffolding. She walked around three sides of the building, scrutinizing the face of each worker. Anxiety and disappointment began to set in. They all appeared to be white skinned. Mary turned and shuffled away, her head down and slumped shoulders.

"Miss Peake!"

Startled, Mary turned. A young man, covered in white dust, waved a hand in the air.

Mary pointed at herself. "I'm sorry. Are you talking to me?"

The man jumped up and down. She walked back and stopped

several paces away. The man looked somewhat familiar. "Shepard. Is that you?" Mary stepped forward. "Dear Lord. Are James and Frank with you?"

"They're right there." Shepard grinned and pointed to a scaffold on the side of the structure. Several large men were standing on wooden planks. They were handing large stones from man to man until the stones reached the top of the wall. There the stone was put in place and secured with mortar. At first, she thought all the men, working side by side, were white. Looking closer, she now saw that two of the men, covered in white cement dust, were actually James and Frank.

James turned and saw Mary. He smiled through his grime-covered face and waved. He kicked Frank, one step below him, in the shoulder and pointed towards Mary. The two men climbed down the scaffolding and walked over to the woman. They wanted to give her a big hug but knew they would soil her pretty dress.

"I'm so glad you're safe," Mary said, smiling with delight and relief. "I just heard that three men escaped from Sewell's Point. I can't believe it was you! How did you ever get here?" She looked from face to face.

James explained the Confederates' decision, and Colonel Mallory's consent, to ship the slaves south to work on more fortifications. He described how they had escaped three days earlier. Mary's mouth hung open. "You rowed across Hampton Roads in a tiny boat. Are you all crazy?"

"We had no choice, Miss Peake. We never would've seen our families again. Never," James said.

"Do you know how long they'll keep you here? I'm so afraid you'll be turned over to Colonel Mallory." Mary's stomach churned.

"Well, General Butler just came by here only a short while ago. He said we could stay here as long as we want. They're giving us a place to sleep and are providing us with meals. And they're even gonna give us wages for our work," James said, shaking his head.

Mary looked around the large building under construction and back to James. "Do your families know you're here and safe?" Mary asked.

James shook his head. "No, they don't. Miss Peake, we'd be grateful if you could tell them we're here and that we'll get home as soon as we can. We're concerned if we go to Hampton the Rebels there will capture and return us. Things are a little crazy right now."

Mary adjusted the bag's strap on her shoulder. "All that matters is that you're all safe. I'll be sure to contact your families when I get back to Hampton, either later today or in the morning." She touched the arms of the three men in turn, as if confirming they weren't an illusion.

She turned and started walking away. After several steps she stopped, turned back to the three men, and waved. They waved back with big grins.

Mary turned down the side street towards the main bridge across the moat. She couldn't wait to tell Thomas about their friends' good fortune.

Thomas and Daisy sat at the kitchen table. They both watched in amazement as Mary mounded food onto her plate. "My, I guess your appetite sure has returned," Thomas said.

Daisy put her hand over her mouth and giggled.

Mary looked down at her plate. "Oh, Lord! I guess I wasn't paying attention. Here, let me put some back." She started pushing food back off her plate.

"What has you so distracted, woman?" Thomas stared at his wife.

Mary looked up and blushed. "Oh, Thomas, I'm so excited."

"What, Mama? What?" Daisy pounded the table with her fists.

She looked from Daisy to Thomas and stood up. "Well, today I went to Fortress Monroe to meet with Mrs. Butler and some other ladies who needed their dresses altered. They were all so nice." She paused and looked at Daisy. "You should see all the birds there, baby. Maybe next time I go you can come."

Daisy nodded and bit into a biscuit.

"And they gave you lots of work?" Thomas said.

"No. Well, yes. But that's not why I'm so excited." She clasped her hands.

"Out with it, woman! What is it?" Thomas impatiently shifted in his chair.

"I saw James and Frank! And the young man, Shepard."

There was a moment's pause.

"They're at Fortress Monroe?" Thomas asked. "I thought you said they're at Sewell's Point with the Confederates."

"They were. But they escaped, Thomas. Isn't that great?" Mary told her husband and daughter about their harrowing journey across Hampton Roads.

"That's wonderful, Mary." Thomas put his fork down. "I was working at Camp Hamilton today. I guess I missed all the excitement. I knew James and Frank would manage somehow. And I'm sure their children must be excited too."

"Oh, their families don't know yet. I got back too late today to tell them. Daisy and I will go to the Mallory farm first thing in the morning though. I can't wait!" Mary returned to her chair.

Daisy listened intently to her parents. She knew her friends had been sad since their fathers were taken away.

"I'm not sure I've ever seen you this excited about anything, Mary."

Thomas thought it was all great news but was surprised by his wife's giddiness. "But you know they'll be returned back to Colonel Mallory."

"That's just it, Thomas. General Butler is giving them sanctuary. He's not going to return them." Mary was grinning from ear to ear. "He's ignoring the laws, Thomas. Isn't this great? Do you know what this means?"

"Now, Mary, don't be getting carried away. It's only a few men. It doesn't really mean all that much. I mean, it's great. And I'm happy for them and their families, but that's all it is." Thomas shrugged.

"No, Thomas. If General Butler is willing to give slaves sanctuary, it could change everything. You told me about the wharves, Thomas. You said every day they're teeming with more and more men and supplies. Why, if the Union could overpower the Confederates in Hampton, or even the peninsula, maybe colored folks would be free to live as they will." Mary stood up again. She was walking around the kitchen, waving her arms. "And no more slave patrols!" She turned to Thomas. "Don't you see, Thomas? General Butler is the key. He's the key!" Mary put her arms around her husband's shoulders from behind. "I'd be able to teach again!"

Daisy jumped up and down in her chair. "Yeah! I can't wait, Mama."

Thomas put his hands on Mary's arms, draped around his neck. "Mary, it's not that easy. I don't want to disappoint you, but it's only three slaves. There are thousands more in and around Hampton. The general can't give them all sanctuary."

Mary looked at her husband and smiled slyly. She kissed him on the side of his face. *We'll see about that*, she thought. Mary sat down and plunged into her dinner.

ALTHOUGH SARAH'S PEACEFUL BREATHING nearby had provided comfort, Butler rose early after a restless night. Sitting on the edge of the bed, he stretched his arms high over his head. He stood and walked over to the washbasin. With the heavy bags under his eyes, the mirror reflected a face of a much older man than forty-two, he thought.

Throughout the night, he drifted in and out of consciousness, rehashing the meeting with Major Cary and his decision regarding the three escaped slaves. Claiming them to be contraband of war was a spontaneous response to the Confederate officer, but it was, as he thought about it more, quite logical. Perhaps, it was even brilliant.

Not only could he deny the Confederates labor to build fortifications, he was able to secure that labor to support his own needs. The key difference was that Butler was determined to treat the three men fairly—providing decent sleeping quarters and adequate food and provisions. In addition, he insisted on paying the three men a proper wage.

He finished breakfast and checked in on his wife, who was still sleeping soundly. After her overnight boat ride from Annapolis a day earlier and her first orientation to Fortress Monroe, Butler knew she must be exhausted. He carefully closed the front door and set out for his office.

Passing the bake house, Butler could see that the apprehension masking the faces of James and Frank the prior day was now gone. Both men smiled and nodded at Butler. Shepard, feeling some personal bond with the Union officer, yelled out and waved, "Morning, General." Butler nodded at the two men and chortled at Shepard. He was surprised by his growing fondness for the young man.

An agenda for his morning staff meeting sat on his desk. The open requisition for horses was now a standing topic. Butler tapped his pen on the desk. For whatever reason, the army had difficulty filling the requisition for the large Virginia fort. He suspected a conspiracy was underway to undermine his ability to take action against the Confederacy.

Butler and his staff sat around the table. He slapped the table with his hand. "Without horses, we can't venture very far from Fortress Monroe or take any aggressive action. Why would Washington do this?"

His staff sat quiet, wondering whether Butler was expecting an answer or if the question was rhetorical. Finally, Pierce offered, "General, perhaps Washington intends for us to be only a defensive force at this time."

"That would make sense, Pierce, if we only had a few thousand troops. But we'll soon have over 10,000 men at Fortress Monroe and nearby encampments," Butler said. He shook his head in frustration.

The meeting was interrupted by a knock at the door. Private Pierce walked over and opened it. He turned to General Butler with a perplexed look. "Excuse me, General," he said. "I think you need to come here."

Butler, muttering under his breath, got up from the table and stormed towards the door. "Private, what is so important that ..." Butler froze in place. Outside his office, accompanied by four Union guards, were eight slaves. "What's going on? Who are these men?"

One of the guards moved to the front of the group. "General, these men arrived at our picket line north of Mill Creek a short time ago. They claim to be slaves from Hampton. Some of them were being sent south to support the building of Confederate fortifications. They heard about the three escaped slaves from Sewell's Point." The guard paused. "Sir, they're asking for refuge here as well."

Captain Haggerty walked up behind Butler. "Sir, we can't use the same argument of contraband of war for all of these men. Some may not actually be helping the Rebel forces."

Butler turned to his aide. "I realize this, Captain. But it is the intent of the Confederates to utilize these men in the same way against us. If they're not using them now, they soon will be."

Butler turned back to his junior aide. "Private Pierce, a large shipment of provisions arrived this morning. Have these men assigned to the main wharf to support the unloading and storage of these provisions. When completed, see to it they're engaged in productive work. Treat them as the other three, providing quarters and meals. Report back to me by day's end."

"Yes, General." Pierce saluted and closed the door to Butler's office.

"General, do you believe this is a wise course of action?" Fay asked. He tapped the table surface in agitation. "Three escaped slaves is a somewhat trivial issue and can even, perhaps, be overlooked. Now they number eleven."

"I'm aware of this, Major, but until I get further direction from

Washington, I intend to ensure their safety and to productively and fairly utilize their services," Butler said. "I don't understand though." He scratched his head. "The three escaped slaves only arrived two mornings ago. And my meeting with Major Cary occurred yesterday. How is it that this news can travel so quickly outside the fort? There was no known communication between these three men and other slaves." He placed his hand on his chin. "They've been in the fort under our supervision since they arrived. Yet these new slaves seem to know with certainty how those three men were received and treated."

None of his aides had any answer.

The balance of the day progressed without further incident. Private Pierce reported back in the afternoon. With the unloading of provisions quickly accomplished, the eight slaves were assigned duties within the fort. Three were assigned to the bake house, three were assigned to help fortify the north wall of the fort, and the remaining two were assigned to laundry services.

The following morning started somewhat better for Butler. He slept well and enjoyed a hearty breakfast with Sarah. On his way to the office, warm breezes hinted of hot, humid weather soon to come. Butler passed by the bake house and noticed there were now six contraband slaves busy on the construction site.

Feeling good about his decision to keep the eight men yesterday, he rounded the corner and spotted a mob of people in the distance, outside the entrance to his office. Private Pierce, seeing the General with a look of shock on his face, intercepted him. Pierce said, "General, these colored folks were outside the fort this morning. There were so many they blocked Mill Creek Bridge. The guards thought it was best to bring them here. I counted forty-seven of them, sir."

Butler started walking around the perimeter of the group. He stopped and pointed. "Edward, these are mostly elderly folks, women, and children."

"Yes, sir. Based on my inquiries, the ages seem to range from three months to eighty-five years," Pierce said, not without the ghost of a smile. An infant wailed over the din of the group.

Children screeched as they chased each other through the roses and around the side of the building. Butler was spellbound. He realized he hadn't seen children playing like this in a long time. The sight of two boys wrestling in the grass reminded Butler of his own two sons, ages six and nine. Butler's older son, Paul II, was named after his firstborn, who died eleven years earlier at the age of four. Paul II had visited his parents in Annapolis in early May. He hadn't seen his youngest son, Ben-Israel, since leaving Massachusetts over a month ago. Butler's daughter, Blanche, the oldest at fourteen, helped with house duties for a short time in Annapolis, but she was sent home with the increased threat of Rebel attacks.

Butler turned back to the large group of desperate people and grabbed Pierce's arm. "Edward, assign these people to quarters. We're short of space, so I'm not sure if we even have room inside the walls. We may have to use tents for now. Find productive uses for the healthy men and women. Perhaps the kitchen or laundry could use additional support. Some of the new troops may need officer's aides. I'd like a full report by the end of the day regarding their disposition."

"Yes, General," Pierce said. "Sir, what about the elderly and children?"

It was difficult enough trying to house the increased troop levels, he thought. This just added to the challenge. But he had cracked open the door when he provided sanctuary to James, Frank, and Shepard. Now the yearning of the human spirit to be free poured through.

"Edward, we'll pay the healthy men and women who work a daily wage. Inform the parents of the children and caretakers of the elderly we'll deduct the cost of feeding these dependents from their wages. I believe this is an equitable arrangement."

"General, you're being more than fair," Pierce said.

Butler rested his hand on Pierce's shoulder. "Well, Edward, we're no longer dealing with a military situation. This is now a humanitarian issue."

"Yes, General," Pierce acknowledged. "I'll report back this afternoon." Pierce walked over to corral the large, noisy group.

Butler entered his office. Finalizing plans to occupy Newport News and accommodate the growing troop presence was now made even more urgent by the influx of the slaves.

After his staff meeting, Butler summoned Colonel Phelps to his office. "Colonel, a few days ago, a group of us explored an area on the bluffs west of Fortress Monroe. We tried to reach it by land but were running out of daylight, so we steamed up Hampton Roads to the mouth of the James River and disembarked onto a small jetty there."

Butler led the tall man to a map on the wall. He pointed to the area in question. "You'll find that it's a very pleasing setting. It's high on the bluffs with excellent views west up the James River toward Richmond, south across the river towards Norfolk, and east across Hampton Roads." Butler swept his hand around the map, highlighting the panoramic views. "Take three regiments of New York, Massachusetts, and Vermont volunteers, along with a detachment of regulars to occupy this area called Newport News Point."

After receiving additional instructions, Phelps left promptly to gather the troops and necessary provisions to last for several days.

With that important business taken care of, Butler sat behind his desk and reflected on the day's events. The growing group of contrabands was the main topic of concern among the Union troops. More importantly, the supervision and logistics of the group were increasingly consuming Butler's time. He decided to appoint someone to relieve him of this burden.

When Private Pierce stopped by Butler's office later that afternoon, Butler asked his friend to take a seat. "Edward, I'm appointing you Commissioner of Negro Affairs. You have full responsibility to manage the needs of these people, to ensure that they are productive and helpful, and to see that they are treated fairly."

From their relationship in Boston, Butler knew Pierce to be a compassionate and efficient young man with impressive leadership skills. In the past two days, he had proved his ability to effectively manage the growing contraband population.

Butler pushed the piles of paperwork aside and decided to write to General Scott. He informed the head of the U.S. Army that the Rebels were using male slaves to construct batteries and, based on discussions between Union soldiers and these men, their wives and children would be sent further south. Butler stated that many families were now in the fortress where he was able to employ the healthy men and women.

He explained his decision to charge the able-bodied people for the expenses of care and sustenance of the nonlaborers. Of the slaves, twelve had escaped from Sewell's Point. He believed that the departure of these men, and his decision to provide refuge, had severely impacted the Confederates' ability to complete the Sewell's Point battery. Butler forwarded parts of the letter to Secretary of War, Simon Cameron.

What Butler didn't realize was that the exodus from the countryside to the fort had only just begun. Later in the afternoon, slaves of all ages arrived. By the end of the day, there were well over a hundred more people seeking refuge in Fort Monroe, many of them children.

Butler was relieved that his day was almost over. His head was pounding. As he tidied his desk in preparation for the next morning, Major Fay entered and informed Butler, "General, there's a elderly planter from Hampton here. He'd like to speak with you."

Butler was tired and only wanted to retreat to his quarters and enjoy a warm meal with Sarah. Massaging his temples, he said, "Show the man in, Major."

The old man shuffled in. He placed his bony hands on the edge of Butler's desk and launched into his speech. "My name's Samuel Jones. I have a farm just outside of Hampton. When I returned home from church this morning, I couldn't find any of my slaves. I called Margaret to take my coat, but she didn't come. I went into the kitchen for a meal, and there was no one there. I went into the garden, and that, too, was abandoned. I went to the Negro quarters behind my house, and there was no one there either. They've all disappeared." He put his hand over his heart. "And they did this while I was at the house of God."

He continued rambling, "So I went back into my house and summoned my body servant, Charles. He informed me that all the slaves had gone to the fort. This fort, sir!" He slammed his hand on Butler's desk. "So I told Charles he'd have to perform all the duties of the fleeing slaves. And I asked him to fetch me some whiskey. Charles went into the kitchen, and I waited and waited. When I went into the kitchen to find him, he was gone too. What am I to do?" His gesture in Butler's direction was not without animosity.

"Mr. Jones," Butler started. He looked down to conceal his smile. "I can't confirm whether your slaves are within our walls. We've received many Negroes from the area only today and are still preparing records. However, if they're here, they have sought refuge, and I intend to provide that refuge." Butler stood up. "So while I'm sorry for your situation, I must bid you good day. Major, please have Mr. Jones escorted to the main entrance."

The old man scowled at Butler. Fay took his arm and led him to the door.

Butler gave a big sigh as he put his jacket on. Shaking his head, he let out a soft chuckle and walked out of his office.

As Samuel Jones was being escorted through the fort towards the main entrance, he looked around and noticed a large number of escaped slaves performing duties. He couldn't tell if any of them were his slaves. His eyesight wasn't sharp anymore and the sun was low in the sky.

Approaching the gate, he heard a familiar sound: the squeal of a wheel, thirsty for lubrication. Samuel turned and noticed a man pushing an old wooden cart. His cart. Samuel called, "Charles, is that you?" Charles looked up and waved to his former master. With a broad grin, Charles pushed the cart down the street and around a corner.

GENERAL BUTLER STOOD AND SHOOK HANDS with two U.S. Naval officers. After a briefing regarding the Union blockade, he thanked the men for their report. This was his first meeting at the Hygeia. The luxury hotel, decorated with yellow lilies and purple irises, rekindled fond memories of his life in Boston. Fortunately, the war hadn't yet affected the outstanding food and service, unique to the area.

Gloved valets opened both doors for General Butler as he exited the hotel lobby onto the veranda. The bright sun was burning through the morning fog. Several children tossed flat stones into the foaming green waves. A lone boy, perhaps four or five years old, was off by himself, busy trying to ensnare a blue crab in a homemade net. Butler leaned against the railing and intently watched the child evade the crab's pinchers.

His firstborn son, Paul, died when he was about the boy's age. Had he survived his illness, Butler reflected, Paul would have been fifteen. He and Sarah couldn't imagine how they would survive the loss of their dear four-year-old boy. A year later, though, they were blessed with their daughter, Blanche. Somehow, they managed to go on, despite the deep pang Butler always felt whenever he saw a young boy playing or laughing on the street.

Thinking he may have overindulged at breakfast, he wished he could return to his quarters for a brief rest, but with pressing matters awaiting him, he knew that wasn't possible. The wharf area swarmed with soldiers unloading containers from a steamship.

Butler looked into the wide moat as he walked over the bridge. Passing through the large entrance, he couldn't believe it had been only five days since his arrival at the granite fortress. So much had happened since. He thought about the contraband slaves now under his protection who were proving to be quite useful working on a range of projects throughout the fort.

The long walk to his office seemed to aid his digestion. His mind drifted back to the small boy and the crab along the water's edge. He thought he heard a child's scream and stopped. Looking from yard to yard, nothing unusual caught his eye. Shrieks grew louder. A wooden hoop, over two feet in diameter, appeared, rolling across the lawn and into the road. After spiraling a few times like a large coin, it came to rest at his feet.

Several children burst through a side yard, across a flower garden, crushing everything in their path, and into the street. Butler watched a boy pick up the hoop and hit it with a wooden dowel. The hoop accelerated down the road. Screeching as they ran, the children gave chase. Butler recognized the boy from the previous day and suspected they were part of the recent influx of slave families.

Butler stood there, shaking his head. He knew this wasn't an appropriate environment for the children. It was only a matter of time before a confrontation would erupt with the Confederates. The children needed some structure during the day to limit potential interference with important military business.

During Butler's staff meeting, the dilemma of the children was discussed, but no one could think of a good solution. After the meeting, he decided to take a ride outside the fort to clear his head.

Butler proceeded into the nearby countryside, past Camp Hamilton on the north side of Mill Creek, and along fields of wheat and corn. Butler could feel the temperature and humidity rising, a sure sign that summer was around the corner.

The growing population of escaped slaves under his care and particularly their children, weighed heavily on his mind. Butler was contemplating how to deal with this issue when he thought he heard the gentle voices of children. He stopped his horse and craned his neck. Nothing. Perhaps it was the sound of the wind whistling through the nearby crops, he concluded.

Gently kicking the sides of his horse, he heard the clear sound of a child reciting letters of the alphabet. Butler dismounted and slowly guided his horse around a grass path. He came upon a clearing near a large oak tree. Two children—a girl, maybe four or five, and a boy, several years older, sat in the shade, leaning against the massive tree trunk.

Standing in the brush, he took pleasure in observing the children for a few minutes. The boy patiently sounded out vowels for the young girl to recite. "Millie, the 'a' in cat sounds different than the 'a' in plate."

A loud whinny from Butler's mount startled the children. The boy grabbed the girl's hand and pulled her behind the tree.

Tying his horse to a tree branch, the Union officer walked over. "Good morning. I was riding nearby and heard your voices. I didn't mean to frighten you." For every step forward, the children took a step backwards. "You're both very smart."

Keeping his distance, Butler circled the tree to face the children. The boy shielded the small girl from the stranger. Butler was surprised that the boy was taller than him. "My name's General Butler. I come from Fortress Monroe." The girl peeked out from behind the boy who immediately pushed her back. "It's okay. I won't hurt you. Are you from around here?"

Butler watched the boy's gaze shift from his face to the pistol in his holster. "We're staying at the fort," the boy mumbled.

He thought he recognized the boy as one of the children chasing the wooden hoop that morning. "When did you arrive?" Butler smiled.

"We went to the fort yesterday. We were told our father was there." He put his arm around his sister. "We hadn't seen him since the middle of April."

"Well, I'm glad you're now united. Who would your father be? Perhaps I know him." Butler took a step closer.

The boy took a step back with the girl. "His name is James. James Townsend." He itched his nose. "Mine's James Townsend too. James Jr."

"Well, well! I do know your father, James Jr. In fact, he's been helping us build a new bake house since arriving a few days ago. He's a hard worker." Butler frowned. "How did you learn to read so well?"

Millie leaned her head around her brother. "From our teacher."

"Hush up, Millie." He put his hand over his sister's mouth. Young James looked at Butler, frightened.

"It's all right, son." He bent over with his hands on his knees. "That's a pretty name, Millie." Millie stepped out from behind her brother.

"Her real name's Amelia, but we call her Millie," James Jr. said. His voice had thawed a bit, but his arm remained protectively around his sister.

"Who's your teacher?" Butler asked.

"We're not allowed to tell," James Jr. said.

"Oh, really? Well, that's okay." Butler scratched his head. "Where's your school?"

James Jr. wouldn't respond. Millie pointed to the tree. Her brother quickly pushed her arm down.

"Is your classroom here, under this tree?" Butler asked, looking around. Millie nodded. "It's a really nice place. How often do you have lessons?"

"We used to have them most days," James Jr. said. "But we haven't had any lessons for a few days. Some men from town beat up on our teacher." James Jr. pulled Millie close to his side.

Butler recalled a briefing from Colonel Phelps after disrupting the secessionist vote in Hampton. The Vermonter had mentioned something about rescuing a local woman from an assault. In fact, Butler recalled, Phelps described that it had occurred in a field near a large oak tree.

Rather than pressure the children any further, Butler decided to obtain the woman's identity from Phelps. He walked over to his horse and climbed up into his saddle. Turning back to the children, he smiled. "Now be sure to keep up with your lessons."

He nodded and guided his horse onto the main road.

Arriving at Camp Hamilton, Butler immediately went to see Colonel Phelps. "Sir, I recall she said her name was Mary Peake. I offered to have some of our men escort her and the children back to town but she refused. I'm afraid that's all I know, sir."

Butler thanked him for the information and continued on to Fortress Monroe. *Well, at least I have a name. That's a start.*

Before returning to his office, Butler walked to his quarters to enjoy a brief lunch with Sarah. He described his morning and the children playing near the shoreline. "It would be so nice to have our children visit here this summer. They would enjoy the area so much." Sarah cleared the dirty dishes from the table.

"Sarah, as much as I would love to see them, I'm afraid it's too dangerous at this time. Let's see how things progress." He wiped his mouth on a napkin and stood. "Oh, I almost forgot. The strangest thing happened. I was riding just west of Camp Hamilton and came upon two children, a young girl and an older boy, perhaps a few years younger than Blanche."

He cleaned the dust off his boots and started putting his jacket on. "They said they attended classes outdoors under a large oak tree. Can you imagine?" He fastened his buttons. "I'm going to ask Haggerty to see if he can find the woman. She might be the answer to my dilemma with all these children running around the fort."

"Do you know her name at least?" Sarah asked.

"Ha! Well, the children refused to tell me. I think they were protecting her so I didn't push the issue." He talked while making his way to the front door. "I think I told you about a woman's run-in with some men from Hampton. Turns out she was teaching the children when it happened. Fortunately, Phelps arrived just in time. I just stopped to see him. He said the woman's name is Mary Peake." He closed the door and walked down the steps.

Sarah flung open the door. "Benjamin! That's the woman I told you about that's making my dress. Mary Peake."

"How can that be, Sarah? That would be some coincidence." Butler frowned, standing halfway down the stone path.

"She did say that she lived with her aunt in Alexandria for ten years attending school. So she is educated. That's also where she learned to be a seamstress." Sarah was giddy with excitement.

"Do you know where she lives, Sarah?" Butler walked back towards the house.

"I don't. But I understand Private Pierce had arranged for her to come meet with me. I suspect he must know." She walked to the edge of the porch.

Butler climbed the steps and kissed his wife on the cheek. "You just made my day a lot easier."

Captain Haggerty and his men arrived at Mary's home. He walked up the front path and knocked, leaning over to look in the front window. Daisy opened the door and looked up at the man and at the group of soldiers behind him on their horses.

Mary called out, "Daisy, who's at the door?"

Daisy was frozen with fear and didn't reply. Mary put the pattern for Sarah's dress down on the table and jumped up from her chair. She hustled to the door. "Can I help you, sir?"

"I'm Captain Haggerty from Fortress Monroe, ma'am. Are you Mrs. Peake?"

"Why, yes, I am."

"Ma'am, General Butler has requested your presence. He asked that I come and escort you to his office." Haggerty politely waited for Mary's reply.

The name and reputation of General Butler were now well known throughout Hampton. Mary had no idea why the General would want to meet with her. She thought, *Surely they must have people there that can alter and repair the men's uniforms.*

"Please give me a few minutes, Captain. I need to bring my daughter next door to stay with our neighbor. Should I bring my sewing supplies?"

Confused, Haggerty replied, "Um. I don't think so, Mrs. Peake. I'm not sure why the General wants to see you, but he said nothing about sewing supplies."

Butler lost track of time, immersed in paperwork. It seemed like he had just ordered Captain Haggerty to find Mrs. Peake, yet two hours had gone by. Hearing a knock, he looked up with a start. Standing in the doorway was Captain Haggerty and an attractive young woman with light brown skin. She was nicely dressed and groomed and had big, brown, intelligent eyes.

Haggerty introduced them. "Mrs. Peake, this is General Butler, commander of Fortress Monroe. General, meet Mrs. Peake." Butler stood and walked around to the front of his desk.

He extended his hand. "Mrs. Peake, it's a pleasure to meet you. Thank you for making the journey here. I hope we didn't interrupt anything important." He looked at Haggerty. "Captain, you can leave us. Thank you."

Mary stood eye to eye with the Union officer. As a woman of average height, she was surprised that such an important man was so short in stature. She remembered Thomas's comments about seeing the general the day he first arrived. "It's nice to meet you as well, General. We've all heard of your kind treatment of the slaves seeking sanctuary here. After entering the fort, I have seen it for myself. Is there something I can do for you?"

Butler escorted Mary to his desk and pulled out a chair. Her hair was parted down the middle and pulled back behind her head.

Three-tiered earrings dangled below delicate earlobes. "Please have a seat, Mrs. Peake." Mary sat down across from Butler and looked around the room. There were several tall stacks of paper on a table behind the General. Three large maps hung on the walls. She could make out one map of the Virginia Peninsula, one of the Hampton area, and the last she didn't recognize. The afternoon sun warmed the room to an uncomfortable, stuffy temperature. Mary could feel perspiration forming on her forehead.

Butler placed his hands on the desk with fingers interlaced. "Mrs. Peake, I understand you're making a dress for my wife. For the gala in a few weeks." He waved his hand in the air.

"Yes, sir. I was working on the pattern when your men arrived." Mary frowned. *Did he actually summons me here just to discuss his wife's dress?*

"Oh. Please don't tell Mrs. Butler that I interrupted your progress." Butler chuckled warmly.

The man seems kind. After meeting Sarah, she was not surprised that her husband would be equally pleasant. Mary could feel the tension slowly leaving her body.

"The reason I asked you here is, well, I was riding in the countryside just north of the fort." He pointed. "I came across a clearing quite by mistake and found two children reading and reciting the alphabet."

Mary's smile slowly disappeared. Her body became rigid. She felt her throat constrict and her heart race. Beads of perspiration formed on her upper lip.

Butler continued. "Are you their teacher?"

She was proud of what she did even though the law forbade it. While Mary was careful, she knew the day would most likely come when she would be caught and punished. After being rescued by Union soldiers the other day, Mary had assumed all Yankees would look the other way at her transgressions. Sitting across from this important man, she realized her fateful day had finally come.

Mary looked directly at the General through glistening eyes. She swallowed hard. "Yes, sir, I teach these children." She bit her lower lip. "I know it's against the laws of Virginia, General, but I strongly believe education is the key to a better life for all people, not just white children. Illiteracy is like a closed door." Her chin started to quiver. "I'm only trying to open the door for some of these children." She leaned back in the chair with her head down and her hands in her lap. "General, I'm proud of what I do, and I'm prepared for any consequences," she said softly. Mary pulled out her handkerchief and dabbed her eyes.

She wondered how the Union officer could sit there with his silly, crooked smile and act so relaxed and smug while confronting her. *He must be so coldhearted. How could Sarah be married to an awful man?*

"Mrs. Peake." Butler leaned forward. "I don't think you understand. I didn't ask you here to take you to task for teaching these slave children." His right eye looked directly at her. "Quite the contrary. I asked you here because I'd like you to establish a formal school." Butler gestured to Mary and continued, "For your students and the other children in Fortress Monroe."

Speechless, she sat staring at Butler. "Yes, I need your help, Mrs. Peake." Butler nodded. "But before we work through any details, I was hoping to learn more about your background. I understand from my wife that you attended school in Alexandria."

When speaking to white people, particularly white men, Mary always spoke with a certain measured economy, choosing her words carefully. Under the current circumstances, however, her head spun from whipsawed emotions. Mary sat forward in her chair and the words tumbled effortlessly. Her soft Southern accent was warm and appealing An occasional word would slip out with a formal English accent, a tribute to her father's heritage.

Butler was quite taken with the woman's dedication. "Well, I saw your outdoor classroom. In fact, that's where I met two of your students, James Jr. and Millie."

"Oh, General, I cherish my students. And I'm particularly fond of those two," she giggled. "Especially James Jr."

"Mrs. Peake, I'm curious, where did this passion to teach come from?"

Mary hesitated, organizing her thoughts. "At an early age, my father stressed the importance of an education. He was born in England and attended the best schools there. He insisted that I attend school. That's why I moved to Alexandria to stay with my aunt. Unfortunately, my father died when I was away at school."

"He must've made quite an impression on you."

Mary looked down at her fidgeting hands. Through tearful eyes, she said, "There's no question my father planted the seeds of my passion, General. But when I was in Alexandria, I saw firsthand the value of an education." Mary dabbed her eyes with a handkerchief. "Particularly for colored folks."

"How so, Mrs. Peake?" He sat forward.

"My aunt lived on the same street as the Hepburn family. Although Mr. Hepburn was a lot older, he and I had a lot in common. We both had a white father and a colored mother. Mr. Hepburn was educated in Pennsylvania and became a successful businessman and civic leader in Alexandria. He insisted his children all have good educations. I attended school with his son, Moses Jr., and we became close friends. We spent lots of time together studying and playing. So it wasn't just my father's words that affected me, General. I witnessed what an education meant to a colored family and how they could live as well as any white family because of that."

Butler smiled. "There's nothing like a concrete example to reinforce a parent's wish. So, Mrs. Peake, are you interested in setting up a formal school for your students?"

Her brown eyes were full and wide. "I can't think of anything I'd want to do more. But I do have a question for you, if you don't mind."

"I'll do my best to answer any questions you might have, Mrs. Peake."

Mary thought about how to best phrase her question. She didn't want to offend the Union officer. "There are men in Hampton who roam the streets enforcing laws against colored people. This includes teaching our children. Will you be able to protect us from these people?"

"Mrs. Peake, everyday hundreds more troops arrive from the North. I can assure you that no one will threaten you or the children."

"Oh, thank you, General. That's a big relief." Tears streamed down her cheeks. She swiped them with her hand. Mary started to ask another question but hesitated.

"Mrs. Peake, please feel free to ask your questions."

"General, do you think the Union will defeat the Confederates? I mean, if you do defeat them, would that mean that slavery would end?" Mary sat back, glad she had asked the question but afraid to hear the answer.

"Mrs. Peake, the future of slavery is a difficult issue to address. It's common knowledge that the Southern states seceded over fears slavery would be abolished. While I'm certainly not a proponent of slavery, my presence here is to help reunite our great country. If slavery falls as a result of our efforts, so be it."

"General, do you think it will be difficult to defeat the Confederates?" Mary winced in anticipation.

"There's no question they are committed to their cause, as are we. But we have overwhelming strength. We're hopeful that this conflict will be over soon. Perhaps by year's end."

"That would be wonderful." Mary placed her hands over her heart.

Butler smiled. "Do you have any other questions, Mrs. Peake?"

"No. Thank you, General. You've been most patient."

"Then, do we have an arrangement?" Butler asked.

Mary nodded in reply.

"First, you'll need to locate a place for your school. Unfortunately, we're too crowded in the fort. When you're ready, we'll provide daily transportation for the children from and back to Fortress Monroe. We'll also ensure that there's no disruption from any local Hampton citizens," Butler said as he stood. "I'll have Captain Haggerty bring you back home."

He walked around to the front of his desk. "Mrs. Peake, you're an impressive and brave woman. It was a pleasure meeting you." Butler escorted her outside his office where Captain Haggerty was waiting.

Mary turned at the door and said, "General Butler, thank you for your support to our people and for your kind offer."

Butler smiled and nodded. "We'll be in touch in a few days to get started with our plans."

Haggerty followed Mary to the front door, looking over his shoulder to Butler with a puzzled look.

MARY AWOKE EARLY AND DRESSED, EAGER TO start her busy day. She was bursting with excitement. After a quick dress delivery, the rest of the day would be spent looking for a suitable place for her school. Thomas had already left for Fortress Monroe. Daisy stumbled into Mary's bedroom, holding her bird book in one hand and rubbing her half-opened eyes with the other. "Why are you up so early, Mama?"

"Well, good morning, Miss Sleepyhead." She bent over and kissed her daughter on the top of the head. Mary pointed to a red satin dress on a side table. "I have to deliver this dress to Mrs. Boyd. She needs it for some function later this morning."

Daisy placed the book on Mary's bed and crossed her arms. "Oh, that awful lady again."

"Daisy, you shouldn't speak poorly of Mrs. Boyd. She's a good customer and she means well. Well, most of the time. Okay, maybe only some of the time." Mary smiled and steered Daisy out of her bedroom.

"Now go get dressed. After breakfast, I'll bring you next door until I get back. I'll only be gone a short while."

Mary wound her way through Hampton. The east-to-west oriented streets glistened in the rising sunlight. Streets running north and south were still shaded. At each turn, Mary alternated between sun and shade, warm and cool. At this time of the morning, the warm sun definitely felt better, she thought. In a few hours though, Mary would seek the shaded streets.

Wagons and carriages crammed with boxes and small pieces of furniture filled the streets. She was surprised it was so busy this early in the morning. The flow of people seemed to be heading west and north, away from the town. *Perhaps it is always like this*, Mary thought. She was rarely out walking at this time of day.

As she got closer to the Boyd's home, Mary became increasingly nervous. Mary wondered if Mr. Boyd knew that his two slave catchers were detained in a jail cell at Fortress Monroe. Maybe she'd be lucky and he either wouldn't be home or he'd be too busy to bother with her. *I pray so,* she thought as she crossed the lane.

Turning up a tree-shaded street, Mary spotted three carriages in front of the Boyds' home. Several of their slaves, men and women, were busy carrying boxes from the house down the long walkway to the carriages. Even from this distance, Mary recognized Mr. Boyd entering the house, waving his arms, and yelling at Dennis.

She slowed her pace, hoping to avoid another altercation with the bully. Only after seeing Melinda Boyd emerge from the front door, Mary resumed her pace. Hoping to make a quick exchange, the dress for payment, Mary tried to time her strides to arrive at the carriages at the same time as the woman.

Only several paces away, Mary could see that Melinda Boyd was in some distress. Matted hair stuck to her sweat-drenched face. Her pink cotton dress was a deeper shade where sweat clung to her back. Large wet rings encircled her sides, extending well below her arms to her waist. Mary was grateful they were outside in the open air. She approached the woman. "Mrs. Boyd, what's going on?"

Startled, Melinda turned around quickly. Her eyes were red and puffy. Mary wasn't sure if she had been crying, if the sting of perspiration irritated her eyes, or both. "My husband insists we leave immediately. With all these awful Yankees roaming around Hampton, he fears it's only a matter of time before all-out war erupts. He says we're surrounded by Union soldiers."

Mary handed Melinda her tailored dress. It was carefully wrapped in paper to prevent it from getting soiled or wrinkled on her walk. Melinda took the dress, rolled it in a ball and threw it into an open box in the carriage.

Taking a step back, Mary looked up at the large mansion, with the top half now lit by the rising sun. "But your beautiful home! Where will you go?"

"My sister and her family live in Williamsburg. We'll go there." She leaned against the carriage to catch her breath. "At least for now. Then we'll decide whether to settle there or, hopefully, come back to here," Melinda said. "When it's safe." She looked around suspiciously.

The slaves carried more boxes down the walk and stacked them onto the carriages. Two were already full. The third was almost full. Mr. Boyd and Dennis stepped out of the front door, straining under the weight of a large wooden crate. "We're only taking Dennis with us. The other Negroes are staying here," Melinda said. "We don't have room for them in our carriages or at my sister's home."

Dennis shuffled backward down the walk, wincing from the

weight of the box. He shot a troubled glance at Mary, clearly not excited about joining the Boyd family on their journey. Mary thought the other slaves, however, looked relieved. The five Boyd children climbed into the carriage seats, fighting for position. Since the family appeared to be leaving soon, Mary decided to stay. She couldn't imagine a more pleasant way to spend her morning than to watch the Boyd family leave town. Especially Mr. Boyd.

Melinda and her younger daughter climbed into the carriage driven by Mr. Boyd. Their three sons climbed into the second carriage. The older daughter climbed into the last carriage, driven by Dennis.

Mr. Boyd noticed Mary for the first time, standing in the walkway. He pointed at her and yelled, "You haven't won. Don't think you've won. We'll be back, damn you. And damn all of you Negroes and your Northern supporters! You'll see."

Mary stood with her arms crossed, trying not to smile. Then he turned to the slaves standing near the carriages. "Now you do what I told you. You go hide in the forest. Those Yankees will surely beat you and sell you off." He pointed at his house. "And stay the hell out of my house. We'll be back soon and everything better be in perfect shape."

With a crack of the whip the carriages lurched forward. Dennis grimaced over his shoulder at Mary. The caravan proceeded down the road leaving a trail of swirling dust. The mood of the six slaves turned from relief to joy. Mary walked over to them. "Don't worry about the Yankees. They won't bother you."

"Oh, we're not worried, ma'am. We're gonna be just fine," one of the men said with a big grin.

They watched the carriages turn a corner to the main road, heading west. The slaves patted each other on the back and strolled up the long walk and into the main house.

Mary turned to walk home. She realized Melinda Boyd never paid her for altering her dress. *Oh well, the sight of her sweating through her clothes was worth it.* Mary sang all the way home.

The steady growth of Union troops caused most of the citizens in Hampton to abandon their homes. Like the Boyd family, many moved north toward Williamsburg or Yorktown. Some of the abandoned homes were quite nice and still contained large pieces of expensive furniture.

The key test for the remaining slaves in Hampton was whether they could survive without their master's care. Most of the slaves lived in one-room wooden shanties in the rear of their master's house with dirt floors and open fireplaces. Many slaves remained in these primitive, crowded quarters even though big, beautiful, empty homes stood only a short distance away. They lived on the remains of food in storage and on vegetables in the gardens. Over time they set up stands on the street selling cakes, oysters, and other items to support themselves. Some approached the Union encampments at Segar Farms and Newport News Point to serve the increasing officer population.

News of the Hampton exodus reached General Butler. Concerned for the remaining slaves, he sent a group of thirty soldiers to ensure that they had the means to support themselves. He also instructed the soldiers to prevent plundering of the abandoned houses.

Mary was overjoyed with the departure of the Boyds. She wasn't even concerned about the loss of Melinda Boyd's business. With her reputation quickly spreading among the Union officers' wives, she had more than enough business just from Fortress Monroe. And with the mass withdrawal of white citizens from Hampton, it was the perfect opportunity to search for an appropriate dwelling for her school.

As she walked through the town, Mary marveled at how quickly her fortunes had changed from only a few days earlier. It was now safe to go about her business of educating the slave children without fear of punishment. *No more slave patrols. No more Mr. Boyd breathing down my neck.* That morning, for the first time in months, the sun seemed brighter and the air seemed fresher.

After an hour of searching block after block, she discovered nothing suitable. She recalled that when she would lead the children to the large oak tree for their lessons, they passed an old abandoned cottage. It was located along the shore of Hampton Roads on the other side of the creek near the Seminary. She was pretty certain the cottage hadn't been occupied for several years.

As visions of classrooms packed with eager children filled her head, Mary glided across Hampton Creek Bridge. About a quarter-mile down the main road, she turned south towards Hampton Roads and entered a sandy path that led down to the old, brown cottage.

She pushed the front door open. The rusty hinges groaned as the stale, inside air mixed with the fresh sea breezes. Mary stepped into a small foyer. Steep stairs led to a second floor. To her right was another door. Pushing it open, she entered a large room that occupied most of the first floor. Mary thought it could have been a sitting room at one time, perhaps filled with elegant furniture and smartly dressed people.

At one end was a fireplace. Along the front wall, with a southern exposure, were several large but dirty windows filtering light into the room. Some of the windows were broken. She walked over and cleaned a small area of the glass with her sleeve. The views of Hampton Roads in the distance were stunning.

The floors creaked as she walked. Cobwebs hung from the ceilings. She could hear rustling in the fireplace and assumed some creatures had made a nest there. The sight of the dilapidated structure would have disheartened anyone else, but Mary could only see its potential. It was maybe large enough to hold forty to fifty children. She imagined how the desks and chairs would be oriented. The fireplace would provide warmth in the winter and the windows would provide plenty of natural light to read. She let out a deep sigh. *It's perfect!*

She walked back out to the vestibule and climbed the staircase. The old boards creaked under her weight. *How long has it been since someone was here?* Upstairs were two rooms she assumed were once bedrooms. In the larger one, a broken boudoir and half-eaten acorns were scattered across the floor. A dead, decaying bird rested on an old, musty mattress near a broken window. She shuddered and closed the door.

Arriving at the bottom of the staircase, Mary's gaze swept across the large room. Excited by the prospect of a new schoolhouse, she closed the front door to the cottage and hurried home.

The main topic of conversation at the Peake residence that evening, as with the rest of Hampton, was the exodus of Confederate sympathizers. But Mary was equally excited about her discovery. Sitting at the kitchen table, Daisy split open a pod and was busy picking out the peas with her fingers. One rolled onto the floor. "Whoops!"

The heat from the oven made the small room uncomfortable. Mary opened a window, but the air outside was as warm as inside, providing little relief.

Mary sat down and pointed to the floor. "Please pick it up, baby." She turned to her husband. "You should see this place, Thomas. Refreshing breezes blow off the water. There's plenty of grass for the children to run around and play. The cottage has a large front room. Although the windows are a little dirty, they should provide plenty of natural light once they're cleaned."

Mary walked over to her husband and stood behind his chair. Leaning over, she put her arms around his shoulders. "Unfortunately, though, it does need some repairs and a good cleaning. If only I knew a big, strong man who was handy with tools." Mary looked at Daisy and winked.

Thomas reached up and clasped Mary's hands and leaned his head back. "I'll be happy to help get this place in shape," he said. "But are you sure you want to be all the way on the other side of Hampton Creek? Isn't there any place in town?"

Mary kissed Thomas on the cheek and stood behind him with her hands on his shoulders. "Thomas, I looked everywhere. And I thought about that. Some of the students will be coming from Hampton. These children were already walking by the cottage on the way to the oak tree, so it'll actually be a little closer for them. And General Butler said there are children from Fortress Monroe who will attend. The cottage is midway between Hampton and the fort, so it should be convenient for everyone."

"Well, it's clear you've thought this through. We can go there first thing in the morning so I can see what repairs and tools will be needed," Thomas said. "Who would've thought you'd have your own school? Sanctioned by the Union army, no less!"

Aromas of bacon and johnnycakes filled the house. Thomas and Daisy arrived at the table at the same time, amazed at the hearty spread awaiting them. Thomas looked at his wife. "You must've woken up early. Why the feast?"

"We have a big day ahead of us," Mary said. "I want to make sure my workers are well-fed and have plenty of energy."

She patiently waited as Thomas and Daisy cleaned their plates and helped themselves to seconds. Mary grew more anxious as the sun rose higher in the sky. While Thomas was still taking his last bite, Mary grabbed his plate and took the fork from his hand. Thomas watched as she placed the dirty dishes in the basin. He looked over at Daisy who quickly shoveled the food from her plate into her mouth.

"Oh, Daisy," Mary said, as her husband started to chuckle. "That's not very ladylike!" Daisy's cheeks bulged like a chipmunk's as she chewed.

As the Peakes headed out, Hannah Townsend, James's wife, and their two children, James Jr. and Millie, joined the cleanup crew. It took less than twenty minutes for the group to arrive at the brown cottage. Of course, this was at the rapid pace set by Mary. They stood outside the cottage and caught their breath. Thomas looked out over the water and whistled. "Look at that view." He turned to Mary and smiled. "Well, you certainly can't beat the location."

Mary, her family, and friends entered the dusty, stale cottage. Thomas stood in the large front room. "Maybe you should have your classes outside," he teased, looking around. He walked along the windowed front wall and looked up at the sagging ceiling beams. "Are you sure you want this as your classroom? I'm afraid this whole place could collapse."

"Oh, Thomas, it just needs some love and attention," she said, hugging her husband's arm.

"I'm not sure that's all that's needed." He shrugged. "But, if this is what you want, we'll do our best."

The group began its mission by cleaning out the first floor's great room. Thomas spent much of the morning going from the cottage back to Hampton to fetch needed tools and supplies.

By late afternoon the space looked clean and almost presentable. After some adjustments, the windows were even functional. Fresh air blew off Hampton Roads and soothed the sweaty, tired faces of the work crew. During the day, Mary had obtained permission to use several tables from the nearby seminary that'd been recently replaced by newer ones. Thomas made a few additional tables and benches from long planks. The only thing remaining now were the children to sit in them.

Mary looked around the room and frowned. "Oh, Thomas! We forgot to clean out the fireplace," she said.

"No problem. Daisy and I can do that in no time." They pulled straw and sticks from the flue, trying not to make a mess in the clean room. Thomas quickly pulled his hand away and put his arm in front of Daisy, shielding her. "I think there's something in there."

A moment later, three squirrels jumped onto the floor and scampered around the room. Daisy shrieked, immediately giving chase and laughing. Mary ran over to the front door and pulled it open. Everyone joined the wild pursuit to herd the frantic rodents towards the front vestibule. After twenty minutes, the group was exhausted but triumphant. Two squirrels fled the swinging brooms out the door and onto the front lawn. One squirrel jumped through an open window and scrambled up a nearby tree.

With the excitement over, Daisy and Millie went to explore the rest of the cottage. Screams echoed through the upstairs floorboards. Thomas bolted for the stairs, scaling them three at a time. James Jr. was quick on his heels. Thomas burst into the dark, stuffy room. Daisy ran to her father and clung to his leg. Millie ran out of the room, past James Jr., and down the stairs to her mother.

"Papa, it's a dead bird." Daisy pointed. "On the mattress."

Mary joined the group, her heart pounding. "Oh, baby, I know. I saw it yesterday. It's so sad."

"It's a mockingbird, Mama," Daisy said. "What happened to it?"

"I don't know, baby. Maybe it got trapped in here and starved. Or it could have just been sick and died." Mary hugged her daughter.

Daisy looked from Mary to Thomas. "Can we bury it? Please?"

Mary nodded to Thomas in approval. Thomas pulled a rag out of his back pocket. He bent over and gently wrapped the bird in the white cloth.

Thomas, cradling the bird, led the procession down the stairs and out the front door. With her head bowed, Daisy walked down to the water's edge and picked up a stick. She used it to dig a hole in the sand while the group stood in a semicircle watching. James Jr. grabbed another stick and helped dig the grave. Thomas carefully placed the dead bird, shrouded in the white rag, into the hole. Daisy slowly brushed the sand with her hands until the hole was covered. She pushed a stick into the small earthen mound as a marker. "Mama, why do things have to die?"

"Well, when people and animals are finished serving the Lord on earth, they go to heaven to join Him." Mary leaned over and stroked her daughter's hair.

"But why does God need birds there?" Daisy persisted.

"Well, even heaven needs sweet music, baby." Mary smiled.

After all the excitement and hard work, everyone was tired and hungry. Daisy and Millie wanted to go home. Mary gave James

Jr. a big hug for being so helpful. The group left, but Mary stayed behind.

With the sun low in the sky, Mary felt the classroom was ready. She looked around the room with her hands on her hips. While not as picturesque as the big oak tree under which Mary was accustomed to teaching, the brown cottage would certainly be more comfortable. It would also provide shelter from inclement weather. Perhaps best of all, she could store books and other learning aids there instead of hauling them from her home each day.

Mary closed the door to the brown cottage and looked across the shimmering water to Fortress Monroe. Mary couldn't wait to hear from General Butler and for the schoolchildren to arrive.

At the main road leading to Hampton Creek Bridge, she smiled to herself, deciding to take a detour. Mary strolled around the large grass clearing. Birds swooped and darted into and out of the oak tree, busy feeding hatchlings and reinforcing their nests. Despite the incident with those two awful men, this place still filled her heart with a sense of warmth and comfort. She walked over and affectionately placed her hand on the rough bark, tracing her fingers in the deep grooves. Only a few days ago, Mary had wondered if she would ever be able to teach again. Now she had her own school and a whole new beginning.

13

WITH THE WALLS OF THE NEW BAKE HOUSE completed, workers were busy framing the roof. The unexpected but welcome assistance of the contraband slaves allowed construction to progress much more quickly than expected.

Confederate Colonel Charles Mallory and his family, and most other families sympathetic to the Rebel cause, had abandoned their Hampton homes and traveled further north up the peninsula. Union forces roamed freely and had complete control of the vicinity. No longer concerned about being recaptured, Frank and James decided to move their families back to their shanties behind the Mallory farmhouse. They were grateful for the protection of the Union soldiers at Fortress Monroe but wanted to settle back into their old routines.

Butler sat behind his desk feeling good about all the loose ends he had recently tied up. It was certainly his good fortune that he had stumbled across the two children while riding outside the fort only two days earlier. He was thrilled to have met Mary Peake and couldn't wait for her classes to begin.

Running a knife along the edge of an envelope, he opened a dispatch from Secretary of War Simon Cameron. Butler had heard rumors that his actions regarding the escaped slaves and his subsequent letter to Cameron and General Scott had caused quite a stir in Washington. President Lincoln was upset that the delicate balance to placate the states bordering the North and South was now at risk.

The letter began, "Your action with respect to the Negroes who came within your lines from the service of the Rebels is approved." Butler slapped the desk in relief. But as he read on about the obligations of the federal and state governments, Butler took careful note of the closing. "You will employ such persons in the service to which they will be best adapted, keeping an account of the labor by them performed. The question of their final disposition will be reserved for future determination."

The last sentence brought a smile to Butler's face. He knew Washington was struggling with his actions, and this gave him a sense of satisfaction. Butler was thankful that he wasn't ordered to return the slaves to their owners. He summoned Private Pierce, Commissioner of Negro Affairs, to his office.

Pierce entered and greeted his commander "I just received approval from Secretary Cameron regarding the contrabands. I've been giving the question of how best to use them careful thought." Butler stood and walked around his desk, leaning against the edge. "Even though we're well-protected to the north, I have concerns we may still be susceptible to attacks there."

Butler led Pierce to a map on the wall and pointed. "I'd like breastworks constructed from the old cemetery here northward to the new cemetery." He turned back to Pierce. "Many of our troops are busy either here at the fort or in Newport News. Using the contrabands will not only help us, but it will keep them occupied. Besides the work will be close to their homes, and they'll be able to return there in the evenings," Butler said. "You'll need assistance to supervise the work. You can select from our troops, as you deem appropriate. Given the hour of the day, it's probably best you assemble and begin work in the morning."

"Yes, General," Pierce said. "I'd like to organize the supervision and requisition the needed tools now, though, so we'll be ready at daylight." Pierce saluted Butler and left his office.

The next morning Pierce and his assistant supervisors walked through the temporary housing in and around Fortress Monroe and through the streets of Hampton. The men were told to assemble later that morning at the courthouse yard upon the ringing of the bell.

James stood in the hot sun with Frank and Shepard, wondering why he and the others were summoned here. He spotted Mary's husband Thomas in the shadow of a large tree and nodded to him.

Standing on the courthouse steps, Pierce looked out over the group of sixty-five men. "My name is Private Edward Pierce in Company L of the Third Regiment of the Massachusetts Militia. Many of you have come to the Union lines requesting sanctuary, which we have justly provided. Some of you are free men of whom I'll make the same request. The Rebels have used many of you to build their entrenchments, aiding in their fight against the Union. Now we need your help." Groans and sighs grew loud.

Pierce held up his hands. "I know what you're thinking. You may have been treated harshly by the Rebels, overworked and abused.

We're not asking you to do anything different from what our own soldiers would perform and have performed."

He took two steps down to the ground and walked around the perimeter of the group. As he did, he looked into the eyes of the men he passed. "You'll be treated kindly. You will not be asked to work beyond your capacity. Whereas the Rebels paid your masters for your hard work, we'll pay you for your services. And you'll be furnished with a full soldier's rations." Some of the men mumbled quiet approval and nodded their heads up and down. Many, however, remained suspicious.

James called out, "We're willing to help. What do you want us to do?"

Pierce smiled his gratitude. "We need breastworks constructed from the old cemetery near town north to the new one. With the help of all of you, this should be quick work. As you may know, this entails digging a ditch and creating a barrier to the height of a man's breast, which will provide protection as he fires over it. We don't expect any impending attacks by the Confederate forces, but we believe this is a necessary precaution. Remember, this is for your own protection as well." More heads nodded in approval. "You'll be supplied with shovels, picks, and other tools as needed," Pierce said.

An old man, leaning against a fence post, yelled out from the crowd. "I have a bad back and am suffering from rheumatism. I can't dig no holes." He spat at the ground.

Pierce walked over, put his hand on the man's shoulder, and looked across the crowd. "No one will be asked to perform work he's unable to do. If you're old or have a condition preventing you from helping, you'll be dismissed or asked to perform a task within your physical abilities." He walked over and climbed the stairs. "In a few minutes, I'll have you line up and enter the courthouse. We need to record some basic information about each of you so we can process your payments and rations."

With the departure of the Confederates from Hampton and little to do on the farms, many of the men had become restless with inactivity and welcomed this opportunity. The men lined up and entered the courthouse. Each provided their name, age, and specifics about any dependents. It was explained to them that the Union would furnish rations for children or the elderly, but that the costs of this would be deducted from their daily wages. The men generally felt this was a fair arrangement.

James, Frank, and Shepard stood in line waiting their turn. Shepard turned to his two friends, stooped over and bracing his back with his hands. "My back's been bothering me something bad. I think I got rheumatism like that old man."

James looked down at Shepard and poked his finger into the young man's chest. "You think they aren't checking to see who's lying, you fool? We need all the help we can get to do this work. These Yankees helped us when we needed it. Now it's our turn to help them. Besides that, they're gonna pay us and feed us, Shep. They gave us their word. Now shut your face and do what they say."

Shepard pushed James's hand away. "Well, words are cheap. I got plenty of words. My pockets are spilling over with words. But they can't fill my stomach when I'm hungry."

Thomas finished his interview. He walked over to the three men and they exchanged greetings. James said, "What are you doing here, Thomas? I thought you were constructing housing in the fort."

"I am," Thomas replied. "We're waiting for a shipment of lumber to arrive. It should get here sometime next week, so I figured I'd work here until then. Besides the money's not bad, and they could use help measuring and cutting posts and supports for the revetment."

James approached the desk where Pierce was seated. He recognized the Union soldier from his meeting with Butler several days earlier. James nodded at the young soldier.

Pierce smiled. "Good morning, Mr. Townsend. We appreciate your help here and your words of support earlier." Pierce recorded the required information that James gave him. "I understand you have a wife and children, is this correct?"

"Yes, sir," James said. "I have two children. My wife and I've been together for many years, but we're not really legally married."

"How is that?" Pierce looked up at the tall man.

"Well, we never had the chance to marry with a preacher and all," James said.

"Very well, Mr. Townsend. If you wait over there with the others, we'll dispense tools when the interviews are finished."

James stepped aside and leaned against the wall. Frank came forward and provided his name and age. "Are you married, Mr. Baker?" Pierce said.

"I have two children like James here. My first wife was sold off. This is my second wife." Frank shifted from one foot to the other.

"Your first wife was sold?" Pierce placed the pen on the table and looked up, this time in alarm.

"Yes, sir," Frank said. "Many years ago. So was my son. Haven't seen them since."

"Were you legally married to your first wife, Mr. Baker?" Pierce said.

"Not legally, no." Frank shrugged. "I guess I'm not legally married now either."

Shepard approached Pierce. After answering his routine questions, Shepard leaned over with his hands on the table. "You say we're gonna get paid for this work. When's that gonna happen?"

"Your wages and provisions will be provided by week's end," Pierce said, sitting back and crossing his arms.

"Yeah, well, that better happen. I ain't working for nothing, you know." Shepard tapped his finger on the table.

James watched the exchange and winced. He was relieved to see Pierce suppressing a smile. "Mr. Mallory, your only concern is to do a good job on the breastworks. If you do, I assure you, you'll be treated fairly."

Shepard turned and strutted over to James and Frank. James crossed his muscular forearms and glared down at the young slave. "What?" Shepard said. "I didn't do anything wrong."

With the interviews completed, Pierce stood and addressed the group. "Thank you for your patience. Let's go outside, and we'll hand out the tools. Then you'll be dismissed until two o'clock this afternoon. When you hear the next sounding of the bell, you're to assemble here."

With the sun bearing down and the humidity uncomfortably high, two o'clock arrived sooner than anyone wanted. The courthouse bell rang, and the men sluggishly assembled. Pierce completed the roll call and asked the men to pick up their tools and follow him from the village to the nearby cemetery.

Facing the group, Pierce explained that a military earthwork, or breastwork, could be constructed in different ways. "An earthwork consists of three main components—a trench, a parapet, and a revetment. The parapet is a protective mound of earth that might contain logs or stones, referred to as the fill. In our case, we'll use stones as the fill since they seem plentiful." Some heads nodded in understanding. "The revetment is the side of the parapet where the soldier stands.

It serves as a retaining wall. The revetment could be comprised of planks, sandbags, or stones; anything that would hold the vertical side of the earthen parapet in place. We'll use planks for this purpose. The soldier stands behind the parapet for protection and places his weapon on top of the revetment to steady his aim."

James was fascinated by the details. From Sewell's Point, he was certainly familiar with the hard labor involved in constructing a breast-work. But he and the other slaves had only been told to dig here or dig there. No one ever explained why. He looked around at the other men seated in the shade of the cemetery. James noticed that maybe only half were paying attention. The others were engaged in their own side conversations. To his surprise, Shepard seemed mesmerized by the soldier's talk. James tapped Frank on the arm and nodded towards Shepard. Frank looked at the young man, seated with his legs crossed, and turned back to James smiling.

Pierce continued. "A trench can be constructed in front of the para-pet or behind it. The preferred method, if time permits, is to construct the trench in front of the parapet. This would, essentially, create a dry moat, providing an additional layer of defense and making it more difficult for advancing enemies. The disadvantage is that it requires more time to build the higher parapet as the soldiers are standing behind it at grade level."

Shepard yelled out, "So which one are we gonna do?"

"That's a good question, Mr. Mallory." Pierce turned from the young man back to the group. "Well, considering the high tempera-tures and the quarter-mile length of our earthworks, I decided to construct the alternative 'rifle trench' method."

"What's that?" Shepard asked.

"Rather than constructing a trench in front of the parapet, the rifle method uses a rear interior trench," Pierce explained. "The advantage of this method is that the earth removed from the trench simultaneously lowers the area where the men stand and raises the height of the parapet wall. Instead of standing at grade, the men stand in the ditch, lower than grade, and rest their weapons on top of the parapet wall."

"Yeah, I like that one." Shepard nodded, as if Pierce had requested his approval.

Pierce chuckled. "Well, I'm glad you approve, Mr. Mallory."

James shook his head at the exchange.

The men were given instructions where to start digging. Some were only used to light household duties. Between the intense heat and the strenuous nature of the work, several of the men began to wane. Pierce instituted regular breaks of fifteen minutes almost hourly to allow the men to rest in the shaded cemetery. He also made sure that they drank plenty of water.

James was sprawled out on the grass. He stretched his arms and legs with his eyes closed, thankful for the rest. A large tree provided welcome relief from the intense sun. He turned to a large, ornate headstone on his right. In large engraved letters it read, "Nathaniel Ambrose Boyd, died 1849." He nudged Frank, who was resting nearby. "Hey, you think this is the ancestor of the Boyds that Mary talks about? You know, the guy who sent the slave patrols after her?"

Frank turned towards the headstone. "Damned if I know." He smiled. "Damned if I care either."

"I understand he built his plantation and made all that money on the backs of slaves." James twirled a long piece of grass between his lips thoughtfully.

"Yeah, well good riddance to him." Frank turned to James. "While he's laid here to rest, we're laying to rest right on top of him." Frank chuckled. "I guess we're on his back now."

At six o'clock, Pierce led the men back to the courthouse. The slaves carefully placed their tools in areas where they could easily identify them. Some actually hid their shovels or picks in discreet places. James watched Shepard place his shovel behind a door and looked around the room to see if anyone saw his hiding place.

"Shep, what're you doing? Why're you hiding your shovel behind that door?" James smirked.

Shepard looked around the room again. He shoved the large man and said in a low voice, "Don't be telling anyone where my shovel's at, James."

James walked away shaking his head. He nudged Frank. "I swear, sometimes I think that boy is dumber than a stump."

Pierce stood up in front of the dirty, sweaty group. "We'll begin tomorrow morning with the ringing of the bell at four o'clock." Groans echoed throughout the courthouse. "This schedule is best for your health. As we saw today, the sun is most intense in the middle of the day. If we find that this approach is too taxing, I'll consult with you about changing it." The crowd dispersed, most men heading back to their small shanties behind the large, empty homes of their masters.

After cleaning up, Pierce returned to the fort and entered the mess hall for a late meal. Two Union soldiers from Pierce's regiment sat cleaning their plates. One man hit the arm of the other and yelled out, "Look who's here! The Massachusetts liberal who became a Virginia slave-master." They both roared with laughter.

Pierce smiled and walked over to the two men. "Very funny. I'll tell you this much. Some may consider these slaves indolent people. But after working by their side for just one day, I find them as industrious as any white man."

The next morning, Pierce decided to give the men a few extra minutes and rang the bell at a quarter past four. To his surprise, the men were quite prompt and quickly assembled with their tools. He completed the roll call and led the men back to the construction site in the dark.

Within thirty minutes of the work bell sounding, all the men were busy with their assigned tasks. They made excellent progress for the next few hours. At seven o'clock, they were dismissed for an hour. Following roll call at eight, the men continued on the earthworks, with regular intervals of rest in the shaded cemetery and water breaks. As the day reached maximum temperatures and humidity, Pierce dismissed the men at eleven, requesting that they reconvene at three o'clock in the afternoon.

After roll call, the men resumed work until six o'clock, when they were dismissed for the day. Pierce inquired whether the men were still objectionable to the work schedule. Without exception, they all felt that it was the best approach to the hot summer temperatures.

On the third day of construction, General Butler stopped by to check on progress. Butler dismounted his horse and walked over. "You appear to be making good progress, Edward."

"Yes, General," he said. "The men are working hard. They seem to be pleased they're no longer idle." He smiled. "And I suspect their humane treatment is also contributing to their productivity and dedication."

"Is there anything here that needs my attention?" Butler asked.

"I don't think so, sir. But a few peculiar things surfaced from our interviews and subsequent conversations." Pierce wiped his grimy hands on his pants.

"What's that?" Butler watched two men lift a large log.

"Well, we discovered that the married men aren't actually legally married." Pierce shrugged. "They have children and seem to have lived loyally with the same women for many years. But it appears they were never given the opportunity to formally and legally make their marriages official," Pierce said.

"Well. Not a surprise, I'm afraid. Anything else?" Butler watched the men dig as the sun shimmered on their sweaty skin.

"Yes, sir." Butler turned to hear more from his junior aide. "Many of the men expressed an interest to learn to read and write. Some of them were exposed to the alphabet and reading basics by white playmates when they were younger. Some tried to learn on their own with primers," Pierce said with a troubled smile.

"Well, Edward. I wish we could do something for them, but we already have our hands full." He climbed into his saddle. "If you can think of anything, though, let me know." He nodded and road away.

At the end of the day, Pierce instructed the men to meet him in an empty building adjacent to the courthouse after they deposited their tools.

James, Frank, and Shepard entered the building along with the other men. They all stood in amazement. Pierce waved his arm over the piles. "Each man will get five days' rations. For those of you with dependents, as you told us during the interviews the first day, you'll be given half rations for each dependent."

James stood and stared at the crates and boxes. He had never seen so much food in one place, not even on the Mallory farm after fall harvest. Before him was a culinary palette of red, orange, yellow, green, and brown. His nostrils flared, inhaling the delightful aromas. His mouth watered and his stomach churned anticipating his dinner that evening and for many evenings to follow. James did the quick math. With his wife and two children, that would be another man and a half worth of rations, he calculated.

Fortunately food and provisions at the fort were plentiful even as war approached.

"The cost of these rations will be deducted from your daily wage," Pierce reminded them.

As the rations were distributed, James couldn't believe how much he and the other men received. His pile included hard bread, beans, salt beef, coffee, sugar, rice, candles, and soap. As he hefted the sacks into his arms, he thought his family could easily live on these rations for much longer than five days.

James looked at Frank. "I'm not sure how I'm gonna get all this back to our place."

Frank laughed. "I don't care if I have to make a hundred trips, James. It's all coming with me." He slapped James on the back.

Even Shepard, always the skeptic, seemed to be at a loss for words. He muttered under his breath, "Well, butter my buns." He looked up at James.

James, grinning with glistening eyes, said, "See that, Shep?" He pointed to his pile. "I told you. Those aren't just words you're looking at and smelling."

14

THE PIERCING SHRIEKS OF CHILDREN AND THE clopping of horses' hooves echoed through the trees. A swirl of dust trailed the wagon as it came to a halt in front of the cottage. The herd of new students piled out, laughing and shoving. It was Monday, June 3, the first day of Mary's classes. Waiting for lessons to start, the spirited boys and girls ran around the old house or dashed inside to explore the rooms.

Mary thanked the driver. He would return at three o'clock. She corralled the children into the large front room and settled them into their seats. Her enthusiasm was dampened by anxiety as she looked around the room and counted over twenty-one students, including Daisy. Her classes under the large oak tree numbered less than ten children. On most days, it was only four or five.

Her voice cracked as she spoke. "Good morning. It's so nice to see everyone. My name is Mrs. Peake." She scanned the room and spotted the children of James Townsend and Frank Baker. It was a comfort to nod and smile at James Jr.'s familiar face. "We'll start the day with each of you coming to see me one at a time. I need to record your name and age."

Due to the large class size and with the numbers expected to grow, Mary knew she needed to break the children into groups. "Then we'll do some fun tests so that I can assess how well you can read and write." She would use these results, along with the child's age, to determine placement into one of four groups.

Since some of the children didn't know their ages, Mary had to rely on their reading aptitude and her initial observations of their maturity level. Once she began assigning students to groups, she immediately ran into a problem. "I'm not going in that group. It has little kids in it! I'm no dummy," Jessey said, standing in defiance with his arms crossed.

Mary walked over to the thirteen-year-old. "Jessey, I organized the groups by everyone's ability to read. If I place you in the next highest group, either you'll fall behind and get frustrated or the group will be held back." Mary placed her hand on his shoulder. "What if you stay in this group and I work with you after school? As soon as I think you're ready, I'll move you into the next group." She smiled. "I promise."

"We'll see." Jessey unfolded his arms with a scowl. As he was sitting down, another boy kicked the bench over from beneath him. Jessey tumbled onto the floor, and the children roared with laughter. With the reflexes of a wild animal, Jessey sprung up and pounced on the other boy. The two wrestled around on the floor, grunting and knocking over more benches. Everyone scattered to make room for the fight and to make sure they didn't get dragged into it.

"Boys! Boys!" Mary grabbed Jessey by the back of his shirt and pulled him up. The other boy kept swinging. James Jr. came to her aid and held the other boy back with his long arms. Although only twelve, James Jr. was the tallest and most muscular of the boys in her class. No one wanted to get into a tussle with him. The threatening look on James Jr.'s face was all that was needed to encourage the other boy to slide away on the floor.

The day dragged on as Mary dealt with shoving matches, arguments, and restless children with short attention spans. She heard the carriage from Fortress Monroe pull up to the cottage and realized with guilty relief that it was the end of her first school day. Mary cleaned up the classroom, and she and Daisy shuffled home.

Mary couldn't ever remember feeling so tired. In a weak moment after dinner, she confided to her husband. "I don't know, Thomas. Maybe I took on too much. My children under the oak tree were never this unruly. Instead of teaching, I spent most of the day breaking up fights and disciplining the boys. Thank God James Jr. was there. He was such a big help."

"Listen, Mary. No one said this would be easy. And you're the one always telling me, anything that's truly important is worth fighting for." He leaned over and kissed his wife on the cheek. "I know how important this is to you. So, like it or not, this is your fight. And I know you can do this." He helped his wife out of her chair. "Why don't you go to bed? I'll clean up and get Daisy settled."

Later Thomas tucked Daisy into bed and went to check on his wife. The sun was still low in the sky, but Mary was sound asleep. He smiled and closed the door.

Mary's second day was, unfortunately, not much better. Five more children showed up, bringing the classroom total to twenty-six students. She went through the same exercise to place the five children into their appropriate groups. One of the new boys insisted the lessons were a waste of time. He complained, "What's the use? I'll always be a slave like my parents. We'll all just be slaves. I'm only here because the soldiers made me come."

Mary shot back. "How do you know that? Things could change. Why, they could change in the next few years—or maybe even sooner. You need to be prepared for a future where you can depend on your own abilities to survive. Not on those of others. How will you do that if you can't even read, write, or do simple math?" Mary closed her eyes and put her head down. The children stared at their teacher in silence. Mary realized she might have reacted too harshly. She was tired, frustrated, and her usually boundless patience was worn thin.

She wondered whether some of the children were too boisterous or perhaps too disinterested to be taught. But recalling Thomas's words of encouragement, she pressed on. Mary continued to nurture the troublemakers while reinforcing the virtues of an education.

Each morning Mary used a spiritual song to settle the children down and get them focused. It took a while to get the children to cooperate, and eventually they could complete a song without interruption. The high-pitched sounds of the younger children pleasantly mixed with the deeper voices of the older boys. Even the mischief-makers seemed to enjoy and acknowledge what they had accomplished as a group.

Mary continued following her lesson plans. She had already made a few changes to the composition of the groups based on her growing knowledge of some of the children. By the third day, the class size had swelled to thirty-two, yet she was already seeing signs of improvement. Less of her day was spent breaking up fights and more was spent working with each group while the other three completed assignments.

General Butler led his two aides down the main road. They were returning from Newport News Point where they had inspected the Union's new encampment, named Camp Butler in his honor. He knew this was the third day of Mary's class and wanted to see her progress firsthand. Approaching the cottage, Butler was captivated by the expansive views along the shoreline. Fortress Monroe rose in the distance like a mountain of stone.

To his surprise, there was a large group of adults milling around the cottage. Heads were craned to the open front door and windows. Many of the younger children from Hampton were escorted to the brown cottage by one or both of their parents. Rather than leaving the children and returning at the end of class, some would linger outside listening to the lessons.

Frank and James saw the general dismount and tie his horse to a tree. The two slaves walked over to greet the Union officer. "Afternoon, General," James said, extending his hand.

"Mr. Townsend. Mr. Baker. What a surprise! I thought you'd be busy on the breastworks outside of town." Butler smiled and greeted the men, shaking their hands.

"We're on a break 'til three, sir. Private Pierce dismisses us at eleven so we don't have to work during the hottest part of the day. We already got cleaned up and ate and are on our way to the breastworks now. But we heard about Mrs. Peake's classes here and thought we'd stop by to look in," James explained.

"Well, that's a coincidence. I'm here for the same reason." Butler looked at the crowd of men and women and pointed. "Do you know why there are so many people standing around out front?"

James smiled. "Oh, they're listening to Mrs. Peake's lessons, I guess. They're interested in learning too," he said sheepishly.

"Are your children attending the classes?" Butler asked.

"Yes, sir. James and I each have two children in there." Frank leaned his head in the direction of the cottage.

Butler crossed his arms and hesitated for a minute. "Can I ask you a personal question?" He looked up at the two, much taller men.

Both men nodded. "Sure," James said. "What is it?"

"Pierce tells me the two of you have wives and children but have never been married?" Butler frowned. "Is that true?"

James looked at Frank, perplexed by the question. Frank shrugged his shoulders. James turned to the Union officer. "General, we've both been together with our wives for many years. Like most colored folks, especially slaves, we've never been married in a church or had any legal kind of ceremony, if that's what you're asking."

"I'm curious, Mr. Townsend. What actually does happen then? I mean, to signify your marriage, that is?" Butler asked.

"Well, first I had to ask my master, Colonel Mallory, for his permission to marry a woman on his farm." James looked off into the distance, recalling the day. "Then we had a 'jumping the broom' ceremony." James raised and dropped his thick, dark eyebrows and massive shoulders in unison.

"And what kind of ceremony is that?" Butler said, curious about the slave's description.

"You see, in most cases, the wife and the husband put a broom at their feet. They both step across the broom at the same time and hold hands. This means that they're married," James said, grinning as he remembered the special day so vividly.

Butler, listening intently, couldn't believe that a marriage would be consummated with such a simple, seemingly meaningless ceremony.

"And that's it? Mr. Townsend, you said in most cases this was the ceremony. Was this how yours transpired?"

"Well, no," James said, his big grin frozen in place. "We did it a different way. Folks held the broom about a foot above the ground. But only the broom was behind us instead of in front of us. My wife and me, we had to jump backwards over the broom. If only one of us makes it over, that person's the boss of the home." He looked at Butler's face and swept his arm through the air. "Forever!"

Seeing James's toothy grin, Butler assumed he had clearly prevailed. "So, Mr. Townsend, you're the boss of your household then?"

"Well, no," James said with a sly smile. "We both made it over at the same time. So there'll be no bossing in our house."

Butler gave James an affectionate pat on the back, and the three men shared a hearty laugh. Butler turned to Frank with a broad smile. "And what about you, Mr. Baker. Did you fare any better?"

Frank's grin abruptly turned to a grimace. "My first wife and son were sold to pay off my master's debts. Soon after, I was sold to Colonel Mallory. I've never seen them since." James put his hand on his friend's shoulder. Frank bit his lower lip. His eyes glistened.

"I'm sorry to hear that, Mr. Baker. That's terrible. So this would be your second wife?" Butler asked.

"Yes, sir. I met Sallie while running an errand in Hampton for Colonel Mallory." Frank wiped his eyes and smiled. "Was she ever beautiful! Unfortunately, she lived on another farm. For months, I would sneak off and see her once or twice a week. Whenever I could. Finally, I worked up the nerve to ask Colonel Mallory if we could get married." Frank wiped his nose with his hand and sniffed. "The Colonel, like most masters, only wants marriages among slaves on his own farm. He says it helps keep us in our place and lowers the chance we might run away."

"So what happened?" Butler asked. James watched with surprise as Frank explained his situation. *Why would such an important man like the General care about a slave's background?* he thought.

"Well, I kept bugging him, and eventually, Colonel Mallory relented and gave his consent." Frank smiled. "So we jumped the broom but continued living on separate farms several miles apart. I spent a few years only able to visit my wife on Wednesday and Saturday nights. The Colonel insisted that my work on the farm always took priority." Frank put his hands on his hips. "With my wife pregnant with our first child, I started bugging Colonel Mallory for another big favor—to purchase my wife from her current owner."

Frank took a big swallow and continued. "Because of what happened before, I knew I had no rights to a child and that my wife's master had ownership of any offspring. My child and wife could be sold off at any time, and again I'd be helpless to do anything about it." Frank paused, glanced down and then back up. "You see, I knew my wife's owner was elderly and could die at any time. It's not uncommon for slaves to be sold in an estate or be split among survivors as inheritance." Frank shrugged. "So I needed to act quickly."

Butler was captivated by the man's story. "That's so terribly sad, Mr. Baker. Were you able to do anything about this?"

Frank thought for a few minutes. He wiped the corners of his eyes with his forearms. "Well, you see, Colonel Mallory's son Luke was playing in the barn with some sharp tools one day. I'm not sure how it happened, but, somehow, he got cut really bad. I mean, really bad. I heard the boy scream, and I came running from the garden near the barn. He was just lying there in a pool of blood, not moving. The blood was gushing out of his arm. He was bleeding something awful." Frank shook his head.

"I thought the poor boy was dead." He squinted at Butler. "But I felt his heart, and it was still beating. I put my hand on the deep gash in his arm to stop the bleeding. While I squeezed his arm, I picked him up and carried him to the house for help. After the doc came and sewed him up and all, he said I saved the boy's life."

He paused. Tears were now streaming down his cheeks. "He was a good, kind boy. I'm so glad he didn't die." He hesitated for a moment, unable to speak. James put his arm around the man's shoulder. "So, after that, Colonel Mallory said he wanted to thank me for saving his boy's life, and asked what he could do." Frank wiped his nose again and smiled at Butler through blood-shot eyes. "So I asked him to buy my wife." Frank hesitated again. He took a big swallow. "And he did it right quick. We've been living together on the Mallory farm for almost six years now. There've been some tough times, but mostly we've been okay—treated fair and all. But we've never been really married—in a church and all."

Butler pulled out his handkerchief and pretended to wipe his forehead but dabbed his eyes and nose. "What a remarkable story, Mr. Baker. I'm glad everything turned out to everyone's satisfaction in the end."

A bell rang in the distance, indicating that the work crew had ten minutes to assemble at the breastworks. The crowd around them roused itself with murmurs and shuffling feet. "General, we need to skedaddle. That's our warning bell," James said. The two slaves waved farewell to him and turned up the sandy path towards Hampton.

Shortly after, Butler heard the sound of horses and wagon wheels coming down the road. Children poured out of the brown cottage. Some lined up for the wagon while others ran to their parents and hugged them. Mary walked out into the sunshine and was shocked to see General Butler standing there with his arms crossed. "Why, General Butler, what a pleasant surprise!"

"I thought I would come to check on my favorite teacher." Butler smiled below his bushy mustache.

"Would you like a tour?" Mary waved her arm towards the front door.

"That would be great." Mary showed Butler around the large front room and the two rooms upstairs. As they walked, Butler asked, "Mrs. Peake, I noticed quite a few adults standing around the front of the house. Are they there all day?"

Mary led the officer down the stairs. "Well, a few of them are. Others come and go during the course of the day." She looked over her shoulder to the officer. "I suspect they're curious. Or maybe they're trying to learn what they can." Mary smiled. "I'm sure many of them have never been to school. They're happy their children are in school but probably wish they could be as well."

Butler paused at the bottom of the stairs. "Did you ever consider having a class for adults? I mean, for the parents of these children?"

"Oh, General. We're already so blessed to be able to teach these children. To be able to teach their parents as well..." She clasped her hands in delight. "Well, it would be truly wonderful."

Butler shrugged. "When can you get started?" They both laughed.

Mary straightened a few tables and benches. "I think I could start early next week. I'll let the children's parents know tomorrow morning."

"Excellent. Excellent." Butler followed Mary out the front door.

"General, you've been so supportive, and I'm so grateful. I don't know how to thank you. I only wish there was something I could do to repay you for your kindness."

Butler stood in deep thought for a moment. He squinted in the bright sun. "Well, Mrs. Peake. There just might be."

M ARY'S FOOTSTEPS ECHOED OFF THE WOODEN
boards of Mill Creek Bridge. Foaming waves churned and
broke against the rocky shoreline. Their salt spray filled the
air. Mary turned her body to shield the delicate package she carried.

After class ended, Hannah Townsend had agreed to take Daisy to
her home until Mary could pick her up. Mary immediately set out for
Fortress Monroe. Her thoughts drifted to her discussion with General
Butler the previous day and his special request. She was spinning with
enthusiasm and ideas. Panic hadn't set in yet, even though she only
had two days left to prepare. Mary was too busy to worry.

She arrived at the big white house and climbed the stairs.
Squeaking boards alerted Sarah, and Sarah greeted her new friend at
the front door with a smile and warm hug. "Mary, it's so nice to see
you. I can't believe you finished the dress already." Sarah's dark hair
had been pulled back in a bun previously, but today her hair fell in soft
waves along her long, elegant neck onto her shoulders.

"Good afternoon, Sarah. Well it's not quite finished yet." Mary entered the home and placed the package on a table. She untied the string that secured the paper wrap. The stark interior of the house from her last visit was now warmly decorated with elegant but practical furnishings.

Sarah clasped her hands in amazement. "Oh, Mary! It's so beautiful." She reached out and caressed the soft fabric. "You're so talented."

Mary flushed with embarrassment. "It's not finished yet," she repeated. "I'd like to see how it fits, though, before I go any further." Mary held up the French blue silk gown with white lace trim. "I had enough lace ruffle for the shoulders, but I need more to finish the overskirt. The store I usually go to in Hampton is all out. They said it's due to the Union blockade." Mary grimaced. She immediately wished she could take the words back. "What I mean to say is, the store owner told me there might be some in Yorktown. Maybe I can convince my husband to take me there tomorrow." She set the dress down on the table.

"Perhaps I can have my sister send me some lace from Boston." Sarah tapped her lips with a finger. "But it would likely take a few weeks to get here." Her face twisted. "I guess that would be too late."

"I'm sure I'll find some near here." Mary handed the dress to Sarah. "Would you mind trying it on?"

Minutes later, Sarah sauntered into the room and spun, center stage, around in a circle. "It fits perfectly. Oh, Mary, it's even more beautiful on."

Mary's keen eye traced the lines of the dress. "I think the bodice is a little snug. Let me place a few pins here so I can make adjustments when I get home." She opened her bag and retrieved a pincushion. "Hopefully I'll find some lace ruffle tomorrow and have the dress finished by early next week."

"That would be wonderful, Mary. Let me change back and we can have some tea." Sarah glided off to her bedroom.

The two women visited for another hour, sharing stories and laughs as they tightened the bonds of friendship. On the way home, Mary felt like she was walking on air.

Mary draped her arm around Daisy's shoulder. She reached over and touched her husband's arm as he sat in the front seat of the wagon. "Thanks for taking me, Thomas. It's going to be such a hectic next few days. I'm not sure how I would have ever found the time to go to Yorktown."

"It's no problem." Thomas smiled. "Besides I needed to get some supplies there anyway." His hands gripped the reins. "Fortunately, Mr. Peterson let me use his wagon, otherwise the trip would've taken us the better part of a day."

That morning Mary had asked the driver from Fortress Monroe to return at noon for the children. Thomas met his family at the brown cottage, and they immediately left for Yorktown.

Mary opened a basket carrying biscuits and jam. They snacked as the carriage rattled over New Market Bridge. Although the springs under the bench absorbed some of the bumps, they could still feel every uneven board. Daisy pointed at the churning waters of the Southwest Branch of the Back River. "Look, Mama. Fish." Crumbs sprayed from her mouth.

"Oh, Daisy. You shouldn't talk with your mouth full." Mary brushed the pieces of biscuit off her lap. "That's not very ladylike."

"She was just feeding the fish, that's all." Thomas chuckled.

Daisy latched onto the new idea. "Can I? Can I feed the fish some of my biscuit?" She pleaded.

"Absolutely not, young lady. We don't waste food. Besides the fish have plenty to eat." Mary put her hand out. "If you don't want your biscuit, I'll wrap it up and save it for you for later." Mary punched her husband in the shoulder.

Thomas turned and smiled. Rubbing his shoulder, and winking at Daisy, he teased, "The mosquitoes are out awfully early today."

The wagon stopped on the other side of the bridge. Thomas shielded his eyes from the bright sun and studied the intersecting roads. "We can take a few different routes." He pointed to his right. "I think the north route may take a little longer, but it's heavily shaded. With this heat, I think it's better to go that way. We can come back through Big Bethel when the sun is lower in the sky."

Mary smiled and shrugged. "Well, you're the driver."

The long ride through the countryside was certainly restful, but it soon became wearisome. With each mile, the poorly padded bench seat felt more like a pile of rocks. Each bump in the road reverberated through their bodies. To break up the boredom, Mary and Daisy sang and played games. One of their favorites was seeing who could spot the most of a species of birds. Daisy almost always won.

By midafternoon, Mary could feel a slight cooling in the hot, humid air. Seagulls swooped over the tall pines, a sure sign they were approaching the port city along the York River. Arriving at the outskirts of Yorktown, large farms transitioned to smaller homes spaced closer together. An occasional store or specialty shop wedged its way in.

The wagon pulled up to the fabric shop on the outer edge of town. Frilly, feminine fabrics of all colors and patterns hung in the window. Thomas winced. "I'll wait in the wagon. You and Daisy can go in."

Five minutes later, Mary walked out into the sunlight holding a package in one hand and Daisy's hand in the other. Thomas helped them up the steps and onto the bench seat. "All set," Mary said.

"Great! They had what you needed?" he asked, picking up the reins.

"There was one small piece of the lace bolt left. It's not the exact shade of white, but it'll do. There may even be a little left over in case I make any mistakes." Mary laughed and tucked the package under the bench.

They rolled down the street leading to the center of Yorktown. "One quick stop at the general store, and we can head back home," Thomas said.

Mary groaned. "We're going to have to soak our rear ends in a bucket of hot water when we get there." They all laughed.

Turning the corner onto the main thoroughfare, Mary glanced up and down the street. The faces of passersby grew increasingly pale and even more hostile than she'd remembered the town being. Her heart began to race and her body grew rigid. She could feel her temples pulsing. Daisy pressed up against her.

Thomas pulled back on the reins in front of the general store. He looked around. "I think you two should come inside with me." Mary and Daisy quickly walked into the store with their heads down. Thomas was close behind with his hands on their shoulders.

As Thomas walked through the aisles, Mary scanned the street through the front window. Within a few minutes, Thomas joined them, nodding towards the door. They walked outside and went directly to the wagon. Thomas loaded the wagon and climbed up next to Mary and Daisy. The wagon lurched forward. Mary felt like they were navigating through a pit full of poisonous snakes.

The sidewalks were teeming with Confederate soldiers—hundreds of them. They were everywhere. Wagons filled with supplies and guns lined the road. Horses pulled small canons. The place was a beehive of activity.

Mary stared straight ahead with her hands in her lap and tried to look inconspicuous. Once they reached the edge of the town, Mary grabbed Thomas's arm. "Dear Lord. What's going on, Thomas?"

"What, Mama? What's the matter?" Daisy looked from her father to her mother.

"It's okay, Daisy. Nothing's wrong. We just want to get home," Thomas said.

Thomas snapped the reins and the wagon kicked up dirt. For the next few hours, they traveled at a brisk pace, only slowing down occasionally for the horses to rest. Coming around a wooded bend to the intersection of two main roads, the wagon approached Big Bethel. Thomas pulled back on the reins, and the two horses reared with their front legs in the air.

"No, Thomas. Dear Lord, no!" Mary whispered in a panicky voice. Her throat was constricted and she felt light-headed.

Several hundred Confederate soldiers were busy digging earthworks around the village. Large guns were positioned facing east towards Hampton.

"Thomas, we need to leave. Quickly! Don't let them see us." Mary pleaded.

He guided the horses into a side trail, circumventing the soldiers. Unable to use the bridge, they followed Brick Kiln Creek north until they found an area shallow enough to cross safely. Reaching the other side, Mary grabbed her husband's arm. "Thomas, stop." Mary looked back at the Rebel activity.

"I thought you wanted to get out of here." Thomas frowned.

"I do. But before we leave, I want to see how many soldiers and guns there are. And where they're digging." She turned back to her husband. "Thomas, we need to let General Butler know what's going on. Immediately!"

An hour later, they arrived in Hampton. "Mary, Daisy's asleep on your lap. She's exhausted. Can't we see the General first thing in the morning?" Thomas said.

"No, Thomas. We need to go tonight. We can drop Daisy off at the neighbor's. If you don't want to bring me to the fort, I'll walk. But I am going. Tonight!" Mary's fists were clenched.

Mary rapped at the door while Thomas stood by her side. She watched through the window as Sarah came to the door. "Oh, what a nice surprise, Mary. Come in. The guards told us you were coming." When she saw her friend's face, she studied Mary with a worried look. "Is everything all right?"

Mary entered, followed by Thomas. "Sarah, this is my husband, Thomas. We just returned from Yorktown. We were able to find more lace ruffle." She smiled tightly.

"It's nice to meet you, Thomas." Sarah nodded but looked confused. "Mary, it was so nice of you to come by and let me know, but it could've waited until tomorrow." Sarah pointed to the parlor. "I was just sitting down for tea. Would you like some?"

"No, thank you. Actually, Sarah, We're here to see your husband, General Butler. Is he at home?" Mary looked through the door to the dining room.

"Benjamin? Oh, he's just finishing his meal. I'll go get him." Sarah frowned and turned to leave.

"Oh, please wait. Please let the General finish his meal. We can wait until he's done," Mary said.

"Don't be silly. Believe me, it won't hurt him to push away from the table for once." She left the room laughing.

A minute later, General Butler walked into the parlor. He extended his hand and greeted the couple. "Mr. and Mrs. Peake. It's so nice of you to stop by. I understand you want to see me."

"We're so sorry for interrupting your evening, General. My husband and I just returned from Yorktown. On the way home we drove through Big Bethel." Mary swallowed hard. "Sir, there are hundreds, maybe thousands, of Confederate soldiers everywhere." She couldn't keep her heart from racing. The fear on her face was apparent.

Thomas added, "There are several earthworks under construction at the intersection of the roads in Big Bethel. Large guns are being positioned to fend off any attacks."

"Interesting. Very interesting." Butler smoothed the corners of his moustache. "We had heard that Lee sent Magruder to Yorktown to organize the opposition. I guess it's true. Please have a seat." He motioned to the sofa. Butler sat down in an armchair.

For the next half hour, Butler questioned Mary and Thomas. The long trip to and from Yorktown, along with the stress of seeing the Confederate soldiers, hit Mary like a wall. She was overcome with fatigue.

Butler stood up. "I can't thank you enough for coming by, especially after such a long day. Your information is most helpful. I'll be sure to have our scouts follow up tomorrow."

Thomas helped Mary stand and put his arm around her waist as the walked to the front door. Mary turned. "General, are the Confederates preparing to attack?" She bit her lower lip.

"I'm not sure, Mrs. Peake. But I don't think so. They wouldn't bother to build earthworks if they were on the offensive. My guess is that they are preparing for potential advances by our troops. In any case, we should know more tomorrow." He shook hands with Mary and Thomas. "It's nothing you should be concerned with though. We have more than enough troops and munitions to deal with the Confederates."

Mary nodded. "Well, thank you." She turned to Sarah. "I should have the dress completed by Monday. Can I bring it by later in the afternoon?"

"That would be fine, Mary," Sarah said. "I can't wait."

The two women hugged. Mary and Thomas stepped onto the porch and down the stairs. Butler stood in the doorway and called out. "Oh, Mrs. Peake?"

Mary turned in alarm.

"I almost forgot to ask you. Are our plans coming together for Saturday?" Butler's awkward silhouette was framed by dim light.

"They are, sir." Mary waved. "Good night, General."

They walked to the wagon. As Thomas helped her up, he whispered, "Saturday? What's that all about?"

"I'll tell you on the way home."

M ARY LOOKED OUT INTO THE GATHERING OF black, brown, and white faces. Slaves gratefully sat next to the soldiers who protected them and provided refuge. People continued to filter in through the large open doors. The smells of sweet incense and burning candles swirled through the air, mixing with the low rumble of voices.

Thomas sat halfway up the center aisle, beaming with pride. Daisy and the rest of her class stood behind Mary in five neat rows. General Butler leaned against the back wall with his arms crossed. As their eyes met, Mary acknowledged Butler's nod with a nervous smile.

Chaplain Fuller of the Sixteenth Massachusetts Regiment approached the altar of Old Saint John's Church. The building, dating back to well before the Revolutionary War, was the center of the Hampton community. The chaplain looked to Mary and mouthed, "All right."

Mary quietly cleared her throat. Her legs felt like melting candles, barely able to support her weight. She placed her hand on her abdomen, trying to calm the sensation of flying insects pinging off the walls of her stomach. Mary looked around the room. Everyone was now seated. She took a deep breath and let it out slowly. As the melodic words of Ave Maria filled the room, the church instantly fell silent and all heads turned forward to see the source of the beautiful voice.

Her students joined in the soulful song. The younger children were fearless. Gradually, the older boys worked up the courage to sing louder. Their lower voices pleasantly mixed with the high pitch of the young girls and boys. All eyes were on the popular teacher and her class.

Halfway through the song, the procession of couples entered the rear of the church. Arm in arm, they walked down the main aisle to the altar. Everyone stood and craned their heads to watch. James and Hannah passed by Thomas, who reached out and patted the tall man's shoulder. James turned to his friend. Tears streamed from the eyes of both men. Directly behind them were Frank and Sallie. In all, sixteen couples walked down the aisle, passed the altar, and filled the front pews.

Chaplain Fuller stood next to the American flag. Its thirty-four stars still included the states recently seceding to form the Confederate States of America; President Lincoln had refused to allow any stars to be removed. "Welcome, everyone, to this happy occasion. We are gathered here to witness the marriage of sixteen couples under the flag of our great country."

Following a prayer and another song from Mary and her students, each couple approached the altar. As with the other couples who had children, James and Hannah exchanged vows with James Jr. and Millie by their sides. The ceremony continued for close to an hour, culminating with a prayer and passionate applause. Chaplain

Fuller held up his hands to get everyone's attention. "Following the ceremony, there will be a feast next door. We hope all of you will join us." The wedding couples lined up and strolled down the aisle as Mary proudly sang the recessional song.

The church slowly emptied out, walking by and congratulating the line of officially married couples. They all lingered in the bright sunshine exchanging well wishes before heading to the planned feast. Butler walked over to Mary. "That was a beautiful ceremony, Mrs. Peake. Thank you."

"General, it's I who should be thanking you. I was so excited when you proposed this earlier in the week." She looked at the crowd of people hugging and laughing.

"I had heard that your teaching talents extended to singing." Butler's eyes glistened. "But, I must say, I was not prepared to be over-come by the beauty of your voice."

"To me, they're one in the same, General." She placed her hand over her chest. "They both fill my heart with joy." Her eyes narrowed as she changed subjects. "Is there anything new with the Confederates?"

Butler's expression turned more serious too. "I have several parties scouting the countryside as we speak. We'll have a better understanding of their movements and intentions by the end of the day." Thomas and Daisy waved from across the lawn. "Well, I think your family is calling you. I'll let you go to them." He nodded in their direction.

"Good day, General." As Mary walked to her family, soldiers and friends reached out to praise her hard work and contributions to the ceremony.

Daisy ran to Mary and threw her tiny arms around her mother's waist. "Mama, that was so much fun!"

Thomas hugged his wife. "Well, you did it. I told you everything would be fine." He picked up Daisy. "And you." He tickled her. "You and the other children sounded amazing."

Mary let out a heavy sigh. "I'm glad everything went well. But I'm also relieved it's over." They walked into the building adjacent to the church and joined the feast.

Revelers passed by tables of fresh meat, oysters, and recently harvested vegetables, filling their plates. Several wedding cakes of various sizes and flavors were displayed on a corner table. James walked over to Frank, extending his hand. "Did you ever think we would see a day like today?" They shook hands. "Just look around." Children were chasing each other around the room. Soldiers and slaves were engaged in conversations like close neighbors.

Frank glanced across the room and smiled. "Not in my lifetime."

"Hey, I didn't see Shepard anywhere." James squinted at the crowd. "In fact, I don't think I've seen him all day."

"Yeah, you're right. It's not like Shepard to miss out on a feast like this." The two men laughed.

James casually glanced out a front window and saw Shepard talking with Butler. He hit Frank on the arm. "Hey, look. There he is. I wonder what he's talking about with the General."

Shepard was waving his arms around passionately. Butler was listening intently and nodding. After shaking hands with Shepard, Butler mounted his horse and headed towards Hampton Creek Bridge.

James and Frank walked outside to their young friend. "Hey, Shep! What's going on?" James nodded in the direction of Butler. "What were you two talking about?"

Shepard shook his head. "We were talking about some business, James. That's all I can say." He looked into the tall man's eyes.

"What do you mean, business? What kind of business would you have with the General?" James persisted.

"James, I can't talk about it, so let it go. All right?" Shepard said.

Frank didn't let it drop, but instead joined the inquisition. "And you've been gone all day. Where've you been?"

Shepard held his hands in the air. "I told you, I can't talk about anything. So that's all I'm saying."

Laughter erupted from the nearby building. Shepard's serious expression turned to a big grin. "Hey, I heard I missed a wedding ceremony. Congratulations." He looked from the festivities to the two men. "Is there any food left?"

S TERN FACES REVEALED HINTS OF DOUBT. Butler's war committee sat around a large table in anxious silence. Heads were slumped and lips pursed. *Is this disbelief or fear?* Butler thought to himself. Finally, Major Fay stood up, placing his knuckles on the table. "With all due respect, General, are you suggesting that we attack the Confederates based solely on the word of some local mulatto woman and a young slave? That seems awfully risky!"

Butler looked around the table and studied each officer. Trying to hide his growing disdain, he leaned forward on his elbows. "Don't be ridiculous, Major. I had our own scouts reconnoiter the area yesterday." He pounded his fist on the table. "Why, we should be grateful to Mrs. Peake for alerting us in the first place. And this so-called slave you refer to risked his life to infiltrate the area and bring back precious intelligence."

Captain Haggerty held up a hand. "We have nothing against Mrs. Peake or the slave, General. Our own intelligence indicated that

Magruder was in the area and building troop strength. But do you think it's wise to initiate an attack until we're sure what the Rebels' intentions are?" He shook his head in disbelief. "Sir, we don't even have any horses!"

Butler's joyful memories of the wedding celebration a day earlier had soured under the dire subject of war. After Mary's urgent visit Friday evening, Butler had two of his soldiers bring Shepard Mallory to his office the following morning. In prior conversations, the young slave had offered his services and impressed the Union commander with his local knowledge. Shepard was initially upset that he would miss the big wedding ceremony that Saturday. But he knew the urgency and importance of Butler's request.

"Well, what do you think we should do then, Captain? Maybe I should just waltz over there and ask Magruder why he's building his troop levels and digging earthworks." Butler shrugged. "Perhaps they're just looking for worms to go fishing." A few officers snickered.

"Now let's stop this nonsense and get down to business." Butler stood up and walked over to a cabinet, opening a drawer. "Estimates of Rebel forces range from 500 to 2,000. Even at the high end of this range, with our superior numbers, we should easily overwhelm them. As Captain Haggerty was good enough to point out, we don't have horses." Butler shook his head, pulled out a large map, and walked back to the table. "So we'll need to rely on our men to carry supplies and draw the artillery equipment. Unfortunately, this will also necessitate leaving the larger, more effective guns, at the fort."

He set the map down in the middle of the table. Pointing at a crossroads, he said, "Our intelligence tells us the Confederates are constructing several earthworks in an area known as Big Bethel. Two major roads intersect here just south of Brick Kiln Creek. Open fields and swamps surround the area, so the Rebels have picked a strategic place to defend. There are a few patches of wooded areas just east and west of the main road here." Butler brushed his hand across the map.

With a mischievous smile, he said, "Even though we outnumber the Confederates, to ensure victory, we'll march at night and surprise them with a dawn attack." The officers looked at each other. A few nodded in approval. Butler could see some were skeptical about his plan.

The group spent the balance of Sunday morning forming the details of the attack. Union forces at Camp Butler were located due south of Big Bethel at Newport News Point. Additional Union forces were east of Big Bethel at Camp Hamilton on the other side of the town of Hampton and Hampton Creek.

Butler traced the roads with his finger. "The main routes from the two camps intersect a few miles before Big Bethel, near a country church at Little Bethel. This will be an ideal location for the two Union forces to unite and march on to Big Bethel." With the basic logistics agreed to, the group went on to further develop their complex plan.

Butler stood and summarized. "At midnight tonight, two New York regiments will leave Camp Hamilton as an advance force. Shortly after, two more New York regiments will follow. They'll pass through Hampton and follow the main road northwest, over the Southwest Branch of the Back River. Mr. Mallory, the young slave," Butler glared at Major Fay as he said this, "discovered that New Market Bridge was destroyed by the Rebels. So we'll need a wagon containing planks and other materials to repair the bridge."

He looked around to make sure all eyes were on him. "The New England battalion, comprised of the First Vermont and Fifth Massachusetts Regiments, will advance north from Camp Butler." He pointed to Newport News Point on the map and traced the route with his finger. "The New York Seventh Regiment will follow this group. Two howitzers will be drawn by our men instead of horses."

Butler crossed his arms and said confidently, "As a united and overwhelming force, we'll march on to Big Bethel, where we're sure to overpower the smaller Rebel force in a morning assault."

A seasoned Union officer sat at the end of the table. The man was a combat veteran and a distinguished graduate of the U.S. Military Academy. Butler could see that he was listening intently and knew the officer considered Butler more of a politician than a soldier. Butler wasn't surprised by his reaction. "How can you be so sure of an *overwhelming* victory, General?" he challenged. "War is unpredictable. And there are most likely many more Confederates throughout the peninsula. Perhaps our intelligence is flawed."

Butler was prepared for the dissenting viewpoint. He walked over to a map on the wall. "The Virginia Peninsula is ninety miles long and ten miles wide. It's bordered by two navigable rivers." He pointed to the York and James Rivers. "And who controls them?" He slapped the map with his hand. "We do! And what's at the eastern tip of the peninsula?" He pointed to Fortress Monroe. "The largest moat encircled fort in the South. This fort! How can Magruder effectively control this much land?" With a wry smile, he said, "Besides I suspect he has his hands full just dealing with the crushing flow of his loyal citizens fleeing the lower peninsula." He walked over and sat down. "Now let's discuss who's going to lead this mission."

The group deliberated for several minutes. Unable to check his impatience, Butler stated, "I prefer to have Colonel Phelps." He scanned the faces of his men for a reaction.

"But, General," Haggerty challenged his commander, "military protocol requires that the most senior officer be placed in charge. After all, this will be our first major battle on the Virginia Peninsula."

"Yes, Captain. I'm quite aware of this." Butler rolled his eyes.

"Sir, I believe General Pierce is the most senior officer." Fay said.

Butler winced at the man's name. Unrelated to Private Edward Pierce, General Ebenezer Weaver Pierce was a descendent of the Mayflower and a native of Massachusetts. As a graduate of the U.S. Military Academy, he was an obvious and qualified choice. But Butler wasn't impressed with the elder Pierce.

"Very well, then." Butler hesitated and swallowed. "General Pierce shall lead the mission." Butler was comforted only by the belief that the Union forces would easily take the Confederate positions and victory was all but certain.

A critical component of the attack from the two camps was the night march. Butler and his officers debated the potential complications of this risky move and the challenge of distinguishing a Union soldier from a Confederate soldier in the dark. The group debated various schemes. One officer suggested, "Perhaps the troops could carry lit torches."

Butler immediately extinguished the idea. "Sure, then the Rebel scouts can see our men coming long before our own troops."

After listening to similarly impractical suggestions, Butler addressed the group. "We need to instruct the men to wear white armbands on their left arms." He placed a hand around his upper arm. "This should enable our troops to easily identify each other. As an additional precaution, the men should identify themselves with a password."

Butler turned away from the group and paced around the room. As the thought, he rubbed his lower lip with a thick knuckle. With a look of satisfaction, he said, "In order for the troops to further distinguish themselves from the enemy, our men should say 'Boston' when in an uncertain situation." The group nodded or shrugged in agreement.

Pleased with their plans and certain of a quick and decisive victory, Butler dismissed the group and left the war room. His officers hastily dispersed to ready the troops for the nighttime assault. Butler knew that Magruder was a West Point graduate and shrewd military officer. But Butler also knew of his opponent's reputation as a womanizer and philanderer. "How could such a person be an effective leader?" he mumbled to himself as he walked through the rain. Butler was certain his Union forces would make quick work of the Rebels.

The downpour finally ended, but the humidity still hung in the air like a damp, heavy blanket. Troops at Camp Butler and Camp Hamilton were restless and concerned about the looming confrontation. Even the crickets were silent with apprehension.

It was a moonless sky, and midnight was fast approaching. Butler was wearing a path in the rug as he paced the parlor floor. Sarah opened the door from the bedroom. "Benjamin, why are you still awake? You should come to bed."

He had been in deep thought. His wife's silhouette in the doorframe startled him. "Sarah, my men are forming for battle at this very minute." His eyes were tight, his skin pale. "Maybe I'm making a mistake. I should be there leading my troops."

Doubts emerged around the offensive. "I knew this day would come." He rubbed his chin with the cup of his hand. "And the battle should be quick and decisive." Butler sighed. "I just hope our men are ready." He thought about General Pierce leading the troops and closed his eyes.

Sarah walked over and put her arms around her husband's waist. "Benjamin, you have capable officers." She guided him to an armchair. "Now sit down and I'll put some coffee on." She headed towards the kitchen with a grim look on her face. "I suspect it's going to be a long night."

Mary lifted her head off the pillow. She was having trouble sleeping. Visions of Rebel forces at Yorktown and Big Bethel strangely mixed with the wedding ceremony the day before. She craned her head. Low, synchronized shudders, distant but growing in intensity, seeped through the open window. Mary sat up.

"What's the matter?" Thomas turned. "Can't sleep?"

"Thomas, listen!" Mary held up her hand.

"What the devil is that? It sounds like beating drums." Thomas frowned.

"No, I think soldiers are marching. Listen, it's getting louder." Mary climbed out of bed. "It's coming from the bridge and passing south of the town."

"What are you doing?" Thomas sat up.

"I'm getting dressed. I'm going to see for myself." Mary slipped off her nightgown and climbed into a dress.

"Mary, it's the middle of the night." Thomas threw his legs onto the floor and stood up.

"Thomas, I need to see what's going on. I feel responsible. Remember, I'm the one who insisted on telling General Butler about the Confederates. The General didn't directly tell me, but he certainly implied they would take some action." She slipped on her shoes. "I just didn't think it would happen this soon."

Thomas followed her to the foyer. Mary opened the front door and turned. "I'll only go a few blocks to the edge of town," she assured him and quietly closed the door.

Thomas opened the door and called in a hushed voice, "Be careful."

Mary weaved through the dark streets. She noticed several people standing on their front stoops. Some leaned suspiciously out their windows. Within a block of the thoroughfare connecting Hampton Creek Bridge to towns west and north of Hampton, the thunder of marching troops was ominous.

Mary stood motionless under a tree until the last soldier disappeared around a broad bend in the road. She wiped her tears away with shaking hands and slowly walked home with her head down.

Sarah had finally convinced Butler to go to bed only after she promised to wake him up at daybreak. A loud knock at the door woke them both out of a sound sleep. Butler picked his head up off the pillow. It was still dark outside. "Who would be at the door at this hour?" Sarah wondered.

Her husband jumped out of bed. "I don't know, but I fear it's not good news." He hustled to the door in his nightshirt and pulled it open.

Major Fay stood with his hands by his side. His expression was grim. "Fay, what is it?" He motioned with his hand. "Come in."

Fay shuffled into the home. "General, we just got word from our troops. Pierce requested we send our reserve units to the battle. The news is muddled, but it appears there was a confrontation outside of Little Bethel. Casualties should be arriving soon."

Butler shook his head in disbelief. "How can this be, Richard? Our reports showed that the Confederates had a minimal presence there. They were massing at Big Bethel. Why, we should have marched right over them!" Butler ran his fingers through his disheveled hair as he looked down at the floor. "What the hell is going on?"

Sarah stood against the door, unsure of what to say. "Benjamin, should I put some coffee on for the two of you?"

Butler looked up. "No, Sarah. I need to get dressed. Richard says there'll be casualties coming in. I need to be there."

Butler and Fay arrived in Hampton as sunrise cast long shadows down Court Street. Soldiers were unloading the wounded from two wagons. Medics were waiting in the courthouse, which they had quickly transformed into a makeshift hospital. Screaming, writhing men were carried in and placed on crude operating tables. Butler turned to his senior aide. "Why are these wounded being brought here? Camp Butler's much closer."

"General, they were instructed to bring the men to Fortress Monroe as the wounds are quite severe." Fay added, "We sent the medics here to meet them to lessen their travel time and give them medical attention sooner."

Butler nodded. "Yes, that makes sense. Good work, Major." He looked at the torn and bloodied bodies. "We need to send for boats. Once the wounded are stabilized, we'll ferry them to the hospital." The Hampton General Military Hospital was along the Hampton Roads shoreline, adjacent to Fortress Monroe.

Fay nodded and left.

Butler hustled over to help. A medic grabbed a soldier under the arms. Butler held the wounded man's ankles as they carried him into the courthouse and maneuvered him onto a table. Blood from the man's leg wounds coated Butler's uniform and boots. Butler retraced his blood stained footsteps to the door. His feet stuck as he walked. Agonizing screams filled the air. Everywhere Butler looked he saw open flesh and splintered bones.

He hurried down the steps. He unfastened his top buttons and gasped for air. Overwhelmed by the carnage, he leaned over behind a bush. His stomach clenched. With his hands on his knees, he vomited several times. The putrid, yellow-brown fluid splattered onto his bloody boots. He stood weak and unsteady. Butler wiped his mouth on his sleeve and shuffled back to the wagon.

A soldier limped towards the courthouse. Butler recognized the man from the New England Battalion. As he helped him up the stairs and into the courthouse, Butler asked, "How did all these injuries occur, private?"

Butler helped the man onto a table. He didn't appear to be severely wounded. "We were approaching Little Bethel as planned. We heard gunfire in the distance." The man swallowed hard. "But instead of in front of us, it came from behind us." The soldier hesitated. "Sir, when we doubled back and arrived at a clearing, it was total chaos the Seventh was engaged in a fierce battle. Musket fire seemed to coming from all directions." The man met Butler's eyes. "But mostly from across the road. It wasn't until we heard men shouting that everyone stopped firing."

"Why would you stop firing because the enemy was shouting? Isn't that the intent, private? Were they surrendering?" Butler asked, totally perplexed.

With his chin quivering, the private said, "Sir, they were shouting 'Boston'."

It took a minute for Butler to process the words. He took a few steps back, almost losing his balance. "Private, were we firing on our own men?"

The soldier cowered.

Butler looked at the mangled bodies on the tables and the corpses piled high outside on a wagon. His throat tightened. "You mean we did this to ourselves?"

The private nodded. There was nothing more to say.

After seeing marching troops in the thick of the night, Mary was unable to sleep. She went back to bed but couldn't settle down. Mary was troubled by her role in any ensuing hostility. Finally, she got up to let Thomas get some rest. She curled up on the couch.

The sky was just brightening into a thin, gray dawn. Hearing voices outside the house, she sat up and looked out the window. First there were one or two people at a time hastily walking down the road. Then several groups hustled by.

Mary went into the bedroom and woke her husband. "Thomas, something's happened. People are hurrying to the center of town." Mary quickly changed back into her dress. She stepped outside her front door. James came running up the walk.

"Mrs. Peake, we were working on the earthworks this morning." James gasped for air. "Private Pierce dismissed us because there's been some battle with the Confederates. He said that he had to go because wounded were coming in," James said, sprinting backwards towards the road. "I'm going into town to see if I can help."

"Wait, James! I'll come too. Let me tell Thomas first." Mary opened the door and called to her husband.

James and Mary arrived at the courthouse several minutes later. The streets were crowded with people. Some were standing and gawking. Others were running into and out of the courthouse. Wagons were haphazardly parked. A large, stained canvas was draped over one of the wagons. Mary was drawn to an object dangling below the cloth. Her squinted eyes opened wide when she realized it was a man's arm.

"Oh, dear God! James!" She pointed to the wagon. "Some of these men are dead." Mary buried her face in the big man's chest. James put his arms around her and patted her back.

"Mary! There's the General." James pointed.

They watched Butler emerge from the courthouse and descend the stairs. "James, I need to speak with him. I'll be right back." Mary wove her way through the congested street and intercepted the Union commander as he untied his horse's reins.

"General!" Mary called out as she approached. Butler turned. She opened her mouth to speak but nothing came out. Bending over, she covered her face with her hands and wept uncontrollably. Butler retied the reins and hurried over.

"Mrs. Peake. There, there." He put his hand on her shoulder. "You shouldn't be here. Please let me have one of my men escort you home."

Mary wiped the tears from her face. "Oh, General. I'm afraid I caused this."

"Mrs. Peake. Mary. That's just nonsense and certainly couldn't be farther from the truth." He held her hands in his. "Sooner or later, a conflict would have occurred. Both sides have been building up to this for weeks. It was only a matter of time." He looked around. "In a way, you prevented the outcome from being much worse." Butler didn't have the heart to tell her that Union soldiers had inflicted the carnage on themselves.

"Is it over, General?" Mary looked hopeful.

"I'm afraid not. I understand the battle is still underway. I was just on my way there when you came over." He stepped over to his horse. "Will you be all right, or should I have someone bring you home?"

"I'm with James." She pointed to the big man standing across the road. "I'll be fine, thank you."

Butler looked over and nodded. James returned the acknowledgment.

She watched Butler untie the reins. "General, please be careful." Mary turned and slowly walked back across the street, wringing her hands.

Butler placed his foot in the stirrup as Major Fay came running over. "General. I just received word that the battle is over. Our troops are presently returning in good order."

The general climbed into the saddle and bowed his head in relief. "That's some good news at least, Richard. Any word on additional casualties?"

"I'm afraid not, sir."

By early afternoon, the returning Union troops approached the north end of Hampton. Crowds lined the streets in horror. A column of ragged, dirty, and tired soldiers shuffled down Court Street. After supervising the transport of the wounded to the military hospital and quickly changing out of his soiled uniform, Butler had returned to the courthouse. He waited anxiously for more casualties.

General Pierce was mounted high on his horse above the troops. He rode over to where Butler was waiting outside the courthouse. The two men exchanged strained greetings.

Pierce began to brief Butler on the series of battles. He described the friendly fire incident outside Little Bethel. "The men were confused. It was too dark to even see the armbands. The situation was most unfortunate," Pierce explained. His words were distant, cold, and absent of any culpability. In disgust, Butler turned to the doors leading into the courthouse and the resulting carnage.

Butler's dread only began to dissipate as Pierce described the larger battle at Big Bethel. "The men performed well," Pierce said. "We were outmanned and outgunned. The Rebels had between 4,000 and 5,000 men. The earthworks were over thirteen feet high and well defended with as many as twenty guns."

Butler realized that they must have grossly underestimated the size and preparations of the Confederate forces. Seeing the fresh casualties being unloaded from the field wagons, Butler turned to Pierce. "Are these the extent of the injuries and dead?"

"Yes, General," Pierce said. "We returned in good order and collected all the dead and wounded from the battle field."

With Pierce dismissed, Butler walked back to the courthouse to personally supervise the care and transport of the wounded. He noticed two soldiers with dejected looks standing at the door. One of them, not bothering to even come to attention, looked up at Butler and said, "I heard what Pierce said. He's wrong." The soldier spat onto the wooden floor. "The battle was filled with confusion. Our attacks were uncoordinated and poorly executed.

"Pierce never recovered command of our troops after Little Bethel," the soldier continued. "And the battle at Big Bethel was filled with uncertainty and missteps."

Certainly, Butler was upset that Pierce had not told him the truth in his debriefing. But Butler was outraged by the description of the withdrawal.

"Our retreat was hasty and cowardly. Our rear was unprotected and many wounded were left in the fields. We disobeyed orders and tried to collect as many wounded as we could, but the Rebel guns continued to fire upon us." Beneath the grime and blood, Butler could see the look of clear disgust on the soldier's face.

Butler briskly exited the courthouse. He arranged for a small group to return to Big Bethel with medical supplies and wagons to collect the remaining wounded and transport them back to the court-house for medical attention. The group was somewhat apprehensive to return to the battlefield even though they hadn't tasted the blood of the first volley. Still, with some cajoling, they departed to retrieve the wounded and dead.

The recovery unit arrived outside the Confederate earthworks as the sun beat down overhead. They carefully navigated the surrounding woods and fields, expecting the stench of bodies ripening in the heat. None could be seen from either side of the confrontation. The men even searched the Rebel earthworks. The entire area was totally abandoned.

They promptly returned to Fortress Monroe and called on Butler's quarters, as he had instructed. The leader of the group stood at atten-tion. "General, we searched the entire area and couldn't find a single body."

Butler was totally confused. He thanked the soldier and sat down, massaging his temples. *How can I receive such contradictory views of the battle and of the treatment of casualties?* he thought.

In Hampton, Mary sat at her dinner table. Her face was buried in her hands. Thomas knelt by her side with an arm around her shoulders. Through sobs, Mary described the sickening events at the courthouse. She had never seen so much blood. As Thomas tried to console her, she said, "Oh, Thomas. It was so awful. There was a wagon with dead bodies piled high. A man's arm hung down below the canvas. What bothers me the most," she paused through the sobs, "what I just don't understand is, how men can do these horrible things to each other." She shook her head "I just don't understand."

"Try not to think about it, Mary." Thomas stood and put some food on Mary's plate. "Try eating something." Daisy watched her parents in terrified silence.

"Thomas, what makes matters even worse is the defeat of the Union soldiers. What if the Confederates retake Hampton? The slave patrols could return. And my school would have to close." She turned to her husband "It would be awful. Everything would go back to the way it was. Or even worse!"

Mary sat staring at her plate. Daisy watched her mother push the cold food around with a fork. "Mama, I'm afraid."

Mary looked at her daughter through a tight smile that did not hold. She thought of this precious child, of her sweet laughter, of all the hardship she may have to live through, and her eyes brimmed with tears.

Thomas tried to change the subject. "Mary, why don't we go into the sitting room? You can work on Mrs. Butler's dress."

Mary latched onto her husband's suggestion like a vice. "Oh, Thomas. With the wedding and all the commotion today, I forgot all about Sarah's dress." Thomas and Daisy followed Mary into the next room.

Mary sat down with the dress in her lap. She pushed the needle through the lace ruffle and silk material and pulled it out through the other side. Her thoughts immediately drifted to the courthouse and the medics stitching the open wounds of the soldiers. She bit her lower lip and stared out the window. Exhaustion washed over her. Too upset to concentrate, she placed the dress back on the side table. She shuffled into her bedroom. Within minutes, she was fast asleep.

A veil of fog seeped through the trees and floated across the damp ground. Mary stood in the dark, barefoot and in her nightgown. She was mesmerized by the canvas-covered wagon. A vulture was perched on the corner of the seat. Its bare black head and sharp eyes followed her every move. The dangling, limp arm of a dead soldier had haunted Mary since seeing it earlier.

As she approached the wagon, Mary became more and more perplexed. The arm appeared much smaller than she had remembered. She was close enough now to touch it. But it wasn't a soldier's arm. It was the arm of a small child. *How could that be?*

Mary gently pulled the canvas back. Her heart hammered against her ribcage. Her breathing was labored and shallow. She gasped for air. Her legs weakened. She struggled to support the weight of her body. Her mouth opened to scream. No sound came out.

Daisy's lifeless body lay among the pile of corpses. Her tiny arm hung down. Next to her were the mangled, bloody bodies of Thomas, James, Frank, and some students—all those dear to her.

She reached out to Daisy with both hands. The wagon lurched forward. With every frantic step Mary took, the wagon seemed to accelerate. She watched helplessly as the wagon started rolling down the road.

Mary heard hysterical laughing from the wagon seat. She looked up. Weston Boyd sat holding the reins. He pointed at her and howled, "I told you I'd be back." He cracked the whip. Daisy's eyes opened. She extended her dangling arm. "Mama! Mama! Help me! Help me!" Weston Boyd's head transformed into the head of a vulture. His hands became sharp claws. Gasping for air, Mary chased the wagon down the road. She reached out and called to her daughter. The wagon disappeared into a thick mist.

"Mama! Mama! Wake up! Wake up!" Daisy vigorously shook her mother's shoulder.

Mary opened her eyes and looked into her daughter's terrified face. "Oh, baby." She reached out and pulled Daisy in.

S UNRISE WAS JUST HOURS AWAY WHEN SARAH
finally convinced her husband to go to bed. Butler made her
promise to rouse him by eight o'clock. He walked into the
kitchen holding a mug of steaming coffee. "Thank you for waking me,
Sarah. The few hours of rest did me well." He sat down at the table.

"Benjamin, I wish you stayed in bed longer. You still look
exhausted." She set down a plate of fried eggs, biscuits, and bacon in
front of him. "Eat, Benjamin. You need a good breakfast. I suspect
your day will be a long one."

As Butler devoured his breakfast, he confided in his wife. "I'm
still puzzled by the details of what happened yesterday." He wiped
his mouth on the linen napkin. "These are people I trust. To get such
varied and inconsistent accounts of, of..." Butler gestured with his
hand, struggling to find the words.

Sarah walked up behind her husband and placed her hands on
his shoulders. "There, there, Benjamin. Don't go getting yourself all

worked up. I'm sure you'll get to the bottom of this today. You always do," she said through a tight smile.

Butler stood and put his jacket on. As he fastened his buttons, Sarah said, "I hope you're going to take your morning walk. The exercise will do you good and help relieve some stress."

Butler kissed his wife on the cheek. "I don't think there's anything I can do to relax today. I need to get right to my office. General Scott and the rest of the Washington bureaucrats will be breathing down my neck soon enough."

As Butler sat behind his desk, Major Fay entered, pale and unsteady. "General, there's a Rebel officer at our north gate under the flag of truce. He claims that he has word regarding our dead and wounded." Fay hesitated. "Sir, he also claims to have the body of Major Winthrop."

Without waiting for Fay to continue, Butler immediately rose from his chair and headed to the stables to mount his horse and meet the Rebel officer.

Even from across Mill Creek Bridge, Butler could see the man's teeth glinting in his smug smile. They, and the brass buttons on that dastardly gray uniform, seemed to taunt Butler as he pulled his horse level to the man.

"Well now," said the Southerner, "if it isn't the General whose men beat a hasty retreat at Big Bethel."

Butler checked his horse's reins. "They did no such thing," he said, hoping to call the man's bluff. He hated how sweet and easy Magruder's emissary rested in his saddle.

"Oh, but they did," he said. "They left a trail of dead and wounded behind. Why, the only soldier with any courage among all of them was

Major Winthrop. Unfortunately, he's among the deceased. But we did honor him with a special ceremony." Butler's shoulders slumped as the Rebel continued. "General Magruder made us collect your soldiers from the battlefield before the vulture's got them. We buried the dead and transported the rest to Yorktown for medical attention." The man inspected his hand. "I'll be digging blood and dirt out from my fingernails for weeks."

Butler felt queasy. "Thank you. Please thank the rest of your infantry for treating my men with dignity."

The man nodded and his brashness softened. "General, I came to escort your men back to Yorktown to retrieve the wounded."

Butler instructed a small group of his men to follow the Confederate soldier with wagons. Later that day, they returned with the wounded and reported to Butler. They explained that they were treated justly by the Confederates and were well fed before departing. They had the body of Major Winthrop and his personal effects. Butler was deeply distressed that his worst fears were true regarding the chaotic retreat from Big Bethel and the abhorrent act of leaving the dead and wounded behind.

Butler felt grateful to Magruder for his treatment of the Union dead and wounded, but, in a series of communications, he nonetheless entered into a testy exchange of words with him. Each blamed the other for the confrontation. Through their interchange the realization finally hit Butler that the Union was defeated by a Rebel force one-third its size.

The following day, Butler was unable to operate with a clear mind. His thoughts constantly fell back to the Big Bethel battle and the missteps leading to his embarrassing defeat. He assembled a small group of men including Fay and a few aides. They ventured past Brick Kiln Creek, now clearly in Confederate controlled territory, and on to Big Bethel.

There, Butler rode around the earthworks and personally surveyed the terrain. Standing with Fay behind the Rebel earthworks, Butler pointed and said, "See how these are strategically placed? They had a perfect vantage point. They were positioned to repel attacks both head-on and around the flanks."

He also determined, however, that the description of the earthworks was grossly overstated. "I was told these earthen walls were thirteen feet high. Why, they can't be more than three feet." He rode around to the front. "And the ditches can't be more than a few feet deep."

Butler kicked his horse in the sides and rode out about twenty feet. Turning and facing the earthworks, he guided his horse directly at the fortification, easily jumping the ditch and earthen wall in one leap. He pulled his horse to a stop and said with disgust, "Had our men been equipped with the appropriate cavalry, we would have easily overrun them." He threw his hat to the ground.

Butler returned to his office that afternoon, upset that the battle was lost, in part, due to the unavailability of horses. He sat behind his desk and opened a letter dated four days earlier on June 8. Written by a close friend in Washington, the letter's contents were like acid spilling down Butler's throat.

His friend described a conspiracy at senior levels in Washington to prevent Butler from having the horses he requisitioned. He had once thought the lack of horses was due to incompetence in Washington. Now he realized it was an intentional act.

Butler pounded his fist against his desk. "I knew it," he yelled. He looked around his empty office. "Damn that Scott! Damn them all! How can they blunt my ability to mount an effective offense?"

Butler sat in his chair contemplating the challenge of fighting against the capable Confederates that was made only more taxing by deceitful bureaucrats in Washington. Mentally and physically exhausted, he stared out the window into the dark sky. He had never felt so far from home.

O VER A MONTH HAD PASSED SINCE THE UNION'S fiasco at Big Bethel. Life in Hampton was slowly returning to a steady and comfortable rhythm. The contraband slaves now numbered close to a thousand. Some remained in and around Fortress Monroe. Many still lived in the shanties behind the homes of their fleeing masters. Any doubts whether the abandoned slaves could survive on their own had long been dispelled. Most adequately supported themselves by providing goods and services to the growing Union forces.

Shaken by the embarrassing defeat at Big Bethel, Butler had been busy reinforcing his positions on the lower Virginia Peninsula. Large guns capable of firing 400-pound shells almost a mile were mounted on top of the massive granite walls surrounding the fort.

Major Fay entered Butler's office. "Sir, we just received word that the telegraph lines have been energized and are functioning."

"Good, good," Butler replied, looking up from his desk. "Now

I don't have to worry about communicating with Camp Butler and Camp Hamilton in an emergency."

The condition of the fort had substantially improved, particularly since his first inspection in late May, two months earlier. Butler was feeling more confident in his role. He began sending expeditions into contested areas between Hampton and Big Bethel intended to gain knowledge of Rebel movements and to harass the enemy. As a result of Union actions, hostility gradually escalated.

News spread of another Union defeat a few days earlier, on July 21, near Manassas Junction, Virginia, just outside of Washington. While Butler was not pleased about the loss, he was relieved that it took Washington's focus off him and the loss at Big Bethel.

Butler looked up from his briefing report at Major Fay. "Richard, this conflict outside Manassas—they're calling it the Battle of Bull Run—is eerily similar to our own experiences at Big Bethel."

Fay walked over and sat across from Butler's desk. "How so, General?"

"It appears the Union's plans were overly complex." But shook his head. "In retrospect, not unlike ours. Their plan required perfect synchronization of troop movements. The Confederates must have been aware of Union troop strength and our positions." He placed the report on his desk. "It appears that Rebel reinforcements arrived throughout the battle. Eventually, they broke through Union lines and sent our men retreating back to Washington."

"I guess the two battles are similar in that regard," Fay replied. "Two losses! Not a particularly stellar start for the Union, I'm afraid." The two men exchanged concerned looks.

"Well, one fortunate difference is that citizens from Washington came to witness the spectacle at Manassas. This report says that our fleeing soldiers became entangled with horrified onlookers as they all chaotically stampeded across narrow bridges and down roadways. Thank God there were no spectators at Big Bethel," Butler reflected.

With this new insight about the Confederates and recent battles, Butler turned to the prospect of mounting an attack on Yorktown and perhaps even Norfolk. "Richard, I've been thinking. A hard lesson learned from Big Bethel is that accurate intelligence about the enemy and careful preparation are critical." He frowned. "Clearly, both were inadequate." Butler walked over to the window and looked at the empty stables in the distance. "And, of course, there's the issue of horses. After personally witnessing the inadequacy of the Rebel earthworks at Big Bethel, a capable cavalry could have made all the difference. And it will be vital to any future engagement."

Despite the continuing expeditions into disputed Rebel territory, Butler still felt he lacked the intimate knowledge necessary to launch a major attack. He was confident Confederate troop strength was growing, and he was becoming increasingly concerned with potential Rebel attacks on isolated Camp Butler.

Butler placed a newspaper in front of his senior aide. "Richard, I'd appreciate your thoughts on a matter. There's an aeronaut, a John LaMountain, who pilots a hot air balloon high into the sky. Over 2,000 feet, this article claims." He pointed to a picture of LaMountain standing in front of his hot air balloon. "Can you imagine the knowledge we could gain if we had this vantage point?"

Fay started reading the article and looked up. "Oh, I remember you telling me about this man. I thought you wrote to him a few weeks ago. Did you ever hear back?"

"I did. He's due to arrive within the next few days." Butler picked up the newspaper and examined the picture of the aeronaut and his balloon. "I'm not sure if he can help our cause, but we'll find out soon enough."

He unfastened the top button of his shirt. "Richard, can you please open a window? It's stifling in here. This humidity is unbearable." Butler wiped his forehead and upper lip on his handkerchief.

"I'll open the window, but I doubt whether it will bring much relief." Fay walked over and pushed the window open and stared, dumbfounded. "What the hell is that?"

Butler looked up. "What?"

"I'm not sure, General. There's a large cloud of dust coming from the far end of the parade grounds. It looks almost like a sandstorm."

Butler stood up and walked over. He looked out the window and scratched his head. "I'm going to see what's going on."

The two men walked out of the office and turned down the road leading to the large open field. As they approached, Butler could feel the ground rumbling beneath his feet like muffled thunder. He stopped and watched the cloud of dust approach. Other than the sight of his children, who he dearly missed, the sight before him was the next best thing.

With a wide grin, Butler raised his arms in the air. "Horses!" he yelled.

Not just a few, but hundreds. The sounds of pounding hooves and sharp whinnies were music to Butler's ears. Two months after his formal requisition for horses, and multiple pleas later, the stables would now be full of his very own cavalry. Butler stood grinning and watched the powerful animals make their way across the field. His nostrils filled with the sweet smells of muck and sweat, mixed with a faint manure odor, as the beasts galloped past him towards the stables.

Back in his office, Butler realized everything was neatly falling into place. Fortress Monroe and the surrounding Union camps were fully equipped with armaments. He had several thousand troops under his command. And now he finally had horses.

Construction of the earthworks, begun several weeks earlier, was finally completed. As the group of workers walked back to the courthouse to deposit their tools, Pierce asked the men to assemble in the yard.

They gathered around Pierce, peering over shoulders to see the Union soldier they had come to appreciate and respect. James stood near the man and could see the Yankee's eyes glisten in the sun. He reached out to Pierce. "Are you all right, sir?"

Pierce looked at James and smiled. He put his hand on the big man's shoulder and gave a gentle squeeze. "I'm fine, James. Thank you."

Pierce slowly pivoted in a circle to address the group of men patiently standing around him. Despite being covered in dirt with perspiration dripping down their backs and faces, they gave Pierce their full attention. "We've finally completed the earthworks we began in June. You've all worked with great diligence through the hot summer. Harder than any group of men I've known, in fact. Perhaps even more importantly, your behavior has been a shining example for all. I dare say any group of white men wouldn't have been able to work as you have without an utterance of profanity."

Pierce paused to compose himself. He could feel his stomach twist and his legs weaken. Looking from face to face, he knew each man by name, and the specifics of each of their families. "This is the last time I'll have the honor and pleasure of meeting with you." Gasps and sighs broke out among the group. Heads turned in denial.

Soft utterances were heard among the men. "No, no." "Say it ain't so."

Pierce continued, "Tomorrow morning, I'll be leaving for my home in Massachusetts. I shall be pleased to report to all there of your industry and high morals." Pierce, again, had to pause. He looked down at the ground.

He knew how unique this opportunity was for a white man from New England to address sixty-four slaves. He looked from face to face. "There is one more thing I'd like to add. Every one of you is as much entitled to your freedom as I am to mine, and I hope that someday soon you'll secure it."

Men nodded and commented. "Believe you, boss." "God bless you." "May we meet in heaven." Pierce's chin began to quiver. He placed a hand over his eyes.

James put his arm around the Union soldier and said, "Hey, now. You treated us with respect. That's something we've never felt before, particularly from a white man. All we want is a chance to be free and to make a life for our families and ourselves. You gave us a taste of that and we're forever grateful. We all wish you a safe journey home. Please don't forget us."

Pierce looked into James's eyes and then around at the other men and smiled. "I may forget my childhood playmates, my college classmates, and my professional associates. I may even forget my comrades in arms. But I'll always remember you and your blessings until I cease to breathe." He paused and reached down into a pouch at his feet. "I don't have much to give, but I want to make a present to each of you with some tobacco."

Each man came up to accept his gift and to wish the private well with a strong handshake or embrace.

"What bird is that?" Mary pointed to a tree near the path. "See how it's walking down the trunk upside down. Isn't that peculiar?"

"Oh, Mama, you know what bird that is. It's a white-breasted nuthatch. It's looking for food in the tree bark. Woodpeckers do the same thing, but they walk up the trunk and use their tails for balance."

"You're such a smart little girl. I don't remember reading about that in the bird book when I was little," Mary said. Mary was always amazed by her daughter's ability to retain information.

"Nuthatches stuff seeds into the bark. Then they hit the shell with their beak to break the seed open and eat the inside." Daisy pointed. "See, Mama! It's doing it now."

"Isn't that interesting?" Mary reached down and grabbed Daisy's hand and they continued walking. "Can mockingbirds walk upside down like that?" Mary said, smiling.

"Of course not." Daisy shook her head and giggled. "But they sing the best of all the birds. They can imitate all the other birds, so they can sound like any bird they want."

"Well then, I guess I'm honored to be a mockingbird." Mary and Daisy looked at each other and laughed as they rounded the corner. They almost collided with James.

"Oh, so sorry, James! We should've been watching where we were walking," Mary said, smiling warmly. "You look like you lost your best friend," she teased.

James made a faint attempt at a smile. "Hi, Miss Peake. Hello, Miss Daisy." He nodded. "Well, in a way, I guess I did."

Mary looked into the man's face and noticed his eyes were red and glassy. "Why, what happened?"

"Private Pierce, the soldier that's been leading us at the breast-works, is leaving for home tomorrow morning." James looked down and then in the direction of the wharf.

"I'm so sorry, James. I know you were fond of him," Mary said.

"Yeah, well. I've been…" James started to talk and suddenly stopped. He scuffed the ground with his big foot, stalling to gain his composure. "I've been thinking. Most of these soldiers have been real good to us and all. But they're all from the North. And some day they're all gonna go back. We'll be here by ourselves again. Alone. If things don't go our way before they leave, everything could turn back to the way it was. All this would all be for nothing."

James's comments hit Mary like a weight of stones. Something had been lingering in the back of her mind like a distant dark cloud, and now she realized what it was. Mary quickly said her goodbyes, took Daisy by the hand, and walked home in silence.

Later that night, lying in bed, Thomas turned to face his wife. With his elbow on the bed, he leaned his head against his hand. "Mary, you've been awfully quiet this evening. Is everything okay?"

Mary twisted the sheets between her hands. "I don't know, Thomas. I don't know whether to feel happy or sad. I was so excited when the slave patrols and all the Confederate loyalists left Hampton. Then the tragedy at Big Bethel was such a terrible shock. It seemed like things were finally settling down these past few weeks," she said.

She lay on her back to stare at the ceiling. "I saw James today. That Union soldier, Private Pierce, the one managing the breastworks outside the town, leaves tomorrow for his home back north. James was pretty upset, which I guess I can understand. I'm told Private Pierce was good to all the men working there." She turned to her husband. "But James said something that I guess I always knew but haven't been willing to admit."

"What's that?" Thomas said. He moved closer to his wife and put his arm around her waist.

"He said that all these men from the North would go home some-day and leave us here to fend for ourselves. If the Union doesn't prevail, things could go back to the way they were. Oh, Thomas, that would be terrible." Mary buried her face in his chest.

He caressed the back of her head. "Mary, listen to me. You told me General Butler thought this conflict would be over by the end of the year. And he's convinced the Union will prevail. I'll admit, Big Bethel was a setback, but I've been doing work almost every day in the fort. There are so many men and guns arriving each day that they don't even know where to put them. There's even been talk the Union may be thinking about an attack on a major city. Maybe Norfolk or possibly even Richmond. Don't be so quick to give up. Brighter days are ahead. You'll see. I just know it."

"Oh, Thomas, I hope you're right."

Mary kissed her husband on the lips and turned on her side. Thomas curled his body around Mary's back. Within minutes Thomas could hear a gentle snore coming from his wife. He smiled and closed his eyes.

L IKE MOST MORNINGS SINCE ARRIVING AT
Fortress Monroe, Butler arose early, unable to sleep. Throughout
each night, he tossed and turned, his thoughts constantly
cluttered with military affairs and the challenges of protecting throngs
of slaves. Today was different though. It wasn't the burdens of his
office that led to his restless night. It was anticipation. Butler had been
looking forward to this day for weeks.

He ate eagerly as he briefed his wife. "Can you believe it! We
finally received our horses, hundreds of them in fact. Our stables are
finally full."

"I heard the commotion when they galloped across the parade
grounds," Sarah said.

"And today, Mr. LaMountain arrives on the late morning transport." Butler wiped his mouth on a napkin and stood abruptly. "I need
to get to the office early so I can finish my paperwork in time." He
kissed Sarah on the cheek and hurried out the door.

Butler took his usual circuitous route to stretch his legs and clear his head. The sun's rays were just peeking over the granite walls warming the dawn air. He could already feel dampness collecting under his armpits and down his back. It would be another oppressively hot day.

He watched honeybees busily collecting pollen from summer blossoms that blanketed the flowerbeds. Swarms of hovering dragonflies patrolled the grounds for invaders, greedily plucking pesky mosquitoes out of midair and devouring the unsuspecting pests.

Sitting behind his desk, Butler tried to concentrate on processing his mountain of paperwork, but he was hopelessly distracted. Even throughout his morning staff meeting, his mind seemed to be somewhere else. As the officers disbanded, Major Fay lingered behind. "General, is something troubling you this morning?"

Startled from his thoughts, Butler turned to Fay. "No, Richard." He smiled guiltily. "I suppose I'm preoccupied with the arrival of Mr. LaMountain. His steamship is due at eleven o'clock."

When the hour came, Butler hurried down to the wharf in time to see the steamship enter Hampton Roads. Several minutes later, LaMountain disembarked and Butler greeted him. While nowhere near as tall as the President, the aeronaut's resemblance to Lincoln was uncanny, even down to the bearded chin and bushy eyebrows. Butler was impressed by the man's neat, formal appearance. His bowtie was expertly tied. "Welcome to Fortress Monroe, Mr. LaMountain," Butler said, shaking the man's hand.

LaMountain grinned broadly as he scanned the vast horizon. "Even though I've heard and read about this fort, I must admit I was rather stunned by its size as we approached. It's truly impressive, General," LaMountain said.

"We've been anxiously awaiting your arrival. How soon can we get started?" Butler rubbed his hands together. He was giddy with excitement.

"We'll need to unload my supplies and transport them to a suitable location. An enclosed building would be ideal. I've news there may be a storm approaching from the west this evening and into tomorrow." He looked to the horizon. "You could feel the humidity already starting to build. So I think we could conduct our first launch on the morning after tomorrow," LaMountain said.

The frown on Butler's face revealed his obvious disappointment. "General, I know you're anxious to get started," said LaMountain assuaging him. "But it's important we take all precautions. We rely totally on the weather and the winds. I would like to understand the layout of the area, where Confederate positions might be located, and those areas where you wish to gain more knowledge."

While LaMountain went to his quarters to unpack, his two assistants and several Union troops unloaded two deflated balloons, fuel tanks, baskets, and other supplies. In the afternoon, Butler met with the aeronaut to provide him with a comprehensive overview of the peninsula's geography. Butler expressed particularly interest in the area from Big Bethel north to Yorktown.

Butler said, "Mr. LaMountain, all these Confederate positions on the peninsula are important to us, but it'd also be most helpful to understand their troop strength at Sewell's Point. If we want to advance on Norfolk, this information would be critical. Is it possible to see two miles across the water?"

LaMountain considered Butler's question. "General, if we can find a suitable area for takeoff and landing, it might be possible to see that far." LaMountain looked up from the map. "Of course, the day would have to be clear, and I would need to get to an elevation of at least 2,000 feet. Another option is to attach the balloon to the deck of a steamship. Using mooring ropes to secure the balloon, we could sail into Hampton Roads. If I can get close enough to the south shore, but still out of range of the Confederate guns, I might be able to get a clear view of the encampment." LaMountain glanced back at the map "I've never tried this before, but with ideal weather conditions, it should be possible. I might even be able to see farther south towards Norfolk."

Since contacting LaMountain weeks earlier, Butler often thought about the views birds must have from the air. Back in Boston, he recalled seeing extraordinary aerial photos of the city taken by James Wallace Black. Butler remembered how clearly he could distinguish the Trinity and Old South Churches, Washington Street, Milk Street, and hundreds of structures in fine detail from the photographer's 2,000-foot vantage point. Butler suspected this would be the first time an untethered hot air balloon would be used for military reconnaissance.

"Mr. LaMountain, if you're not too tired from your journey, Mrs. Butler and I would like to host you for dinner tonight." Butler pulled his jacket on and fastened the buttons.

"That's very kind of you, General. It would be an honor. I look forward to meeting Mrs. Butler." LaMountain followed Butler into the thick afternoon air. Just as LaMountain had predicted, the skies were shrouded in gray-black clouds.

Over dinner, Butler learned from LaMountain that the Union had attempted to use a hot air balloon at the Battle of Bull Run. "Although it would have been tethered to the ground, the balloon flight was intended to provide military intelligence on Confederate troop positions in the Maryland countryside," LaMountain said.

The man's perilous adventures fascinated Sarah. "Were you there, Mr. LaMountain?" She leaned forward with her hands clasped. Her cheeks were flush with wine, further enhancing her beauty.

He swallowed a piece of potato and said through a tight smile, "Believe it or not, Mrs. Butler, ballooning is quite competitive. There are several of us vying for the coveted position as head of the Army balloon corps. One of my contemporaries, a Mr. John Wise, actually accompanied the Union at Manassas."

Butler sat back and wiped his mouth on a linen napkin. "I'm curious, Mr. LaMountain. How does one inflate a balloon in the field?"

"That's a good question, General." LaMountain put his fork down. "Well, as you'll soon see, I'll actually be making the gas here with the supplies I brought. Wise, however, rather *unwisely* chose a different path." He chuckled at his own pun and took a sip of wine. "He decided to inflate his balloon with city gas first and then move it into location. I'm told the advance of the Union troops was substantially hindered by the awkwardness of the floating balloon. You see, they needed to keep it away from trees along the route. So to help speed progress, the officer in charge ordered the balloon to be tethered to a wagon." LaMountain shook his head.

"Oh, dear!" Sarah gasped and took a sip of wine. "I think I see where this is going." They all laughed.

"Yes, well, I'm afraid you're right, Mrs. Butler." LaMountain cut off a piece of beef with his knife. "The fast pace of the horses caused the balloon to be blown off course and into some branches along the road. The balloon became tightly lodged in the trees. So the officer ordered the wagon to reverse direction in order to free the balloon." He shrugged. "The fabric was quickly torn." He chewed and swallowed the tender meat. "And poor, dejected Mr. Wise departed for Washington with his damaged balloon, void of any triumphs of flight." LaMountain tried to hide his smug expression behind his napkin.

After finishing their hearty dinner, the three toasted to future successful flights. LaMountain thanked his hosts and returned to his quarters. With a full stomach and more wine than he was used to consuming, for the first time in weeks, Butler slept soundly through the night.

The following morning was windy and wet as LaMountain had predicted. Butler walked to a large storage building in Fortress Monroe that housed the balloons and other equipment. LaMountain and his assistants were already unpacking boxes and organizing the needed supplies for his first flight when Butler walked in and greeted the aeronaut. "Good morning, Mr. LaMountain. I trust you were comfortable last night. Let's hope our weather tomorrow will be an improvement over today."

"Good morning, General," LaMountain replied. "I did sleep well, thank you. And the meal last night was splendid. I so enjoyed meeting your wife." He looked to the door. "I suspect this storm should blow through by this evening. Tomorrow should be clear enough, but perhaps a little windy. We'll have to see what the day holds for us then."

Butler looked around the big room in wonderment at all the exotic supplies needed to support balloon flight. In addition to the 5,000 pounds of iron fillings, about the size of Butler's desk, LaMountain transported almost five tons of sulfuric acid, as well as various hoses, tanks, and of course, the balloons. The mound of materials could easily fill the rooms of a good-sized house. "I must say, Mr. LaMountain, I never would have thought all this stuff is needed to make a balloon fly." Butler waved his arm around the warehouse.

LaMountain smiled. "Well, other than the balloon itself and the basket, most of the material is used in making the gas."

"Yes, you mentioned this last night. So what actually happens here?" Butler asked.

The aeronaut explained. "The process of inflating a balloon is long and tedious. Like I said last night, normally, balloons are inflated with city gas." LaMountain placed a box he was holding on the floor. "The closest source is Washington, so it's just not practical to inflate the balloon there and then transport it as far as Fortress Monroe. Fortunately, a man named Professor Thaddeus Lowe invented a portable hydrogen gas generator, which provides us balloonists with more geographic flexibility." He walked over to the crates containing the supplies. He put his hand into a barrel containing fine, silver-gray particles. "Lowe's process uses these iron filings and sulfuric acid. Through a complex process of mixing the ingredients and filtering the resulting gases, a clear stream of hydrogen is produced."

Though Butler was himself an exceptional student and well educated, he found that most of this explanation was over his head. "Yes, well, I'm sure you know what you're doing, and I'm probably only in your way. I'll leave you to your work." He shook hands with LaMountain.

"Are you going to join us tomorrow?" LaMountain asked as Butler headed for the door.

"Why, of course! I've been waiting for weeks. I wouldn't miss this for anything." Butler smiled.

"Well then, we're going to head out at about six in the morning for Camp Hamilton. I suggest you stop by midmorning after the balloon is mostly filled."

Butler wished him well and stepped back into the rain. As he walked to his office, Butler felt like he was floating in a balloon over the puddles of water. He entered his office, removed his jacket, and sat behind his desk. Despite the dreary weather, Butler was in unusually high spirits.

He thought about the excellent state of the fort, the extensive troops under his command, a stable brimming with horses, and now he was only days from military intelligence most officers could only dream about. He was eager to start the morning staff meeting where he would commence planning for attacks on Yorktown and perhaps even Norfolk.

Even the embarrassment of Big Bethel was a fading memory. Butler committed to learn what he could from the disastrous battle and move forward. Key to that knowledge was the need to better understand the size and movement of Confederate troops, which he was about to address in a most unheard-of way.

The following morning, LaMountain's balloon was transported to a small field just north of Mill Creek adjacent to Camp Hamilton. Butler, frustrated with the long wait leading up to this day, arrived to witness the launch. He was as giddy as a schoolboy as the whooshing sound of the hot gas filled the expanding balloon cloth. Fortunately, he had arrived after the inflation process was well underway. Though it took about three hours to completely fill, the balloon was almost ready.

LaMountain and his crew of two men positioned the balloon and made their final adjustments. Butler gasped as LaMountain climbed into the basket while his assistants held the anchor lines. "Well, aren't you coming?" the man called to Butler with a smirk.

Butler held his stomach and laughed. "Surely you jest, Mr. LaMountain?"

"General, when it comes to flying, you'll learn that I'm all business. I figure you waited all this time for me to arrive, so the least I can do is to repay you with an experience of your life." LaMountain extended his arm, inviting the officer to board.

As Butler reluctantly approached the basket, he thought about Sarah. *How will I ever explain this to her? Perhaps I better not even tell her. I do wish my children could witness this though. The boys would be thrilled.*

Butler stepped onto a stool and over the basket edge onto another stool inside. He gripped the edge of the basket with both hands.

"Are you ready, General?" LaMountain asked, handing the stool to an assistant.

Butler nodded weakly. His face was as pale as his white mustache.

LaMountain's assistants released the anchor lines. Gradually gaining elevation, the balloon drifted up and west towards Hampton. LaMountain put his hand on Butler's shoulder. "General, you can open your eyes. I've done this many times in the past. I assure you we'll be safe. Besides I'm only planning to go a short way just to experience the wind direction and view the nearby terrain."

Butler watched the ground recede below them as the balloon rose. Men shrunk to the size of squirrels. Homes became small boxes. Roads became ribbons of sand. The tears streaming down his cheeks could have been from fear or joy. It didn't matter. He was flying!

Mary and Daisy were holding hands and swinging their arms as they walked to the brown cottage. The heavy rains and powerful winds that battered the area had blown through the prior evening. It was a perfect summer morning—a deep blue sky, gentle sea breezes, and low humidity. Puffy, white clouds dotted the distant horizon over Chesapeake Bay, like pillows floating on the water.

Daisy kept her eyes on the sky and trees, hoping to spot some bird species for the first time. She heard a familiar sound and smiled. Following its direction, she spied a cardinal hopping around in the grass. She pointed with her free hand. "Look, Mama. A cardinal."

"Oh, they're so pretty, Daisy. I know they're your favorite," Mary said. "That's the male, right?"

Daisy nodded with a smirk. "The female must be nearby. They mate for life, you know." She looked down at the ground and turned to her mother. "Mama, why are birds able to fly and not people?"

"Wow. That's a tough question for so early in the morning." Mary placed her free hand to her forehead. "Let me think. I guess it's because birds are lighter and have wings covered in feathers."

"I know that, Mama. What I mean is, do you think people could fly? Not with their arms, but maybe if they made big wings and somehow attached them to their arms." Daisy flapped her free arm. "Do you think they could fly then?"

"Why, I don't know, Daisy. I would imagine, though, if that was possible, someone would have figured it out by now." Mary looked over at her daughter and smiled. "Do you remember me telling you about the story of Icarus and his father, Daedalus?"

Daisy frowned. "Who are they? Do they live in Hampton?"

Mary laughed good-naturedly. "No, baby. They lived on the island of Crete in ancient Greece. Daedalus was an inventor, and he angered the king one day. They had to flee for their lives, so Daedalus made wings out of wax for him and Icarus. They had to make sure they flew high enough so the seawater wouldn't dampen their wings but not too high, or the sun would melt them," Mary said while walking.

"So what happened?" Daisy eyes were wide as she looked up at her mother.

"They were able to escape the island, and Icarus started to get a

little uppity. Ignoring his father's warnings, he flew high into the air."
Mary stopped and flapped her arms rapidly. "And the sun melted his
wings and he crashed into the ocean, never to be seen again." Mary
squatted, pretending to crash to the land.

"Are you teasing me, Mama?" Daisy asked.

"What do you think?" Mary laughed, tickling her daughter's sides.
"My, you're awfully inquisitive today."

Daisy saw a large bird swoop over the trees, heading towards the
shoreline. Its white underside and black mask clearly revealed the bird's
identity. "Oh, it's another mean, old osprey." Daisy slowly turned her
body, following the bird's flight as she walked. Daisy was walking
sideways and about to walk backwards when a shadow cut across her
view. The girl came to an abrupt stop, pulling on Mary's arm.

Mary turned and leaned over. She looked into her daughter's
shocked face. "Daisy, what is it?"

Daisy didn't look back at her mother. With her mouth wide open,
she pointed up into the sky. "What's that?"

Mary followed Daisy's pointing finger. She looked into the sky but
was initially blinded by the brilliant morning sun. She was about to
ask her daughter what she was pointing at when a huge object crossed
in front of the sun and came into view.

"Why, I think it might be a large balloon! I've read about them and
have seen pictures, but I've never seen one in person. See the basket
under the balloon?" Mary pointed. "There's a man in it. Two men
actually. They must be controlling the flight of the balloon somehow."
Mary and Daisy watched the balloon slowly pass over their heads.

Daisy waved at the men in the basket. "Mama, those men are
flying like a big bird!"

"Well, I guess people can fly after all," Mary said. They both
laughed.

The balloon was too high for them to recognize General Butler as one of the occupants. Mary and Daisy watched the balloon drift west until it disappeared behind some trees.

The balloon was crossing over a dirt road, and Butler could see a woman and young child pointing up at the balloon. He smiled and waved. The little girl was jumping up and down while waving back. He couldn't see their faces from the high altitude, but he was pretty certain it was Mary and Daisy on their way to school. Butler looked south to the shoreline and could just make out the small brown cottage through the trees.

Gliding along the gentle breezes coming off Chesapeake Bay, the balloon drifted across Hampton Creek. The town of Hampton lay sprawling to the north, like a child's blocks. LaMountain eventually guided the balloon to 1,400 feet. They could see a river farther to the west, flowing south. Butler yelled, "That must be the Southwest Branch of the Back River." To the west, Confederate-controlled land was fast approaching.

LaMountain didn't want to be too aggressive during his first flight in Virginia, particularly with General Butler on board. He planned to land in a large field just east and south of New Market Bridge, where a wagon was waiting to transport the two men, the balloon, and its basket back to Fortress Monroe.

LaMountain pointed to the horizon and said, "We're high enough now to see over ten miles. With more altitude and on a perfectly clear day, I'd be able to see about thirty miles in all directions."

Butler was dumbstruck as he scanned the peninsula below.

"Ideally, I would want a flight path further south where I could safely travel more to the west." LaMountain pointed to the coast on the south shore of Hampton Roads. "I might even be able to detect Rebel positions at Sewell's Point."

The balloon suddenly dropped several feet. Butler squatted and looked openmouthed at LaMountain. "It's nothing to worry about, General. We just hit a small air pocket. Air turbulence happens all the time." The aeronaut tried to assure the officer.

Butler slowly stood. The balloon sailed across a heavily wooded area. LaMountain reached up and held a long cord that ran up to the top of the balloon. "When I pull on this, a small valve opens at the top of the balloon and hot air escapes." He handed the cord to Butler. "Pull on it slowly. The air temperature in the balloon will decrease, and we'll slowly descend."

Butler nodded and hesitated. With LaMountain's encouragement, he carefully pulled on the cord. The balloon drifted down. LaMountain took over the controls as the ground approached. With a jarring thud, the balloon landed about a hundred yards from the planned site. "Well, what do you think, General?" LaMountain helped the officer climb out of the basket as his waiting assistants secured the balloon.

Butler shook his head. "It's hard to describe, Mr. LaMountain. As much as I've dreamt about this and imagined what it would be like, it was beyond my wildest expectations." He smiled. "Thrilling. Absolutely thrilling."

"I'm planning to go up again tomorrow morning, but I will launch further south than today. Assuming the wind directions are similar, my hope is to travel west and land just south of Little Bethel." LaMountain helped his two assistants manage the deflating balloon as the gas seeped out.

"I think I'll let you fly solo tomorrow, Mr. LaMountain," Butler said. Both men laughed. "I need to return to my mundane duties at the fort."

The following morning was even more spectacular than the previous day—it featured a deep blue, cloudless sky with gentle easterly breezes. This time LaMountain launched his balloon in a small field just south and east of Hampton Creek. With the help of the same crew, the balloon was quickly airborne. He remained in the air for almost two hours, covering over five miles of terrain at a height of 2,000 feet. LaMountain could see a large encampment, surrounded by earthworks on the north side. He assumed it must be Camp Butler at Newport News Point.

He was well into the second hour and estimated he could only travel another mile before needing to descend to the preset landing area. LaMountain had nothing yet to report back to Butler. He gnawed his lip. The general would be disappointed.

He could see a burned structure where three roads intersected to the north. He assumed this was Little Bethel, the site of the now-notorious friendly fire incident by the Union. LaMountain scanned the western horizon and worked backwards to his position. Using field glasses, he had to be particularly careful to see among the heavily treed landscape.

As he was about to make preparations to begin descending, LaMountain spotted about 500 men near Water's Creek. He followed the road further west and almost dropped his field glasses over the side of the basket. From studying the maps at Fortress Monroe, he believed the area was Young's Mill.

LaMountain estimated that from 4,000 to 5,000 Confederate soldiers were encamped there. His heart began to race as he made careful notes of the two positions. He had to make a rapid descent as he had traveled longer than expected and overshot the planned landing area.

Back at Butler's office later that day, the Union officer could hardly contain his emotions as LaMountain described his Rebel sightings. "This is incredibly valuable information, Mr. LaMountain. I have been concerned about Rebels attacking Camp Butler. I've ordered the men stationed there to be extra vigilant. The new armaments we recently installed should also be a substantial deterrent. However, the location of these Rebel forces indicates an attack may be imminent. I'll be sure to place the troops on high alert."

After LaMountain left, Butler walked over to his office window. Fortress Monroe was a beehive of activity. Men were busy drilling on the parade grounds. Ammunition, food, and other provisions that arrived almost daily were being transported from the wharf area to storage buildings.

Butler could see the roof of the stables from his vantage point. As a result of his orders, the horses were being exercised regularly. He looked back at the large table in his office. He had spread out several maps, highlighted with notes and arrows, each representing alternative battle plans to advance on a major Confederate city.

With the intelligence gathered from LaMountain's flights, Butler knew he needed to act quickly before his information became old news. He eagerly waited for his war committee to assemble and make a final decision regarding which city to attack first.

Captain Haggerty entered his office. "General, a special boat has just arrived with a telegraph from General Scott." Haggerty handed Butler the envelope.

Butler, expecting approval of his plans to advance on a major Confederate city, opened the message and anxiously began reading.

Haggerty could see the blood drain from Butler's already pale face as it slowly contorted. "What is it, General?" Haggerty said.

Butler finished reading and sat down behind his desk. He gazed down at the message again as if questioning its contents or even perhaps its existence. He looked up at his aide. "General Scott has requested we send four and half regiments to Washington by way of Baltimore. That's over 4,000 men!" Butler shook his head in disbelief. "With the defeat at Bull Run, our leaders in Washington have come to the realization that this war will not end quickly. They're concerned with the prospect of a Rebel attack on Washington." Butler looked back down at the message hoping that somehow he might have misread it, but the words remained unchanged.

"Which regiments is he requesting?" Haggerty asked.

"He's only stated he wants four and half regiments, including Colonel Baker's California Regiment," Butler said. "I think it's best we send the Third, Fourth, and Fifth New York regiments as well. Of course, this will mean we'll have to withdraw our remaining troops from Hampton." He looked out the window. "It also reduces our troop levels at Camp Butler at the worst possible time." He shook his head.

Haggerty stood next to Butler's desk. "What of the contrabands living in Hampton, General?"

Butler put his face in his hands and thought about the large number of people under his protection, living in and around the village. He knew there were many women, children and elderly who had sought refuge with the Yankees.

The contraband men were performing various useful duties within and around the fort. The women had also been quite helpful cleaning the soldiers' clothes or cooking in the kitchens. Butler knew these people had been earning their keep and the extra rations provided for any children or elderly. Butler had grown quite fond of them and felt a deep obligation to protect them.

The prospect of moving them from their homes closer to Fortress Monroe would be difficult. But he knew there was no other alternative that would ensure their safety. "With the loss of so many soldiers," Butler said, "we'll have to move the slaves across Hampton Creek within our lines for protection. Unfortunately, this will mean they must break up their homes and move whatever possessions they have." He slapped his hand on the desk and stood. "Captain, please organize a party of our men to help these folks move. We should start first thing tomorrow morning. I'll gather our staff shortly and give the orders for the regiments to muster first thing tomorrow. This message indicates that steamships will arrive in the morning to transport these troops to Baltimore."

"Yes, sir," Haggerty replied and exited Butler's office.

Butler sat quietly with his head slumped down, staring at the message from Scott. He was dumbfounded. To finally have all the necessary elements to mount a successful offense only to have everything dashed in an instant. He realized it wasn't only his plans that had been affected, but also all of the contrabands living in and around Hampton.

"The best-laid schemes o' mice an' men," Butler mumbled.

MARY WOKE UP EARLY TO MAKE FLAPJACKS for her family as a special treat. She poured several blobs of thick batter into the pan and smiled as they spread. The elongated shapes reminded her of the hot air balloon she and Daisy spotted two days earlier.

Thomas and Daisy inhaled the sweet aroma as they sat at the table, forks in hand. Mary set the steaming plate down, and Thomas smacked his lips. "These look delicious," he said, winking at his daughter. He speared a flapjack and dropped it in Daisy's plate.

Five days had passed since Mary's discussion with James. She was deeply troubled by his revelation that the Union troops would vacate Hampton at some point in the future. It was inevitable. The large population under their protection would have to fend for itself. She felt a little better after her discussion with Thomas that evening and his assurances that the Union was building its capabilities, not tearing them down. Mary couldn't explain why, but on this day her spirits were soaring like the hot air balloon.

But a distant rumble of measured drumbeats brought back memories of the marching Union soldiers on their way to Big Bethel. Mary craned her head and looked at Thomas with concern. "Listen. Do you hear that?"

Thomas stuffed a large piece of flapjack into his mouth. Chewing as he walked into the front room, he said, "I guess the rumors of a Union advance on Yorktown must be true."

Mary followed her husband, leaving Daisy to devour her breakfast. They stepped out onto the front stoop. Hundreds of soldiers were on the move, but rather than marching west towards Yorktown, they were headed east towards Hampton Creek. Mary frowned. "There's so many of them. Why are they heading back to Fortress Monroe?"

"Well, I'll be there all day working, so I suspect we'll find out soon enough." Thomas put his arm around his wife's waist.

They watched for another few minutes before returning to the kitchen. The plate of flapjacks was empty. Daisy sat slumped in the chair, holding her stomach. "Did you eat all of those, you little piggy?" Mary pointed to the plate, smiling.

Daisy nodded and let out a muffled belch. "Excuse me," she said with her hand over her mouth.

After cleaning up, they all left. Thomas walked across Hampton Creek Bridge with Mary and Daisy. A few lingering soldiers and wagons were headed in the same direction. At a fork in the road, Mary and Daisy said goodbye to Thomas and turned towards the shoreline and the brown cottage. He continued on to Fortress Monroe.

Two wagons pulled up to the brown cottage and over thirty children spilled out. Mary walked over to one of the drivers. "Can you tell me what's going on? Why are so many soldiers leaving Hampton and heading back to the fort?"

The large, heavy man tipped his hat. "I don't know the details, ma'am, but I understand some troops are heading to Washington." He shrugged. "That's all I know, I'm afraid."

Mary would find out more when Thomas stopped by the cottage at noon. She saw her husband lingering around the front door and stepped out of her classroom. "Thomas, what a treat! Are you here to help me teach?" She chortled.

Thomas gave a strained smile. "Mary, you wouldn't want that. Trust me." His expression turned serious. "I found out what's happening. Over four regiments are leaving for Washington."

"Oh, one of the wagon drivers told me," she replied. "I guess I can understand. But that won't change things, will it? I mean, it can't be that many soldiers?" By now many of the Hampton residents had heard about the disaster at Bull Run, yet another Union defeat. With all the soldiers at Fortress Monroe, it was no surprise that some would be sent to help protect the nation's capital.

"Mary, I don't want to upset you, but that's more than 4,000 soldiers. Half of all the men around here are leaving." Thomas looked at his wife, waiting for a reaction.

Mary looked confused. "I don't understand, Thomas. What does all this mean?"

He shook his head and placed his hands on her shoulders. "It means that they can't protect us anymore in Hampton. General Butler wants everyone to move east of Hampton Creek, either into Fortress Monroe of near Camp Hamilton." He looked into his wife's eyes. "We need to leave our home, Mary."

Mary peered across Hampton Roads at the large granite fort. "So James was right. They are leaving us."

"No, Mary. They're not leaving us. They'll still be plenty of soldiers. And they have all those big guns around the fort." Thomas hugged his wife and gently rubbed her back. "General Butler is just being careful, that's all." He stepped back and looked into her face again. "They'll be sending soldiers and wagons starting tomorrow to help everyone move their things."

"Where will we go?" Mary pointed at Fortress Monroe in the distance. "Will we have to move there?"

"Well, that's one of the reasons I came here. I remembered there are two rooms upstairs. I want to check on them. They may be big enough for us to move into." Thomas smiled weakly. "You wouldn't have to walk very far to school. Besides it'd be temporary until the soldiers returned. They're expected back in a month or so."

Mary turned to the cottage. "Well, I suppose it would better than living in some tent."

Over the next several days, near-chaos ensued. The streets were filled with men, women, and children loading wagons with crates of food, clothing, and treasured personal items. Furniture and other large items were left behind.

Mary and Thomas were busy going from room to room, setting aside whatever they planned to bring. Mary stood next to her favorite upholstered chair. "Thomas, can't we bring this? I do all my sewing here."

Thomas shook his head. "Mary, the only things we'll be able to fit in those two rooms are the beds, a small side chair, and this table." He placed his hand on a rectangular table only large enough to hold a lantern.

Daisy was tired of all the activity and sat in the corner reading her bird book.

"But how will I cook? And where will we eat?" Mary asked, with her hands on her hips.

Thomas shrugged. "We'll have to use the fireplace in your classroom to cook. The desks can be our kitchen table."

"Oh, Thomas." Mary's face crumbled.

Thomas put his big arms around her shoulders. "It's only for a short time. We'll manage."

Aided by two soldiers, they finished loading the wagon. Mary looked around her home, decorated simply but comfortably. Her heart was heavy as she closed the front door and walked to the wagon.

The wagon rolled slowly down the road. Mary looked back at her home. Thomas reached across Daisy, snuggled closely next to her mother, and squeezed Mary's hand. "Don't worry, Mary. It's not like our house is going anywhere. We'll be back before you know it." She looked at Thomas through tear-filled eyes and smiled tightly.

At the Mallory farm, James, Frank, and Shepard were busy filling a wagon with the few possessions the three slaves and their families had. The wagon contained mostly Union rations distributed earlier and saved for an emergency. Also important to the three men were their tools. Although worn with use, they represented the future for the three slaves, a future that would enable them to lead productive lives.

The three families were less disturbed about leaving the tiny shanties in which they lived behind the Mallory farmhouse. While the new accommodations would most likely not be as comfortable or familiar, the children saw this as a big adventure. James guided the wagon across Hampton Creek Bridge. His wife Millie was seated next to him along with Frank's wife, Sallie. Frank, Shepard, and the four children walked behind the wagon as curls of dust wafted in the soft breeze.

Butler sat behind his desk, composing a letter to the Secretary of War, Simon Cameron. In a rather lengthy letter, he confirmed the execution of Scott's orders to send over 4,000 troops to Washington. Butler highlighted the resulting need to move folks from Hampton into Union lines to ensure their safety.

Frustrated by Washington's failure to provide clear direction on the growing contraband population, which was only made worse by the departure of soldiers for the capital, Butler described the unfortunate event. "Indeed, it was a most distressing sight to see these poor creatures, who had trusted to the protection of the arms of the United States and who aided the troops of the United States in their enterprise, be thus obliged to flee from their homes and the homes of their masters who had deserted them, and become fugitives from fear of the return of the Rebel soldiery who had threatened to shoot the men who had wrought for us, and to carry off the women who had served us, to a worse than Egyptian bondage."

Butler continued writing for several more minutes. He looked at the multiple pages he had written and wondered if Cameron would have the patience to carefully read the entire letter. He felt that he logically presented his case, and if Cameron took the time, the war secretary would understand the issue. Butler knew that the brass in Washington, and President Lincoln particularly, was troubled by his contraband decision. Nonetheless, Butler felt it important to force the President's hand and that of Congress.

While Butler may have opened the door with his decision to provide sanctuary to the three escaped men, he knew slaves throughout the border states had been fleeing across Union lines. Without a clear policy from Washington, each commander had to decide how to deal with the problem. Many Union officers still complied with the Fugitive Slave Act and returned slaves to their owners. Others, like Butler, provided Union protection to the fleeing slaves and families.

Never one to shy away from stating his mind, Butler thought it important to reveal his personal thoughts on the matter to Cameron. He continued writing: "I confess that my own mind is compelled by this reasoning to look upon them as men and women. If not free-born, yet free, manumitted, sent forth from the hand that held them never to be reclaimed."

He thought about this logic for a few minutes and added, "Of course, if this reasoning, thus imperfectly set forth, is correct, my duty as a humane man is very plain. I should take the same care of these men, women, and children, houseless, homeless, and unprovided for, as I would of the same number of men, women, and children who, for their attachment to the Union, had been driven or allowed to flee from the Confederate States."

Butler reflected on the conflicting approaches officers exercised when dealing with slaves fleeing across Union borders. He knew that General McDowell, as an example, treated the slaves quite differently than he, generally forbidding fugitive slaves from coming within his lines.

Reading the letter from the top, Butler was quite pleased. Slightly concerned with his tone and realizing he was addressing a complex issue, he wrote in closing, "Pardon me for addressing the Secretary of War directly upon this question, as it involves some political considerations as well as propriety of military action. I am, sir, your obedient servant, Benjamin F. Butler."

Butler was eager to achieve a meaningful victory in battle. He wondered how long it would take for the 4,000 men to return to his command and when he could resume planning for attacks on key Confederate strongholds.

A knock interrupted his thoughts. Major Fay opened the door and escorted John LaMountain into the office. Butler stood and warmly greeted the aeronaut. "Mr. LaMountain, it's a pleasure to see you. I was just finishing a letter to Washington. I'll only be a minute more. Please have a seat." Butler sat down and signed the letter. He sealed it in an official envelope and handed it to Fay.

"Please see that this makes its way to Washington with urgency, Major." Butler nodded to his senior aide.

"Yes, General." Fay nodded back and left the room.

Butler turned to LaMountain. "So how are your flights going? Have you been able to gain any intelligence at Sewell's Point?"

"General, due to the orientation of the peninsula and the easterly wind, I'm afraid I can't launch the balloon far enough south without risking the chance of getting carried out over Hampton Roads." LaMountain shook his head in frustration.

Butler sought for a possible solution. "Mr. LaMountain, on the day you arrived here, you indicated it might be possible to have your balloon tethered to a boat and pulled?"

LaMountain, recalling his comment, said, "Well, if the connection is secure and the balloon is kept leeward of the boat, it could be possible. I would think the main challenges would be upon launching and then landing the balloon. But, yes, I think it could be done. If you can have someone show me the boat we would propose to use, I will spend tomorrow trying to solve these issues."

Later that day LaMountain headed down to the wharf to inspect the gunboat called *Fanny*. He determined the boat was sufficiently sturdy and powerful to pull the balloon against the expected wind resistance. Also there was adequate space on the deck to secure a windlass of sufficient size along with the required mooring lines. Based on the easterly winds of the past few days, which were expected to continue, LaMountain thought it best if they could launch the balloon as far west as possible and then travel east into the wind.

After talking with some of the soldiers, the decision was made to load the partially inflated balloon and basket onto the *Fanny* and to travel to the vicinity of Newport News Point. While holding the boat steady into the wind, the balloon would then be fully inflated. As the balloon began to rise, the windlass would crank out additional line so that the balloon could slowly gain altitude. Once the balloon achieved maximum height, the boat would slowly proceed east through Hampton Roads towards Chesapeake Bay where LaMountain would have a clear view of Sewell's Point.

Early the next morning, *Fanny* left the wharf and headed west towards the James River. People along the northern shore stared at the boat with its strange cargo on deck. LaMountain instructed the sailors to travel as far as Newport News Point, not quite into the James River but just south of Camp Butler. At that point, the boat reversed direction and reoriented into an easterly heading, dropping anchor. The crew carefully guided the partially filled balloon over the rear deck. As the boat held steady in the waves, LaMountain completed the tedious process of filling the balloon.

With the balloon fully inflated, the basket was only a few feet off the deck. LaMountain climbed into the basket, as crewmembers slowly turned the crank on the large windlass to begin unwinding the mooring line. The balloon slowly gained altitude as winds pushed LaMountain away from the boat. The process continued for thirty minutes until the mooring line was fully extended and the balloon reached a height of over a thousand feet.

The boat slowly headed east back towards Fortress Monroe. LaMountain was shocked by the view looking south. He was certain he could see Norfolk and the surrounding area. He noted several Confederate positions in and around Norfolk.

Continuing east, the boat was careful to maintain an adequate distance from the south shore, staying beyond the range of Confederate guns at Sewell's Point. They continued east towards Camp Calhoun in the middle of Hampton Roads. At that point, the boat stopped as LaMountain carefully observed the Rebel fortification at Sewell's Point. He took out a sketchpad and drew a detailed map of what he saw, showing earthworks, tents, and batteries. Strangely enough, the boat, with its extended crow's nest, seemed to go unnoticed by the Confederate troops.

The boat slowly steamed back to the wharf, stopping about 200 feet short. The process used to launch the balloon was reversed. The windlass was rotated in the opposite direction to pull the balloon in. The men quickly realized that it was much easier extending the mooring line than rewinding it. They took turns so they wouldn't tire quickly. After an hour of hard work, the balloon almost reached the deck. LaMountain slowly released the balance of the hot air from the balloon and the basket gently settled onto the deck of the *Fanny*.

Back at Butler's office, LaMountain reviewed his sketch of Sewell's Point and described his observations around Norfolk. Butler's enthusiasm for the aeronaut continued. With the military intelligence he now possessed, Butler could recommence planning attacks on Yorktown and Norfolk as soon as his troops returned.

"General, I can probably complete two more flights before I anticipate running out of gas. Perhaps one at sea and one on land," LaMountain said.

"Well then, let's make the best of it and hope we have a good grasp of all Confederate positions. Even if we're not able to use the information for immediate offensive purposes, we'll at least understand where we're vulnerable to attack until our troops return," Butler said.

On LaMountain's last flight, he encountered sporadic cloud cover as he drifted over the countryside. His view was partially obstructed, so he failed to spot a large Confederate force moving towards Fortress Monroe. With 4,000 infantry, 400 cavalry, and a howitzer battalion, the Rebels were only a few miles west of Hampton.

S EVERAL DAYS HAD PASSED SINCE OVER 4,000 Union troops departed for Washington. The Hampton streets were eerily quiet, abandoned by inhabitants over the past week for the security and protection of Fortress Monroe. Only a few people remained; too elderly, too ill, or too stubborn to move from their homes. Even the Confederates were conspicuously calm. Despite a few minor incidents west and north of Hampton, no major altercations had taken place since Big Bethel.

The sun was low in the sky. Butler sat slumped in his favorite stuffed chair holding a generous glass of red wine. His uniform top was thrown haphazardly onto the floor. He was in a pensive, melancholy mood. The first week of August was a trying time for Butler. In addition to the troops leaving, Sarah had departed for Massachusetts. He recalled her parting words, pleading with Butler to join her. She knew that the burden of duty weighed heavily on her husband, and she was reluctant to leave. But after being away from her children for over two months, she was desperate to be reunited with them.

Butler's hand trembled as he read his wife's letter. He took a swallow of wine. "You will not be surprised at this deep sadness which held me even up to our gate, without one throb of pleasant expectation at sight of home and all until I heard the sound of the voices of the children playing in the evergreens.'

He set the goblet on a side table and leaned forward. "They saw the carriage and ran to us with shouts of delight. The driver stopped, and they clambered into the hack with such a noise, screaming, 'Here is mother, and we thought father was coming too. Where is he? And why did he not come?' They think you ought not to be away so long." Butler set down the letter on his lap and stared at the blank wall. *How long has it been?* he thought. "Let's see," he calculated out loud, "I left Boston on April 18 and it's now it's August 6. Three and a half months." He closed his eyes and shook his bowed head.

A picture of his children in a gold frame stood on the table next to the half-empty wine bottle. Butler took a sip of wine and set the glass down. With a sorrowful look, he held the picture in both hands. It had been taken in a portrait studio just before he departed for Baltimore earlier this year. His beautiful daughter Blanche was fourteen but looked so much older. Paul II was nine, and Ben-Israel was six. He suspected they would have grown a good inch or two since he last saw them. How he missed them all. He put the picture down and pulled out his handkerchief. He wiped his eyes and blew his nose.

The next morning Butler woke well before sunrise, back to his restless, sleepless nights. He walked down to the wharf area to see LaMountain off. The aeronaut had completed his last flight before exhausting his supplies. With the help of several troops, his balloons and other paraphernalia were loaded onto an early morning steamboat. Butler thanked the man for his invaluable support over the past few weeks and bid him farewell. Based on the aeronaut's intelligence, Butler was well prepared for the Confederates spotted from the air outside Young's Mill. He had sent reinforcements to Newport News Point and alerted his troops there to be prepared for Rebel attacks.

That very morning, General Magruder tried provoking the Union into a battle by displaying his forces outside Camp Butler's earthworks. Hoping to draw the enemy into the open, Magruder was disappointed as Union troops remained safely within their heavily armed entrenchments. An unexpected windfall for the Confederates was the discovery of a telegraph line suspected to connect Camp Butler with Fortress Monroe. After failing to obtain a device that would enable the Confederates to intercept Union transmissions, Marguder ordered the line to be severed.

Daisy was frantic. After class ended, she ran upstairs to rummage through the two makeshift bedrooms. Mary was busy organizing the benches and desks in the large classroom after wagons arrived to retrieve the children. The tapping of her daughter's footsteps and the scraping of shifting furniture reverberated through the second story floorboards. Mary looked up at the dusty ceiling and followed the sounds of her daughter's movements.

Making her way back down the stairs and into the front room, Daisy shuffled over to her mother. Her lower lip drooped and her shoulders slumped. "Mama, I can't find my bird book." She pulled on Mary's faded flowered dress and looked up. "I looked everywhere. Have you seen it?"

"Oh, Daisy. I remember seeing you reading it a few days ago when we went back home for some dishes. Do you remember?" Mary held her daughter's face gently between her hands. "Do you think you left it there?"

"Darn! Darn!" Daisy stamped her foot. "Can we go get it, Mama? Please?"

"Daisy, it's not necessary to throw a tantrum. I'm sure your book is safe," Mary said.

"But I want it. Can we go now?" Daisy persisted.

Mary placed her hands on her hips. "I'll tell you what. When Papa gets here, we'll ask him if we can all walk back home. I need a few things myself, but I could use his strong arms to help me carry them." She smiled, leaning over and pinching her daughter's nose. "Now please put these books on the shelf, and then you can help me prepare dinner. We're having Hoppin' John stew." Mary smiled.

"I hate cooked peas," Daisy pouted as she collected the books. "They're all mushy."

The sun was low in the sky as Mary, Thomas, and Daisy walked across Hampton Creek Bridge. A wagon and several Union soldiers were at the far end of the bridge. The men were milling about inspecting the wooden structure. A few men seemed to be prying up boards with a large iron bar. The activity stopped when they noticed Mary and her family approaching the western end of the bridge.

"Mr. Peake! Miss Peake!" Thomas and Mary turned as they passed the men, startled by the sound of their names. "Where're you going?" Shepard climbed over the railing and approached the family.

"Shepard, what a surprise! What are you doing here?" Mary asked.

The young slave turned and pointed. "I'm with these soldiers. I'm not sure what we're supposed to do yet, but I was sent to help." He shrugged with a crooked smile. "We just got here a little while ago."

"We're just going back to our home to pick up a few items." Mary draped her arms around her daughter. "Daisy left something very precious there. It seems like we go back almost every day to get something we either forgot or need." Mary smiled at the young man who had bravely scouted for Butler and the Union.

The shout of a soldier quickly ended the conversation. "Well, I guess I better get back." Shepard nodded and walked away.

When they got within sight of their home in Hampton, Daisy bolted up the walk and slammed the front door open. By time her parents reached the stoop, Daisy appeared with a gratified grin. Her arms were wrapped around her beloved bird book. While walking past her into the house, Mary smiled and patted her daughter on the head. "You found it! I'm so relieved." She rolled her eyes at Thomas, who chuckled.

Daisy followed her parents into the kitchen. Mary searched the cabinets for a special pot. She knew it would be large enough for a big batch of stew. And with a heavy metal handle, it was ideal for hanging on the pot crane in the cottage fireplace. Cooking at the brown cottage was a challenge. Mary missed her home and especially her oven.

"There it is." Mary bent over and pulled out the scratched, dented pot. She cringed as other pots and pans clanked and tumbled into the void. "Just one more thing and we can leave." She smiled at Thomas, who patiently watched from a kitchen chair.

Daisy walked over, placed her bird book on the table, and climbed onto her father's lap. "Papa, can we spend the night here?"

Thomas helped his daughter up. "Daisy, don't you remember? We moved our beds to the cottage. There's nowhere to sleep, baby." He supported Daisy with his hands as he moved his leg up and down, given her a little ride.

"W-w-h-h-e-e-e-e!" Daisy laughed. "We could sleep on the floor. And the sofa is still in the sitting room." She reached up and threw her arms around the big man's neck. "Please, Papa! Please?"

Thomas's knee went still as he turned to his wife. "You want to help here?" He looked at Mary through desperate eyes.

Mary sat on the kitchen floor. "Oh, Thomas, I guess it wouldn't hurt to spend the night here." She smiled lovingly at her husband while suppressing a laugh. "It may be weeks before we can move back. Besides it's getting late." She angled her head to the side. "And it might even be kind of fun."

"Yah!" Daisy shouted in celebration with her arms high in the air.

"You call that help?" Thomas said to his wife, more as a statement than a question. He shook his head and winked, breaking into a big grin.

Daisy was curled up under a light blanket on the sofa, sound asleep. Thomas and Mary were on the hard floor, poorly padded with some old blankets. For the past hour, Mary had shifted from side to side trying to get comfortable. She thought she could feel every ridge and ripple in the wooden planks. Morning couldn't arrive soon enough, even if it would bring aches and pains with it. After a string of deep sighs and groans, she and Thomas were both finally breathing peacefully.

Mary rolled onto her back. Half asleep, she thought she heard voices pass by their home, just outside the window. She craned her head, listening intently. Not detecting anything after a brief moment, Mary suspected it was most likely a dream and closed her eyes. Her nostrils flared as the smell of burnt wood wafted from the stove. It seemed peculiar to her, particularly since it hadn't been used in almost a week. Then again, she thought, she's never slept on the floor and so close to the kitchen. Her childlike smile faded as she drifted off again.

A short time later, a loud pounding echoed through the house. Mary, in the fog of sleep, noticed a hazy light coming in from the front window. She was surprised but grateful that their agonizing night was almost over. "Did you hear something?" Thomas mumbled, groggy and still lying on his side but sensing Mary's movement.

Through bleary eyes, Mary watched the daylight shimmer and flicker as she lay on the floor. *What an odd sensation*, she thought. *It must be the trees casting shadows on the window.* "I'm not sure. I think it was something outside. But the sun's finally coming up, thank the Lord." She smiled as she closed her eyes and yawned.

A second loud knock startled them both. Mary and Thomas sat up. She was disoriented, her neck was stiff and her head dizzy as she looked out the window. Her nostrils flared with the smell of smoke, more intense now. The pattern of sunlight through the window was unnatural. "Mr. and Miss Peake, wake up!" Someone yelled from outside.

Mary jumped up and staggered to the door, pulling it open. Shepard stood on the front stoop out of breath, a wide-eyed and panicked look across his face. The heat from outside surged into the house. Mary's initial reaction was that the air was unusually warm, even for the middle of the summer. "You need to get out!" he shouted.

Looking over Shepard's shoulder, Mary spotted flames rising from the small wooden homes across the street. The dark sky radiated an orange, raging fire. Still groggy, she stepped out onto the front stoop. The town was aglow in every direction. But it wasn't morning. It was still nighttime. Smoke filled the air. Excruciating cries and a few gunshots could be heard in the distance. "Hurry! We don't have much time," Shepard pleaded.

Thomas appeared by her side, holding Daisy in his arms still wrapped in her blanket. "Quick, get your shoes on," he yelled to Mary.

Mary and Thomas, clutching Daisy, followed Shepard into the road. Looking around, Mary realized that they were in the middle of a blazing inferno. Flames climbed up the exterior walls of their home and licked the roof. The curtains in Daisy's upstairs bedroom window glowed red. Thick smoke stung Mary's eyes and poisoned her lungs. The hissing and popping of burning wood filled the air.

"Follow me," Shepard waved to the family. "Put something over your nose and mouth and run low." As they fled, Thomas covered Daisy's face with the blanket.

Shepard led the group down a side street. In the distance, Mary could see smoke billowing from the tower of Saint John's Church. The bells clanged discordantly as the heat and the heavy wind made them swing to and fro. Red and orange embers sparkled as they soared from the courthouse roof. Strong southern winds fanned the fire, which leapt from home to home and building to building. After several days of dry weather, the flames quickly spread on wood thirsty as kindling.

Staggering through the thick smoke, the group shielded their faces with their arms. The heat was so intense, Mary thought her eyes would melt in their sockets. She was surrounded by gusts of sweltering air that rushed in behind searing updrafts. It was difficult to determine where the road ended and the fiery lawns started. Mary held on tight to Thomas's shirttail. Clutching Daisy close to his body, he closely followed Shepard through the blistering labyrinth.

A large flaming tree fell across the road only several paces in front of them. "This way!" Shepard screamed, pointing to the left. He led the group through a side yard, between two homes engulfed in flames. Mary spotted a child's toy horse on a windowsill, leaning against the glowing glass.

Wheezing and holding her cramping side, she stumbled to the ground. Mary watched the back of Thomas's shirt disappear into the swirling smoke. She looked down at the tree root that snagged her foot. Her ankle throbbed in pain, and her mouth tasted fire. *How did this start?* She was disoriented and couldn't remember in which direction the group fled. Certain that she was about to perish in the flames, Mary hoped that Thomas and Daisy would make it out alive.

A hand from behind pulled her to her feet. "Stay low, Miss Peake. Follow me."

"I can't walk. I injured my ankle." Mary yelled.

"Lean on me. I'll help you." Shepard pulled Mary's arm around his neck and wrapped his arm around her waist. Supporting much of her weight, he guided Mary through the mayhem. They broke through the smoke and stumbled into the road on the next block where Thomas was anxiously waiting with Daisy. The air there felt slightly less oppressive, and the smoke seemed to be thinning. Mary's breathing was shallow and labored.

"Where're you taking us? The bridge is that way." Thomas pointed down King Street.

As they hobbled, Shepard looked back. "The bridge is out. We need to go this way."

"What do you mean it's out? Did it burn?" Thomas said as he cradled Daisy and gasped for air. Daisy was crying and coughing under her blanket.

"No," Shepard said as they turned towards Hampton Creek. "The Union soldiers dismantled it so the Rebels couldn't cross."

Thomas winced against the heat. "You didn't know this when you saw us earlier?"

As they neared the edge of town, Shepard stopped in a large clearing of dry grass and trees. "They told me after you crossed." Thomas sat Daisy on the ground. All three adults were leaning over with hands on their knees, coughing and gasping for air. "I figured you must still be in town since the bridge was out and you couldn't get back," Shepard said.

Thomas softened his tone between gasps. "Well, thank you for remembering us."

Mary's face and clothes were covered in soot and sweat. Her dress was torn, and her knees were dirty and bloody from the fall. She rubbed her eyes. "Shepard, we're so grateful you came for us. There's no telling what would have happened if…" Mary placed her quivering hand to her mouth unable to finish the sentence. She looked at Daisy and turned back to the town, tears streaming down her grimy cheeks, leaving crooked streaks in their wake. Daisy wrapped her arms around her mother's legs. "Dear Lord, it's like fiery demons are fanning the flames of hell," Mary muttered.

"After we finished the bridge, I went back to the Mallory farm to get some tools." Shepard stood up and wiped his face on his sleeve. "When I was coming back, that's when I saw those crazy Rebels running through the streets torching everything in sight."

"The Rebels did this?" Mary looked at the blazing town in disbelief. "It doesn't make any sense. Why would they burn the town? Some of these men have homes here." Mary frowned. Grabbing Shepard by the arm, she looked into his bloodshot eyes. "Where are the Union soldiers? Why aren't they here? Why aren't those big guns from the fort firing on the Rebels?" She turned to Thomas and shouted. "You said they could reach Hampton!"

"I don't know, ma'am." Shepard shook his head and shrugged.

Thomas was still bent over, breathless and parched, with closed eyes and clenched fists.

After failing to draw the Union into battle at Camp Butler, Magruder positioned his troops outside Hampton. While he was observing the town through the thick brush, someone handed the Confederate general a Northern newspaper. With great interest, he read an article discussing the evacuation of Union troops for Washington. Scanning the same page, another article revealed Union plans to use the vacant homes of Confederate-loyal citizens as winter quarters for the returning soldiers and the growing contraband population. Magruder was outraged. Rather than let the enemy use Hampton as a haven for runaway slaves and allow the Union to further denigrate Confederate homeland, he gave the order to set fire to the town.

Some of the Confederate soldiers were shocked by the proposed action, particularly those men who owned homes there. However, word had spread that some Union soldiers had written obscenities on the walls and had even used some homes as latrines. Ultimately, they agreed to sacrifice their own homes but expressed concern over the likelihood of the whole town perishing.

There was one request by local soldiers, which the Confederate officers reluctantly granted. They knew of thirty to forty citizens, ill or aged, still residing in Hampton. A small group of Confederates were granted a brief time advantage to empty the town before others, carrying torches, were fast on their heels.

Magruder knew he would never be successful attacking Fortress Monroe, but hoped that the conflagration would draw Union troops from Newport News Point. He had positioned troops along the route to engage them. LaMountain's aerial observations had proved enormously useful to Butler and the Union. However, on his last flight, clouds had obstructed the view of Magruder's troops, lurking outside Hampton, posed to attack.

"We need to go." Shepard led them down the bank towards Hampton Creek.

"Shepard, we can't cross the river!" Thomas cried, looking to the distant shoreline and the violent, foaming rapids in between. "We're not good swimmers, and Daisy can't even tread water. Besides the current's too strong." They followed Shepard along the water's edge through tall reeds. Waves lapped up on the rocky shore.

"There're two small boats up ahead we use for fishing. Take one of them across the river, and you'll be safe." Shepard led the group to a small sandy area. The boats lay side by side far enough from the water to not drift away in high tide.

Thomas put Daisy down in the grass near Mary. He helped Shepard pull one of the boats so that the bow entered the water. "Are you going to take the other boat?" Mary asked.

"I will. But I have to go back to town to make sure Mr. and Mrs. Brown are safe." He anxiously looked back at the roaring inferno.

"No, Shepard, it's not safe," Mary pleaded, grasping the young man's arm.

"I have to. They're very old, and Mrs. Brown can barely walk. I know I can get there and back with them safely. I'll be fine, Miss Peake." Shepard nodded. "Now you need to get going. Climb in and I'll push the boat out into the water."

Daisy had never been in a boat before and was in shock. Mary waded into the shallow water, and Shepard helped her climb in. Thomas picked Daisy up and set her into the boat next to Mary. The small vessel rocked from side to side. Daisy clung to her mother with panicked eyes. Shepard guided the boat into deeper water and Thomas carefully climbed in. With a gentle push, the boat glided out into the river's turbulent current. Thomas grabbed the oars and watched as Shepard turned and ran up the riverbank, disappearing into the churning smoke.

"Oh, Thomas. I'm so worried." Mary clutched Daisy with both arms, determined not to let her daughter out of her sight again.

Thomas rowed the boat into the middle of the river towards the eastern shore. Mary looked back at the town's skyline. Buildings were no longer distinguishable in the firestorm. Her world was disappearing as smoke ascended high into the heavens.

Union troops had advanced to the eastern shore of Hampton Creek. With a large section of the bridge dismantled by their own men earlier, they could only fretfully watch the town burn. Butler sat on his horse in the distance, witnessing the devastation. He shook his head in disgust and guided his horse back to the fort. Easily within range of the guns of Fortress Monroe, the Confederates were surprised that no Union action was taken.

The Rebel troops lingered along the town perimeter until just before sunrise. Horrified soldiers watched as the town was consumed in the blaze. A local newspaper would later capture the sentiments of a Confederate soldier who helped ignite the fires. "By the time we had reached the corner of King and Court Streets, the Baptist Church was burning like an inferno—the flames belching out of the steeple like a furnace. The smoke ascending toward the heavens reminded me of the ancient sacrifices on the altar to many deities and our little town was being made a sacrifice to the grim god of war. As we filed out of the town, there rested in the hearts of each of us the realization of a great sacrifice nobly made, and the heroic satisfaction of a soldier's duty well performed."

23

BUTLER SAT SLOUCHED ON HIS HORSE WITH the reins loose in his hands. A handful of soldiers followed the Union commander as they wound their way through the streets of Hampton. The somber mood and plodding pace were reminiscent of a funeral procession. Ashes swirled in the warm, dusty breeze as embers still smoldered where houses once stood.

The beauty and vastness of the deep blue sky was in cruel contrast to the blackened, scorched landscape. The strong scent of charred wood saturated the air. Butler was shocked that an entire town could vanish overnight. Of the approximately 500 homes and buildings, he estimated that maybe only seven or eight still stood.

It was early afternoon. Troops had repaired Hampton Creek Bridge that morning so that it was now passable. Butler entered the town with a full Union regiment in search of survivors and casualties. He knew that some people were unable to evacuate the town days earlier, either too ill or elderly to do so. A few wouldn't leave their possessions behind in fear of pillaging.

He passed by Old Saint John's Church and paused. Constructed on the site in 1762, Butler had heard that the church was heavily damaged in the Revolutionary War and the War of 1812. After repairs and a series of additions over the years, the church served as a religious beacon to the Hampton community. He recalled the joyful day two months earlier, when sixteen contraband couples were married there in a formal ceremony. All that remained of the church were its blackened walls. Butler shook his head and whispered under his breath, "What a shame."

A Union war correspondent accompanying Butler was visibly shaken. He wiped his eyes with the back of a hand and shook his head in disbelief. He would later write, "There was nothing left but a forest of bleak-sided chimneys and walls of brick homes tottering and cooling in the wind, scorched and seared trees and heaps of smoldering ruins."

The correspondent said to Butler. "I've never seen such a picture of desolation."

Butler bit his lower lip. He gripped his reins and gently kicked the sides of his horse, trying to outrun the images flickering in his mind. The group followed closely as they approached an intersection.

Captain Haggerty, with several troops and a wagon in tow, came from the opposite direction and rode over to Butler. "Sir, we found bodies along the east riverbank." He pointed to the canvas covered wagon. "It looks like they tried to swim across Hampton Creek and drowned. We're making our way through the town looking for more casualties."

"How dreadful. This whole thing is such a calamity," Butler said in disgust. He was transfixed by the wagon. His body shuddered, recalling the dreadful aftermath of the Big Bethel fiasco and the lifeless bodies mounded on a wagon. "How many casualties are there, Peter?"

"We found four so far, sir." Haggerty's expression turned somber. "Sir." Haggerty hesitated. "The young slave Shepard was one of them."

Butler almost fell off his horse. "Oh, Peter," he groaned. "Tell me it's not so. Are you sure?" His gaze shifted back to the wagon.

"I'm sorry, sir. We retrieved his body a short while ago." Haggerty watched his commander with concern. "It appears he made it across the river but was shot in the back," he said, wincing. "He was lying next to a boat he must have used to cross."

Butler stared at the wagon. He found himself light-headed and swallowed hard. "Thank you, Peter. Please let me know if you find any more casualties." Butler nodded and continued down the road with his head down.

Traveling another few blocks, Butler could see people in the distance searching through the ruins. Concerned with scavengers, he urged his horse forward. As he approached, Butler recognized the familiar faces of the Peake family. He pulled back on the reins.

Mary looked up, startled by the whinny of a horse. She and Thomas were picking through the charred timbers that once held up the roof of their incinerated home. She wiped the soot and sweat from her forehead onto a soiled sleeve. Mary carefully stepped through the debris and walked towards the road. With a strained smile, she said, "Good afternoon, General."

Butler dismounted. "Mary, I'm so sorry about your home." He nodded to Thomas who was sifting through rubble where their kitchen once stood.

She looked around at the remains of her home, the neighborhood, and her town. The enormity of the devastation overwhelmed her.

Mary put her face in her hands and wept. Thomas stepped over the smoking embers and put his arm around his wife. She buried her face in his broad chest.

"I'm deeply sorry for your loss," Butler said, looking at Thomas. He had trouble finding any more words to console the couple and fumbled with the buttons on his jacket. They all stood in silence for a few awkward minutes.

Eventually Mary turned her head. "We lost everything, General. Our furniture and all our other possessions." She pointed to an object lying under a large charred beam. "The only thing left is my stove. And I'm not sure it can ever be repaired." She shrugged weakly. "But our home can be rebuilt and our furniture can be replaced or remade." She attempted a determined look. "A wise Greek philosopher once said that happiness resides not in possessions and not in gold, but dwells in the soul." Her tired eyes scanned the horizon like a hunted animal, reconciled that it was about to be slaughtered. "At least, we're all safe."

Daisy was weeping, sitting on the scorched grass that was once their modest front yard. Her face and hands were covered with dirt and ash. She held a blackened book. Its pages were burnt beyond recognition.

Butler looked down and nodded at Daisy. "What's she holding?"

Mary walked over to Daisy and kissed her daughter on the top of her head. The usual calming lemon scent of her hair was replaced by the bitter smell of smoke and cinders. "It was her favorite book—a birding guide. My father gave it to me when I was a young girl. And I gave it to Daisy." She let out a deep sigh and looked back at Butler. "Daisy forgot it here a few days ago. We came back last evening to get it and a few other things. We decided to spend one last night and..." Her words trailed off as she looked back at her razed home. Her chin quivered. Mary took the burnt book from Daisy's hands.

Butler's body went rigid. "You mean you were here during the fire?" Deep creases lined his forehead and his mouth gaped open.

"Yes, we were so lucky to get out alive," Mary said, recalling the dreadful escape.

"If it wasn't for Shepard, we wouldn't be here," Thomas added, shaking his head.

Butler shuddered. "Well, I'm so relieved you're all safe," he said, thankful but also suddenly uncomfortable.

Mary noticed his change in mood. "Was anyone injured in the fire, General?"

"I'm afraid there were a few casualties." Butler shifted from one foot to the other not meeting her eyes. "We found an elderly couple still in their bed. And we heard that the Confederates captured a few slaves and may have pressed them back into service."

Mary turned to her husband. "Oh, Thomas. Shepard went back to get Mr. and Mrs. Brown. I hope it wasn't them." She turned to Butler. "Do you know the names of the coupled who died?"

Butler shook his head. "I'm sorry, Mary. I'm afraid I don't." Butler opened his mouth to say more but stopped.

Frowning, Mary asked anxiously, "Do you know which slaves were captured?"

"I don't, Mary. I'm afraid we're just collecting that information." Butler shrugged. "And some people are still unaccounted for."

"I hope Shepard wasn't captured. I would feel just horrible. He saved our lives."

Butler's face was as pale as ash. "He wasn't, Mary."

"Oh, I'm so grateful, General." Mary hesitated, noticing Butler's distraught expression. "What is it? Do you know something more about Shepard?"

Butler looked directly at Thomas and nodded. His drooping

mustache partially hid his lower lip, which was wedged under his bite. Thomas closed his eyes and reached over to hold Mary.

She looked from one man to the other, terror dawning across her face. "What is it? What aren't you telling me?" she shouted.

"I'm so sorry, Mary." Butler's eyes glistened.

Mary could feel her throat constricting, her heart pounding in her chest, and the sound of blood rushing through her ears.

"We found Shepard this morning." Butler extended a hand to comfort her.

Mary slapped it away. "What do you mean, you found him?" Mary was wide-eyed. She pushed Thomas away and put her face in front of Butler's. Bordering on hysteria, she demanded, "Where is he? What's happened?"

Thomas reached from behind and restrained his wife. Mary struggled to remove his hands.

"Some of our soldiers found his body on the east shore of Hampton Creek."

Mary's face shriveled in anguish.

"Mary, I'm so sorry." Butler hesitated. With his head down and eyes closed, he said in a low voice, "He was next to an overturned boat."

Thomas asked quietly, "Did he drown?"

Mary was weeping so hard she had trouble catching her breath. She still held the burnt book under an arm. Butler shook his head. "It appears he made it across the river. We found a few other bodies. They must have tried to swim across the river but didn't make it."

"But you said Shepard made it to the other side. He had a boat. We used the other boat to cross ourselves. What happened?" Thomas pressed.

In a soft whisper so that the child could not overhear, Butler said,

"He was shot in the back." He swallowed hard. His voice was strained. "I suspect once he crossed, the Rebels chose to shoot him rather than let him go free."

Mary turned. Her face was dripping with tears. She was breathing heavily. Her words started softly and controlled. "Why didn't you stop them? You have all those men and guns. Why couldn't you stop them?" She looked at the Union officer in desperation.

With slumped shoulders, Butler said, "Mary, this was a decision that the Confederates made to burn their own town. It wasn't my business to stop them. My responsibility is to my men and the fort."

Her voice grew louder. Her tone became sharper. Her fist and teeth were clenched. "But you were protecting us. You gave these people shelter. They trusted you. This was their town too." She waved her arm around, enraged. "Now there's nothing. Just look! There's nothing left."

Butler stood still with his arms by his sides. He closed his eyes.

"What good are all those guns? You could have easily stopped them. You let this town burn and people died because of that." Mary was shrieking. Thomas tried to restrain her, to calm her down in front of their daughter and the general, but she pushed him away. She pointed at Butler's chest. "You killed Shepard just as if you pulled the trigger yourself." She stepped forward and pounded Butler's chest with her fist. "You killed Shepard! You killed Shepard!" she yelled, bursting into tears.

Two soldiers moved in to restrain Mary. Butler held up his hand to stop them. "I'm sorry, Mary. I'm sorry you feel this way, and I'm certainly sorry about Shepard. I was fond of him as well." He grabbed her wrist gently. Thomas moved to aid his wife. Soldiers stepped in to block him.

"I did what I thought was appropriate and necessary." Butler shook his head and spoke softly. "I don't expect you to understand, Mary. And I didn't know you and your family were here last night." He looked at Daisy and then back to Mary. "If I had, I assure you I would've sent in my troops." He released her arm. He nodded to his men to release Thomas.

Butler placed his foot in the stirrup and mounted his horse. "I'm sorry, Mary. I am so, so sorry," he said.

Mary wiped the tears streaming down her cheeks. "Go back behind your big stone walls where you'll be safe and let us pick through the ashes of our lives." She flung the burnt book at Butler; pages fluttered as the book narrowly missed his head.

Butler rode back through the town with his head lowered in deep despair. Back in his office, sitting behind his desk, he tried writing to General Scott, but his hand couldn't stop shaking. He knew he urgently needed to capture the tragic event in a full report, but his mind kept drifting back to Mary and the ravaged town.

His thoughts also turned to Shepard. He recalled when he first met the young, spirited slave in his office. At that time Butler never could have imagined Shepard would have become so useful to the Union cause as a scout. He sat back and closed his eyes, trying to erase the memories. Within minutes he was fast asleep.

Over an hour later Butler was startled awake by the sound of cannon fire. He leapt out of his chair and staggered to the window, his head still groggy. He sighed in relief when he realized his troops were conducting artillery practice.

He sat back down and dipped his pen in the ink well. Organizing his thoughts, he started in on the letter. "A more wanton and unnecessary act than the burning, it seems to me, could not have been committed. There was not the slightest attempt to make any resistance on our part to the possession of the town, which we had before evacuated, as you were informed by my last dispatch. It would have been easy to dislodge them from the town by a few shells from the fort, but I did not choose to allow any opportunity to fasten upon the federal troops any portion of this heathenish outrage."

Remembering Mary's stinging words, he rubbed his left temple and continued. "I confess myself so poor a soldier as not to be able to discern the strategic importance of this movement." He informed Scott that the earthworks recently constructed near the cemetery were not destroyed.

Having learned from Captain Haggerty that the motivation of the Rebel action was to prevent the Union troops from using the Hampton homes as winter quarters, Butler added, "The poor citizens were told by their friends that this destruction was to prevent the use of their village as winter quarters for our troops. But I am sure it never entered my mind, and, I take leave to believe, the mind of the Commanding General, that there was the furthest intention of wintering any portion of the federal troops at this point outside the garrison."

Butler informed Scott that the Rebels had completely withdrawn back across New Market Bridge. He acknowledged his decision to evacuate Hampton after many of his troops were sent to Washington. He continued writing. "I regret the military necessity, to which I yield the cordial recognition of my judgment, which called for the withdrawal of the four and a half regiments, which caused the evacuation of Hampton, not for our sakes, but because of the loss which has thereby been brought upon the inhabitants."

He placed his pen down and ran his fingers through his thinning, gray hair. Butler thought about the extreme hatred the Rebels had shown the Union by destroying their own homes out of spite. He picked up the pen. "This act upon the part of the enemy seems to me to be a representative one, showing the spirit in which the war is to be carried out on their part, and which perhaps will have a tendency to provoke a corresponding spirit upon our part, but we may hope not."

Butler stood up and walked back over to his office window. Looking at the troops and horses exercising in the parade grounds, and the large guns mounted on the granite walls, he was amazed at the awesome power at his disposal. Yet as he thought about his confrontation with Mary earlier that day, it all proved useless in preventing the destruction of a town and the pain and suffering of so many people. He wondered out loud as he stared at his reflection in the glass, "Should I have done more to protect the town?"

He massaged his temples, trying to relieve a looming headache. He wished that he had left with Sarah and was back home with his children, away from the violence of Hampton Roads. Butler closed his eyes and quietly sobbed. Mary's harsh words pierced his heart like a bayonet. The worst of all, he knew she was right.

After staring out the window a while longer, he returned to his desk. Butler slumped in his chair and wondered if he had the strength to carry on through this dreadful conflict. Haggerty had placed the notes of the Union war correspondent who witnessed the fire on the corner of his desk. Butler picked up the paper and shuddered as he read the haunting words. "House after house and building after building melted like wax before the fiery element, and threw the lurid glare up to the sky. A long, heavy line of clouds floated away from the Fortress Monroe as if crying for help for the poor village."

24

BUTLER'S ARMS FLAILED AS HE DESPERATELY reached for the woman. Union soldiers held his shoulders tight, struggling to restrain him. Mary howled in pain. With arms extended, her hands flexed open, begging for help. Red and orange flames licked her body. Her legs were quickly weakening, about to collapse beneath her. Shimmering sparks ascended into the air from where dark hair once covered her head. Her soft skin was melting like wax. Blood streamed from the corners of her big brown eyes, dripping off her chin.

He ordered his men to release him, but they wouldn't comply. Butler shouted at them, totally bewildered as to why they wouldn't go to Mary's aid or at least let him rescue the poor suffering woman. He reached out his arm and called to her in desperation. Mary turned slowly and lifted her head. She pointed at Butler. Arm and hand lacked flesh. Pale bone glowed red. As she collapsed backwards into the raging inferno, Mary called out in a low, prolonged moan, "Why?"

Captain Haggerty shook the general. "Sir, wake up! Wake up!"

Butler's body lurched forward. Startled, he realized it had been a horrible nightmare. His heart raced as his chest heaved to catch his breath. Beads of sweat dotted his forehead and upper lip. Butler held up his hand. "I'm fine, Captain. I must have fallen asleep." He shook his head trying to erase the horrifying images.

"We've all been under a lot of stress lately, and we haven't had much sleep, sir. Especially you," Haggerty said, hoping to ease the officer's embarrassment. "General, a letter just arrived from Secretary Cameron. I thought you would want to read it immediately. I know you've been awaiting his response to your letter for over a week now."

Butler dabbed his head and face with a handkerchief. "Thank you, Captain." Haggerty handed him the sealed envelope. Butler nodded. "It's certainly taken longer than expected."

It was late in the afternoon, and Butler had trouble focusing. He knew it was just a dream, but he couldn't erase the image of Mary ablaze and writhing in pain from his mind. It had seemed so real. Ever since his confrontation with Mary the day before, she constantly entered his mind. He was very fond of her, and their estrangement was troubling to him.

Butler unsealed the envelope and began reading. "The important question of the proper disposition to be made of fugitive slaves from service in the states in insurrection against the federal government, to which you have again directed my attention, in your letter of July 30, has received my most attentive consideration."

Countless letters had been sent to General Scott and Cameron seeking direction or guidance concerning the contrabands. Not only for Butler's sake, but for the many Union forts throughout the North and their border states. Butler was relieved that direction was finally being provided.

He read on. "It is the desire of the President that all existing rights in all the states be fully respected and maintained." He knew President Lincoln was troubled by Butler's decision to label the escaping slaves as contraband of war. Other Union officers were also offering escaped slaves sanctuary; some even declared them free.

The Secretary cited Congress's approval of the Confiscation Act on August 6. Butler was aware of this, having received a copy of the act and the results of Congressional voting. Permitting the confiscation of any property used to support the Confederate independence rebellion, including slaves, President Lincoln had reluctantly signed the bill.

Butler knew that the act authorized court proceedings to strip slave owners of any claims. Unfortunately, it didn't clarify whether the slaves were actually free. Due to this ambiguity, many Union officers interpreted the act as making the U.S. government responsible for the care of the slaves.

Butler sat back and thought about what he had read so far. The Confiscation Act and Cameron's letter confirmed that the steps he had taken were appropriate and were now law. Butler thought about all the women, children, and elderly people under his protection. There was also the issue that some of the male slaves within his lines had not been supporting the Confederates. Butler was disappointed that the act didn't clarify how these specific groups should be addressed.

He continued reading Cameron's letter, nodding in agreement when he got to the following section: "It seems quite clear that the substantial rights of loyal masters are still best protected by receiving such fugitives, as well as fugitives from disloyal masters, into the service of the United States and employing them under such organizations and in such occupations as circumstances may suggest or require."

"Excellent!" Butler said aloud and slapped the desk.

Knowing Butler all too well, Cameron went on to warn the General, "You will, however, neither authorize nor permit any interference by the troops under your command with the servants of peaceable citizens in a house or field, nor will you in any manner encourage such servants to leave the lawful service of their masters."

Butler knew he had never encouraged any of the slaves to seek refuge within his lines. In fact, he was deeply puzzled as to how the community even found out that he had granted sanctuary to the first three slaves. He felt somewhat gratified, believing that the Confiscation Act and Cameron's broader interpretation would certainly result in an acceleration of slaves seeking protection.

Optimistic about Cameron's letter, Butler decided to immediately write to Washington. He was anxious for the return of his troops and eager to plan his next offensive. After a bleak and depressing twenty-four hours, he was feeling slightly more upbeat.

While Butler was writing to Washington, General Winfield Scott, Butler's commanding officer in Washington and head of the U.S. Department of the Army, was writing a letter to Major General John Ellis Wool. "It is desirable that you repair to and assume control of the department of which Fortress Monroe is the place of headquarters. It is intended to reinforce that department (recently reduced) for aggressive purposes. Is your health equal to that command? If yes, you will be ordered thither at once. Reply immediately."

Over the next three days, Butler's mood fluctuated between hope and despair. His spirits were lifted with the prospect and anticipation of returning troops and with thoughts of planning an attack on a major Confederate city. However, he was still deeply troubled by the destruction of Hampton, reminded of the incident every time he crossed Hampton Creek Bridge to travel to Camp Butler. Nightmares of Mary being consumed by flames continued to haunt him. He desperately wanted to speak with the woman, hoping this would end his sleepless nights and mend a treasured friendship.

The crushing blow came that evening, when Butler received President Lincoln's order for Wool to replace him. Butler was initially distraught. He felt betrayed by everyone in Washington. The only person he could trust was Montgomery Blair, the Postmaster General, who also happened to be a close friend to Lincoln.

He sat glumly in his quarters, holding a near empty goblet of wine. A bottle of Bordeaux and a tapered candle stood sentry on the table, flanking him on each side. He set the glass down and began his letter to Blair. "I send enclosed a copy of an order which I have received this morning, without a word of comment or explanation from any source. What does it mean? Why this? I supposed when I last saw the President that I had his confidence. Now I am superseded and no duty assigned me. What have I done or omitted to do? Why this sudden change of policy?"

He thought about his anguish over the past several days. Could this be retribution for the burning of Hampton? He continued, "I have witnessed the disgusting scene of a burning village when I had only 2,000 men against 5,000 and could not oppose it. The enemy was coming down solely because they knew I had *no troops*."

What could have motivated this drastic action by Washington? In closing his letter to Blair, he wrote, "Is this because Scott has got over his quarrel with Wool, or is it a move on the part of the President, or is it because of my views on the Negro question are not acceptable to the government? I suppose the last. Meanwhile I am in the dark. Please give more light."

He put the pen down and grasped the neck of the wine bottle.

Butler was mentally and physically spent, drifting into a haze of alcohol. Swirling the bottle in the candlelight, he realized it was empty. With a heavy sigh, he set the bottle down and put the goblet to his lips, draining the remaining contents. Butler stared at the candle, hypnotized by the flickering flame. After a jarring shudder, he leaned over and blew into his cupped hand behind the candle. He sat in the dark for several minutes.

It was mid-August. The late morning sun was beating down on the parade grounds. Channels of sweat drained down Butler's stomach and back, pooling at his waist in the humid air. The shirt beneath his jacket seemed fused to his body. Soldiers were assembled to welcome Major General John Ellis Wool as the next commander of Fortress Monroe. One of the army's most distinguished officers, Wool had served in the War of 1812 and the Mexican War.

Butler felt that President Lincoln, as well as General Scott, knew that Wool might be too old to undertake such a position. Butler had seen the letter from Scott questioning whether Wool was even in sufficient health to take on the assignment. At age seventy-seven, many considered Wool's appointment a slight to Butler.

It was not long before General Wool's carriage arrived at the front gates of the fortress. Wool stepped down from the vehicle, surveying his new post. His gray hair was combed forward to hide his balding temples. Despite his age, Butler thought the man looked remarkably fit.

Butler roused himself and walked forward to meet the man. Though Butler was uneasy, he was also aware of the thousands of men who watched their meeting. "Welcome to Fortress Montroe, General Wool," he said, extending his hand.

"I am pleased to be here, General Butler," the older man said, shaking Butler's hand.

Over a strong cup of coffee the next morning, Butler stared at the stack of letters from Sarah pleading for him to come home. Even Major Fay, who had returned to Massachusetts in early August, reached out. Butler picked up his former aide's letter. "I write in great haste, wishing to catch you before you leave the Fortress, to beg you on no account to let them force you to resign. My feeling is that your resignation would be construed as an acknowledgement of incapacity for your position."

Falling deeper into despair, he continued reading. His back straightened as he read with interest. "Whichever way you come home, however, you will find many friends who have stood by you through thick and thin, and who will be heartily glad for their own sakes to have you among them again." Butler smiled weakly. He had known Fay for many years. The man had always been a loyal friend.

Contrary to those close to him, though, Butler saw his situation as an opportunity. There was no order to relieve him, so he felt he was obligated to stay with his troops. Later that morning, Wool stepped into Butler's office. "I have no specific orders or objectives other than to assume command of the Fortress Monroe and the Departments of Virginia and North Carolina," the older officer confided.

Butler watched the man talk with keen interest. He was impressed that Wool had been mentioned as a Presidential candidate in the past, an aspiration that crossed Butler's mind from time to time. But the old man wanted nothing to with politics and had declined to run. Butler was also pleased that such a prominent war hero was actually shorter than himself. At five feet two inches, Wool was a good two inches shorter than Butler. Assuming no one else was in the room, Butler almost felt tall when standing near Wool.

From their conversation, Butler got the impression that Wool might not want to instigate any major campaigns against the Confederates. Perhaps the new assignment would allow the elderly officer to serve out his last few years in a more leisurely manner. Or, Butler thought, more likely Scott believed Wool's advanced age, like Scott's, would preclude any reckless acts on the peninsula.

Wool sat with a rigid back. His hands were on the desk, fingers interlaced. "Major, I know that this situation must be awkward for you, but I hope you'll stay on."

"General, I won't pretend that this hasn't been an embarrassment. Many of my close acquaintances believe I've been wronged," Butler acknowledged. "And my wife has taken particular advantage of my circumstances to lobby hard for my return home." The two laughed. "I suspect General Scott still holds a grudge against me for my actions in Baltimore earlier this spring." He shrugged. "Either that or our defeat at Big Bethel is still fresh in his mind."

"General, I must confess, General Scott and I are not on the best of terms either," Wool admitted. Butler thought that this could become an ideal arrangement. Perhaps he could be free to conduct the Union's business while Wool would take full responsibility.

Only a few days after his arrival, on August 21, Wool would make his intentions clear. He issued the following order: "Major-General Butler is hereby placed in command of the volunteer forces in this department, exclusive of those at Fortress Monroe." This position would include the regiments at Camp Butler and Camp Hamilton, as well as the Union Coast Guard.

Meeting to review his orders, Butler encouraged the new commander to solicit Washington for more troops. As Wool wrote the dispatch, he joked to Butler, "I suspect it would be easier to attempt to fly than get any more troops from Scott!"

Butler chuckled and said, "Well, actually, let me tell you about that." He went on to astound the old officer with the aerial feats of LaMountain.

Any hope that Scott might have had in containing Butler with the appointment of Wool was quickly vanishing. Under the cover of Wool's leadership, Butler quickly began formulating new battle plans. Since he no longer commanded the troops within Fortress Monroe, Butler looked further down the coast. He had been monitoring two forts on the North Carolina coast, Fort Hatteras and Fort Clark. With insiders still loyal to the Union, Butler was receiving regular updates on the building of the two important Rebel strongholds.

Wool was settling into his routine at Fortress Monroe. Butler decided the timing was right to present his North Carolina plans. He assured Wool that Camps Butler and Hamilton were well fortified and not likely to be attacked by the Confederates. They knew the Confederates had retreated to Yorktown, realizing that Newport News Point and Fortress Monroe were too heavily garrisoned to successfully assault.

Butler baited his new commander. "General Scott's confident you won't take any action in your assignment here. He'll not let you do anything any more than he'd let me." Butler leaned forward. He looked into the aging officer's tired eyes and said softly but purposely. "But a victory while you're in command of this department will result in great glory to you as the first considerable success of the war."

Butler reviewed the details of the combined army and navy expedition with Wool. Butler left it to the more experienced officer to recommend required troop levels and supplies needed to support the attack. On August 25, Wool issued Special Order Number Thirteen: "Major-General Butler will prepare 860 troops for an expedition to Hatteras Inlet, North Carolina." Excited to finally taste warfare Butler immediately made plans to depart.

The following evening, Butler was ready to set out, except for one important matter he had to address. Still haunted by his horrible nightmares, he wanted to visit Mary before departing for North Carolina in the morning. Under the glow of a brilliant sunset, he wound his way down the dirt road leading to the Hampton Roads shoreline and the brown cottage. Looking at the deep red sky reflecting off the water, he was reminded of the awful night of the fire almost three weeks ago. He hadn't seen Mary since.

Butler's legs felt weak as he dismounted and tied his horse to a low tree branch. He was hoping to visit with Mary alone, but as he walked to the open front door, he could see a few dozen adults through the front windows, seated and attentive. Not wanting to disturb the class, he stood by the door but remained out of sight. It was late, and he expected the class would end soon.

Mary stood at the front of the room. As he listened to her teach, he noticed that she would occasionally break into a coughing spell. Butler hoped she wasn't getting a case of grippe, knowing that, as a teacher, she was most likely exposed to many sick children. He could hear adult men and women attempting to read, slowly pronouncing letters as one might expect from children. Butler admired their determination to become literate.

He was concerned how Mary would react to seeing him. Her parting words, accusing Butler of killing Shepard, still stung. Hearing a deep raspy voice through the open doorway, and despite feeling apprehensive, Butler couldn't suppress a grin. "When the sky is red, and the sun is set, the pigs must be fed."

"Very good, James," Mary said before breaking into another coughing fit. After recovering, she collected the book from James. "Excellent progress, everyone. Our next class will be Wednesday evening at the same time." As the adult students rose, the sound of benches scraping the floor echoed in the room. The group filed out the front door, past Butler, enthusiastically discussing the evening's lesson.

Butler and James made eye contact at the same time. Butler noticed that the big man's curved lips compressed into a tight, troubled grimace. James walked over to Butler and nodded. "Evening, General."

"Mr. Townsend. It's been a while. I hope you've been well." Butler shifted his weight nervously.

Friendly but reserved, James said, "I've been okay, General. You here to see me?"

Butler looked past the man's wide body into the doorway. "No, I came here to see Mary. Mrs. Peake." He smiled weakly.

James peered over his shoulder into the classroom and back to Butler. "Does she know you're coming?"

"No, I'm leaving tomorrow for several days and wanted to see her before I go." Butler hesitated. "I'm afraid things didn't end well when we last met." He looked down at the ground.

James put his hands in his pants pockets. "Yeah, so I heard. We're all pretty upset about Shepard." He shook his head. "I know he could drive a person crazy, but he meant well."

"I was quite fond of him, Mr. Townsend." Butler's eyes glistened. "Actually, I thought he was quite extraordinary." His mouth twisted. "His death haunts me constantly." Butler crossed his arms. "I suspect you're angry with me as well."

"General, I owe you my life. You've always treated me with respect. For that, I'm grateful." James tilted his head to the side. "I am confused though. Why didn't you do something about the fire?"

"It's complicated, Mr. Townsend. I had just lost over 4,000 soldiers and still had to protect Newport News, Camp Hamilton, and Fortress Monroe with the remaining troops. I thought by bringing everyone near the fort, they would all be safe." He frowned. "I never could've imagined the Rebels would burn their own town."

"General, I'm not happy about the whole thing, but I don't have a bone to pick with you on this." James shrugged. "I mean, I love Mrs. Peake and all. But this is between you and her."

James could see Mary walking towards the front door. "Well, I'll let you two visit. I hope you can work things out, General." James nodded and strode up the path.

Mary stepped through the front door and stretched her arms high into the warm, thick air. She didn't notice Butler waiting nearby. She was startled when the Union officer stepped from the shadow of a tree with his hands by his sides. Gold buttons shimmered against his dark jacket. Attempting a feeble smile, her eyes narrowed. "Good evening, General. What brings you here?" Mary folded her arms across her chest.

"I'm leaving for several days, but I wanted to see you first." He hesitated a moment. "Mary, I was hoping we could clear the air." Butler bit his lower lip.

"General, I..." Mary stopped to cough into her hands. Butler watched with concern as Mary wheezed and gasped for air. After a few minutes, she swallowed and said, "I don't know what you want me to say, General." Mary shrugged and shook her head. "You can't bring Shepard back. And you can't bring our town back." Her face softened. Her big brown eyes were sad. "I suppose I was a bit harsh with you. I was upset." Her chin quivered. "I guess I'm still upset."

"Mary, I wish there was some way I could convince you how sorry I am," Butler said. "Had I known you and your family were at your home that night, I certainly would have acted differently."

Mary stepped forward from the shadow of the cottage into the evening sun's low rays. Her shrunken face took Butler by surprise. Her skin stretched tightly across sharp cheekbones. It was obvious to Butler that she had lost weight since he had last seen her. "General, I don't want this to stand between us either." She extended her hand in the direction of Hampton. "But I don't know how we'll ever rebuild our town. It's all so senseless. And it's overwhelming."

Butler nodded sympathetically. "I know, Mary. It'll take time for everything to get back to the way it was. But I promise, I'll do whatever I can to help."

"General, I'm glad you came by. Maybe with time, our friendship can get back to the way it was as well." Mary's paused. "I should go. I suspect Daisy's still up." She looked up at a second floor window. "Thomas always has a hard time putting her to bed." She turned back to Butler and sighed, smoothing her dress with her hands. "It's been hard living here, but we'll have to get used to it." She shrugged. "We don't have a choice anymore, do we?"

Butler winced. "Well, I should be getting along anyway." He untied his horse. "I leave for North Carolina early in the morning."

Mary turned her head and coughed.

"Mary, do you mind if I have one of our doctors come by to see you?" Butler asked. "I hope you don't mind me saying, but you don't seem well."

She shook her head. "Thank you, General. That won't be necessary. I suspect I caught something from the children. A few of them have been ill." She turned and walked towards the cottage. "I'm sure I'll be fine soon enough." Mary stopped at the door. "Besides I'm sure you have more important things to worry about than me. You made that clear the night of the fire."

Butler climbed into his saddle shaking his head. He straightened his jacket. "Please, Mary. Let me send a doctor."

Mary pondered his request. "If it'll make you feel better, General." She nodded.

Butler smiled cautiously with a slight bow. "Thank you, Mary. Have a good evening. And my best to Thomas and Daisy." He nudged his horse several feet and stopped. Turning back to Mary, still standing in the doorway, he said, "Mary, I'm glad we had a chance to talk."

Mary tucked her hair behind her ears and gave a faint wave, fighting back tears.

As Butler road back to Fortress Monroe, his mind quickly turned to his anticipated voyage to the North Carolina coast.

GENERAL BUTLER BOARDED THE STEAMER
Adelaide, traveling all night and day to Fortress Monroe from his expedition in North Carolina. After a brief assault on Fort Hatteras, the Rebel forces had fallen to the Union. Realizing defeat was all but certain, and anxious to spare further bloodshed, the Confederate commander offered to surrender the fort "with the arms and munitions of war; the officers to be allowed to go out with side arms and the men without arms to retire."

Butler quickly countered: "The terms of surrender are these: Full capitulation; the officers and men to be treated as prisoners of war. No other terms admissible." Within an hour, the Confederate officers accepted Butler's terms. In addition to over 700 prisoners, the Union forces obtained a substantial quantity of arms and provisions. Butler returned to Fortress Monroe exhilarated by his first victory.

Seated across from General Wool in his former office, Butler provided a detailed account of the expedition. As a key element of Washington's orders, Butler was instructed to sink two vessels in Hatteras Inlet with the intention to stop up the passageway and prevent any future Confederate travel. Butler crossed his arms with determination. He informed his new commander, "I defied the order." He watched the old man's face for any hostile reaction. Wool sat expressionless. Butler continued, "I believe that, by holding Fort Hatteras and keeping the inlet open, the Union can control the coast from Virginia to South Carolina."

Wool squinted below sagging eyelids. "I agree, General." He nodded. "In fact, I consider this victory so important, I'm directing you to Washington to report the engagement firsthand." He stood up and walked with Butler to the door. "But before you leave, though, there's a gentleman from New York, a Reverend Lockwood, who wishes to meet with you."

Reverend Lewis C. Lockwood sat across the desk from the victorious Union officer. Butler was tired after his long trip and anxious to begin packing for Washington. Lockwood spoke slowly and softly. "General, thank you for seeing me. I understand you just returned from a long and arduous journey. Your time is most appreciated."

"Yes, Reverend. I understand you represent the American Missionary Association." Butler's leaned forward. His fingers tapped the desktop. "How may I help you?"

Lockwood put both feet on the floor and spoke with greater urgency. "With the flood of escaped slaves seeking the protection of the Union and, of course, the favorable treatment by you and your soldiers, the AMA thought it'd be appropriate to establish a presence here on the lower Virginia Peninsula." The thin man smiled below his pointy, beak-like nose. His dark, beady eyes blinked. "I was recently commissioned by the AMA for this very purpose."

"I recall receiving a letter from Mr. Tappan in early August," said Butler. "I apologize that it'd taken me several days to respond." Butler frowned as the horrific images reemerged. "The Confederates had just fired the nearby town of Hampton. It was a difficult time."

"How awful, General. I read about the incident." Lockwood shook his head. "I can't even imagine the scale of destruction."

"In any case, Mr. Tappan offered to receive our refugees in free Northern states and provide them with employment." Butler shifted in his chair. "Of course I thanked the AMA for their offer but assured him that these unfortunate people would be protected and treated well here." He met the man's eyes. "I did request clothing and shoes for them though."

Lockwood sat up. "Oh, I did bring some with me, General. Almost a wagon full, in fact."

"Thank you, Reverend. I'm sure that will be very helpful." Butler leaned forward impatiently. "I need to leave for Washington this evening. What is it you need from me?"

"Of course, General. Education and religion are two essentials of my mission. I'd like to investigate the living conditions of these people and understand their basic needs. The AMA believes that you have shown great compassion, and for that we are most grateful," Lockwood said. "It's my hope to begin Sabbath classes as well as weekday and evening classes to teach the children and adults, most of whom I suspect are illiterate."

Butler nodded. "Well, Mr. Lockwood, you may be pleasantly surprised by what you'll find. We have a woman living nearby. She had a home in Hampton but..." Butler frowned, waving his hand through the air. "In any case, she has a special gift for teaching. She's truly exceptional and has been teaching the slave children of Hampton for many years."

Lockwood's mouth hung open. Butler shrugged. "We all know that laws prohibit this. She would lead the children to a small clearing near Hampton Creek. Under a large oak tree, she conducted her lessons in secrecy." Butler recalled the woman's accomplishments with pride. "Her name is Mary Peake. As the population grew and more families with children sought our protection, I approached her and proposed to formalize her classes. With our arrangement, the children were cared for during the day, and their parents were free to support important Union activities."

Lockwood gripped the edge of the desk. "Where might I find Mrs. Peake, General? This could make my mission here much easier. I was concerned with finding an acceptable teacher. Locating qualified teachers is often difficult as many who choose to teach are preyed upon by local white citizens opposing our mission."

Butler pointed across the room. "If you leave through the main entrance of the fort and follow the road over Mill Creek, you'll pass by Camp Hamilton to the west. Follow the road until you almost reach Hampton Creek. Just before the bridge, there's a dirt path on the left that leads down to the Hampton Roads shoreline. You'll see two dwellings there. The larger one to the west is the seminary. Adjacent to it is a small, brown cottage. Mrs. Peake conducts her classes there on the first floor." His fists clenched, thinking of the condition Mary had been in the last time he had seen her. "She lives on the second floor with her husband and daughter."

"Thank you, General. It seems as though my only challenge now is to organize evening classes for adults and, of course, to find a teacher," Lockwood said as he stood. "Perhaps Mrs. Peake could give me some recommendations."

Butler straightened his jacket while walking to the door. A big grin covered his face.

"Is that humorous, General?" Lockwood asked. "Don't you think it's possible to teach adults reading and math?" His long, sharp nose rose high in the air. "Let me assure you that the AMA has been quite successful at this."

Butler shook his head as he opened the door. "Mr. Lockwood, I'm not amused because I don't think it's possible. I'm amused because this is yet another activity that will require little of your attention."

"General, I'm not sure I understand," Lockwood said, looking puzzled.

"Reverend Lockwood, Mrs. Peake has been teaching the adult community, many of whom are parents of her daytime pupils, for much of the summer." He patted the man on his back. "You should be delighted that your mission here will be easily achievable. In fact, much of it is already happening." Butler laughed and extended his hand.

Lockwood shook his hand with a twisted smile. "Thank you, General. You've been most generous with your time."

Butler departed for Washington later that evening. He arrived at the home of Postmaster General Montgomery Blair, which stood opposite the White House, in the middle of the night. Butler was exhausted from the long day of travel. He was surprised to find his friend still awake and visiting with Assistant Secretary of the Navy, Gustavus Fox. Both were excited to hear the news of Butler's victory and insisted they immediately tell President Lincoln.

Butler was reluctant to wake the President, but the two men persisted that Lincoln would want to hear the good news. Fifteen minutes after the men arrived at the White House, the President came out and greeted the three men in his nightshirt. Butler provided a quick overview of the Hatteras incident. President Lincoln shook Butler's hand.

"You've done all right, General. Come tomorrow at ten o'clock, and we'll have a cabinet meeting to cover it in more detail."

Waiting in the corridor outside the White House's Cabinet Room, Butler contemplated the last four and half months. He had rescued the USS Constitution, opened the way through Annapolis for troops to save Washington, thoroughly executed his mission at Fortress Monroe, and by taking Hatteras, atoned for any misdeeds at Baltimore and wiped out the residual repercussions of Big Bethel. Perhaps most significant, Butler had provided Lincoln's administration with a clear and logical path towards resolving the dilemma of slavery. The only other meaningful Union activity during that timeframe was the thrashing by the Confederates at Bull Run.

Butler reached into his pocket and pulled out an old letter from Sarah. He carried it with him everywhere as a reminder of what he was sacrificing by being away from home. He reread the sentence about the children asking for their father. "Here is Mother, and we thought Father was coming, too. Where is he? And why did he not come?" Butler sat back and stared at the blank wall opposite him. He tried to recall the last time he had been home. *It must be fifteen or sixteen weeks now. Perhaps even longer.*

He thought about his firstborn son, Paul, who had died eleven years earlier at the age of four. His heart ached. He deeply missed his other three children. At that moment, he made the critical decision to return home. *I've accomplished so much in just over four months—much more than anyone else. Yes, I've earned the right to go home.*

After the Cabinet meeting, Butler met with President Lincoln in private. "Sir, I haven't been home since April 16. Would you be kind enough to relieve me and allow me to return there?"

The President extended his hand. "You have every right to go home, General, for a little rest, but study out another job for yourself."

He reminded Lincoln of an earlier conversation. "When I accepted my commission with which you were kind enough to honor me, I told you that we have disagreed in politics, but that so long as I held the commission I should fully and faithfully sustain all the acts of your administration. And when I felt that I could not do that, I would return the commission. But you asked me to promise to lay before you any matter upon which I disagreed with you before I took that step."

The President sat up with his hands together. "And what would that matter be, General?"

Swallowing hard, Butler shared his thoughts. "As you know, the Governors of the Northern states control the troops and appointment of officers." He watched Lincoln nod in agreement. "Since most governors are Republican, they recruit friends and like-minded associates to these posts. As a result, most officers and troops are Republican. If this practice continues, sir, the war will be viewed as heavily partisan and could even result in a division of the North."

"Yes, General. There's meat in what you say." Lincoln rubbed his bearded chin.

After a deep breath, Butler made his proposal. "Rather than relying on the states to recruit troops, I believe the President should draft men for the service of the United States."

Butler requested the authority and funds to recruit troops in New England, focusing on Democrats but not rejecting Republicans. The President agreed with Butler and asked him to draw up an order. On September 10, the Secretary of War and the President signed and approved the order. "Major General B. F. Butler is hereby authorized to raise, organize, arm, uniform, and equip a volunteer force for the war in the New England states, not exceeding six regiments."

Butler returned to Fortress Monroe to organize his personal effects for transport home. He had hoped to visit Mary before his departure. While their last meeting began to address issues between the two, he still felt there was lingering tension in the friendship. Butler was also concerned about her health.

Since he had to immediately return to Boston to meet with the New England governors, he decided to get an update from Dr. Browne. Unfortunately, the Union doctor was visiting Newport News Point for a few days so Butler left him a note, thanking him for looking after Mary and inquiring about the state of her health.

Lockwood walked through the main gate of Fortress Monroe and over the long, wooden bridge. The morning air was warm but not as humid as it had been. The dry, crisp autumn weather of New York would soon arrive on the Virginia Peninsula. Lockwood followed Butler's directions and found himself standing outside the brown cottage, already buzzing with activity this early in the morning.

The first floor schoolroom was filled with children eager to start their lessons. As was typical of each day, Mary began with prayers and a song. Lockwood arrived as the group of over sixty children was singing "There is a Happy Land."

He was spellbound as children of all ages sang with the passion and sensitivity of a professional choir. Lockwood was familiar with the hymn and couldn't recall ever hearing such a moving version. At the conclusion of the song, Mary organized the children into their learning groups and said, "Please study your lessons while I greet the gentleman at our door." The children all turned to see the stranger standing in the doorway.

Lockwood smiled as Mary walked over to the door. After exchanging greetings and introductions, Mary invited Lockwood to observe the class. Mary was thrilled with the prospect of the AMA's support and instructional material.

As the day progressed, Mary's exceptional abilities were abundantly clear to Lockwood. Her teaching style went beyond having the children memorize their lessons. Mary took the time to explain theories and concepts, relating the classroom material back to her own experiences or to those of the students. Lockwood was delighted.

Mary had explained to the reverend her strong belief that educating the young would lead to more productive lives as adults. In the absence of an education, these children would face closed doors. Lockwood had singled out one young girl who exhibited truly exceptional abilities in the classroom. Mary smiled with pride as she said, "That's my daughter, Mr. Lockwood. Her name is Hattie, but we call her Daisy."

Lockwood bent over and nodded his head. His dark, tiny eyes blinked rapidly as he spoke. "You're quite smart, Daisy. I've been observing you closely."

Daisy smiled. Lockwood turned to Mary and said, "Do you mind if I look around the classroom, Mrs. Peake? I can't begin to tell you how excited I am."

"Not at all, Reverend. Please go right ahead." Lockwood hopped between the desks, watching the children with delight.

Daisy tugged on her mother's dress. Mary leaned over, "What is it, Daisy?"

Daisy cupped her hands around her mother's ear. "That man looks like a woodpecker."

"Oh, Daisy. That's not funny." She looked away, hiding her smile.

The next morning, an additional wagon pulled up behind those carrying the children. Lockwood walked over to Mary and explained. "I have new primers for the children. There're also catechisms and other religious books you may find interesting."

Mary was elated. "Oh, Reverend. This is wonderful. The children will be so happy. I'm sure we'll see a great deal of improvement in their reading and math skills." The driver of the wagon, James Jr., and a few of the other bigger boys helped Lockwood carry the boxes into the classroom.

Butler strolled down the main boulevard of Lowell, Massachusetts; chest thrust high, spine straight and rigid, ego on full display. Gold stars adorned his shoulders. Two columns of nine brass buttons each, shimmering in the sunlight, marched abreast down his long coat. Waves of lank hair curled over his upright collar, which was embroidered with oak leaf clusters.

Sarah's left hand clutched the crook of her husband's elbow. Her scarlet dress flowed and swayed with each long, elegant stride. Pointed black boots, laced above her dainty ankles, embossed with roses on each side, clicked on the sidewalk. With two-inch heels, Sarah tried to appear no taller than her husband.

To his other side, the long fingers of Blanche's hand were interlaced with her father's short stubby fingers. Paul II and Ben-Israel circled and weaved in and out of the group as they greeted passersby. Arm in arm, hand in hand, the Butler family was on full display. They were the talk of the town, and everyone wanted to see and be seen with them.

Butler had arrived home to a hero's welcome, family and friends showering him with endless adulation. Even strangers stopped on the street to shake his hand and acknowledge his accomplishments. Some just stared in awe. Having lived in Lowell for most of his life, Butler was perhaps the most recognizable person in the city.

One day as he and Sarah dressed for another night on the town, she noticed his military attire still hanging in the wardrobe. "Benjamin, aren't you going to put on your uniform? You look so handsome in it."

"I thought that if I wore my regular clothes, I might blend in better," he said while slipping on his shoes. "At first it was a boost to my ego. Now I find all this attention a bit intrusive."

Butler wore his dark gray trousers, lawyer's coat, and slouch hat. Paul II sat next to him on the carriage bench, thrilled to be holding the reins for the first time. Sarah, Blanche, and Ben-Israel were settled behind into comfortable carriage seats. Butler provided careful guidance as they wound their way through the streets of Lowell. The carriage pulled up to the curb in front of an exclusive restaurant. Under his father's watchful direction, Paul II pulled back on the brake lever. Despite Butler's more discreet attire, crowds gathered around the famous family, applauding as they stepped down from the carriage and strolled up the walk to dinner.

A week had passed since Butler arrived home. It was mid-September, and crops were being harvested in the fields. Days were sunny and pleasant. Nights were cool, crisp, and growing in length. The brilliant red, orange, and yellow leaves of the sugar maples were a sure sign that winter was around the corner. Butler was ramping up his recruiting efforts.

Returning from Boston where he'd met with Governor Andrew, Butler noticed a letter sitting on the kitchen table. Seeing it was from Dr. Browne, he tore off the end of the envelope and anxiously unfolded the letter. His eyes scanned the pages. Routine activities of the fort were summarized in the first several paragraphs. He pulled out a chair and sat down as he held the last page. "I stop by to see Mrs. Peake regularly on my way to Camp Butler. Unfortunately, she continues to lose weight, as she doesn't seem to have much of an appetite. Her zeal to teach is still strong, however, and her class size continues to grow with the support of Reverend Lockwood and the AMA." Butler looked up. "Well, that doesn't tell me much." He mumbled to himself.

He continued reading. "I will be certain to keep you informed of any changes to Mrs. Peake's health. I hope that you are in pleasant spirits finally being home and in the heart of your family.' Butler set the letter down. *If Mary's condition was serious, I'm sure he would have said so*, he thought with relief. *And she must be well if she's teaching.* Notwithstanding, he vowed that the next time he visited Fortress Monroe or even Washington, he would make sure there was sufficient time to visit Mary.

GENERAL BUTLER RODE ACROSS THE FAMILIAR bridge spanning Mill Creek. The clopping on the wooden deck gave him a strange sense of comfort. It was mid-November and more than two months had passed since he'd left the Hampton area for Boston to head the Department of New England. It seemed much longer, though, since he had commanded Fortress Monroe and the thousands of troops in the surrounding area. So much had happened in his four months there. He smiled as he passed the exact spot where he met with Confederate Major Cary in late May, denying Rebel demands to lift the Union blockade and return the three escaped slaves.

A cool breeze off Chesapeake Bay sent chills down his back. He fastened the top button of his coat and pulled the collar up around his neck. Butler had heard the winters could be difficult on the Virginia Peninsula, but he suspected they couldn't compare to the harsh, dark winters of New England. A flock of gulls flew over his head and glided into Mill Creek.

Butler guided his horse down the dirt road towards the shoreline of Hampton Roads. Arriving at the small brown cottage, Butler dismounted and tied his horse to the porch railing. In the distance, he could see Daisy running through the tall grass along the water's edge. As she chased two other children, she spotted the Union officer and waved.

Butler was always impressed by the young girl's intellect and perceptiveness. He sometimes wondered how her life might have been different if she had been born white or lived in New England instead of Virginia. Yet with her obvious aptitude, especially at such a young age, perhaps she would flourish regardless of her race or environs. Butler certainly hoped so.

He walked up to the front door with his arms by his sides. Butler had received a few more letters from Dr. Browne, but none went into detail about Mary's health. On this recent trip to Washington, he had an opportunity to go to Fortress Monroe and was determined to visit her. Standing at the door, he hesitated to knock, concerned he might be disturbing her, and took a step back. Despite a thawing in their relationship when they last met, he and Mary hadn't spoken in over two months. *I wonder if she's still upset with me*, he thought as he knocked.

While he waited for someone to answer the door, Butler looked around the outside of the old house. He knew it had been abandoned for several years before Mary and Thomas had converted it into her schoolhouse. He was told that they were still living on the upper floor.

There were signs of minor improvements and renovations to the outside of the cottage, but Butler could see it was still rundown. He suspected that Thomas's attempts to save the decaying house were futile. Large gaps around the window frames were certain to let in the cold winter air. A few panes were missing and crudely replaced with small boards. Through the front windows, he could see makeshift benches and desks facing one end of the main room. It was a Saturday, so he suspected there were no classes this day. Butler wondered how many students were attending Mary's classes now.

There were no sounds coming from inside the home. Perhaps Mary was busy preparing lessons and Thomas was out working. He decided to return at a later time and stepped off the porch. While untying the horse's reins, Daisy came sprinting around the corner. "Hi, General Butler."

"Daisy! How are you? You sure can run like the wind." He patted the top of the girl's head. "Is your mother home?"

"She's upstairs. She probably can't hear you knocking though. She usually keeps her door closed. I'll go tell her you're here." Before Butler could inquire about her mother's health, Daisy opened the front door and ran up the stairs.

Butler looked out at the schooners anchored in Hampton Roads. He could see the south shore of the large waterway in the distance and wondered how many Confederate troops now occupied the fortification at Sewell's Point. Butler thought about the three slaves who had made their courageous and dangerous escape across the massive waterway several months earlier. He never regretted his decision to give them sanctuary, despite the angst it caused in Washington. With a deep sigh, he thought about Shepard, his contributions to the Union's efforts, and his horrible death.

Daisy came bounding down the stairs and took the last two steps in a giant leap. "Mama says you can come up." Daisy grabbed Butler's hand and pulled him into the doorway and up the stairs. At the top of the second floor landing, Butler could see daylight through gaps in the wood plank floor. Daisy pushed the door open.

Butler took a step into the dark, stale room. Everything in it seemed gray and drab, a depressing place even for someone not ill. Frayed cloth framed the slightly open windows. Fresh air slowly infiltrated the room, but it did not do much to alleviate the smells of camphor and salves. He almost didn't recognize Mary. She was lying in bed under a threadbare blanket pulled almost up to her neck. Her body was barely detectable under the covers. Her normally big, bright, brown eyes were dull and sunken.

Her thin gaunt hands held a needle and a tattered dress. She smiled weakly at Butler. "General, this is a surprise. Please excuse me for not getting up to greet you." Mary held up the dress. "I've been busy altering all my clothes. It seems that everything is too big on me these days."

Butler forced a smile. "Good morning, Mary. I'm so happy to see you. You're looking well."

Mary squinted at the Union officer standing in the doorway. "That's very kind of you, General, but you and I know that's not true. It's good to see you too. I thought you were based in Boston now."

Butler looked around awkwardly, clearly uncomfortable. He thought Mary would be in an upstairs sitting room, not in her bedroom—and certainly not in bed. Daisy had dragged him up the stairs so quickly, he didn't have time to ask where she was leading him. "I am, but business required me to be in Washington and then briefly to Fortress Monroe," he said. "I thought I'd take some time to check on my favorite teacher." His smile revealed stained teeth below his bushy mustache.

Mary turned to Daisy who was standing next to her bed. "Why don't you go out and play with your friends in the fresh air? The General and I would like to visit for a little while. All right, baby?"

"All right, Mama. But I want to come back to say goodbye to the

General when he's ready to leave." Daisy looked from her mother to Butler.

"I'll be sure to see you before I go, Daisy," Butler said.

Satisfied with the arrangement, Daisy abruptly turned, marched out of the room with her nose in the air, and closed the door behind her. She ran down the stairs, intentionally making as much noise as possible on the wooden boards. Arriving at the front door, she opened it wide and then swung it closed loud enough to echo throughout the house. The windows in the front room rattled. She covered her mouth with both hands realizing that perhaps she flung the door a little too hard. Daisy slowly turned, looked up at her mama's room, and surreptitiously started climbing back up the stairs.

She knew the staircase by heart, which boards creaked and which ones were safe. Daisy managed to avoid the bad spots most of the way up. She knew the last two steps were the worst and had to be extra cautious. There were no safe spots.

To help her balance, she placed her left hand against the wall, stretched across the last two steps with her right hand, and put it on the top landing. She swung her tiny right leg up to the landing and carefully shifted her left hand to the last step. Daisy was now sideways on the stairs. Her legs straddled the last two steps. She had never tried this complicated maneuver before and started giggling.

Taking a deep breath, she pushed off on her left leg and threw herself onto the landing. She cleared the two squeakiest stairs but realized she had made more noise than she planned. She lay quietly on her back for a few minutes. Then satisfied that no one heard her, she slowly stood up. Daisy carefully placed her ear against the bedroom door, as she had done so many times before when Dr. Browne visited.

"I think she's grown two or three inches since I last saw her," Butler said inside the room.

"She's the light of my life." Mary frowned at the closed door for several seconds and turned to Butler. "General, I'm glad you came. I know we tried patching things up last time we met, but I'm afraid I was still angry with you." Her eyes welled up. "I've had a lot of time to think about what happened. You were right. Your first obligation was to your troops. Not to all us colored folks."

Butler opened his mouth to talk, but Mary held up her hand. "Please let me finish." She took a deep breath. "I didn't have a chance to thank you for your kind treatment to all the escaped slaves." She shrugged. "Actually to all of us. If it wasn't for you, I never would have been able to teach again. I've been meaning to write to you, but I am grateful I can tell you in person." Mary watched Butler take a seat near the open window. "You took a big risk protecting James, Frank, Shepard, and all the others who followed. We all know what you did was against the law. It was a courageous thing to do."

"Mary, I am sensitive to the plight of the slaves and conditions here in the South. But in all honesty, my actions were more selfishly motivated. My orders here were to defeat the Confederates in the hope we could reunite our great nation. That's still my goal and, I believe, the goal of the North."

Butler smiled at Mary, who was watching him closely. He continued. "While many of us are repulsed by slavery, our goal wasn't, and still isn't, to end slavery necessarily. By giving those three men sanctuary, and the others who followed, I was depriving the Confederates of their labor. At the same time, of course, we had the benefit of their hard work, and in fact, we still do. So my actions weren't as benevolent as you might think. Besides it was the actions of those three brave men that were courageous. They could have encountered many grave circumstances that evening." Butler looked down at the floor and around the room, finally resting on Mary's expressionless face. He hoped he hadn't disappointed her, but the intricacies of politics and war were hard to explain.

Mary stared at the Union officer for a few minutes. Her lips were pressed tightly together. Slowly the corners of her mouth started to turn upward. "You can't fool me, General. I hear what you're saying, but even I know your decision was difficult and controversial. And I'm sure President Lincoln wasn't all too happy with you either."

He chuckled. "That's an understatement, I'm afraid. But Fortress Monroe wasn't and isn't the only Union location giving shelter to escaped slaves. As a result of our collective actions, the Confiscation Act was passed last August. As you may know, it stripped slave owners of any claims to those who escaped, but unfortunately, it didn't clarify whether the slaves were free."

Mary set her dress down on the bed. "Well, I suspect at least they're better off now than they were, General. Who knows? Perhaps there'll be a day when this dreadful war will be over, and they'll truly be free."

"I hope you're right, Mary. I truly do. But I'm afraid it won't be anytime soon." Butler slowly shook his head

"Do you think the war will continue much longer?" Mary strained to sit up.

"When we first met several months ago, I told you the war would be over by now or certainly by the end of the year. I'm afraid it doesn't look that way anymore. I suspect it could go on for at least a few more years, unfortunately." Butler didn't want to upset Mary, but he thought it best to not mislead her either.

Mary turned away. Butler could see Mary's shoulders shudder. He stood and walked over to her side. He extended his arm to comfort her, but pulled it back. "Mary, please don't be upset. I can't imagine things getting worse in Hampton. With the Union presence at

Fortress Monroe, I would think living conditions here should only improve. You mustn't worry."

"You don't understand, General." Mary said through gentle sobs. "My goal was initially a modest one. I wanted to ensure that the oppressed children of Hampton could read and write. I dreamt of a day when they could lead a free life. A life without closed doors. I wanted to prepare them for that day."

She turned back to Butler. Tears streamed down her sunken cheeks. "Then you arrived. Followed by more soldiers and guns, I thought, perhaps naively, the Union forces would soon prevail and these poor people would be free. I tried to help in my own limited way. And when you gave James, Frank, and Shepard sanctuary, the dream of freedom seemed within our grasp. You see, General, you were the key!" Mary stated. "Now I'm afraid I'll never witness that dream. I suspect that sounds silly to you."

"No, Mary. It doesn't." Butler leaned over and grasped her hand. "I share your dream of a quick end to the war. I'm sure most of us on both sides want that as well. It'll end. And I'm certain the Union will prevail. Then we'll all have something to celebrate."

"You just don't understand, General." Mary turned her head away. A few minutes passed. Butler stood, shifting his weight from foot to foot. A look of puzzlement and concern filled his face. She squeezed Butler's hand. "I'm running out of time. I have consumption," she said.

Butler opened his mouth to say something, but then closed it and just looked at Mary. He knew many soldiers suffered and died from the disease, that it filled their lungs with blood and bile, and that there was no known cure. "Mary, you mustn't give up hope. Others have recovered. Certainly you can as well. I'll have Dr. Browne come by today to see you."

Mary released his hand and clutched the corner of the blanket, wiping her face. "Thank you, General. Dr. Browne has been most kind. He comes here regularly and is taking such good care of me. I feel guilty. I know he has more pressing matters at the fort." Mary looked at the door. "Daisy, you can come in."

The door slowly opened, and Daisy poked her head through. "Sorry, Mama."

"It's all right, baby. You can come in and sit down." Mary smiled and looked at Butler. "I'm afraid Daisy has a habit of eavesdropping, General."

Butler watched Daisy cross the room and sit in a chair in the corner. "Well, there's certainly nothing wrong with your hearing," Butler said.

Daisy looked at Butler sheepishly, raised her eyebrows, and shrugged her shoulders. "I just want to make sure my mama is okay." She turned to her mother. "Were you crying, Mama?"

Butler smiled at the little girl. "We'll make sure your mama has the best care, Daisy. Hopefully she'll be well soon." He looked back to Mary. "You said you tried to help our efforts in your own way. I have no doubt in your abilities, Mary, but what did you mean?"

Mary looked out the window next to Butler, and slowly shifted her gaze back to his face. "Shortly after those three men escaped to Fortress Monroe, I delivered a dress to Sarah, I mean Mrs. Butler, and I saw them. James told me that you decided to keep them at the fort and protect them." Mary started to say something and stopped. She shrugged her shoulders in the same way Daisy did when she was caught eavesdropping at the door. Butler realized with a soft smile how remarkably similar mother and daughter were in appearance and mannerisms.

"And in the following days, tens and hundreds of slaves came into the fort seeking sanctuary," Butler finished Mary's thought. He smiled and shook his head. "I wondered how the news of my decision spread so quickly outside the fort. It was you, Mary, wasn't it?" Butler wasn't angry. In fact, he seemed relieved to finally figure out one of the many missing pieces of the puzzle.

Mary tried to smile. "Let's just say it was a little bird that told everyone, General." She looked at Daisy and smiled. Then she turned back to Butler. "A mockingbird."

THE SEMINARY WAS BRIGHTLY DECORATED WITH evergreens and red ribbons in celebration of the holiday season. In addition to the little brown cottage, the old building was one of the few to survive the great fire in August, primarily because it was located east of Hampton Creek. Families streamed in and quickly filled the pews. Joining them were soldiers and officers eager to see the children perform and longing for their own families back home.

A large platform was constructed at one end of the room upon which some of the children were taking their positions. Standing still and attentive, Chaplain Fuller opened the ceremony with a warm welcome and led the large group in the singing of "My Country, 'Tis of Thee." The Chaplain followed this with a celebratory prayer and a reading of the Nativity of Christ.

Over the next hour, different age groups took turns on the stage and serenaded the audience. Intermittently, the children recited special holiday stories. All the children were stars that evening, but the highlight of the festival was a solo performance by Daisy. The audience was completely mesmerized, overcome by the young girl's beautiful voice.

As Daisy sang, tears filled her eyes. Thomas sat in the audience, beaming with pride. Sitting next to him were James and Frank and their wives. Their children were participating in the concert as well.

At the conclusion of the festival, Chaplain Fuller led everyone through a closing prayer and then addressed the audience. "I would like to thank all of the children for this glorious performance." Everyone broke into applause.

He continued, "We have someone special to thank for this but, unfortunately, she could not be with us to celebrate this remarkable occasion. Mrs. Mary Peake, the children's teacher, has worked tirelessly over the past few months to prepare them for this festival. The children are disappointed she could not be here due to illness. They have, however, requested that we bring the celebration to her. So we've decided to carry decorations and refreshments from this room to the brown cottage where we will decorate the first floor classroom and conduct an encore performance for Mrs. Peake." The crowd rose to their feet, cheering with enthusiasm.

The procession of adults and children eagerly exited the seminary and slowly assembled outside. It was a short stroll along the Hampton Roads waterfront to the brown cottage. Those not carrying decorations or refreshments carried candles that flickered in the cold, evening wind.

The decorations and refreshments filled the first floor room where many of the children and adults attended weekday classes. Christmas trees already stood in the corners, covered with the children's handmade ornaments. Tables were pushed against the wall, overflowing with treats.

Dr. Browne heard the commotion outside and peered through the second floor window. He was startled to see well over 200 people gathered around the brown cottage. Mary had finally dozed off and was comfortably resting. He hesitated to wake her. As the sounds of "Hark! The Herald Angels Sing" flowed through the windows and up the stairway engulfing the room, a smile emerged on Mary's face; her eyes still closed.

Dr. Browne, noticing her reaction, gently put his hand on Mary's shoulder and said, "Mary, I think you have visitors. I dare say that most of Hampton is downstairs."

Mary opened her eyes and responded, "I'm so excited, Doctor. I feel well after resting. I'd like to greet them."

With help from Dr. Browne and Thomas, Mary slowly made her way down the stairs, leading to the vestibule and classroom. The crowd filling the room and surrounding the cottage broke into the song "It Came Upon a Midnight Clear." Mary beamed as she watched the children.

Chaplain Fuller, speaking for the group, informed Mary that the children insisted upon bringing the festival to her doorstep. Over the next hour, the children performed for their teacher with even more vigor than they had earlier. Finally, Daisy sang her solo, looking directly into her mother's eyes as the words flowed effortlessly. Tears of pride and joy slide down Mary's face as she gazed upon her daughter.

After all the revelers left, Mary, Thomas, and Daisy sat on a bench looking around the richly decorated classroom. Mary spotted a wrapped package under a fir tree covered with red ribbons. Neither she nor Thomas could recall who brought it and placed it there. She pointed. "Daisy, can you please go over and get that package near the tree?"

Daisy walked over and picked up the thin package, covered in white and red-striped paper and a large red bow. "There's a note, Mama."

"What does it say, baby?" Mary shakily stood up.

Daisy handed the package to her mother. "Here, Mama. You can read it."

Mary opened the envelope and held the note in her hand. She gave the package back to Daisy. "It says, 'Dear Daisy, I hope you have a very Merry Christmas. General Butler.' It's for you, baby."

Daisy's eyes opened wide. She carefully undid the wrapping paper, folding it neatly. She held the present high over her head. "It's a new bird book. Mama, Papa, it's a new bird book! And it's even bigger than the one I had."

NESTLED IN TENTS ADJACENT TO CAMP
Hamilton, the contraband community crawled out from under
warm covers into the crisp morning air. The sun's rays reflected
off Chesapeake Bay, creating a shimmering, golden thoroughfare that
faded into the distant horizon. One week had passed since greeting
the New Year. A long frigid winter still lay ahead.

There was a faint rumbling of horses' hooves and wagon wheels
over the boards of Mill Creek Bridge echoing in the distance. Like
rolling thunder, the low roar grew in intensity. Men, women, and children, bundled in heavy coats and blankets, frosted breath swirling in
the air, wandered to the side of the road. Looking in the direction of
Fortress Monroe, they were certain the Union army was on the move,
heading up the peninsula to engage some key Confederate stronghold.

James stood with his arms crossed. He tucked his large hands
under his armpits to keep warm. His dark eyes watched in anticipation
below his creased forehead.

Frank stood nearby. "What do you think's going on, James?"

"Not sure, Frank." Clouds of dust could be seen in the distance. "There're a lot of them coming though. That's for sure." James nodded, shifting his weight from foot to foot.

The first of several wagons came into view. James immediately recognized its driver; sharp cheekbones, twinkling brown eyes, big, white teeth framed in a wide grin. "Why, that's Thomas! What in blazes is he doing with those soldiers?" James walked to the edge of the road and raised his arm.

Coming to an abrupt halt, Thomas jumped down from the wagon seat and shook hands with his friends. "Morning, James. Frank." He nodded. "You want to give me a hand here?" Thomas walked to the rear of the canvas-covered wagon. A caravan of several more wagons came to a halt behind them.

"What're you carrying?" James asked, following Thomas.

"Help me untie these ropes and you'll see." Thomas climbed onto the back of the wagon.

James and Frank eagerly worked the knots on each side. Thomas stood with legs apart behind the bench seat. Like a magician performing for his audience, he flipped the canvas high into the air in a large sweeping motion. The desperate crowd gasped at the treasured contents. A large stack of lumber, in varied widths and lengths, gleamed in the winter sun.

"Where'd all this come from?" James rubbed his hand across the grainy wood in amazement. "What's it for?"

With a big smile, Thomas pointed back across the bridge. "From the fort." He jumped down and walked to the next wagon in the long line. "It was requisitioned by General Butler back in Boston." Thomas slapped his friend on the back. "You better go get your tools, James. We got work to do."

James stood stunned. He looked from wagon to wagon and whistled. "Good Lord! There's enough wood here to darn near build an entire town."

"Well," Thomas said, uncovering the next wagon in line, "that's the plan."

During Butler's visit to see Mary the prior November, Thomas intercepted the General as he was leaving and shared his grief over his wife's illness. He wanted to do something productive to keep his mind busy, so he asked Butler if there was any way the Union could help them rebuild the town. While visiting Fortress Monroe a few days after the New Year, Thomas discovered the lumber had just arrived on a recent steamship. He hoped to lift everyone's spirits by surprising them with the delivery.

The supply of lumber couldn't have come at a more needed time. As the contraband population continued to grow, conditions had become increasingly crowded and difficult. The thin tents did little to combat the frigid air. Unable to grow crops in the frozen ground, and with the war escalating, food was in short supply. The opportunity to rebuild the town served two important purposes. It would help relieve the housing problem, and it would keep the men busy through the long winter months.

Thomas, James, and Frank organized work groups. With their experience building the earthworks around Hampton and several buildings within Fortress Monroe, many of the men had become skilled carpenters. Construction quickly began, reclaiming portions of Hampton that had been destroyed by the fire.

The homes were intentionally built small and close together. Although the lumber provided by the Union was great for framing the homes and provided structural integrity, wood was still needed to sheath the outside walls.

Days were spent wandering the ruins of destroyed homes and buildings looking for additional materials. Fortress Monroe also provided some recycled wood from buildings demolished to make room for newer, larger structures. Bricks were salvaged from chimneys lying on the ground. Over the next several weeks, a new town slowly emerged from the ashes of Hampton.

Four students surrounded Mary's bed, including James Jr. and Millie. Daisy sat on the pillow next to her mother's head. It was mid-February, and Mary was feeling well enough to have visitors. "Are you all keeping up with your studies?" Mary asked the children with a weak smile. Reverend Lockwood had taken over her classes until she was well enough to return.

Thomas poked his head through the open doorway. He could see that his wife was starting to wilt from the energy of speaking with the children. Her large, brown eyes were dull and struggled to stay open. "Okay, children. Time to leave. We need to let Mrs. Peake get her rest." He roused the disappointed students through the door. "Daisy, can you get some water for your mama?"

Daisy nodded. "Yes, Papa." She followed her friends down the stairway.

Mary's cheeks were hollow. Withered fingers pulled the frayed blanket up around her neck.

"How're you doing?" Thomas sat on the edge of the bed, holding his wife's fragile hand.

Mary looked at her husband through red, glassy eyes. "Not too bad. A little tired, I guess." Her chin quivered.

"Why don't you rest your eyes for a bit? I'm going into town to see if James and Frank need anything." He smoothed her hair down with his free hand. "You should see the town, Mary. We're making good progress." Thomas smiled and stood up. He leaned over and kissed his wife on the forehead.

He walked over to the door, stopped, and looked back, leaning against the doorframe. "I'll be back to get lunch ready."

"Thomas?" Mary struggled to lean on her elbow. "If I'm feeling up to it later, will you drive me into town?"

"Of course. I'll ask to borrow one of the wagons from the soldiers." With a sigh of relief and smile, he said, "Maybe the fresh air will do you some good." Thomas closed the door.

Mary wore a heavy brown coat with a thick collar. A faded green wool scarf covered her head. Thomas draped a checkered blanket over her shoulders, which she pulled high over her mouth and nose. White puffs of air seeped through the openings with every breath.

Thomas had heated several bricks in the fire, wrapped them in cloth, and placed them in floorboards of the wagon. Although it provided some relief from the bitter cold, Mary sat close to her husband, sharing his body warmth. Her eyes watered in the chilly breeze. Daisy had decided to stay at the cottage with friends.

The wagon turned from the sandy trail onto the main road leading to Hampton Creek Bridge. Mary glanced to her right. A grass path led to the familiar clearing beyond. She could see the top of the large oak in the distance, rising above the tree line like a steady beacon.

Thomas could see his wife's yearning eyes through the opening in the blanket. "Do you want to stop there?"

"Can we please?" Mary sat up, excited to visit the cherished spot where she had taught the children for so many years. It was a place where she always found peace and tranquility.

The wagon bumped and swayed over the frozen ground and came to a halt near the edge of the tree. "Will you help me down?" Mary tried to stand.

"Mary, are you sure it's a good idea to get down?" Thomas frowned.

She nodded, the strongest she'd looked in weeks. "I want to touch the tree, Thomas."

Thomas lifted his wife from the bench with his strong arms and carefully placed her on the ground. He held her hands until she could steady herself.

Mary shuffled over to the tree and placed her hand on the trunk. It was cold and rough against her thin skin. Her finger traced the gaps in the bark. She recalled the many times she had watched insects crawling along the deep crevices, deciding where to turn, which path to take. Mary thought about her own life and the choices she had made; a path that led to this very spot.

Leaning her head back, she looked up into the massive structure of the tree, its powerful limbs reaching out into the blue sky. A few withered, brown leaves, long dead, fluttered in the cold breeze and clung desperately to gnarled branches.

Mary started walking back to the wagon. A long branch hung low enough for her to grasp. She held it in her hand and examined the new growth in the bright sunlight. Small brown buds were bundled tight against the bitter wind. Waiting patiently for warmer weather to return, they would spring open into healthy green leaves and resume their cycle of life.

Thomas helped her into the wagon. He wrapped the blanket over her shoulders. With a gentle snap of the reins, the wagon wobbled back to the main road.

The biting wind blew off the icy waters of Hampton Roads. Mary could feel every uneven board as the wagon wheels slowly rolled over Hampton Creek Bridge. Each bump rattled the bones in her fragile body. She gripped the edge of the bench, relieved when the wagon finally reached the smoother road beyond.

She and Thomas approached the outskirts of her cherished town. Several months had passed since Mary had crossed Hampton Creek. The devastation was worse than she had remembered. Her sad eyes surveyed the landscape. Behind the blanket, Mary bit her chapped lower lip. Scrawny rodents scampered among the charred timbers and piles of rubble in search of nourishment. Crumbled brick and stone chimneys stood askew like vandalized tombstones. The air was earthy and acrid.

Mary sighed and lowered her head. "How're you doing? You all right?" Thomas asked, reaching out for his wife's hand.

Mary nodded. "I'm all right, Thomas," she said weakly, looking into his eyes. She wrapped her hands around Thomas's arm and buried her face in his side. Swirls of wind kicked up ash and soot, blowing across the once tidy neighborhoods like black snow.

Thomas pointed to a section of the town. "Look there. That's where we've been working."

Mary looked up and blinked. She wiped the frozen tip of her nose with her hand.

Thomas guided the wagon to where homes were under construction. "Well, what do you think?" he asked.

Over twenty homes were framed. A few were almost completed and ready for occupancy, even as new areas were being cleared. "Thomas, it's wonderful." He put one arm around his wife, gently rubbing her back with the other.

A familiar voice called out from one of the homes. Mary looked up. James and Frank lumbered over to the wagon, both grinning wide. "Mrs. Peake, what a surprise!" James said. "It's great to see you up and about." He shook hands with Thomas. Waving his arm across the construction site, he asked Mary, "So, what do you think?"

"It's so exciting to see our town starting to come back to life." Mary pulled a blanket over her mouth and coughed.

James winked at Thomas. "Did you show her yet?"

Thomas put a finger to his lips. "Not yet."

"Show me what?" Mary looked from Thomas to James. Both men grinned.

Thomas turned to his wife. "Why don't we take a ride and see?"

They made their way up Court Street, past the once-vibrant town center. In the distance, Mary could see a large building being constructed where the courthouse had stood. Only the charred shell of the old building had remained after the fire. The wagon came to halt.

Reverend Lockwood was standing outside, watching the progress. Seeing Mary, he quickly came over. "Mrs. Peake, how nice to see you." He pointed to the building. "What do you think?"

Mary frowned. She looked up at the timbers framing the high roof. "It's so large." Her voice was weak. "Bigger than the original courthouse."

"Oh, it's not a courthouse," Thomas said, smiling at Lockwood. "Show her!" He nodded his head.

The Reverend walked over to a tree near the construction site. He picked up a large board and carried it to the wagon. Flipping it over, he held the painted side towards Mary.

The blanket muffled her gasp. Thomas put his arm around his wife's shoulders. Her eyes glistened. Bold black letters on a white background read "MARY S. PEAKE SCHOOL."

Lockwood smiled and nodded to the building. "We'll have

four classrooms when it's done. We're all so eager for you to return. Especially the children." He laughed. "I'm afraid I'm a poor substitute for your skills, Mrs. Peake."

Mary pulled the blanket down to speak. "That's so nice, Reverend Lockwood. I'm happy the people of Hampton will have a new school. But you and I know it's not likely I'll be returning." She smiled through tight lips. "As much as I'd like to."

"Everyone wanted to make building the school a priority." Thomas tried to cheer her up. "The first thing we completed was the sign."

Mary studied her name in big bold letters. Her gaze moved to the new building. She imagined it full of students, eager to learn. And Daisy would be among them. Perhaps her daughter might even be a teacher at this school some day. "I don't know what to say." She wiped her eyes with the corner of the blanket. "I'm so happy for our children." Mary covered her mouth with the blanket and coughed several times.

"I think we need to get you home." Thomas looked at his wife with concern.

Mary nodded. "Reverend Lockwood, it's so nice to see you and the progress you're making." She swallowed hard. "I'm honored that the school is named after me."

"Mrs. Peake, it's the least we can do to celebrate your devotion and hard work over the years."

Thomas waved and snapped the reins. The wagon lurched forward. Mary closed her eyes, grimacing.

The wagon rolled through the streets of Hampton toward the bridge. Mary looked at the contrast between the desolation from the fire and the optimism created by the new school and homes being constructed in the distance. An icy tear trickled down over her sharp cheekbone and disappeared behind the blanket.

As the wagon passed by where their house once stood, Mary grabbed Thomas's arm. "Can we stop for a minute, please?"

Mary looked at the charred timbers, piled like burnt matchsticks, still littering the yard. Her cast iron stove lay on its side, abandoned to the elements. Mary stared into the emptiness. She had trouble remembering what her home looked like. The burnt cover of Daisy's bird book still lay on the ground, half buried and decaying under the soot. Mary thought how fragile and temporary everything seemed.

She covered her head with the blanket. Frosty wind ripped across the landscape. Wiping her moist eyes, Mary turned to her husband. "Can you take me back now, Thomas?"

EPILOGUE

I REMEMBER THE LONG LINE OF PEOPLE WALKING past my mama's still body. It was in a box on the first floor of our little cottage. Most everyone was there; even the soldiers came to honor her. Reverend Lockwood stood at the front of the room where my mama taught us children. I remember him saying how fitting it was to hold these services in my mama's classroom, "a place sweetened by associations of her crowning labors." My papa and his friends James and Frank cried like little boys.

I knew her time was coming, but I prayed it would never happen. Even Dr. Browne slowly turned from hope to despair as her illness got worse. I heard many of the soldiers at the big fort were dying from the dreaded consumption disease. But I never thought it would take my mama. She was such a strong woman.

Dr. Browne, who cared so tenderly for my mama, gave the eulogy. I'll never forget his words. "Mary's thirty-nine years of earthly existence were but a prelude to a life beyond the sky. While her spirit survives the ravages of death, her name shall live in memory. She has erected to herself a monument more enduring than brass or granite, by impressing her own image upon a group of susceptible students in whom she shall live again. We shall never see someone like her again."

Days, weeks, and months drifted by after that dark time. Before I knew it, it was winter again. I was standing under the great oak tree looking out into a crowd of people. I could feel James trembling through his big hand. Everyone from Hampton must have been there. Papa was smiling proudly. There were folks of all shapes, sizes, and colors. I hadn't seen that many people since my mama's service.

James stood tall as he looked out over the crowd. "We're all almost a year older since we lost Mary Peake. She started teaching our children many years ago here under this tree. Mary defied the laws of Virginia and risked brutal punishment to make sure our children had an education." James stopped talking. His eyes were red and shiny. His chin quivered. He took a big swallow and the bump in front of his neck went up and down. "Look around you. Almost everyone here was taught to read and write by this amazing woman. She wanted us all to be prepared for a day when we might be free. She wanted us to be able to support ourselves and lead productive lives if that opportunity ever came. And she wanted our children to have a better life than we all have had."

It was a cold day, and everyone was bundled up. Plumes of chilled air swirled from our mouths like smoke. It was so quiet that only the wind could be heard whistling through the bare branches of the big oak tree.

James looked down at me and then around at the crowd. "I've here a copy of the Emancipation Proclamation. President Lincoln signed it last September, but it took effect only a few weeks ago. None of us knows what it says. I asked you all here so you could hear the words for yourself. Mary would've wanted to be here. I'm sure she would have loved to be the one to read it to us." He looked down at me again. "So I've asked her daughter, Daisy, to read it on her behalf."

James squeezed my hand. I'd never read in front of so many people. I hadn't been this nervous since the Christmas festival over a year ago. James told me to read slowly and loudly so everyone could hear me.

I looked at the paper with all the big, fancy words and wondered if I could do this. I thought of my mama and how she first taught me to read. She always told me if I ever came across a strange word to look at the letters and sound them out in my head. I took a deep breath and started.

I read the opening paragraph. I looked up and saw everyone staring at me. I could feel my heart thumping through my thick coat. I took another deep breath, looked down at the paper, and continued.

I'm not sure I knew what all those words meant, but I thought it must have been a good thing. People were cheering and hugging each other. The two words I did understand were "forever free."

I continued reading. I felt like someone else was moving my mouth and reading the words for me. I could feel my mama within me, as if she was giving a lesson under that tree. Everyone was crying, but they were happy.

Many years have passed since that bright winter day. It's ironic that the reading of the Emancipation Proclamation was near where slavery began in our country many years ago. Folks also said that if James, Frank, and Shepard hadn't crossed Hampton Roads that spring night seeking sanctuary, none of this would have ever happened. Or at least it wouldn't have happened so soon.

Of course, it took a controversial decision by General Butler to provide refuge to those three men and the many colored folks to follow. It was said that the Confederate states left the Union to preserve their way of life and the practice of slavery. That decision led to the awful war. Ironically, slavery probably ended much sooner than it would have if those states had chosen to stay in the Union.

That big oak tree became known as the Emancipation Tree, since it was believed to be the location of the first reading of the Emancipation Proclamation in the South. Some called it the Freedom Tree.

But I like to think they call it the Emancipation Tree because it's where my mama first taught us colored children in Hampton, freeing us from the shackles of ignorance.

I remembered looking up into the deep blue sky that special day. Mama told me she would always be there watching over me from above. The puffy, white clouds were moving quickly, heading south in the stiff winter breeze.

I heard a familiar sound coming from the Emancipation Tree. Its powerful limbs reached into the heavens like strong arms. A bird was perched on a low branch just above my head. It was a mockingbird. It didn't have pretty red colors like a cardinal. But nothing could sing as beautiful as that bird, except my mama.

The mockingbird stopped singing, craned its head, and looked down at me. Then she swooped over the crowd and flew high into the sky.

I knew my mama was happy.

Her work here was done.

The door was open!

Continuing Mary's legacy, General Butler founded the
Butler School in 1863, adjacent to the Emancipation Tree.

———

The Butler School taught children reading, writing,
arithmetic, geography, and housekeeping skills.

———

The roots of the school would later grow into Hampton University.

———

The Emancipation Tree thrives on the Hampton University
campus, greeting students and visitors at its entrance.

THE EMANCIPATION PROCLAMATION

January 1, 1863

By the President of the United States of America:

A Proclamation.

WHEREAS, ON THE TWENTY-SECOND DAY OF September, in the year of our Lord one thousand eight hundred and sixty-two, a proclamation was issued by the President of the United States, containing, among other things, to wit:

"That on the first day of January, in the year of our Lord one thousand eight hundred and sixty-three, all persons held as slaves within any State or designated part of a State, the people thereof shall then be in rebellion against the United States, shall be then, thenceforward, and forever free, and the Executive Government of the United States, including the military and naval authority thereof, will recognize and maintain the freedom of such persons, and will do no act or acts to repress such persons, or any of them, in any efforts they may make for their actual freedom.

"That the Executive will, on the first day of January aforesaid, by proclamation, designate the States, and parts of States, if any, in which the people thereof, respectively, shall then be in rebellion against the United States; and the fact that any State, or the people thereof, shall on that day be, in good faith, represented in the Congress of the United States by members chosen thereto at elections wherein a majority of the qualified voters of such State shall have participated, shall, in the absence of strong countervailing testimony, be deemed conclusive evidence that such State, and the people thereof, are not then in rebellion against the United States."

Now, therefore, I, Abraham Lincoln, President of the United States, by virtue of the power in me vested as Commander-in-Chief, of the Army and Navy of the United States in time of actual armed rebellion against the authority and government of the United States, and as a fit and necessary war measure for suppressing said rebellion, do, on this first day of January, in the year of our Lord one thousand eight hundred and sixty-three, and in accordance with my purpose so to do publicly proclaimed for the period of one hundred days, from the day first above mentioned, order and designate as the States and parts of States wherein the people thereof, respectively, are this day in rebellion against the United States, the following, to wit:

Arkansas, Texas, Louisiana, (except the Parishes of St. Bernard, Plaquemines, Jefferson, St. John, St. Charles, St. James Ascension, Assumption, Terrebonne, Lafourche, St. Mary, St. Martin, and Orleans, including the City of New Orleans) Mississippi, Alabama, Florida, Georgia, South Carolina, North Carolina, and Virginia, (Except the forty-eight counties designated as West Virginia, and also the counties of Berkley, Accomac, Northampton, Elizabeth City, York, Princess Ann, and Norfolk, including the cities of Norfolk, and

Portsmouth), and which excepted parts, are for the present, left precisely as if this proclamation were not issued.

And by virtue of the power, and for the purpose aforesaid, I do order and declare that all persons held as slaves within said designated States, and parts of States, are, and henceforward shall be free, and that the Executive government of the United States, including the military and naval authorities thereof, will recognize and maintain the freedom of said persons.

And I hereby enjoin upon the people so declared to be free to abstain from all violence, unless in necessary self-defence; and I recommend to them that, in all cases when allowed, they labor faithfully for reasonable wages.

And I further declare and make known, that such persons of suitable condition, will be received into the armed forces of the United States to garrison forts, positions, stations, and other places, and to man vessels of all sorts in said services.

And upon this act, sincerely believed to be an act of justice, warranted by the Constitution, upon military necessity, I invoke the considerate judgment of mankind, and the gracious favor of Almighty God.

In witness whereof, I have hereunto set my hand and caused the seal of the United States to be affixed.

Done at the City of Washington, this first day of January, in the year of our Lord one thousand eight hundred and sixty-three, and of the independence of the United States of America the eighty-seventh.

By the President: ABRAHAM LINCOLN
WILLIAM H. SEWARD, Secretary of State

ACKNOWLEDGMENTS

WRITING MY FIRST NOVEL WAS A DAUNTING journey. Looking back, had I known it would have taken several years and countless revisions, I'm not sure I could have prevailed. However, Mary's remarkable life, and my passion to share it, kept me focused.

I am grateful to my family-Karen, my wife, and my children, Megan and Ryan-who were subjected to early versions of my book. Their candid feedback and bemused stares, which communicated more than words ever could, didn't discourage me but, rather, inspired me to press on.

There were several "professionals" who helped transform this book from its embryonic stage to the final product. Laura Morelli provided guidance and counsel regarding where and how to start this long process. Jessica Hatch challenged me to bring Mary, General Butler and the other characters to life. Melissa Wuske applied the final coat of polish to the manuscript. Andrew Newman created a captivating cover concept. Shannon Bodie provided cover production guidance, and developed an inspiring interior design.

To the many historians who have documented the people and events that shaped this great country, thank you.

Lastly, I am grateful to Diane Rehm and her iconic show on NPR for, unwittingly, inspiring me to learn more about General Butler. This led me to Mary Peake and my desire to create this book.

A NOTE ON SOURCES

UNLOCKING FREEDOM'S DOOR IS HISTORICAL fiction. The story was inspired by actual events that occurred in and around Hampton, Virginia during the early years of the Civil War. To recreate the lives of Mary Peake, General Butler, and other characters, I relied on numerous books and articles.

There is much written about Butler, but very little about Mary. Reverend Lewis Lockwood chronicled her life in a brief memoir (***Mary S. Peake: The Colored Teacher at Fortress Monroe***, 1862) based on his short time in Hampton while Mary was still alive. Her commitment to educating the children of slaves, the sweetness of her gentle spirit, and her passion for music were all captured by Reverend Lockwood. The eulogy attributed to Dr. Browne in the Epilogue is actually based on Reverend Lockwood's words from his book.

The challenge in researching General Butler and the Civil War was sifting through the mountains of books and other reference material available and distilling this down to a coherent story. I relied heavily on three books about Butler: ***Autobiography and Personal Reminiscences of Major-General Benjamin F. Butler Part 1***, 1892; ***Private And Official Correspondence of General Benjamin Butler – Vol I*** , privately issued 1917; and ***The Life and Public Services of Major-General Butler***, 1864. The majority of the dialogue in Unlocking Freedom's Door is fictionalized to support the story. However, there are a few exceptions where interchanges are based on Butler's account from his autobiography. These include the meeting between Butler and General Scott (Chapter Two), his meetings with Secretary Cameron and President Lincoln (Chapter Two), and the encounter between Butler and Major Cary (Chapter Nine). Also, the letters cited in the book are from Butler's collection.

Information on James Townsend, Frank Baker, and Shepard Mallory is limited to their names and years of birth. Based on Butler's notes, the three slaves were owned by Colonel Charles Mallory, leased to the Confederacy, and escaped to Fortress Monroe. The resulting flood of slaves into the fort was encouraged by Butler's controversial decision to give the three men sanctuary.

The accounts of Private Edward Pierce and his interactions with the three slaves, and the broader contraband community (Chapter Nineteen), are largely based on Butler's autobiography and an article written by Pierce (*"The Contrabands of Fortress Monroe," Atlantic Monthly, November 1861, 626-640*).

The burning of Hampton by the Confederates was an actual event. The quoted reactions by a Rebel soldier (Chapter Twenty-Two) and the Union war correspondent (Chapter Twenty-Three) were documented accounts of this horrific act.

There is no evidence that Mary had any knowledge of, or interaction with, General Butler or the three slaves. However, since they all lived in the Hampton area at the same time, I took the liberty of creating a story where their lives were intertwined.

ABOUT THE AUTHOR

Portrait by Marshall Photography

K EN WORKED IN THE CORPORATE WORLD FOR over thirty years. He continues to consult and is active on company boards. Throughout his career Ken was able to travel and live abroad, experiencing many different cultures and customs. He enjoys reading historical fiction, where he can continue to learn about the world–past and present–while being captivated by a good story.

He first learned about General Butler while listening to The Diane Rehm Show on NPR. His subsequent research led to the discovery of Mary Peake and his desire to learn more about this remarkable woman. After visiting Hampton University, the Hampton History Museum, the Casemate Museum of Fort Monroe, and Mary's gravesite, Ken decided to write a novel that honors her memory.

Ken is a native New Englander and lives on Cape Cod with his wife.

I hope you enjoyed reading this book.

If you would like to join my email list to learn about events and new releases please visit:

www.unlockingfreedomsdoor.com

www.flatpondpublishing.com

www.ingramcontent.com/pod-product-compliance
Lightning Source LLC
Chambersburg PA
CBHW050537260626
47157CB00002B/331